THE
MARRIAGE
RETREAT

BOOKS BY LAURA ELLIOT

Fragile Lies

Stolen Child

The Prodigal Sister

The Betrayal

Sleep Sister

Guilty

The Wife Before Me

The Thorn Girl

The Silent House

After the Wedding

THE
MARRIAGE RETREAT

LAURA ELLIOT

bookouture

Published by Bookouture in 2023

An imprint of Storyfire Ltd.
Carmelite House
50 Victoria Embankment
London EC4Y 0DZ

www.bookouture.com

ISBN: 978-1-83790-011-4
eBook ISBN: 978-1-83790-010-7

Dedicated to the memory of my mother, Bridie Bolger, who remains forever young, forever missed.

ONE

NO NAME GIRL

I hear the clock. Seconds ticking. I count to three. Tick-tock... tick-tock... tick-tock... begin again.

Sunshine and shadow. Sound and silence. They wipe my tears. Tears that are as meaningless to them as the twitches and jerks and groans. Slippery tears with no purpose other than to let them know I'm still breathing.

They talk about the vegetative state. I think of aubergines. Purple, satiny skin, plump flesh. My favourite. Sometimes they wear gloves. That's when I feel most like a vegetable. A shiny aubergine to be turned and scrubbed and laid out for inspection; prodding and poking – such a lot of that goes on here.

Professor Macken discusses my Glasgow Coma Scale. It's low. A bad sign. He breathes his concern over me. Is garlic a vegetable or herb? They call me No Name Girl and wait for someone to say my name, but there is no one to speak for me.

His face never goes away. Those eyes staring into my soul. I breathe his name. It echoes loud. Louder than the hiss and bleep and dinging alarms. No one turns to wonder at the sound of it. Their hands are gentle when they bathe me and massage my fingers.

I love them for their care, and wonder which one of those hands will pull the plug... tick-tock... tick-tock... tick-tock...

TWO

LORRAINE

The cherry blossom was in full bloom, swathes of pink hanging heavy on the branches as Amy and Gerard Foster—with eyes only for each other—renewed their marriage vows. The out-spanned boughs sheltered them from the midday sun and the pair of doves that came to rest on a branch above them cooed quietly into the afternoon shimmer. *Could any other setting be more perfect?* Lorraine Gordon wondered. The weather had provided this magnificent backdrop, but it was the Rekindle programme she and her husband ran at Serenity Falls that had created this space for the Fosters to take time out and salvage a marriage heading for divorce.

Gerard was emotional. Stiff and resentful when he first came to Serenity Falls, his spine had softened over his five-day stay, and pent-up feelings he had controlled for so long had finally been released. Tears glistened on his cheeks as he spoke his vows, yet he held his wife's hands with an awkwardness that suggested he was trying to recall a once-familiar habit.

The writing of their vows had taken time. Amy had showed them to Lorraine before Fr. Smithson arrived to perform the ceremony. The words offered each other space to be different.

To listen to what the other person was saying and hesitate before giving way to anger. They would react as a united front when it came to the perpetual demands and tantrums of their teenage children. Most importantly, they would establish a date night once a week.

They were not demanding vows. Twenty years of marriage had suppressed more ambitious aspirations and Amy hoped these promises would see them through the next twenty years.

Afterwards, Lorraine would wonder about perfection. How could she have believed, even for an instant, that it existed without blemish? How could she have been seduced by the cooing of doves and a shower of cherry blossom drifting downward? Those questions would haunt her later but, as Fr. Smithson raised his hand to bestow a blessing on the Fosters, she was content. She moved discreetly around the couple and photographed them. She even managed to include the cuddling doves. Excellent publicity shots for the new Rekindle Connections brochure.

Apart from the Fosters, who had decided to stay overnight, the other guests had left Serenity Falls last night. Hugs and handshakes had been exchanged and emotional promises to stay in touch were made, before the ten couples, their relationships rekindled and invigorated, drove away.

Renewing marriage vows was becoming an increasingly popular ceremony at the end of a Rekindle programme. Recently, two couples had asked for a humanist celebrant and were delighted by the moving ritual. Lorraine had even managed to find a druid, who performed a ceremony beside the waterfall and did something wonderful with fire.

She walked back to the courtyard with the priest and waited until he had driven away before climbing the steps to Serenity Falls.

Silence settled over the old house, blissful and restful after the activities of the past five days. The staff had started their weekend break and the cleaners would be arriving shortly to prepare the house for the new guests, who had booked to arrive on Monday. Time for coffee and a brief rest before the next stage. Saturday was Lorraine's favourite day of the week. She could relax for a few hours and reflect on the previous five days. Usually, she and Victor had lunch in the Silver Falls Café and drove into Potters Glen afterwards to shop. But she thought she would forgo lunch today and catch up on paperwork instead. Deciding a herbal tea would be more refreshing, she dropped a teabag into a cup of freshly boiled water and let it steep, before carrying it into her office.

She considered ringing Victor. Checking her watch, she changed her mind. He would probably still be on the podium delivering his speech at the annual Hearts and Vows conference in London. Hopefully, he was stressing the points she had laid out for him. Would he think of her as he listened to the applause afterwards and accepted the compliments he would undoubtedly receive from the attendees? Probably not. The web she had woven with her husband had too many silky strands to separate into individual parts.

She turned her attention to her laptop. New enquiries came every day, not only from Irish couples but from overseas as well. It was gratifying to know that the reputation of Rekindle Connections was spreading far beyond Ireland and the small village of Potters Glen. Soon, she would have new brochures to send to potential guests, but she needed to seriously consider employing someone to handle their online promotions.

The view from her office window overlooked the avenue and the lawns sloping away on either side. The orchard was out of sight and the Fosters were taking their time about returning to the house.

Lorraine had no reason to be alarmed when a garda squad car came into view. The gates leading to Serenity Falls were often mistaken for the entrance to the Silver Falls Café, which

was a short distance further along Cliffside Road. She waited
for the officer to turn the car around once the house came into
view but the driver continued towards the courtyard and
braked.

Two uniformed officers emerged. Despite the heat of the
day, they wore high visibility jackets. The word GARDA was
visible on the back of each one as they turned to stare over
the lawns, and, then, as if sensing Lorraine's presence at the
window, the driver closed the door and adjusted his hat. He
looked as though he had barely emerged from his teens but
the older police officer, a stocky woman with broad, authoritative shoulders, had the seasoned expression of a professional.
They climbed the steps in unison to the front door. Lorraine
lost sight of them when they disappeared behind the
balustrade, and put down her unfinished cup of tea on her
desk when she heard the sharp, commanding blast of the
doorbell. Had someone made a complaint about Rekindle
Connections? A married couple, perhaps, unsatisfied with the
counselling they had received? Not every programme ended
with the dazed happiness the Fosters had achieved. Some
relationships were beyond repair. The Rekindle programme
could be merciless in highlighting such issues but it was
unlikely that anyone would report such an unhappy experience to the gardai. Had she broken the speed limit? New
speed cameras had been installed on the main road leading
into Potters Glen and she was always in a hurry. Such
thoughts ran through her mind as she hurried to answer the
door.

'Are you Mrs Gordon?' The female officer was the first to speak.

'Yes, I'm Mrs Gordon,' Lorraine replied. 'How can I help
you?'

'I'm Sergeant Boyne and this is Garda Morris.' The

woman's eyes were blue and palely expressionless as she nodded at her companion. 'May we step inside, please?'

'Is something wrong, Sergeant—?' Lorraine tried to ignore the unsettling sensation the woman aroused in her.

'Please, if we can talk inside, Mrs Gordon.' Her interruption was quiet but firm.

'Of course.' She opened the door fully and stood back to allow them to enter the hall. A quick glance along the avenue assured her that the Fosters were still in the orchard. Hopefully, whatever had brought the police to Serenity Falls would be sorted and the officers gone before Amy and Gerard returned to the house. She moved smoothly in front of the sergeant and led them into her office.

The sun's glare pressed against the window and for a dazzling instant they seemed haloed in light. It was possible, before Sergeant Boyne spoke again, for Lorraine to believe she was witnessing a mirage. One that would dissolve and leave her to continue an uninterrupted, perfect day.

'Please sit down, Mrs Gordon.' Sergeant Boyne gestured towards one of the two armchairs in the office and waited until Lorraine was seated, before sitting opposite her. 'I'm afraid we have to inform you that there has been a fatal accident on the M1 motorway. A serious one, I'm afraid. Your husband...' She hesitated, and the swallowing sound she made reached Lorraine. 'I'm sorry to have to tell you that Mr Gordon was involved in the collision and—'

'That's not possible...' Lorraine tried to interrupt her, but the sergeant had a message to deliver and was determined to do so. '—an articulated truck heading northwards along the M1 swerved from its lane shortly after exiting the Dublin Port Tunnel and crashed into his car.' Her direct gaze never wavered as she related the horrific facts. 'I'm so sorry, Mrs Gordon, but I have to tell you that the impact resulted in your husband's death at the scene.'

This information was delivered so calmly and sympatheti-
cally it was almost possible to believe her. How could someone
so assured be so wrong? Somehow, Lorraine must stem this flow
of tragic information that was not meant for her but would soon
have to be delivered in the same terrifying detail to another
wife.

'You've made a dreadful mistake.' Her voice shook at the
enormity of this blunder. 'Victor is in London. You've confused
him with another Victor Gordon. This is clearly a case of
mistaken identity.'

'We identified him from his driving licence and the registration on his BMW.' The sergeant leaned towards her. Her closeness, the slight scent of spices – a curry eaten too late last night,
perhaps – caused Lorraine's stomach to heave. 'Victor Gordon
also had other documentation on him in his briefcase, along
with Rekindle Connections brochures.'

'This is ridiculous... his car must have been stolen. He left it
in the long-term car park at Dublin Airport. You need to check
the true identity of the man who died. Victor is giving a speech
at a conference.' Lorraine stood and grabbed her phone from the
desk. 'Check it out. He's staying at the Harlequin House Hotel.'

'When did you last speak to him?' the sergeant asked.

'Yesterday. He told me...' Her throat was parched and her
tongue, struggling with words she was unable to utter, rasped
against the palate of her mouth.

'Did he give any indication that his travel plans had
changed?'

'We'd no reason to discuss his itinerary. I organised it for
him. He's flying home tomorrow... Sunday. I can't understand
how this misunderstanding happened, but you have to believe
me when I tell you it wasn't Victor in that car.'

Lorraine's vehemence reached across the space between
them and the sergeant shifted a little in her chair. 'Please, Mrs
Gordan... Lorraine – listen to me. I wouldn't come to you with

such distressing news if we hadn't checked Victor's identification thoroughly before contacting you. I'm so sorry—'

'Enough... I've heard *enough*.' Lorraine brought Victor's name up on her phone and rang him.

The stranger who answered introduced himself as Garda Lennon and informed Lorraine he was speaking to her from the hospital where her husband had been pronounced dead on his arrival. He spoke with the same sympathetic persuasiveness as the sergeant. Lorraine felt the walls moving towards her and away again, a shift in balance that pressed her eyes closed in case she collapsed. The phone fell from her hand but the younger officer caught it before it hit the floor.

The sergeant conferred briefly with Garda Lennon, who was keeping watch over an unidentified dead man in a north-side Dublin hospital.

'I don't understand...! Victor's in London... how could he be in London and Dublin at the same time?' She was repeating herself, a record stuck in a groove, and unable to stop.

'Mrs Gordon, *please* listen to me,' said Sergeant Boyne. 'You've just reached his phone—'

'No, *you* listen to *me*.' Her knees buckled and Garda Morris, moving swiftly, eased her back into the armchair. 'Someone stole my husband's phone and flew back to Dublin to steal his car from the long-term car park. They would have found all the information they needed to do so on his phone. It's the only reason that makes sense.' She gripped the arms of the chair and drew a deep breath.

'I'm sorry, Lorraine. What you're suggesting is not feasible. Mr Gordon has been correctly identified.' Sergeant Boyne answered her with a new authority, her voice more demanding. *Were her eyes grey or blue?* Her pale gaze seemed devoid of any true colour but was now filled with terrifying certainty. 'I'm afraid you need to hear what we're telling you. Mr Gordon—'

'His name is *Victor*.' Lorraine needed the informality of first names to break down their official detachment and Sergeant Boyne nodded in acknowledgement.

'I'd like to stress that Victor wasn't to blame in any way for the accident,' she said. 'The truck driver suffered a heart attack and lost control of the steering wheel. I'm sorry we had to bring such tragic news to you and be forced to repeat it. Sadly, Victor died at the scene.'

'Instantaneously.' Garda Morris poured a wealth of reassurance into that one word. As if aware of its inadequacy, his face flushed. 'He never suffered.' He nibbled his bottom lip, something he had been doing since his arrival. He was a rookie, raw and unused to the dazed emotions of the stricken.

'Is there someone we can contact?' Sergeant Boyne asked. 'A family member who can come here and be with you?' Her tone had softened, as though she knew the message she had come to deliver was finally sinking in.

'My son Aidan is in Canada.' A scream soared in Lorraine's throat, something wild and unhinged that had to be controlled or it would bend her double. 'I've no intention of contacting him until I know for certain that what you've told me is true.'

'Do you have a daughter?' the sergeant asked.

'No. Aidan is our only child.'

'I see...' When she paused, Lorraine noticed a subtle change in her expression, a flicker of unease that could have been imagined. 'I have to tell you there was a young woman in the car with Victor,' she said.

'A *woman*?' Lorraine's disbelief bounced off the officers and Garda Morris chewed so hard on his bottom lip that she expected to see blood spurting forth.

'His passenger is critically injured and is in a coma,' Sergeant Boyne continued. 'We're unable to identify her as she has no documentation on her. She's probably in her early twenties, has long, black hair, and is of a slim build. Have you any idea who she could be?'

Unable to speak, Lorraine could only shake her head. Her husband was in London. That fact could not be denied: she had organised his itinerary. She knew what he had been doing, and would do, for every hour since he left Serenity Falls on Thursday evening.

The evidence didn't matter. Somehow, an appalling mistake had been made by the police and this latest disclosure about a woman confirmed it.

Sergeant Boyne was describing the clothes the young woman had been wearing: a red jacket, dark blue jeans and black trainers. She was Caucasian, her hair had been tied in a ponytail and her eyes were brown. The sergeant's tone was reasonable and compassionate, the same tone Lorraine used on guests who were afraid to confront the awfulness of their relationships.

'An official identification is important,' said the younger officer. 'When you feel ready, and in your own time, we'll bring you to the hospital where we'll give you all the support and assistance you need. You'll also be assigned a family liaison officer. Her name is Jean Bowden. She'll keep you updated with all the information you'll need to bring you through this process.'

'Process...' Lorraine allowed the word to fall away. Identification was the only answer. It didn't matter about the length of time the police believed it would have taken Victor to fly from London to Dublin. It had not posed a problem for a thief, who was dead, and whose accomplice was in a coma. The sooner she reached the hospital and confirmed that the man whose mangled body had been lifted from the wreckage of Victor's car was a stranger to her, the sooner this travesty would end.

The Fosters came into view on the south lawn. They were walking closely together, laughing, hands clasped, arms swinging. Noticing the squad car they paused, as if offended by the sight of it.

Lorraine needed to reassure them that no shadow had fallen

over the ceremony that had meant so much to them; instead, she was locked into a nightmare that made no sense and could only watch helplessly as they skirted the car and approached the steps to the front door. She heard their footsteps on the parquet flooring as they crossed the hall towards the staircase. Soon, they would descend with their suitcases and expect her to be at the entrance to bid them goodbye.

'I need to ring my manager.' Her voice was barely audible. 'She lives in the lodge at the main gates and won't take long to get here.'

Garda Morris, who was still holding her phone, passed it to her.

Pamela's name blurred on the screen as Lorraine struggled to hold back her tears. She mustn't cry. To do so would give credence to this ridiculous misunderstanding. She hit the number and her friend answered immediately.

'What is it, Lorraine?' Pamela Blake's familiar voice calmed her momentarily. 'I saw the squad car arriving. Is something wrong?'

'I'm not sure.' She cleared her throat, conscious that Sergeant Boyne was ready to take the phone from her if she was unable to continue. 'There's been some dreadful mix-up about Victor. I'll explain it all later but I need you to come here and see the Fosters off. Can you make up an excuse to explain the squad car? Something innocuous?' She saw the officers exchange glances and heard Sergeant Boyne's sigh.

'I'll grab my bike and be there in a minute. Don't worry. I'll look after them.' Pamela's unflappable personality was one of the reasons why Rekindle Connections ran so smoothly.

No questions asked, just action when necessary.

Pamela arrived shortly afterwards, flushed and breathless when she entered the office. Sergeant Boyne stood to offer her the armchair but Pamela remained standing, her eyes fixed on Lorraine as the officer repeated the same appalling details.

'But that's impossible,' she exclaimed. 'Victor's in London. He isn't due home until tomorrow.'

Loraine pressed her hands to her chest in a futile effort to ease the pressure on her heart. 'They're saying that a woman was in the car with him.'

'Then that can't be him.' Pamela spoke directly to the sergeant. 'You don't know Victor. He's not the type—'

'We're not making a moral judgement here.' Sergeant Boyne's sharp interruption silenced her. 'If a mistake has been made, there is only one way it can be cleared up, and that is through an official identification.'

'I'm going with them to the hospital,' said Lorraine. 'Sergeant Boyne is right. That's the only way to sort out this ludicrous situation.'

'You can't go on your own,' Pamela protested. 'I'll follow you.'

'I need you to look after the Fosters... and the cleaners will be here soon...' Her thoughts were spinning with the force of a projectile let loose without direction; and the instructions she needed to issue seemed utterly irrelevant.

'Leave everything to me,' Pamela whispered in her ear as they embraced. 'None of this makes sense. Just hold your nerve until you get to the hospital. I'll follow as soon as I organise everything here.'

The Fosters would have reached their bedroom by now. They had a back view over the grounds from their window and would be unable to witness Lorraine climbing into the back of a squad car.

Garda Morris drove through the open gates and turned left onto Cliffside Road. The river that flowed through Potters Glen became visible, the cliff looming above it. An upward march of gorse and pine obliterated the cliff's rocky face until the vegetation gave way to a churning waterfall. Lorraine closed her eyes against the vision of her father falling through the silvery flow. *Not now... not now...* The past must not intrude on this extraordinary day.

What exactly had Victor said when they last spoke? Had she actually listened to him, or allowed his words to waft past her, her mind on other things? She was not a complacent wife. She understood the dangers associated with smugness. But what would he have said that she did not already know?

The driver slowed as he drove through Potters Glen. The village was quiet, bathed in an afternoon stillness. Spring was giving way to summer and everywhere Lorraine looked, she could see cherry blossom, so vibrant and pink – so ephemeral.

THREE

LORRAINE

Victor's face was cut and bruised, unrecognisable except for his mouth. Lorraine had no idea how it had escaped the fly of glass and crush of steel. She had kissed his lips so often: lingering kisses; fierce, passionate kisses; playful kisses. She knew its swells and puckers, its lop-sided smile, its firmness. His wedding ring was smeared with blood, his fingers broken and swollen, but it was his tattoo that confirmed her worst fears. The orange-red hue of Sedona, that primal sandstone with its furnace-like bluffs and canyons, was visible on his arm, halfway between his elbow and shoulder.

She screamed then, a thin, high howl of recognition.

Sergeant Boyne, who had accompanied her to this place of death, waited quietly by her side as Lorraine's body shuddered with a horrific acceptance and she found the strength to nod.

Jean Bowden, the family liaison officer, took over after Victor had been formally identified and escorted her to the bereavement room. She gently encouraged her to drink the coffee she ordered.

Wrapping her hands around the cup, Lorraine welcomed the burn against her fingers. The liaison officer looked kind and strong. Someone on whom she could lean and be held upright when she was asked if she could identify Victor's female passenger. Black ponytail, a jacket and jeans, the description was too generic to mean anything to her. She had barely been able to recognise Victor's face and if this woman's features were equally disfigured, then there was no chance Lorraine would be able to name her. To travel without identity – who did that these days? Had her phone been lost in the wreckage?

Jean shook her head when Lorraine asked.

'The car and the surrounding areas have been searched,' she said. 'We've been unable to find it. I agree it's unusual for one not to be in her possession. Young people seem to see mobile phones as an extension of their right hand. All we must go on are the clothes she was wearing when the accident took place.'

Lorraine nodded. The words were meaningless and had no connection to her. The numbness was receding and been replaced by a hot, churning sensation that felt like acid in her chest. Anger – what else could it be? One of the first stages of grief. She didn't want that. Victor was the most important person in her life. She had to give him the benefit of doubt.

If there was a rational explanation, then she needed this young woman, who, apparently, was still in the operating theatre, to remain alive so that she could explain it all to Lorraine.

It was morning in Vancouver when she rang Aidan. He would have just returned from the beach. The previous summer, she and Victor had visited him and she knew the routine of his days. She imagined him sprinting on the warm sand before stopping off at a pavement café for a takeaway coffee and a croissant on the way back to his apartment. The sun would be splintering the distant, snow-capped mountains and casting a glassy sheen on the ocean waves.

She tried to break the news gently to him but his stunned reaction tore across the space between them. She wanted to cry with him but she had entered another space. One that was devoid of emotion. Numbness, she guessed, but it allowed her to speak to Aidan in a voice that remained steady as she related the details of the accident. His questions battered her. How, where, when? She struggled to answer him and, somehow, keep the information from him that Victor had lied to her.

Time passed. It could be minutes or hours since she reached the hospital, but she didn't feel inclined to check her watch.

Pamela arrived and rushed to comfort her. They sat together, hands clasped tightly, as they had done throughout their years together, best friends since they were toddlers playing games on the south lawn of Serenity Falls.

Pamela had cancelled the guests who should have been starting the programme on Monday. She had broken the news of Victor's death to the staff, who were appalled and disbelieving that tragedy could strike so randomly. She passed on their messages of condolences to Lorraine, then paused with that same discreet hesitation displayed earlier by Sergeant Boyne, before referring to the fact that Victor had not been travelling alone.

'Journalists have been in touch,' Pamela said. 'Word is out that Victor was one of the victims and that he had a passenger with him. I've been in touch with the Garda Press Office. No information will be released until all family members have been notified. That includes the family of the truck driver. Did you know he was Polish?'

Lorraine shook her head.

'Living here for five years.' Pamela sighed. 'God help his family.' She stopped and ran her hand over her chin. 'The journalists were asking about Victor's passenger. I hung up on them and I'll do so again if they dare to ring me.'

She sounded reassuring and supportive, but what did she

really think about this unconscious woman whom Lorraine was waiting to identify? Was Jean Bowden also wondering about her identity and her relationship to Victor? Perhaps there was no mystery and Victor had simply recognised someone from Potters Glen as he waited for his flight at Heathrow airport... or they could have met by chance in London. She could cling to these possibilities, but there was no avoiding the fact that Victor had lied to her about the time of his arrival home. Deliberately lied about an itinerary she had compiled for him before he left. These thoughts tormented her, yet she found herself joining in the conversation with Pamela and the family liaison officer as they drank coffee and waited for the young woman to emerge from the operating theatre. They even laughed once. How was that possible? Only Jean, seasoned in such situations, seemed unsurprised that they could find laughter in tragedy. What had triggered that need in them? Was it gallows humour, the wall between reality and insanity?

Lorraine's throat was raw. She never remembered screaming, even as a child, yet earlier, when she had stood in the mortuary and identified her husband, it had come to her as naturally as breathing.

Pamela was talking to the family liaison officer about the calls she was receiving from the media when Lorraine went outside, into the hospital grounds. A wooden gazebo, erected for smokers, was empty and offered her some privacy.

She sat down on the bench and phoned Lucy Strong, the event organiser of Hearts and Vows.

Lucy's shock when she heard about the accident jolted her even more savagely into the horror of his death. 'Oh, my *God*. I don't believe it... That can't be true... how *can* it be true?'

Then, as if suddenly aware that it would be an obscenity for Lorraine to tell such an untruth, Lucy asked, 'What on earth happened to him?'

'A driver lost control of his truck and veered into his car.

Victor was killed instantly. I've been told he didn't suffer, but how is one supposed to make such a judgement?'

'We can only hope that it's true. Victor was so... *so* vital. It's unbelievable... Is there anything I can do...?' Her voice trailed away.

In the waiting silence that followed, Lorraine sensed Lucy's helplessness as she searched for the right words to comfort her. 'My *God*... do we ever know what's around the corner? I can't believe he was speaking to us only yesterday. And what an inspiring speech he gave. Everyone was talking about it afterwards.'

Yesterday? Lorraine's heart thumped in her ears, in her pulses. This endless day was still grinding onward and another four hours must pass before midnight. He should have delivered his speech that afternoon. Afterwards, he was to have given a short reading from his latest book and do a book signing.

Right now, he should be having dinner with Lucy and her team. Lies, all lies.

'I never had a chance to talk to him about his speech.' Somehow, she had to probe for the truth without admitting how she had been deceived. 'Did he deliver it in the afternoon?'

'Yes, he did. As you know, he was originally meant to speak today. But when he had to return home early, we managed to rearrange the programme without too much difficulty. He sent a text from Heathrow just before boarding his flight and thanked me for obliging him. Your dear husband was a very courteous man.'

'Yes, he was.' How easily she slid, with Lucy, into the past tense.

'Our attendees are going to be devastated when I break the news to them at the wind-up meeting tomorrow morning. It's incredible to think we were together only yesterday...' Lucy exhaled heavily and, when she spoke again, the shake in her voice suggested Victor's death had triggered a personal grief of her own. 'Bereavement, when it happens so suddenly, adds an extra layer to the pain of losing someone you love. It's not that long ago that my father died from a heart attack. No warning. Nothing to prepare us...' She paused, conscious that she must be adding pain upon pain, and Lorraine, seizing the opportunity, brought their conversation to a close.

She had the information she needed. Victor had returned to Dublin earlier than planned and pretended otherwise. It was as simple and stark as that.

The atmosphere had changed when she returned to the bereavement room. She could tell by the gentle way the liaison officer greeted her that the waiting was over. The patient was back from surgery and ready to be identified. No way to avoid what was to come as Jean accompanied her into the intensive care unit where Sergeant Boyne was waiting for her.

They donned masks and protective clothing before being led towards one of the beds.

She was mindful of the officer's watchful gaze as she stared down at the unconscious figure. Sergeant Boyne had estimated she was in her early twenties. Perhaps her police training helped her to see beyond the bruises and swellings. To Lorraine, this stranger, who was the last person her husband saw before he died, could have been any age. Her hair had been shaved and her head was swaddled in a turban of bandages. One cheek was stitched and the skin around both eyes was so swollen that Lorraine would have been unable to see their colour had she been conscious. The only adornment on her fingers was a pulse oximeter. Her neck was long and a tracheostomy tube was attached to her throat. An oxygen machine hissed its lifesaving breath into her lungs.

Lorraine averted her eyes from the broken figure on the bed and looked at the officer. 'I don't know her. I've no idea why she was in the car with Victor. I'm sure she'll soon be identified by her family. I'd like to be notified when that happens.'

'Don't worry, Lorraine,' Sergeant Boyne said. 'Jean will keep you updated on all developments.'

What was going on behind her impassive expression? Was she seeing Lorraine as a betrayed wife... no... she was no longer a wife. She was his widow, and Victor had left her with a mystery to untangle.

Honesty had been the bedrock of their marriage. On a moonlit Sedona night, the desert wind balmy on their skin, they had made a vow to never lie to each other. That vow had seen them through twenty-five years of marriage. They had built the Rekindle programme around it. Absolute trust. Was that his first lie? Or had there been a pattern before then, and she had been too blinded by love to see it?

This lie involved a young woman who was dying from some unimaginable brain trauma. Lorraine could tell from the sergeant's body language that she was not expected to survive.

It was after ten o'clock when she returned with Pamela to Serenity Falls. Despite the lateness of the hour, the staff had gathered to greet her. Candles encased in glass lanterns lit the avenue, their flames flickering in the darkness. Food had been prepared, and bottles of wine opened. Many tears were shed as they gathered around Lorraine.

None belonged to her.

They left eventually, apart from Pamela, who was anxious to stay with her.

'I need to be on my own to gather my thoughts,' Lorraine told her. 'Once this story breaks in the media, I won't have time to think straight.'

'That's not a good idea, Lorraine. You shouldn't be alone tonight.'

'You're only a stone's throw away if I need you. Honestly, I'm fine. I'll ring Aidan again and see if he's managed to organise a flight. Go on home and get a good night's sleep. We're going to need all our energies for the next few days.'

They stared at the avenue where the candles still guttered but would soon be quenched. Lorraine resisted the urge to hug her friend. Doing so would shatter the frail shell she had created around herself, and she would start wailing questions into the night.

Who was that young woman, with a neck slender enough to strangle?

She should find out soon enough. The liaison officer had said it would only be a matter of time before someone made a report to the police about a missing person.

Only then could Lorraine decide how to frame Victor's story.

'Ring me if you need me, no matter what time it is,' Pamela said, before descending the steps. 'I'll be with you immediately.'

Aidan rang with details of his flight. He still sounded bewildered, his voice rasping as he demanded more details of his father's death.

The driver of the articulated truck was called Janusz. Lorraine hadn't wanted to know his name but, little by little, she had been given information about the man who was responsible for her husband's death, as well as his own. He had been carrying a cargo of frozen prawns that were bound for a ferry to Scotland. She imagined those frozen prawns defrosting. The water dripping like tears. She wanted those tears. Her eyes burned from their lack.

She didn't mention the young woman. How could she answer the questions Aidan would ask once she revealed to him that this stranger had been with his father in the final moments... *hours*... *days*... of his life. Such thoughts were too unbearable for her to share with her son at this stage. Let Aidan grieve without the taint of suspicion adding to his shock.

Her phone rang as she was about to climb the stairs to her

bedroom. Believing it was Aidan ringing her back, she answered it without checking the screen.

'How are you, Lorraine?' The voice was male and instantly recognisable. Her shoulders lifted when she realised, too late, that the unfamiliar number on the screen belonged to Carl Sheridan, a reporter with *Capital Eye.* 'I'm sorry for ringing you at this hour,' he said. 'But I'm on the late shift—'

'This is a private number. How did you get it?'

'I've always had it, Lorraine, but never had to use it until now. I'm ringing to offer my sympathy—'

'How dare you contact me!'

'To offer my sympathy,' he repeated. 'I'm so sorry to hear that—'

She ended the call before he could continue. Switching off her phone, she wondered how long the media could be fobbed off. Victor's advice columns and regular television appearances made him a reluctant celebrity. So, too, did his books. The advice he gave about relationships was all-inclusive yet it was his comments on sex that the media always focused on. He healed relationships, but when couples were no longer able to live together, he created a new path for them to move forward. He was the public face of Rekindle Connections and their marriage – a relationship based on honesty and trust – reflected the ethos of the programme they offered to their guests.

The frail, broken figure lying on a hospital bed could tell a different story, and Lorraine had no way into the mystery surrounding her, no clues that could go into a press statement and silence the speculation that was already circulating. The information was controlled for now, but that would end once Victor's name was released to the media. She imagined the headlines in tomorrow morning's newspapers.

Horrific Crash Kills Love Guru and Critically Injures Mysterious Female Passenger

Once in bed, Lorraine longed to ring Aidan back. But what could she say to him? Nothing but small talk. Anything else was impossible. How could she tell him that his dead father had cut her adrift and left her wandering through the labyrinth of his lies?

Unable to sleep, she tossed back the duvet and dressed quickly in a hoodie and a pair of jogging pants. She left the silent house and took the short cut to the cliff walk. The waterfall cascaded from the rocky crevice and the full moon, reflecting brightly on the flowing torrent, was wondrously fragmented on the flow. It always sounded louder at night, as if it was defying the slumbering world.

Lorraine had never thought of herself as stupid or too trusting. She could read people. They passed in and out of Serenity Falls and she could tell at a glance those who would benefit from the Rekindle programme. No matter what façade they presented, she recognised the disillusioned and unhappy, the deceived and the deceivers, the dominators, the ones who loved too much.

Was she in that last category? Too reliant on a moonlit night when she was giddy with freedom and headlong in love with Victor Gordon?

The waterfall was below her now. She took a step closer to the edge. Suicidal ideation... was that what she was experiencing? This sudden longing was not new. Honesty and its consequences had chewed her up and spat her out on a few occasions. Truth to oneself was hard. It cut into the skin and flayed the soul, but she had always accepted its rigour. Now, she felt rootless, capable of flinging herself into the white fury. Spray rose and settled on her cheeks. Tears by default.

That would have to do for now.

FOUR

Sedona

Twenty-seven years earlier

Lorraine Kilbride was twenty-one and free to go wherever she chose. Airy footsteps and no backward glances. She felt part of the Irish diaspora, but she had no intention of singing sad emigrant songs about the island she was leaving behind. This was her big adventure and she embraced the freedom she expected to find in California. She waited tables, picked fruit and sold jewellery on small roadside stands, all the time stirring dust from California to Arizona – until she reached Sedona, and decided her journey was over.

Everywhere she looked it seemed as if Nature had attacked the landscape with a chisel and gouged into its heart. Rocks, rusted-red and towering, cast shadows on the sun-blasted earth. Sheer buttes and dried-out gullies, boulders with tortured faces and bulbous eyes, cacti and the tall *saguaro* with its upraised limbs... the sights she saw were new, yet had a nostalgic familiarity. They reminded her of cowboy films she had watched with her father, curled up sleepily beside him in the Nook, a bowl of popcorn between them. The Nook was her family's home, separated from Serenity Falls – the hotel her father owned – by a door marked *Private*. Her mother would return from the night shift and scold him for not putting Lorraine to bed earlier but Eloise was always smiling, her voice soft and forgiving.

But such memories belonged to the 'before time'. The friends she made in Sedona were backpackers and trekkers, young like herself, all of them seeking escape from too-ambitious parents, stoned parents, indifferent or callous parents, or parents who had yet to realise that the children they had lost had no intention of being found. They lived in vans painted with psychedelic murals, or they rented rooms above the town's cafés and galleries. Their life stories all had a similar theme and Lorraine said little during these conversations, fearing they would be scornful of the ordinariness of her situation: a mother who died too young, and a father who had allowed the hotel that had been in his family for generations to sink under the weight of his unresolved grief.

She heard about Sedona's vortexes and how these sites radiated special energies that banished negativity and enhanced spiritual growth. Like a sponge that had been wrung too dry, she soaked up this information.

Kelly Nelson, roundly pregnant, was doe-eyed with admiration about a so-called 'vortex guru' who, she claimed, was responsible for her inner peace. She encouraged Lorraine to join her and her husband, Seth, on a hike to Cathedral Rock. This spectacular site was renowned as the most powerful of the vortexes.

The hike would be led by Kelly's vortex guru, who would guide them through a yoga and meditation session when they reached the summit. The group gathered outside Hot&Saucy, the Mexican restaurant where Lorraine worked parttime waiting tables. She had taken the afternoon off to join the hike and when Victor Gordon strode across the square towards them, she experienced a jolt of recognition that had no basis in reality. She was staring at a stranger and yet the sense of familiarity he aroused in her seemed perfectly natural. Had he also felt that same electrifying charge? If so, his expression gave nothing away when Kelly introduced them, but Lorraine was convinced that the strength of his handshake affirmed their connectedness.

On Cathedral Rock, she stood in the shade of his shadow, his tall frame elongated on the dusty, red earth. She guessed he was in his late twenties, maybe early thirties. He was clean-shaven and dressed plainly in a white T-shirt and black jeans. His voice captivated her: a deep yet soft drawl with no sharp edges or annoying twangs. Lifting her arms to embrace the sun, she experienced a powerful energy that spread outwards from the core of her being to her tingling fingertips.

The intensity of his gaze startled her, yet also awakened trust in her. In this vast, mysterious space she believed they were the only two people to feel the sublime power emanating from the majestic landscape surrounding them.

When they returned to Hot&Saucy, he sat beside her in a wooden booth and asked her how long she had been grieving for her mother.

His question wiped her smile away.

He stretched behind her and laid his hand against her spine. A light pressure, yet when it penetrated her thin cotton top, she felt the same searing energy she had experienced on Cathedral Rock; only now it came at her like shrapnel, and stripped aside the pretence that she was happy with her new-found liberty.

. . .

Eloise Kilbride had done her utmost to prepare her fourteen-year-old daughter for the parting that was to come. But, after her death, Lorraine felt as if she had tumbled instantly from a light-filled childhood into a different reality. Was it possible for Serenity Falls to darken, even when the lights were switched on and reflected in glittering mirrors? Eloise had nurtured a softness in her husband that Lorraine was never able to ignite. Arthur Kilbride endured her – that was how she felt. The mote at the corner of his eye, impossible to ignore, yet he seemed incapable of figuring out what to do with her. His sorrow was so isolating that Lorraine felt as if she had lost both parents.

She would escape his bleak silences and run to Falls Lodge, where Pamela's mother would welcome her into the warmth of her kitchen. Rita Blake looked after the gardens at Serenity Falls and supplied the kitchen with fresh produce. The Blake family had moved into the gate lodge when Lorraine's great-grandparents opened the hotel, and the generations that followed had worked there ever since.

When Lorraine had eaten – she was always hungry in those days – she would retreat into the pink, sparkly cheerfulness of Pamela's bedroom. She had wanted her father to marry Rita Blake; then, they would become a proper family. Pamela was horrified when Lorraine suggested this possibility. She was happy to share her mother with Lorraine. Never having known her father – he died shortly after she was born, or so Rita claimed – Pamela had no desire to fill that space with Arthur Kilbride's dour demeanour. The girls planned to travel together. A trip across the United States was worked out in exact detail. But this ambition faded when Pamela met Edward Egan at her twenty-first birthday party and decided she didn't want to travel any further than Potters Glen.

Arthur Kilbride showed no emotion when Lorraine told him she was leaving. She wanted to love him, as she must have done when she was a child and her mother was alive, but her memory of such happiness was almost non-existent. It was easier to pretend love than to try and understand its absence.

'I loved my mother so much yet I was frightened of what she changed into.' In the wooden booth at Hot&Saucy, she whispered the words to Victor, afraid that if she spoke them aloud, their horror would be amplified. 'She was so beautiful and then she was not. Her hair fell out and her face no longer had any shape. All I saw was pain. When I was with her I just wanted to escape. It should have been her pain that upset me but what mattered most was the impact it was having on me. And then none of that mattered after she died. I wanted her back so badly that my grief turned to anger at her for going away from me. It was always about me... me... *me.*'

As she spoke about these conflicting emotions, she didn't realise she was hitting the table with her fist until Victor took her hand and held it tightly.

'You were a child lost in a complex, adult world,' he said. 'And what you describe were just thoughts. Think of them as the froth on a river. It can be blown either which way by the wind, but nothing changes the river's course. It remains deep, constant and true. You never stopped loving your mother, not for an instant, and she would have known that. As for the anger you felt at her passing, that was grief at its purest, but you were defending yourself against its ferocity.'

She was held in the heat of his hands, her fist at ease on the table. She could still feel the imprint of his fingers against her spine, even though he was no longer touching her there, and the sensation acted like a cooling balm that calmed her down. The almost-hypnotic rhythm of his voice allowed her to accept that she missed Serenity Falls with a tightly controlled desperation, yet each time she rang her father and heard his flattened tone, she was reminded of why she had left.

Victor was still speaking to her when Kelly, who waitressed with her, signalled that it was time to begin her shift.

He dined regularly at Hot&Saucy and had a favourite table by the window. He always entered alone but, inevitably, before she had even brought his order to him, he would be joined by women from the tour he had just concluded or those who wished to join the next one. Lorraine would overhear him talking about the electromagnetic power of the vortexes, the *ki* energy they projected and how they had the power to bring the mind to stillness. What were they thinking? she would wonder, as she cleared dishes from the table and observed their rapt expressions. Were they, like her, caught up in some mystifying web he wove with words that touched the core of their being?

His youthful looks were deceptive. She found out from Kelly that he had just turned forty-two. Twenty-one years older than she was. She should have been taken aback by this gap in age, but by then it was irrelevant. Love, mysterious and over-whelming, had claimed her.

She resisted at first. An older man was not in her future plans, yet she was unable to deny what was happening to her.

His vortex tours were combined with a wood-carving prac-tice. When she heard, through Kelly, that he was looking for an assistant to help out in his studio, she applied for the job. She grew accustomed to the haze of sawdust and clusters of wood chippings, the scents of pine and camphor – and sometimes a nutmeg smell that transported her back to the Nook at Christ-mas, stirring Christmas puddings and making wishes. He used juniper, laurel and cypress, cut-offs that he collected from lumber companies and turned into precise replicas of coyotes, bobcats, bears and *javelinas*. They travelled to craft fairs and galleries where his carvings always sold out. Sitting beside him in his dust-covered van with its painted images of *saguaro*s and towering bluffs, Lorraine quivered every time his arm brushed against her.

'Take those stars out of your eyes,' Kelly warned when she called into the studio one afternoon. She collapsed, groaning, onto the nearest chair: she had another month to go on her pregnancy, and was afraid her ankles would never be slim again. 'Settling down is not on Victor Gordon's agenda. As long as we've known him, he's always only linked up with women who are passing through. If they talk about staying on, he takes off to the mountains. Apparently, he fasts for weeks among the rocks, or so I've heard. It adds a whole new dimension to getting your rocks off, if you'll excuse the pun.' She was joking, yet serious in a way that suggested she knew what she was talking about from personal experience. She seemed happy with Seth yet, sometimes, there was a slope to her mouth that belied all her talk about inner harmony.

It was easy to dismiss Kelly's advice. Lorraine had recognised something in Victor that echoed her own loss. She glimpsed it occasionally when he was carving wood, his attention focused on each exquisite turn of a chisel or knife. She would hear him sigh, as if the physical activity of his hands allowed him to drop his guard. His thoughts seemed far removed from Sedona in those instances, and she would wonder at the journey he had taken to reach this red-baked terrain. Kelly had told her he was a qualified relationship and family counsellor, and also a licensed mental-health coach. He had given up his practice in California, settling instead for a nomad life in Sedona where his charisma, rather than his qualifications, brought people to him.

Idyllic. That was how she viewed those first six months in Sedona – but everything changed after Naomi Nelson was born.

Kelly gave birth to her in the back of the van where she and Seth lived. Easy and natural, she told Lorraine afterwards. No drugs, no gas, just Seth with his gentle hands. They didn't register her birth, Kelly said when Lorraine asked. Naomi was a child of nature and would go wherever the wind took her parents. Fate, however, had other ideas. Naomi's tiny presence was short-lived, and remained unregistered. She was only two months old when Kelly, milk-drenched and sleepy in the small hours, lifted her from her wooden cradle and found her floppy and unresponsive. Two days later her parents drove away, a tiny white coffin replacing the cradle. Their dream of freedom crushed, they returned to the anonymous suburb in Chicago from where they had originally escaped.

Lorraine never saw them again, but their departure, and Naomi's sudden death, broke the spell that had consumed her since she arrived in Sedona.

Victor, also, seemed devastated by the baby's death. Lorraine came early to the studio one afternoon and found him at his work bench. He was startled by her arrival, unable to wipe tears from his face. She was surprised to see him so undone. Lines she had barely noticed until that moment had deepened around his eyes and strands of silver were visible in his springy black hair. She was starkly aware of their age difference yet, conversely, having witnessed this unexpected vulnerability in him, that gap seemed bridged and gave her the confidence to put her arms around him. His body shook, as if he was still reacting to such an unexpected onslaught of emotion.

Was he Naomi's father? What else could have caused him to weep so violently?

'I didn't expect you here so early,' he said, as he dried his eyes. 'Sorry you had to witness my distress.'

'Everyone's upset over Naomi,' she said. 'To be taken so young and for no reason. It's so unfair.'

'Life's never fair, Lorraine, yet we're constantly taken aback by this reality. Life is about making decisions and crossing your fingers in the hope that they are the right ones.'

'Have you always made the right ones?'

'Yes.' He answered with certainty.

'But what if your decisions rebound off others in a negative way?'

'Or their decisions rebound off me.' He shrugged. 'We all have to find our own path and keep to it.'

'From where I'm looking, your path seems a lonely one. There's something priestly about you, and priests, I think, are the loneliest of us all. Kelly told me you take to the mountains if any woman shows more than a passing interest in you. Was that her experience?'

'You think I had a relationship with Kelly?'

'I don't know.' She looked away, embarrassed by her boldness yet anxious to continue their conversation.

'Kelly was troubled when she first came here,' he said. 'She believes I was responsible for her healing, but she's wrong. Everything she achieved in Sedona, she did by herself. My only involvement was to guide her forward. That's all I'm capable of doing to anyone. Ultimately, we're all on our own and if we're unable to change ourselves then what hope have we of changing the world around us?'

'I'd wondered about Naomi...' She hesitated.

'If *I* was her father?' His face was still flushed from weeping.

'You're so upset. It crossed my mind.'

'Naomi was Seth's child. And, yes, I'm upset, as are you at such a random waste of a life barely begun.' In the quiet moment that followed she allowed her relief to seep through her and he, as if understanding the effort it had cost her to discuss this with him, gazed steadily back at her.

'Would it matter to you if I'd been her father?' He was the first to break the silence.

'It's none of my business.'

'I think it is, Lorraine.'

His eyes reminded her of pools stained by centuries of bog, fathomless until the sun gleamed like amber on the still waters.

Could he guess at the wildness of her thoughts. Did he share them?

She held his gaze and tasted the salt of his tears when they kissed.

Opening her mouth to him, she lost herself in the plunge of touch, the swelling anticipation, the fervour of discovery. He slipped off her T-shirt and shorts, and she, reaching for him with the same impatience, uncaring that this moment had not been planned, gasped as he lifted her to the workbench, her legs encircling him, enticing him into her, harder, harder... how easily they came together, her lips swollen from the pressure of his kisses. *A rip tide*, she thought. She was in the middle of a desert and drowning in the luminous depths of his dark-brown gaze.

Two months later, Lorraine was wilting under the intense heat of Arizona. She looked at the landscape with new eyes. Whereas, before, she had seen only the beauty of the plants and been amazed by their ability to survive in desert conditions, she was now aware of the dangers they posed: the jumping *chollas* with its vicious bristles, the poisonous bells of the sacred datura and the banks of poison ivy. Spiders, rattlesnakes and scorpions – how could she have ignored the threats they posed in the reddened earth? Even the *javelinas* rummaging with their pig-like snouts in the bins at night frightened her. She longed for the formation of clouds, the sudden downpours, the wind whipping her cheeks.

She was unsurprised when she discovered she was in the early stages of pregnancy. Too late to be careful after their first unheeding loving.

'I'm not cut out to be a father.' Victor's stunned reaction when she broke the news to him filled her with dismay. 'I don't have the capacity within me to nurture a child. It's something I've always known about myself.'

'How can you say that?' she demanded. 'You loved Naomi. I saw how you held her. How gentle you were with her.'

'I minister freely to others because I've no personal responsibilities. Having a child will take that energy from me.' He spoke with such certainty, a visionary with his own sense of self-awareness.

'Are you listening to yourself?' She didn't try to hide her anger. 'You weren't thinking about saving the world when you had me on that workbench. And your energy was charged in only one direction.' She slapped her hand against her stomach, flat and firm for now; but already her body was changing, and she was becoming accustomed to the sudden prickling in her breasts, the waves of nausea and tiredness.

'I've been careful—'

'Afterwards. But not that first time.'

'I regret—'

'I don't want your regrets. I don't want your excuses. I'll give our child the love you're incapable of giving and more... so much more. Take your psychic energy and stick it where the sun don't shine.' She flung open the door of his studio and was about to leave when he slammed it closed and pulled her roughly to him.

'Stop it, Lorraine, and listen to me for a moment! You're right to be angry with me and I'm sorry for reacting the way I did. Your news—'

'*Our* news.'

'It triggered something in me.'

'Like what?'

'Something that happened long ago and is not relevant to this discussion.'

'From your childhood?'

He hesitated then nodded. 'My parents were hippies who believed the grass would always be greener when they reached the next commune. I'd no idea what a normal home was like. Much as I longed for one when I was a boy, I inherited their need to keep moving. But I never wanted to impose that life on a child. That was why I decided I'd never marry or have a family.'

'Then I guess you'd better head up to the mountains and start fasting again.'

'I'm not going anywhere,' he said. 'I'll support you in whatever decision you make. If you decide not to have—'

'There will be no abortion.' Lorraine was no longer angry. She needed to be clear-headed if she was to make a future with him. *Change yourself first before you change the world*, he had said, and she had changed much since she left home. 'You won't have to worry about me,' she said. 'I'm going back to Ireland. My friend is getting married and she's asked me to be her bridesmaid. My father has also been in touch. He's anxious that I return home and run Serenity Falls with him.'

Arthur Kilbride had sounded different when he phoned, his voice no longer dulled or indifferent. He had greeted Lorraine warmly and apologised for what he called his 'absolute self-absorption'. As he outlined his plans for the future, she wondered if he had been seeing a therapist or undergone some fundamental experience that had lifted him out of his depression over the untimely death of his wife. He intended refurbishing Serenity Falls as a boutique hotel with spa facilities and a swimming pool. He needed her with him to make it a success.

'Living like a hippy may have an appeal when you're in your early twenties, but it won't see you through your life,' he had said. 'I want to leave you something with substance when I'm gone.'

She had refused his offer and told him she had no intention of leaving Sedona. But instead of being annoyed with her, he had told her to take as long as she needed to think about his proposal.

'I thought his hotel was defunct.' Victor sounded surprised.

'He's reopening it again,' she said. 'I studied hotel management for two years before I came here. I knew from the beginning that it was not the right career for me so I never completed my degree. But I have a vision for Serenity Falls and I intend to make it come true.'

'Which is what?'

'My father is a businessman. If I go to him with a proposal fully costed and worked out, I believe he'll agree to it. My intention is to create a retreat where couples can come and be spiritually healed, especially those who are coping with difficult relationships.'

'What do you know of such relationships?' Victor asked. 'You're twenty-one years old. How can you possibly understand the demands of love, and all that originates from it?'

'I wish you wouldn't patronise me.' Why was he making her sound like a naïve twenty-one-year-old with grandiose aspirations?

'I'm not being patronising.' He was quick to refute her accusation. 'But what you're talking about would be a massive undertaking. Couple counselling is one of the most complicated kinds of therapies.'

Love, she had often heard him say, was a beast that could never be tamed. It was a pain machine and a wellspring of happiness. One seemed incapable of existing without the other. His ability to find the path in between was what drew people to him. They confided in him and were willing to expose their unhappiness, knowing he would handle their pain with care. Other people's pain, Lorraine thought with sudden clarity. Pain that he could afterwards discard with a handwash and a cooling drink of water.

She had to change his mind. Their futures had been

decided in that initial shock of recognition. The knowledge had been contained within her in a hard kernel of awareness since their first meeting, and was being released to her in tentative stages, each one bringing her closer to Serenity Falls.

Was loss of love the motivating force behind her idea? Yes, that was it, she decided. She had enjoyed unconditional love throughout her childhood and lost it when Eloise died. In Sedona, she had experienced a different kind of loving, more consuming and demanding, more ruthless. A war of sorts, and one she was determined not to lose. Serenity Falls had failed as a hotel and was waiting patiently for rebirth. She would bring the energy of the vortex home with her and use it to establish a haven where love could be rekindled. A marriage retreat that she would run with Victor by her side. Anything else was inconceivable.

'I'll create an environment at Serenity Falls where couples can find happiness again.' She spoke with certainty. 'Even if that proves impossible, they can leave Serenity Falls with a new direction and sense of purpose. It will be a continuation of what you do here in Sedona.'

She was offering him an apple, tempting and ripe. Would he accept it, or head up into the mountains and remove himself from the responsibilities of love, with all its messy skeins?

The answer became apparent as the weeks passed. How could she expect him to give up everything he had achieved in Sedona for a vision that could disintegrate in a puff of smoke he would demand each time she tried to discuss her idea with him? Yet, at other times, she sensed his interest and could almost feel the drag of his indecisiveness. Her own conviction never wavered.

That was the state of play between them when Hamish McAdam, sweaty and dusty from exploring canyons, entered Hot&Saucy where she still worked an occasional shift. He demanded a large beer. The thirst on him would drain an ocean dry, he told her. His laughter was loud as he introduced himself. Hamish by name and harmless by nature. Scottish, Highlands born and bred, but Sedona was more to his liking, especially if there were lassies like Lorraine on the loose. He ogled her and called her bonnie, asked what she was doing when her shift ended.

She was used to men trying to chat her up. She looked upon it as a tedious aspect of waiting tables, but Hamish was not just passing through. He had rented a premises a few doors down from the restaurant, and planned on opening a tattoo parlour.

Victor arrived and took his usual seat by the window. Three women entered soon afterwards and gravitated towards him. From the snatches of conversation Lorraine caught, they had been to the Bell Rock vortex and were interested in hearing about other energy sites.

'Is he the vortex gadgie?' Hamish leaned back on his stool and looked over at the table.

'The who?' Lorraine asked.

'The laddie who does the tours?'

'Yes, he's Victor Gordon.'

As if aware that he was being observed, Victor glanced towards the bar, then turned his attention to one of the women, who had produced a map.

Hamish pushed himself off the stool and made his way towards them. From his unsteady walk, it was clear that Hot&Saucy had not been his first stop-off point.

'Share and share alike,' he said, as he pulled out a chair and forced himself between the women. 'I'm Hamish but harmless.' He handed out business cards to the women and slapped one down on the map Victor was studying before returning to the counter for another beer.

He refused a menu when Lorraine offered it to him. 'You're

food enough for my soul.' He leaned across the bar and cupped her face before planting a moist, noisy kiss on her lips.

'Let her go.' Victor had crossed to the counter and was staring angrily at Hamish.

'Are you her keeper?' Hamish tightened his grip on her and tried to kiss her again.

'No one's my keeper.' Lorraine shoved him away from her. 'You'll have to leave if you don't behave.'

'Stroppy lassie.' Hamish grinned and folded his arms. 'Be nice to me and I'll tattoo your fanny for free—'

Victor's fist sent him sprawling to the floor. Before he had time to recover, Victor had straddled him and was aiming blows at his face with such ferocity that it took Lorraine and two men to pull him off.

Hamish, wiping blood from his nose, had managed to stand upright. 'You sound like a Yank but you've the fists of a Scot,' he said. 'I'll not forget you in a hurry, laddie.'

'We're leaving.' Victor took Lorraine's arm and hurried her from the restaurant. He had been so shaken by the fight that he slumped down on the bench outside, his arms dangling between his knees.

'That man... his hands on you... I couldn't bear it.' She could scarcely make out his halting words. His violent outburst seemed to be as much of a surprise to him as it was to Lorraine. It reminded her of his savage weeping after Naomi's sudden death and was a further indication to her that behind his laid-back image, he was capable of powerful emotions.

'It was nothing, Victor. He was drunk.' She cradled his head against her stomach, stroking his thick strands of hair back from his flushed face.

Hamish staggered past them, having been unceremoniously ejected from the restaurant by the owner.

A tremor passed through Victor as he lifted his arms and encircled her.

'I'm sorry for the way I've behaved,' he said when the Scotsman had entered an empty building a few doors further along the square, presumably his future tattoo parlour.

'I know how much you miss your home yet all I've done is undermine what you proposed without giving it the serious consideration it deserved.' Victor sounded thoughtful. The energy had returned to his voice and Lorraine was aware that something fundamental had changed between them. 'If it's not too late, I want to make amends. Tell me again about this wonderful place you call Serenity Falls.'

FIVE

LORRAINE

Aidan's face was wet with tears when he saw her waiting for him in Arrivals. Exhausted from countless hours in the air and hanging around two airports waiting for connections, he looked so different from the vibrant, sun-tanned man who had waved her and Victor goodbye at the end of their Canadian visit. The distress of his father's sudden death was evident in his pallor and red-rimmed eyes. His hair, as blond as hers, was cut so short she could see the outline of his scalp. Last year he had worn it long. He had grown a hipster beard but that, too, had been shaved off, and his chiselled cheekbones added to his gaunt appearance. *He's shriven*, she thought. She envied his sorrow. It was a straightforward emotion, understandable and, in time, would become endurable. But, lies and betrayal – where was she to go with that combination?

Three days since Victor's death and her fears about publicity had turned out to be groundless. The front pages on the morning afterwards were dominated by a gangland shooting that had taken place the previous night during a wedding reception at a hotel. Carl Sheridan's by-line sat underneath the banner headline *Three Men Dead at Wild West Wedding*.

The motorway crash had been relegated to fillers in the morning papers. No names were mentioned and the stark facts were confined to the location of the accident and the number of dead. This was accompanied by a brief description of the young, still unidentified woman and the clothes she had been wearing.

The shootings had happened on the grounds of the hotel. Photographs had been taken at the crime scene. A smooth lawn and swaying palm trees, a huddle of dead bodies covered with sheets. Three other families were coping with the same news that Lorraine had received that afternoon. One of the victims was the nephew of a known gang leader. It was possible that a revenge massacre could take place very soon.

She should have felt some empathy towards the stricken families, who were coping with the same devastating loss as she was, but her main reaction was one of relief that the shooting had diverted attention from Victor and his passenger.

'Tell me everything,' Aidan said, as she drove from the airport. 'You hardly gave me any details on the phone.'

'I might as well tell you now as later.' She changed lanes, swerving so sharply into the outside lane that the driver behind her sounded an alarmed warning on his horn. 'There was a woman in the car with Victor. She has yet to be identified.'

'A *woman?*' His emphasis was an echo of how the media would react when the names of the dead were released.

'She's young, younger than you, I'd say. I don't know her name or anything about her. She's badly injured and not expected to survive.'

'Why she was in Dad's car?'

'I'm sure there's a perfectly logical explanation, but I don't have it at the moment.'

'How come she hasn't been named? Surely she had identification on her. What about her phone—?'

'She didn't have a phone with her.'

'That's impossible.' His disbelief would have amused her at any other time.

'Apparently not. The gardai haven't found anything on her or in the car that can help them to trace her family. I saw her when she came out of the operating theatre. She'd had emergency surgery on her head. Her face was swollen and badly bruised but I could tell immediately that she was a stranger.'

She followed the signpost for Dublin and veered onto the M1. Traffic pulsed steadily along the three lanes and she had a brief glimpse of the cars on the opposite side of the motorway. That was where the accident had occurred. It had caused a major delay before it had been cleared away. Cars and trucks had been unable to move for ages. She imagined the scene: the flashing lights and hi-vis jackets, the crushed metal, the blood and screams. She could not endure it, and yet she must.

Yesterday, she had met with Malcolm Cleary, the undertaker from Potters Glen. He held her hands in a reassuring clasp and the sympathy he conveyed had the sturdiness of a rope that would hold her secure throughout the preparations for Victor's funeral. A date would be set as soon as the post-mortem was over. It should be a straightforward procedure, according to Malcolm. The gardai had no reason to ask for a postponement, unlike the unfortunate truck driver, whose body had to be repatriated to Poland.

Malcolm had left just as the liaison officer was arriving. Lorraine watched from the window as he stopped in the courtyard to speak to Jean. They both had the thankless task of comforting the grieving.

'How soon can I see Victor?' Aidan asked. He had begun to use his father's first name shortly after he started boarding school.

'Malcolm will let us know when that's possible.' Did she sound as detached as she felt? Her sense of unreality continued to grow. Was that normal? Was 'normal' a word that could be associated with such a situation?

Aidan was silent for a while, his gaze fixed on the traffic flowing past.

'What else have you kept from me?' he asked.

His direct question was impossible to ignore.

'Victor decided to fly back two days earlier than planned.' She brought her attention back to him. 'But I may have been wrong and got the dates mixed.'

'You're never wrong, Mum.'

A quick glance at his solemn expression assured her he was not being sarcastic.

'Do you think that woman was the reason he came back early?'

'I don't know, Aidan. I'm so confused...'

'He would never have...' He hesitated, searched for an appropriate word then spread his hand outwards. 'You know what I mean—?'

'Be unfaithful to me?'

'Yes. *Absolutely.*' He nodded vigorously. 'He never would.'

'I know that. I just hope we find out who she is before she dies.'

'I want to see her.'

'Why on earth—'

'What if she's from Potters Glen... one of my friends? Victor could have been giving her a lift to the village.'

'If that was the case, her family would have reported her missing by now. But no one has contacted the police.'

'She could be working in Dublin or attending uni. Her family mightn't have realised yet that she's missing.'

'I'd have recognised her if she was from the village.' She slowed down, aware that she was breaking the speed limit.

'You said her face was messed up, so how would you know?'

After a pause, Lorraine nodded. 'I'll talk to Jean and see if

that's possible – for you to see her, I mean. She's our family
liaison officer.' She indicated and moved into the lane for the
turnoff to the M50 motorway. It was important to focus...
focus... one slip... that was all it took for unimaginable consequences to blast the future to pieces. She swerved onto the M50
junction and continued an uninterrupted journey towards
Wicklow.

Jean agreed it would be useful for Aidan to see the unconscious
woman. She would check with the hospital authorities and
arrange a time for him to be admitted to ICU. She also
confirmed that the gardai were still waiting for someone to come
forward to report a missing person answering her description.

The young woman's face was more shapeless and swollen than
Lorraine remembered from the first night. Tubes and monitors
surrounded her. A ventilator kept her breathing. Fluids entered
and left her body as she laboured to live. It seemed such an
impossible task for her frail body to undertake.

Aidan shook his head. He touched the woman's face with
his fingertips. Lorraine resisted the urge to pull his hand away.

'Does she understand that we are here?' he asked.

The nurse who had brought them to her bedside told them
quietly that no one truly understood what lay within the subterranean layers of the unconscious mind.

———

Drug gangs and their revenge killings continued to dominate
the headlines in the lead-up to Victor's funeral. Two more men
were dead and a woman, shot on the driveway of her house, was
critically ill in hospital.

Her husband's death, still tragically fresh to Lorraine, was old news in the rolling media circuit.

The melodic voices of Fr. Smithson, Reverend Deane and the humanist celebrant, Alyssa Grant, combined to perform the kind of ecumenical service Victor would have wanted.

Aidan delivered the eulogy. None of the rancour that existed between him and Victor was evident as he eulogised his father.

Writing it had been hard. As he had struggled to piece together his father's early life, Lorraine had realised how little she knew about Victor's youth. She had asked him, of course: questions about his parents, both dead, and hippies even before the word became hip. They had lived in communes throughout the States. She remembered him mentioning California, Arizona, Vermont, Virginia and Tennessee, but he had been born in South Carolina. She was sure there were other states but she could no longer remember. Rootless, Victor had come to her fully formed in Sedona.

Lorraine remained dry-eyed as the organ swelled. 'Panis Angelicus' soared in the voice of a soprano, while the soft, plucking strains of a harpist playing Leonard Cohen's 'Hallelujah' —Victor's favourite song—accompanied Aidan and the five other pallbearers from the church. People reached out to touch her arm and offer sympathetic smiles. If there was curiosity among them, and she was sure there must be, it was masked – apart from Carl Sheridan. The reporter's eyes narrowed as she walked down the aisle. Resolutely, she kept her gaze fixed on the wicker coffin as she moved slowly past him.

The sun stayed out for the afternoon. A lunch reception at Serenity Falls had been prepared for the mourners. They overflowed from the house into the grounds, where the solemnity of Victor's burial was replaced by reminiscences and laughter. He would have enjoyed his send-off and found nothing unusual in the gathering of admirers. *As he lived, so he died*, Lorraine thought, as she walked to the orchard.

She stood on the spot where the Fosters had exchanged their wedding vows. They had attended the funeral and Amy, weeping openly when she entered Serenity Falls, had begged Lorraine to continue the wonderful programme Victor had initiated.

The doves were still cooing but they were off somewhere in the distance, their soft strains melodic and soothing. She pressed her face against the bark of the nearest tree and closed her eyes.

'Please accept my heartfelt sympathy, Lorraine.' Carl Sheridan's voice came from behind her. 'That was one of the most moving funerals I've ever attended.'

'Thank you, Carl.' She turned around to face him.

'An interesting line-up on the altar,' he said. 'Very diverse indeed. But that was Victor – all things to all men and women.' His smile, a clenched grimace, was fleeting enough as to be imagined. 'How are you coping?'

'As well as can be expected under the circumstances,' she replied with equal politeness. 'I have a good team supporting me.'

'That's essential at such a sad time.' His sympathy, with its oozing insincerity, was merely a prelude to the punch he would deliver. He did not forgive easily, she knew, and he was still consumed by a libel action she and Victor had instigated against him. How long had it been since he tried to destroy Rekindle Connections with his poison-pen feature? It must be eight years, but the words he wrote would never be forgotten – and must have also been on his mind as he attempted to outstare her.

'The woman with Victor... I gather she is *not* a member of your team.' He was the first to look away. 'The Garda Press Office has refused to comment but you must know who she is by now. I'm sure you'd like to clear up any misunderstandings that could arise.'

'There is no misunderstanding, Carl. I'm trying to deal with my husband's death and you're hassling me—'

'Lorraine... *Lorraine*, the last thing I want to do is hassle you. I'm trying to get the record straight before others get their hands on the story. You and Victor... you are... were...' He coughed softly. 'Your marriage was the gold standard. Victor's reputation as a love guru—'

'Don't you dare start that again! You invented that ridiculous name and tried to undermine him with it.'

'When have I ever written—?'

'ImplacableX! Don't bother denying it! I know it's your Twitter username. Grow up, Carl, and get over yourself. You libelled us and deserved everything that came your way. I'd advise you to leave my property before I call the police and tell them you're breaking a moratorium that's still legally binding.'

'Really? Let's wait and see how that works out.' He inclined his head towards her and walked away.

Rekindle Your Love at a Cost. As a headline it had demanded Lorraine's immediate attention when the feature had appeared in *Capital Eye* eight years ago.

> *The scenic village of Potters Glen, once famous for its distinctive crockery, is the home of love guru Victor Gordon and his much younger heiress wife, Lorraine. Since they established Rekindle Connections over twenty-four years ago, they have succeeded in amassing a fortune by convincing disillusioned marrieds that their love can be rekindled in the luxurious surrounds of Serenity Falls.*
>
> *Once owned by the renowned hotelier, the late Arthur Kilbride, it passed to his daughter after his tragic drowning,*

and was turned by the couple into a marriage retreat. Since then, it has catered for those who can afford the exorbitant fees they charge participants to confront the reality of their broken relationships. Over their five-day stay, they engage in a Rekindle programme that consists of the love guru's quack psychology, which is reputed to have come to him when he experienced a vision on a mountain top. Cupid's arrow is indeed gilded with gold when he aims it at the gullible.

'A conman with a messianic personality,' was the comment from one outraged participant. 'His champagne life-style is made possible through the credulity of desperately unhappy couples who believe there is a quick fix to their problems.'

The feature had continued for another five hundred words and had been illustrated with a photograph of her and Victor standing outside Serenity Falls.

At first, Lorraine had been astonished rather than angered by the content. Why the vitriol? Had he been drunk when he wrote it? A quick check through her records confirmed that he had never participated in a Rekindle programme, so he could not claim to be a disgruntled guest. The programme had occasional failures, which were always discreetly handled by Lorraine and resulted in a full return of the couples' fee. This had happened just a few weeks before the feature was published, when the marriage of one of the couples imploded towards the end of their stay. They had departed Serenity Falls stony-faced and intent on divorce.

Lorraine was still recovering from this failure when Carl's so-called exposé was published. Her anger, when it came, consumed her. She found out later that the sub-editor had been distracted by some family issue and had allowed the feature to pass without being properly scrutinised.

She wrote a powerful rebuttal which was published under

Victor's name. It included quotes from couples who had stayed at Serenity Falls, and whose marriages, Carl had claimed, were *'mindless and monotonous relationships on the brink of failure.'* The demonstration that took place outside the offices of *Capital Eye* seemed to spring spontaneously from those same ranks but was carefully managed by Lorraine, who notified the media in advance. The serious business of seeking legal recompense dragged on for two years and was finally settled out of court.

She had watched Carl's career self-destruct. Occasionally, she saw his by-line on a report from a county council meeting: sluggish details that he must have loathed writing. His redemption came when he uncovered corruption among some of the county councillors that had been festering just below the public gaze for years. After four years in the wilderness, he had been appointed as *Capital Eye's* crime correspondent, yet his vendetta towards Victor had never wavered.

A last minute settlement agreed on the steps of the courts stipulated that he would never write about them again. But one part of that moratorium had ended: it was impossible to libel the dead, and his speculative gaze before he walked away warned Lorraine that Carl Sheridan was well aware of that fact.

Later, checking Twitter, she saw how he was using his tweets to amplify Victor's link to the mystery woman. *#nonamegirl. #loveguru #unansweredquestions.*

SIX

GAIL

The Night of the Accident

Gail Robinson was working on the final edits of *Generational Carousels* when Carl Sheridan rang.

Seeing his name on the screen, she hesitated. Idle chatter belonged to their past. These days, Carl only rang when he had information to impart that would be of interest to both of them. Curiosity won out in the end and she took his call.

The information he delivered so abruptly and dispassionately didn't allow her time to cushion herself against the rush of memory.

Victor Gordon had died in a car accident.

'Oh, my god! How awful.' She paused to absorb the news. 'Where did it happen?'

'On the M1. The only survivor is the woman with him.'

'Lorraine—'

'No, not Lorraine. No one knows who she is – not yet, that is.'

'Is she badly injured?'

'She's in a coma and not expected to survive.'

'That's so sad. But she must have had some identification on her. A phone, bank cards—'

'That's what you'd expect but, no, nothing. The gardai are waiting on her to be reported missing, which they expect will happen soon. But why was she in his car? That's what I'd like to know.'

'There could be a dozen reasons—'

'Or there could be one.' The silence that fell had a waiting quality as she waited for him to elaborate. She was still trying to absorb the fact that he was dead – that larger-than-life man. The man who had effectively ended her marriage and, in the domino effect that followed, done the same to Carl.

'Are you still there, Abigail?' He demanded her attention.

'*Gail... Must* I keep reminding you?'

'Sorry... sorry. Old habits. You sound stressed.'

'I'm surprised by what you've told me, *obviously*, and I'm busy editing a documentary.'

'Sorry to disturb you. I thought you'd like to know. A personal call is always better than a text or hearing about his death on the evening news. That's if you bother checking out Ireland Inc. anymore.'

'I check RTE news every night at nine. Same political squabbles and health-of-the-nation issues. Some things never change.'

'Oh, they change all right. There's been a shooting here. I'm heading to the scene right now. Otherwise, I'd be covering the Gordon crash and checking out the story behind it.'

'What makes you so sure there is a story?'

'Instinct. I have the scent of it. You can help me out.'

'How so?' At last, he was getting to the point of his call.

'According to my sources, Lorraine has no idea who this woman is. Nor does she know what her husband was doing on the M1 when, apparently, he should have been in London giving a speech at one of those happy-ever-after marriage conferences. It's still running for another day at the Harlequin House Hotel. Far as I remember, that's fairly close to where you live. Call in there tomorrow and find out from the organiser what exactly his timeline was. According to Lorraine, he was supposed to be delivering his speech when the crash occurred. Check what photographs are available—'

'Let me stop you right there, Carl.' He had ruined her night and set loose the fiends of guilt. 'You can brood in the past all you want but I've no intention of joining you there. I'm busy and have a deadline to meet, which is why I'm burning the midnight oil. You have enough sources to fill an encyclopaedia so let them do your snooping. Victor Gordon can rest in peace, as far as I'm concerned, and I hope that that unfortunate woman recovers.'

'That's highly unlikely.'

'Then I hope she dies without regaining consciousness and suffering any more pain.'

'So, you won't help out—'

'How perceptive of you.'

'Please, Gail. I'm tied up with this gangland shooting. Apparently, the crime scene is like a slaughterhouse. I'm not going to have a free moment—'

'I said *no.*'

She heard his intake of breath and then his slow exhalation. 'If that's how you feel—'

'What I feel has nothing to do with it. You need to be careful. The Gordons would have destroyed your career with *Capital Eye* if your father hadn't been one of the shareholders.'

'Every word I wrote about them was true—'

'You distorted the truth for your own ends. You're lucky *Capital Eye* survived.'

'They ruined my life and yours. They established a cult—'

'I never told you it was a cult. That was your interpretation.'

'I got the facts straight from the horse's mouth, if you'll excuse the unfortunate simile.'

His laughter was harsh and intended to offend her.

She wanted to return to her documentary. Highlighting the corrosive impact of long-term unemployment on generations of the same families was preferable to listening to his grievances.

Gail could remind him that she and he together were responsible for his so-called ruination, but Carl was not a listener. She refused to whine with him. What was done was done. That was what she believed each time she was stopped in her tracks by actions that now, eight years on, had a dream-like sequence that could belong to someone else's life story.

'We're not having this conversation again,' she said. 'Goodnight, Carl.'

She ended the call and worked at editing a particularly long-winded exposition by a Tory politician who believed, without actually saying so, that the poor deserved to be kept firmly under the well-polished heel of the elitist boot.

But her conversation with Carl kept bubbling up in her mind. Unable to concentrate, Gail left her apartment and walked along the south bank of the Thames. The river calmed her as it always did but it failed to chase her memories away.

Serenity Falls, a three-storey house with Georgian windows, a stained-glass fanlight above the front door and a cobble-stone courtyard. She could see it standing tall at the end of a sun-dappled avenue lined with poplars. Five days at Serenity Falls. Five emotive, destructive days spent under the spell of Victor Gordon and his willowy, younger wife with her mane of blonde hair and brittle charm.

Gail shook herself free from her reverie and walked back to her apartment. She defrosted a lasagne and rang her mother. Noreen Robinson demanded to know – as she always did – if her daughter was happy. Gail answered in the affirmative and Noreen sighed, knowing she was lying.

Carl was inside her head when she went to bed. They were united by a mutually destructive act that had shaped their futures. The man who turned them in that direction was now a mutilated body in a morgue. She shivered, imagining the sights and sounds that must have brought the M1 to a shuddering standstill.

Morning brought no relief to Gail from her thoughts. It always took a couple of days to shake off the residue Carl left in his wake. She passed the Harlequin House Hotel on her morning jog. A banner hung above the front entrance with the words *Hearts and Vows Annual Conference*.

Unable to withstand the temptation, she entered the foyer. Heart-shaped balloons were everywhere, pink and blue, pink and pink, blue and blue. Love in all its diversity was on display. A poster of Victor Gordon still hung in the foyer and a small table with curved edges had been placed beneath it. A vase of flowers on the table, and an electric candle that released a serene glow, created what looked like a hastily assembled memorial shrine. Wrapped bouquets of flowers were piled on the floor beneath the shrine.

His latest book was on sale at another table. Gail picked up a copy and read the blurb. The theme was adultery. How affairs could be avoided and how, if they occurred, the truth was an essential tool for repairing the inflicted wound. Partners dealing with such heartache could learn from the experience and build a stronger, more enduring relationship. From the back cover, his smugly handsome face stared up at her. She remembered his compelling brown eyes, their magnetic intensity, and quickly laid the book down on the table.

The attendees streamed from the ballroom where the conference was being staged and gathered around a bar to consume their coffees and muffins. A woman carrying a bouquet of flowers crossed the foyer. Her brisk walk and red tailored trouser suit with matching high heels set her apart from the more casually dressed attendees. *Lucy Strong* was the name on her identification badge.

'Could I have a quick word?' Gail caught up with her and gesticulated towards Victor's poster. 'I'd like to speak to you about Victor Gordon. I'm hoping to write a short report for *Capital Eye*. It's an Irish daily newspaper.'

'Unbelievable and tragic.' Lucy stooped and added the flowers to the other bouquets. 'I'm afraid this is not a good time—'

'Just a few quick questions, if you don't mind. There appears to be some confusion over Victor's time schedule—'

'No confusion, just a rearrangement. He needed to return home earlier than planned. Strange to think that if he'd kept to his previous arrangement he'd still be alive. Fate is so random.'

'I agree. The woman with him—'

'I've already spoken to the Irish police about her. He wasn't with anyone while he was at the conference and he said he was going directly from the hotel to the airport. I'd be surprised if she was with him in London. He spent most of his time here and was more than generous when it came to interacting with our attendees.' She looked beyond Gail towards a younger woman who was hovering apologetically and tapping her watch. The attendees were beginning to move towards the conference room. Some couples stopped to stare at the poster. One man joined his hands in prayer, while a woman reached upwards to press her palm against Victor's smiling face.

'Are there any photographs from yesterday—?' Gail asked.

'You'll find some in the press room. They were mainly taken when he was giving his speech.' She spoke directly to the younger woman. 'Jade, will you show...' She paused, distracted. 'Sorry, what is your name again?'

'Abigail.' Gail had abbreviated her first name after her

marriage ended but she used it unthinkingly now, triggered no doubt by memories of her stay at Serenity Falls.

'Nice to meet you, Abigail.' Lucy was already moving away from her. 'Now, if you'll excuse me, I have to run. Jade will take care of you.'

As Lucy said, the photographs showed Victor Gordon on stage or engaging with his audience in workshop settings. *Did he feel a preordained tremor as he laughed and spoke with them?* she wondered. The women surrounding him were mainly middle-aged and older. Clues to the identity of his young companion in the car would not be found here.

Gail returned to her apartment and went online. The Irish media had dealt briefly with the crash, no names released. All their attention was on a shooting that had taken place at a wedding reception. Carl had written extensively about it. Another one of his features outlined the history between the two feuding gangs.

Eight years earlier, when Gail had been living in Dublin, the Charters were never out of the news, especially when a split occurred and spawned the Eastly Boys. The latter sounded more like a downy-faced boy band, but were even more ruthless and brutal than the Charters. Both factions seemed intent on wiping each other out and Carl, who viewed himself as their nemesis, had re-established his career on the back of their notoriety.

She had no intention of telling him she had followed his instructions. Victor Gordon was not a charlatan, as Carl insisted. He was merely a man who talked and others listened. She had listened and then made decisions. Her responsibility. Her choice. It was time for Carl to let go. There was never anything to expose at Serenity Falls except the desperate struggles of couples trying to hold their relationships together. Whatever tangled path Victor was travelling on the day he died had nothing to do with her.

SEVEN

LORRAINE

The family liaison officer rang on Monday morning with another update from the gardai as Lorraine was about to leave Serenity Falls for a meeting with her solicitor.

Over a week had passed since the accident and titbits were all Jean handed out.

No Name Girl. Who were her family? Surely, by now, someone should be missing a daughter or sister or niece or girlfriend or work colleague or fellow student. Someone should be distraught, bewildered, seeking answers, sticking posters to walls and storming social media, yet the police were no nearer to an answer than they were on the day of the accident.

They had released a description of the young woman, yet no one had come forward with information. Jean claimed that they'd checked CCTV at airports and ferry terminals. They were dependent on identifying her by the clothes she wore: her face was too distorted to give a clear indication of her features. CCTV footage on the M1 showed Victor's car seconds before the truck driver veered from his lane but she was not visible, apart from her head and her black hair. The angle suggested she was looking down at something on the floor, and was useless as a means of identification.

Lorraine ended the call abruptly and drove with Aidan to Dublin for the reading of Victor's will.

Jennifer Moore was clearly nervous as she welcomed Lorraine and Aidan into her office. Her grandfather, Brandon Moore, had been Lorraine's family solicitor until his death last year. This was Lorraine's first meeting with his granddaughter, who was now handling his clients. She had sensed Jennifer's anxiety earlier when they had spoken on the phone, a hesitation in her voice as if she was choosing her words carefully.

Her sympathy was genuine but there was something about her easy elegance as she lowered herself into a swivel chair that increased Lorraine's apprehension. She was used to reading body language and the lift of Jennifer's shoulders when she removed a folder from a drawer in her desk, her slow exhalation as she opened it, suggested that something was wrong.

'Mrs Gordon, were you informed—'

'Please, call me Lorraine. This is not the time for formalities.'

'Indeed.' The solicitor leaned forward slightly. 'Lorraine, did your late husband inform you that he'd decided to revoke his will?'

Her bluntness did away with any further small talk.

'Revoked his will?' A band of pain tightened around Lorraine's forehead. 'What do you mean?'

'All I can tell you is that Victor decided that there were some anomalies that he needed to change. He was keen to make an updated will as soon as possible.'

Anomalies? The word had a startling undertone, a prelude to dangerous revelations. 'Can you explain those anomalies to me?'

The solicitor paused before replying. 'That's client privilege, Lorraine. I'm afraid I'm not at liberty to discuss them. All I can say is that Victor wanted to make certain adjustments to his will. Sadly, his sudden death occurred before his new one could be signed and witnessed.'

'This is a mistake. It's ridiculous.' A faint humming in her ears swelled to a louder pitch and her mouth filled with saliva. She could feel the colour draining from her face, her skin prickling in response to the sudden chill that overcame her. She was going to faint. She clenched her fists and the bite of her nails into her palms enabled her to continue speaking. 'We made our wills together. They were witnessed in this office. Brandon organised it. Victor left everything he possessed to me.'

'I'm familiar with Victor's previous will. But, as I said, there were anomalies that in the light of his illness he needed to address.'

'Illness? Victor died in a car crash—'

'I'm referring to his heart condition. He accepted that his time was limited...' Jennifer's voice trailed away as she studied Lorraine's expression. 'You are aware that he had been diagnosed with serious coronary heart disease?'

'Of course.' Lorraine ground out her reply.

'Why didn't you tell me he was ill?' Aidan's surprised expression as he gripped her hand demanded an explanation.

'We'll talk about it later.' She was amazed at how convincing she sounded. 'I'll tell you everything then.'

Jennifer's office was a light-filled contrast to the black walnut panelling favoured by her late grandfather yet Lorraine was groping in darkness. *Trust, the bedrock of marriage. Honesty its core value.* Victor's voice resounded in her head. That dulcet tone that had so captivated her when they first met.

'We'd made an appointment next week to finalise the details and have his new will signed and witnessed,' Jennifer contin-

ued. 'Due to the tragic suddenness of his death, your late
husband has died intestate.'

'What exactly does "intestate" mean?' Aidan asked.

'In your father's case, it should be straightforward enough,'
Jennifer replied. Now that the bad news had been delivered,
she looked more relaxed. 'Lorraine, you'll inherit two-thirds of
Victor's estate and the other third will pass to you, Aidan.
Under Irish law, that's how it works when a spouse dies intes-
tate and his partner has outlived him.'

'How long will it take to organise the intestacy?' Lorraine
asked. 'I have a business to run and will need certainty as I go
forward.'

'If no issues arise, then I don't foresee any delays. But I can't
give you a precise date at this stage. I'm sorry, Lorraine. Another
week and everything would have been settled. I'll make this a
priority and have the legalities sorted out as soon as possible.
The fact that Serenity Falls is in Victor's name...' A faint line
between the solicitor's eyebrows deepened into a cleft. 'Am I
right in assuming that the house belonged to your family for
generations and you inherited it from your father?'

'Yes, it was originally bought by my great-grandparents.'

Lorraine was conscious of the solicitor's gaze, the rise of her
finely arched eyebrows. Jennifer might as well ask the question
aloud, instead of allowing it to hang in the air between them.

'I signed Serenity Falls over to Victor shortly after Aidan
was born,' she said.

'You *what?*' The gasp from Aidan left her in no doubt about
his reaction to the news.

'That was a very generous act on your part.' Jennifer's tone
was guardedly neutral.

Lorraine could only guess at her thoughts. Somehow, she
must make both of them understand why she had made such a
momentous decision.

'It was important to do so,' she said. 'My father had died

shortly after I returned to Ireland. Aidan was born five months later. As well as grieving for my father and coping with a new-born baby, I suffered from severe postnatal depression. I was convinced I'd inherited the same depression as my father, who suffered from it for years. Victor and I weren't married then. He wouldn't have had a roof over his head if anything had happened to me and in my state of mind that was always possible. I signed the house over to him so that he and Aidan would have that security. Victor was wonderful. If it hadn't been for his support, I doubt if I would have made it through that terrible time. I know how crazy that must sound now—'

'Please, don't think like that.' Jennifer was quick to reassure her. 'Very few of us manage to avoid the impact of depression at some stage in our lives.'

Lorraine's heartbeat pounded in her ears. She stared at the deeds for Serenity Falls as Jennifer laid them before her. Her signature was a faint, shaky smear at the bottom of the document. She remembered the strength of Victor's arms, his soothing reassurances. Did he hold her hand to help her sign the deeds? Treacle, dark and sticky – that was where those memories lodged.

She tried to concentrate on the conversation that followed but the solicitor's words seemed meaningless. Her reassurances that she would do everything in her power to move the intestacy process forward as swiftly as possible floated them towards the front door.

Outside, on Merrion Square, the everyday rumble of traffic was muffled by a cacophony of voices from the past, all shouting at Lorraine.

'Why did Victor never put Serenity Falls in both your names?' Aidan asked, as they walked through Merrion Square Park.

'It didn't matter,' she said. 'I knew it would be mine again when he died, and with our difference in age that was likely to be the outcome. Had I gone first, then it wouldn't have mattered who owned the house.'

'But why? That doesn't make any sense.'

'It did at the time. I don't expect you to appreciate my position but you were the reason I gave him the security you both needed.'

'I still don't understand. I *don't*. It's incredible that you signed over your family home—'

'You were my family, Aidan – you and your father.'

'Did he pressure you into doing it?' He was unable to hide his anger. 'I bet that's how it happened.'

'You're wrong.' She strode faster, forcing him to increase his pace. 'It was entirely my decision. Why do you always think the worst about your father? I couldn't have come through that awful time without his support.'

'I've never known you to be depressed. And you had years to change the deeds. Why didn't you?'

'Can we have this conversation another time?' she asked. 'When I'm stronger, I'll explain what it was like back then.'

She could not endure such unbearable memories. Then, as now, they leached the colours from her world and flattened the everyday sounds.

'Why didn't you tell me he was so ill?' Aidan continued. 'I would have come home—'

'He didn't want a fuss.' Lying to her son should not have been so easy, yet her answer slid smoothly towards him. Above them, the birds sang in a piercing, tuneless dirge. 'We would have told you sooner but the accident happened and... well... fate made the decision for us.'

'How do you feel about me owning one third of Serenity Falls and Victor's share of the business?'

'You'll own it all when I die,' she replied. 'One-third is just coming to you sooner than either of us expected.'

Aidan stopped abruptly on the pavement and turned towards her.

'Don't you even dare think about dying on me.' His voice broke on the words as he caught her awkwardly in his arms and pulled her roughly to him. The warmth of his cheek, the strength of his arms – she wanted to sink into him and be cleansed of memories.

He was still unsatisfied with her explanations, she knew. She was familiar with his tenacity, his determination to follow through on answers that didn't satisfy him. Nor had her answers convinced Jennifer Moore, no matter how impassive her gaze.

What woman would willingly cede ownership of her home to her partner, as Victor had been at that time, especially a house that had been in her family for generations?

How to explain to her son about a vision she conceived in the rugged grandeur of Sedona? A dream that became a nightmare when her father died, and all she had to keep her from sinking into the void he left behind was the strength of Victor's arms.

EIGHT

LORRAINE

The light was off in Aidan's bedroom when Lorraine left the Nook and walked through the hall to the office she had shared with Victor. Three generations of Kilbrides stared down at her from the wall, their portraits ornately framed. Each one added to the sense of continuity projected by Serenity Falls, a house she had recklessly ceded to another.

In the office, Victor's presence was still so strong, so evident, everywhere her eyes rested. His desk was tidy, as he always left it, the surface clear of anything except his work phone, computer and a selection of pens in a holder.

She had already searched throughout The Nook but had been unable to find his unfinished will. An *anomaly*. How benign that sounded. A glitch that would have been addressed if fate with its indiscriminate cruelty had not intervened.

She was consumed with the need to discover what he had he written into his new will. Lorraine opened every drawer in his desk but achieved the same result. Nothing even remotely controversial could be found anywhere. The filing cabinet consisted of ten sections filled with files, neatly tagged. The information they contained was specific and easily accessible. All was as it should be, yet the air resonated with secrecy.

The safe was concealed behind the portrait she had commissioned to celebrate their twentieth wedding anniversary. It was hanging slightly askew. Had Victor moved it before he left for London? Why hadn't she checked the most obvious place first? Thinking clearly was impossible when her mind was filled with suspicion and dread. Lifting down the portrait, she entered the combination code and opened the safe. She checked the contents twice, systematically examining each document before admitting defeat and replacing the portrait.

How distinguished Victor looked in the painting. Age had complimented his strong cheekbones and jawline; no sagging chin or bags beneath his eyes, his swept-back silver hair thick and plentiful. The sheen of the oil paint enhanced the smoothness of his skin yet the artist had not flattered him. This had been a true representation of her husband; but Lorraine would never be able to look at the portrait again without remembering the brutal destruction of his face after the crash. She had always disliked her own image in the painting. The artist had emphasised her eyes, their hazel tones, those tiny gold flecks bordering her pupils. Victor said they were the first thing he noticed about her. He had called her 'honey eyes'. At the time she wondered if it was his way of distinguishing her from the other women who grouped around him when he spoke about the powerful energies emanating from the red rocks of Sedona.

When Victor saw their portrait for the first time, he had commented on her self-assured gaze, yet all she saw within the glaze of oil were the secrets she hid.

She sank into his chair and allowed the leather softness to curve around her. His desk was identical to hers, with the same decorative trim edging the front of it. The engraving, consisting of a series of whorls, added to the feeling that her life was spinning out of control. The chair swivelled suddenly and the room seemed to sway with a sickening momentum. Why had he kept his illness a secret from her? Why revoke his will? Why lie about his return from London? And who was that woman? According to Jean, the investigation team was beginning to believe she could be from abroad. Ireland was too small and closely connected for someone to go missing for so long without an alarm being raised. Even if she was a tourist, why didn't she have a mobile phone, a passport or bank cards? Why hadn't she been seen in internet cafés connecting to her family? So many questions. No answers. And still, she clung to life, a tenuous thread that refused to snap.

The dizziness she had experienced in Jennifer's office was returning. She had fought it off then and must do so again. She concentrated her attention on the trim on Victor's desk and gradually became aware that there was a minute difference in the centre of the pattern. The keyhole was tiny enough to over-look in the delicately carved whorls and would open a drawer that she had forgotten existed. A space so shallow that it was useless for anything except pens or keys. She searched without success in the other drawers for the key that would open it and was about to give up when she noticed Victor's dark green waxed jacket hanging from a hook on the office door.

His pockets held tissues and parking tickets, lip salve, and a pedometer he used when he walked with guests along the cliff walk to the waterfall.

Eventually, she found the key in a pocket in the lining of his jacket.

The unlocked drawer slid open. At first, it appeared to be empty but her fingers, sliding forward, touched something that moved slightly to one side. Easing it out, she removed a folded sheet of paper.

Before opening it, she knew what she would read.

This is the last will and testament of me VICTOR GORDON of SERENITY FALL POTTERS GLEN in the county Wicklow I HEREBY REVOKE any Will or Wills by me at any time heretofore made I APPOINT my solicitor Jennifer Moore to be sole executor of this my will I DIRECT her as soon as possible after my decease to pay my just debts funeral and testamentary expenses I GIVE DEVISE AND BEQUEATH Serenity Falls to my said wife...

He had stopped writing at this stage and a number of Xs had been scrawled so heavily across the paper that it was slashed in places.

Lorraine checked the drawer again. This time she discovered a second sheet of paper that had been rolled up and secured with an elastic band. She removed the band and flattened the paper.

The writing was small, slightly loopy but legible, and signed by someone called Megan Ross.

Dear Max,

This letter will come as a surprise to you but I hope you will read it. It has taken time for me to find the courage to make contact with you but I believe this is the right thing to do.

Do you know that Candice is dead? Drugs. Inevitable. I'm sorry to be so blunt but as you were responsible for her entry into this world, then you should know that she has departed it.

Rosanna does not know I'm writing to you. She would forbid it but you are my concern, not hers. She is still angry and refuses to tell me anything about you. She says your name brings bile to her mouth. Can you blame her? You walked away from Lochanar and never looked back.

Do you ever feel a tap on your shoulder and shiver? I am that tap. You will wonder how I traced you. There's always a

*clue if you persist in searching for it. And, oh, how I followed
that trail of breadcrumbs.*

*Email me at 23meganLochanar@redbird.com to arrange a
meeting.*

Megan Ross

The letter, released from Lorraine's hand, coiled back in on
itself. She was reminded of a snake retreating after it had
inflicted its venom on a victim. Who was Max? Who was
Megan... Candice... Rosanna?

The young woman in hospital... Lorraine's thoughts turned
to her immediately as her mind reeled from one grotesque possibility to the next... *Did this mysterious stranger answer to the
name of Megan? No, surely that wasn't possible... and yet she
had demanded to meet Victor... no, not Victor... She had
demanded a meeting with someone called Max.*

Why was the letter in Victor's desk, rolled up beside the
will he had discarded? It made no sense whatsoever. She had to
calm down. Nothing would be gained from falling apart and
splintering the night with her fury.

Once again, she went through his desk and filing cabinet,
searching for names that would link to the letter. Every document she opened was related to Rekindle Connections. Nothing... nothing... nothing... Her husband was dead, and she had
become a spy.

She switched on Victor's computer, used his password and
typed *23meganLochanar@redbird.com* into the search mail. No
emails with that name showed up. She entered Megan Ross
and, again, drew a blank. On Facebook, she typed in the same
name. Numerous faces appeared, a dizzying array of women
smiling back at her. She tried Megan Ross Lochanar and drew
another blank, but other images appeared.

Lochanar was a small town in the Scottish Highlands.

According to the Wikipedia entry, it was located on the shores of a sea loch. She scrolled through photographs of gymkhana competitions – children riding ponies over jumps and standing to attention as they received their rosettes; other photographs must have been taken at Highland Games: bagpipe players marched in unison and cabers were being tossed energetically by men in kilts. Children danced in a swirl of tartan, their legs angled in that customary style of a Highland Fling, their hair tied in neat topknots. The shops on the high street of Lochanar belonged to another era with their many-paned windows and old-fashioned, arched entrances. She imagined bells tinkling, glass jars filled with Scottish tablet and humbugs. The loch had the grey restlessness of deep waters and the boats at the harbour flashed their dark reflections on the surface.

The computer screen blurred. Clamorous questions demanded answers and she had none. She tried to concentrate on the screen but was unable to absorb any further information.

All her joints were fused with pain as she switched off Victor's computer and locked the drawer on his desk. She made her way slowly back to the Nook. Normally, on such a night, guests would be sleeping upstairs. The dining room would still be redolent of whatever food had been served by the chef, Nick Tobin, for the communal dinner. The Chat Room and the consultation rooms used by the relationship counsellors would have been prepared for tomorrow's sessions.

She needed to focus on reopening Serenity Falls. Financial decisions would have to be made –but she was powerless to move forward until she understood why that letter was hidden in Victor's desk. Yes... hidden. Why else would he have locked it in that shallow drawer, along with his uncompleted will?

She opened the patio doors and stood in the walled garden. Herbs scented the air and berries ripened on canes. The weather was warm for May and the garden had responded. Six years since Pamela's mother had died, yet the gardens at

Serenity Falls still carried her distinctive mark. Dawn had risen and a wraith-like mist lay low on the ground. Spider webs slung on the bushes glistened with dewdrops. Such beauty would be seen by so few. Why waste it, Victor used to say, coaxing her from bed to witness the budding of a new day. She longed to cherish such memories. They were supposed to bring comfort to the bereaved and ease their path. A path she must learn to walk alone... except that she was sharing that path with another woman who, more than likely, was the author of that vicious letter. What were the odds? There was only one way to answer that question.

NINE

LORRAINE

She was conscious of colour as she drove westward towards Lochanar – breath-taking sweeps of green and golden swathes of gorse; lochs that appeared depthless in their icy-blue shimmer. Canoeists in red life jackets surged on the lather of rivers while the rocks, with their raddled faces, revelled in the emptiness of their landscape. No ribbon development here, no bungalow blight or clustered homesteads. Instead, just here and there, Lorraine saw a house, an almost furtive sighting, often abandoned and held together by crumbling stone and layers of creeping ivy. The ruins of a castle were a bleak reminder that even nobility had a limited life span.

Lochanar, when she finally reached it, was exactly as it was portrayed online. Houses were clustered along the shore of the loch and the bell tower of a small kirk rose above the chimneys. She had booked overnight into the Running Stag, a pub with accommodation attached. Her room was spotless, with crisp white sheets and pillowcases. Paintings of stags in various postures, mainly combative, hung on each wall.

Downstairs, the woman behind the bar, who also worked

reception, handed her a leaflet about the ruins Lorraine had passed. The castle and its ancient history was a site of interest in the area but the main attraction were the tour boats on the harbour.

Leaving the bar, Lorraine walked towards the centre of the town. Once again, she was struck by the familiarity of her surroundings, which was not surprising when she considered how often she had browsed Lochanar on the internet since she found the letter. The shops were closed for the night, apart from the local Co-op. Further along the road she came to an Italian restaurant, the tables visible through a chink in the slatted blinds. It was filled with diners but she was not in the mood to be absorbed into their conversations and laughter. The smell emanating from a fish and chip shop swept her back to Maria's Marina in Potters Glen. It was now a pizzeria but, in her teens, it had served the best chips in Wicklow, or so she and Pamela believed. Every Friday night they would sit on the wall outside, eating chips from bags that were almost too hot to handle.

She bought a portion of chips and walked to the loch, where lobster boats listed alongside the harbour wall. She picked her way carefully between the lobster pots piled on the pier and sat down on a bench facing the water. A tour boat with a cabin and a viewing deck was moored further along the harbour, along with some smaller fishing boats. She ate her chips and watched the lights in the town come on.

Pamela and Aidan believed she was in London meeting Lucy Strong. They had been surprised when she announced her decision to visit Lucy but understood her need to speak to the event's organiser, who would have been one of the last people to be with Victor before his death.

Was lying to those closest to her going to become common-place? Would a time come when she would no longer wince inwardly every time she did so? Almost two weeks had passed since Victor's death. She should be in the throes of grief. Instead she was struggling with confusion, suspicion and anger, and normal emotions had no space to grow in the maze of deception she was trying to navigate.

She had considered showing the letter to the gardai and allowing them to follow where it led. Almost in the same breath, she had changed her mind, afraid of what they would discover and how it would reflect on Rekindle Connections. She had brought a dream, envisaged in the rugged grandeur of Sedona, to this quiet corner of Ireland and turned it into a success. The future of the marriage retreat could be taken from her hands if she ceded control to the police and allowed them access to the contents of that vicious letter. She needed to follow the trail laid by Megan Ross before she could think about anything else.

She had wrestled with this fact while normality of a kind was restored at Serenity Falls. Pamela dealt with calls from couples who had booked to do the Rekindle programme in the weeks to come and, now, intended to cancel. Victor had been the face of the company, instantly identifiable. Without his charismatic presence, Serenity Falls would be an empty husk, one woman emphatically declared as she demanded back her deposit. Others were willing to keep their bookings but were anxious to know who would be replacing Victor.

Could they continue to operate without him? Pamela asked this question tersely and Lorraine, forcing her attention away from the insidious letter, agreed that they must issue an immediate press release stating their intention of reopening the marriage retreat as soon as certain adjustments had been made.

Her friend was unaware that anything was amiss regarding Victor's will. Lorraine had warned Aidan that what had been discussed in the solicitor's office was to remain between them. She had already been in touch with her stockbroker to sell the shares she inherited from her mother. The money would be used to tide the company over until the intestacy was complete.

Lorraine had never told Victor about those shares. It was the one secret she had kept from him. Had she known instinctively that a day like the one she experienced in Jennifer's office would come, and she would be forced to confront the truth of their relationship?

No... *no*... she could not think like that, not when it took all her energy to put one foot in front of the other. She cried all the time now: sudden surges that sent her running to private places. Here, with just the lap of the loch against the harbour wall, there was nothing to silence this need. Such outbursts didn't help and the questions still remained unanswered.

She balled the chip bag in her hands and walked towards a kiosk, where a rubbish bin was located. An advertisement there showed a picture of the tour boat she had noticed earlier. The advertisement promised sightings of dolphins, porpoises and seals. The sighting of a whale was also possible, but could not be guaranteed during the tours that took place mornings and afternoons.

Enquiries should be made to Rosanna Ross.

Her reaction to the name was primal. Skin-tingling. Victor would have said it was the truth knocking for attention before she was ready to acknowledge it. She leaned closer, the tears still wet on her cheeks, and made out the words *Rosanna's Redemption* on the side of the boat.

Lorraine quickened her pace until she returned to the Running Stag. She was surprised to see that the bar, empty when she left, was now busy. She found an armchair in the only quiet corner and ordered a glass of Pinot Grigio. Some of the customers were hillwalkers, their sticks set aside for the night. A group of fishermen in woollen hats, their skin burnished from salt and wind, sat on stools around the bar. The other type, the sea anglers, wore padded gilets. Seated at a nearby table, they talked animatedly about the curse of strong winds and the finest bait available.

Gradually, the crowd thinned out. Some were staying upstairs, but others made their way out into the night.

The woman behind the bar approached Lorraine. 'Would you like another drink before I close up?' she asked. 'I've odds and ends to do before I call it a night. I'm Maggie, by the way.'

Lorraine's ear was becoming acclimatised to the accents around her and she was tuned into the musicality to this woman's words.

'No, thank you, Maggie.' She smiled back at her. 'I'm hoping to have an early start in the morning and do a tour on *Rosanna's Redemption*.'

'It's worth doing, that's for certain. Rosanna lays on a good trip – well worth the price she charges. Have you booked your seat?'

'The kiosk was closed when I saw the advertisement. I didn't want to phone and bother her this late at night.'

'Nothing bothers Rosanna. I'll give her a quick call if you like.'

'You're very kind.'

'Eloise, isn't that your name?'

Lorraine twirled the empty wine glass by its stem and nodded. 'Yes. Eloise Kilbride.' The softness of the vowels and their rolling resonances transported her back to her childhood and the memory of her mother, smiling, vital and battling until the end.

Maggie disappeared into a room behind the bar. Her voice reached Lorraine but she was unable to make out what was being said.

'That's settled.' Maggie returned and nodded across the counter at her. 'Be on the pier at eight, Eloise.'

Sleep was difficult, despite the comfortable bed. Questions continued to torment her throughout the small hours. What would tomorrow bring? What would she say to Rosanna Ross when they came face to face? How on earth was Victor connected to this town, with its cosy warmth and steely-grey loch? It was so far removed from the scorched rocks of Sedona with their pulsing energies, yet there had to be a key somewhere that would unlock the mystery that had brought her here.

TEN

LORRAINE

Rosanna Ross walked and spoke with authority. She had the build to withstand the lurch of a boat and the force of a sudden gale should one dare to blow towards her when she was out on the loch. She imparted this information with a straight face and then grinned as the tourists, who had congregated around her on the pier, laughed obligingly. Her assistant, an older man named Andy, small, wizened and wiry, handed out life jackets while Rosanna gave instructions on how they should be fastened and worn at all times while they were aboard *Rosanna's Redemption*.

Lorraine had paid for the tour in cash, having taken money from the ATM in the Co-op earlier. She would pay her hotel bill from the same fund. She touched her belt bag where the notes were lodged and turned her head a fraction too late when Rosanna said, 'Glad you could make it, Eloise.'

Andy handed a life jacket to her. *He must be seventy*, she thought, yet he moved with the agility of a younger man. Rosanna's age was more difficult to gauge. She was medium-sized but shapeless under her life jacket. A peaked cap shaded her face and her eyes were hidden behind a pair of large sunglasses.

The skirl of bagpipes accompanied them as they boarded the boat. The piper was collecting for charity and some of the passengers tossed money into his collection box.

"'The Skye Boat Song,'" said Andy, when a woman asked for the name of the tune. He sounded resigned to answering this question, and the glare he gave the piper suggested he had heard the tune too often.

A second man was already at the wheel when they boarded the boat. Rosanna, microphone in hand, pointed towards the sky where clouds were beginning to scatter. She gave a thumbs-up as sun rays spilt onto the deck and added to the impression that this robust woman was in full control of the elements.

She projected her voice towards the crowd. Her accent was similar to Maggie's and fell pleasantly over the group. Everyone listened intently as she described the glacial randomness of the Ice Age and its impact on the loch. It had always been of interest to the scientific community, but was now attractive to tourists thanks to its remoteness and unique marine life. Everyone smiled in response when she praised their discernment in choosing Lochanar instead of the more popular Highland destinations.

The shore had disappeared from view. Adrift on a remote Scottish loch, Lorraine had no point of reference, no reason for being there except a letter wrongly sent to her dead husband. She swallowed bile. It soured her mouth as she remembered the words in the letter written by Megan Ross. *She says your name brings bile to her mouth.*

A collective gasp of wonder distracted her as a dolphin suddenly leapt from the water, and the passengers rushed to one side of the deck. Arching its sleek body into a downward dive, it disappeared but was immediately followed by others, all leaping in harmony. A cheer went up when one of the dolphins performed a double twist before diving back under the waves.

Lorraine wanted to be part of the euphoria that gripped the crowd. She listened to Rosanna describing the dolphin life cycle and felt a memory welling. One that should bear no relationship to this moment, yet it insisted on being acknowledged.

The time Victor almost died from a ruptured appendix. It happened so suddenly – discomfort turning to searing pain, a midnight rush in an ambulance to the hospital. He developed peritonitis and when his fever was at its height, he raved about Sedona. She believed his unconscious mind was calling on the energy of the vortexes to heal him. If that was the case, it succeeded. By morning his temperature had dropped and the danger had passed. But his voice... she allowed herself to hear him as he had sounded then: the unfamiliar cadences so similar to the accent of the woman addressing the crowd.

Lorraine wanted to hold her hands over her ears to block out the memory. It was only a pinprick in the wall of his sickness and she had hardly noticed it at the time. She was unable to remember anything sensible he had said in his fevered state but he had spoken the words, '*Mo grá... mo grá...*' repeatedly. Translated from the Irish language, it meant 'My love,' and Lorraine had believed it belonged to the smattering of Irish phrases he had picked up since his arrival in Ireland.

She leaned over the rail and stared at the heaving dolphins and their rhythmic drive through the waves. She was unaware that she had moaned aloud until Andy stood beside her and patted her arm.

'No need for the nerves, lass,' he reassured her. 'Rosanna has your back, never fear.'

The boat veered around an islet where seals, basking on rocks, gazed impassively back at the barrage of cameras. Rosanna had switched her attention to the life cycle of seals and their habitats. They headed further into the loch where, according to Rosanna, she had spotted a whale earlier in the month. No sightings since then, but it was a hopeful sign that conditions were attracting them to the loch. What a whale of a time they would have then, she said. This time the laughter was not so obliging. The dolphins were the highlight of the trip and people were growing tired of looking at the grey swell of the loch.

The man at the wheel turned the boat in a wide arc and headed back to the pier. Rosanna asked if anyone has questions. One of the passengers queried her belief that it was *actually* a whale she spotted. Could it have been a monster similar to the one in Loch Ness? The group looked hopefully towards Rosanna who remained polite as she outlined the reason why it was most definitely a whale – mainly video evidence.

'Why did you call your boat *Rosanna's Redemption*?' The woman who spoke next had heavily accented English and wore a Bayern Munich football shirt. 'As a German citizen, I cherish the word "redemption" so I am curious as to why you chose it.'

Her blunt question silenced the chatter among the group.

Rosanna pushed her cap back to reveal her high forehead and scratched her head before pulling it forward again. 'I agree with you,' she said. 'It's not a word to be used lightly yet all of us, I'd hazard a guess, have had experiences of redemption. This boat has been my redemption. It gave me hope and a future at a time when my life seemed bleak and meaningless. If you would like me to answer your question even more directly, life only made sense when I had a glass in my hand.' She spoke simply and the group nodded, as if deeply moved by her admission.

An elderly man in a high-vis rain jacket, asked about the earth's crust and its function in creating the loch. Rosanna answered readily and the atmosphere was relaxed as the tour drew to a close.

Lorraine disembarked and waited until the passengers had left the pier. The fishing trawlers were out, as were the boats hired for angling. She sat on the bench and leaned her back against it. Her face stung. She never thought of sunscreen.

Andy came ashore, followed by the younger man, who carried a bottle of water. He stopped and took a long swig from the bottle before looking back and shouting something to Rosanna.

His voice carried towards Lorraine and forced her eyes closed. Victor was everywhere. She saw him in the set of a stranger's shoulders, the cast of a forehead, the movement of hands, the line of a profile and, now, she heard him in this man's tone.

Was this to be her future? Haunted by similarities until her memories of him faded and she was no longer able to see his shade in others or hear an intonation in a voice that echoed his?

'Are you all right there, lass?' Andy stopped beside her. 'You look a wee bit scunnered.'

'No, I'm all right.' She sat up straight and opened her eyes. 'Rosanna was wonderful, so informative.'

'Aye, she's class, fair enough. The boat tours were her idea. Figured Lochanar needed more space on the map so had the boat built to her specifications. It's bringing a tidy number of visitors to the town and if there are more whale sightings... well, who knows?' He turned around to face the younger man who was walking towards them. 'Wouldn't you agree, Evan?'

Not so young, she realised, as Evan drew nearer. Mid-forties, she decided. Until now, she had barely noticed him. He was simply the helmsman at the controls and only partly visible from his cabin.

She half stood as he smiled and nodded in answer to Andy's question. Her hand gripped the side of the bench, the back of her neck suddenly damp. Was she going to throw up? She could blame it on sea sickness or whatever was the equivalent when it occurred on a loch excursion.

The knowledge that she was going to faint came over her

but, in that fraction of time before her senses fell away, she believed joyously that she had awakened from a nightmare: Victor was alive again and walking through the radiant colours of Sedona towards her.

She opened her eyes. Clouds drifted across a blue sky. One of them reminded her of a shark; another formed a perfect swan, its glide soon blotted out by Andy's face. He looked even more wizened than before, his mouth puckered with anxiety. Why was she lying on the ground? And why was Victor at Andy's side when he was cold in the grave?

Tears ran down her face. She was helpless against them but she made no sound as she gathered her wits about her.

'Don't move yet.' Evan – who was not Victor, not even like him except in a most superficial way – pressed a bottle of water to her lips. He lifted her head slightly to help her to drink. His touch was gentle and assured. She gulped water too quickly and her body shuddered in response.

'I'm okay... really,' she managed to gasp, and pushed the bottle away. He helped her to stand. She was still dizzy but she managed to remain upright.

'Let me look at you.' Rosanna was breathless when she joined them.

Minus her lifejacket, cap and sunglasses, she looked older than Lorraine had originally thought but her authoritative voice was unchanged. She lifted her index finger before Lorraine's eyes and ordered her to follow its direction.

'Do you know where you are?' she asked.

'Lochanar.'

'Can you tell me your name?'

'It's... it's...' She felt danger where there was none – just three people helping her to recover her mind and her balance. She ground her teeth and forced herself to concentrate on the reason she was there. Evan had his hands on either side of her shoulders and was still supporting her. His breath was warm on the back of her neck. Was she still sweating? Probably. She stepped away from him.

'I'm Eloise Kilbride,' she said. 'I'm sorry for causing such a fuss.'

'Sit down and take your time.' Observing her, Evan hovered around her for an instant longer.

'You need strong tea,' said Rosanna. 'Nessa will have the kettle on in the office.' She gestured towards the kiosk. 'Lean on me if you feel weak.'

'I'm fine now—'

'You're far from fine, Eloise, and you're under my care until you step off the harbour. We have a blood pressure monitor as well as a teapot in the office.' Rosanna linked arms with her. 'Just walk slowly. That's good. Evan, you'd better get back on board. The afternoon group will be gathering soon.'

'I hope you're okay.' He nodded politely at Lorraine.

'Thank you for your help.' She wanted to understand what it was about him that had caused such a reaction. His brown eyes, perhaps, yet there was nothing compelling about his gaze, just a mild concern as he turned his attention back to the boat. She noticed his indigo jeans, and how well they fitted him, unlike Andy's baggy trousers with bulging pockets. He wore a white T-shirt under an open denim shirt. It was his clothes that triggered her reaction, she realised. They emphasised his physique, a shape that had nothing to do with gym work or pumping iron, and, like Victor, he walked with the long, confident stride of a man at home in his surroundings.

Rosanna continued to support her until they reached the entrance to the kiosk. Inside, it was bigger than it appeared from the exterior.

'Tea's ready, Rosanna.' The woman behind the counter glanced curiously at Lorraine. 'Is everything all right?'

'All okay, Nessa. This is Eloise. She was on the trip but felt unwell after she disembarked.'

'I'm fine... I'm fine...' She was parroting nonsense and Nessa, ignoring her, opened a door and led her into a small galley with a counter and a few high stools. A teapot sat on a hob set into the counter. The shelf above it held a biscuit jar, a first-aid box and, as Rosanna said, a blood pressure monitor.

At Rosanna's command, she sat on the stool and allowed the cuff of the monitor to be strapped around her upper arm. She studied a framed photograph on the counter. It was partly obscured by a breadbin but she could make out a Christmas tree and figures sitting in front of it. The pressure on her arm tightened then eased as the cuff slowly deflated.

'It's low, Eloise,' Rosanna said. 'Do you have problems with your blood pressure?'

'No, never.'

'Then you need to get this checked out. There's a medical centre in Loch—'

'I can't, Rosanna, but thank you for your concern. I've to meet someone and I'm late already. I'll visit my doctor as soon as I return home.' She pointed towards the photograph. 'What a lovely family you have.'

'Aye, they're bonnie, sure enough.' She returned the monitor to its box. 'Do you have bairns?'

'What?'

'Children.'

'Oh, yes. A son. He's grown up now.'

'It happens fast. That's what I tell Nessa and Evan when they complain about their boys.'

Lorraine leaned forward and pulled out the photograph. It showed Rosanna sitting on a sofa between two boys, who looked to be in their early teens. Nessa, Evan and Andy stood behind them. Once again, she felt that weakening sensation as she studied the features of the taller boy. 'What are their names?'

'The older lad is Maxwell. Callum is the younger.'

'Maxwell. I don't hear that name very often.'

'It was his grandfather's name. It's a tradition in Lochanar to call the eldest son after his grandfather. Not that I'm a believer in that particular tradition but Evan decided to continue it so that was that.' She turned abruptly away and poured tea into a mug.

'Does your husband also work on the boat?'

'My husband is dead.' Her expression hardened as she set the mug down in front of Lorraine with a brisk clatter. 'Drink this down,' she said. 'And relax here as long as you like. I've to head back to the boat. The afternoon tour starts in an hour and I need to ensure that everything is in order. Nessa will look after you. Do get yourself checked out, Eloise. Our health is our wealth and stress will leave us all the poorer. I've had my share of it in my time, but the boat keeps me centred.'

'Your redemption?'

'Aye, indeed.' She left the galley, a host of unanswered questions following her. Lorraine wanted to scream each one after her.

Instead, she clutched the mug of tea and turned her gaze back to the family photograph, her attention focused on Maxwell, the older boy. She had no idea what Victor looked like when he was a youth, yet her quickening heartbeat told her that the resemblance to Maxwell would be uncanny.

Nessa opened the door. 'Are you okay there, Eloise?'

'I'm fully recovered, thanks. I've been admiring your family. Rosanna is a lucky woman to have two such handsome grandchildren.'

'Rosanna makes her own luck. But she throws it away, too.'

'I'm sorry to hear she lost her husband.'

'She lost him a long time before he died. Evan was just a baby when he scarpered, so he never knew his dad. You don't miss what you've never had, at least that's what he tells me.'

'What happened to Evan's father?'

'He walked into an ocean and was never seen again. Rosanna says her only regret is that she never had a chance to dance on his bones.' Nessa shrugged and laughed. 'What can you say to that?'

'They never divorced?'

'No. She didn't bother. One brush with marriage was enough to put her off for life.' She looked towards the outside counter. The little office was still empty. 'Here's me gossiping again. Rosanna says my mouth runs faster than the Spey and she's right. If she heard me talking about Max—'

'Don't worry. I'd never dream of repeating anything you've told me. Your husband was very kind to me when I fainted. Is he Rosanna's only child?'

'Well, he is now that Candice has gone.' She sighed. 'She died young. She was a lost soul, but least said soonest mended.'

The kiosk door opened and Nessa looked relieved that she could stop talking: the first of the new group to set sail on *Rosanna's Redemption* had arrived to collect their tickets.

'You still here, lass?' Andy entered behind the couple, a rope slung over his arm.

'I'm on my way.' Lorraine zipped up her jacket. She had drawn too much attention to herself and the small kiosk was beginning to fill with customers.

She waved goodbye to Nessa and walked out into the fresh air. She longed to faint again. To stay lying down, out cold and unthinking. Victor had taught her to meditate. She had sat with him in the shade of towering rocks and travelled inward. In a landscape charged with energy, it seemed possible to do so but, even since she'd left Sedona, she found it difficult to achieve the stillness she advocated to the guests at Serenity Falls. She always felt like a fraud, her calm voice persuading others to let go and pay attention to their breathing, while her mind was running ahead to the next session, the next meeting with their bank manager, the next book she needed to write to keep Victor's name in the public domain.

'How're feeling now, lass?' Andy had caught up with her.

'Reasonably okay,' she replied.

'Are you staying overnight in Lochanar?'

'No, I'm moving on.'

'Ah, that's a shame. I'm off for the afternoon and was hoping to buy you a wee dram in the Stag.'

His hopeful expression penetrated her thoughts. She was flailing through information that could have everything, or nothing, to do with her. The desire to walk away was powerful. Coincidence, that's all this was: a letter misdirected to Victor, and she had followed it like a bloodhound on a false scent.

Yet she found herself nodding in agreement and arranging to meet him at the bar in an hour.

Lorraine showered and packed her overnight bag. Candice... Rosanna... Megan. The names made a scatted jigsaw and she was terrified of where the pieces would join when they fell.

Two glasses of scotch were already on the table when she met Andy in the Stag.

'Edradour whisky.' The mellow-gold liquid sloshed in the glass when he handed it to her. 'It's the smallest distillery in Scotland and it'll put life back into you in no time at all.'

He drank it neat but advised her to use a small amount of water. The alcohol, warming her, rushed colour to her cheeks. 'Told you so, lass.' He chuckled. 'Ready for another?'

'Only if you let me buy this round.' She gestured towards Maggie, who brought fresh glasses to the table.

'Have you family, Andy?'

'No bairns, if that's what you mean. Nor wife.' He shook his head. 'A curse and a blessing in equal measure, I'm told. So, who knows what I spared myself? Rosanna's my sister-in-law and Evan... well, I guess you could call him my almost-son. I've done as much for him as any father could do. Wish I could say the same...' He stopped and knocked back his drink. 'Aye... that hits the spot and bounces back again. Where are you from, lass?'

'Ireland.'

'I thought so. Never been there but it's on the bucket list.'

'Our countries have a lot in common... including language.'

'Aye, that's a fact. Whisky is one of them. Your lot pushed an "e" into the bottle for no good reason.'

'That's true...' She laughed. 'With or without an "e", this is one smooth drink.'

'Can I tempt you to another?'

'No, thanks. You don't want me fainting on you again.' She paused, then continued: 'Going back to language, how do you say "my love" in Scots Gaelic?'

'*Mo ghràidh*,' he said, and grinned. 'Don't tell me I've turned your head, lass.'

'It's *mo grá* in Irish... and you're capable of turning any woman's head.'

'I believe you, though thousands wouldn't.' He grinned again before shouting to Maggie: 'I'm being shifted, Maggie. What d'ya make o' that?'

'Away with you, you old goat.' She laughed good-naturedly and busied herself hanging glasses from a rack above her head. 'I'm thinking you'll need to run for the border, lass. He's lazy enough not to catch you.'

'Tell me about Candice,' Lorraine said, when he turned his attention back to her. 'Nessa said she died young.'

'Candice.' His puckered eyelids closed but not before she saw the sudden glisten of tears. 'She was my sunbeam,' he said. 'I adored her, but she's gone now, God rest her.'

'How did she die?'

'Let her be.' He straightened and opened his eyes. 'A last

dram, then I'm off home to sleep it off.' He lifted his finger towards Maggie. 'Will you join me, lass?'

'Yes.' She had a plane to catch but she was in no condition to drive to the airport. It no longer seemed to matter. She was not used to drinking spirits. An occasional glass of wine with guests at the end of a Rekindle programme was her limit, but each sip was smooth as velvet as it went down. 'Candice is such an unusual name. Is it Scottish?'

'No. I seem to remember Rosanna called her after some African queen. Funny that. Rosanna's never put a boot outside Lochanar yet she calls her wee bairn some foreign name. Maybe that's what gave Candice the need to run as far as she could from here. Megan, too, she's cut from the same—'

'Who's Megan?'

'Rosanna's grandchild...' His voice faltered. 'Candice was her mother.'

'She's not in the family picture I saw in the kiosk.'

'That's because she'd gone wandering again.' He ran his fingertips across the table in imaginary flight. 'Last we heard she was in Peru. She and Rosanna never saw eye to eye on anything. Bad blood and too much history. In your country, you lot thrive on bad blood yet it got you your independence. We're still fighting for ours. Three hundred years under the thumb o' the Sassenach.'

He was loud and belligerent. It would be impossible to prise any further information from him. Did she want to do so? The triumvirate of names had fallen into place. Three generations, riven by bad blood and tragedy.

Maggie cast a resigned glance towards them and said, 'That's enough, Andy. You know the rule. Politics have to be left outside the door. Do you want to be barred again?'

'You're a bonnie lassie and I'm thinking it's time to bide away.' He rose to his feet and lifted Lorraine's hand. Bending forward he kissed her fingers before walking steadily towards the door.

Her legs were trembling. No way would she be able to walk from the bar with the same stability.

'Are you all right, lass?' Maggie collected the empty glasses and watched her anxiously.

'I'm not used to drinking.' She could still speak clearly which surprised her. 'Will it be okay if I stay another night?'

'Don't you have a flight to catch?'

'I'm not able to drive. I'll cancel and rebook.'

'What you need is a strong cup of coffee and something to eat. Come with me.'

The bar swayed when Lorraine stood and Maggie grasped her arm. 'As the saying goes, "I can walk on water but I stumble on Scotch.' She laughed as she guided Lorraine towards a door at the side of the bar. 'I'll open the parlour for you and you can have some privacy there.'

Inside the parlour, which was more like a small hall for social gatherings, Maggie gestured to one of the armchairs. 'Sit yourself there and relax. I'll bring the coffee shortly, and some food to sop up the alcohol.'

The room smelled musty and must only have been opened for special occasions. A shuttered bar at the end of the room and a well-worn, wooden floor suggested it had seen many decades of dancing. Photographs covering the walls provided a record of such events. Some were sepia-tinted and others had the sharp clarity of more modern times.

She had seen some of those images online: children performing gymnastics or dancing, musicians playing fiddles and accordions, pipe bands and lone bagpipe players leading processions. Wedding photographs were also on display, so the parlour must also serve as a reception venue. The photographs looked dated. Today's bridal couples preferred a more stylish location. She searched for Rosanna in the montage and recognised her among a group of women in a number of recent photographs. Recognising a young Rosanna could be difficult but none of the faces she examined in the more faded images looked like her.

She crossed to a cabinet with glass doors. Rows of photographic albums lined the shelves. The door was unlocked. The year each album was compiled was dated along the spine. She took one out and opened it at random. Images from the eighties – all those scrunched perms, exuberant hairstyles, leg warmers and padded shoulders. Every event that took place in the Running Stag has been captured. She found Rosanna's wedding photograph in one of the seventies albums. The colours had faded into a predominance of yellow but she was recognisable. So young then, still sturdily built, round-faced, her hair hanging limply to her shoulders, her eyes fixed on the young man beside her. She must have still been in her teens, eighteen or nineteen, but she could have been younger, a girl startled from childhood into sudden maturity. The slight rise of her stomach under her wedding dress gave the reason.

The man beside her, just as young, wore an ill-fitting suit. Unlike Rosanna, he did not attempt to smile. His dark hair fell over his forehead and shaded his eyes, but his mouth revealed his discontentment.

Victor... Breathing his name, she longed to be mistaken. In Sedona, she had met a man who was almost other-worldly, yet assured and sophisticated. His gaze compelled, his voice enticed and seduced the unwary like her. She still couldn't – wouldn't – believe it... yet she recognised his tight-lipped fury at being trapped by circumstances of his own making. She remembered that expression. She had seen it through the sheen of post-natal depression when she feared he would leave her.

She had willed herself to forget that time but now, as she stared at his resentful expression, she was forced to confront that repressed memory.

They hadn't divorced, Nessa had said. Rosanna never bothered or, perhaps, until news of his death reached her, she had carried the hope that someday he would return. Had she let him go then, oblivious to the fact that he had reinvented himself? A disguise so thorough that he had managed to deceive Lorraine until his death compelled her along this journey of discovery?

She replaced the album and stepped away from the cabinet.

Maggie entered with a tray. 'Here you are, Eloise.' She had made a cheese and ham toastie and cut it into neat triangles. She set a bowl of Scotch broth and a pot of tea on a small table beside the armchair. 'I've been talking about you to my husband,' she said. 'He's heading for Inverness in about thirty minutes. If you like, he can drive you in your rental to the airport.'

Lorraine tried to concentrate on what she was saying but the only word she heard was inside her head, a word that kept repeating with a rhythm of a drumbeat... *bigamist... bigamist... bigamist...*

How had his granddaughter tracked him to Serenity Falls? And had others been aware of his past, or was Megan Ross acting alone? Surely if anyone else had known where she was going, they would have arrived by now to claim her and reveal the truth about Victor?

'*Eloise*, you should eat.' Maggie's voice jolted her from her thoughts. 'Let me know if you want Geoff to drive you to the airport. It's no problem. He'll easily get a lift back from his friend, who works in security there.'

'Thank you, Maggie.' Why did she sound so serene? Primal screams, the ones she unleashed when she identified Victor's body, would be more appropriate but within the fuzziness of her mind, she was cognisant of the need for control. 'Andy has quite a way with words.'

'He's a rogue, always has been.' Maggie sounded indulgently resigned to the behaviour of her customer. 'But he's got a heart of gold behind it all.'

'He told me he was a surrogate father to Rosanna's children.'

'Aye. Evan and Candice were blessed with him when they were bairns.'

'What about Megan? He spoke a lot about her.'

'Megan's a headstrong lass. A bit too streetwise for my liking. That's her there.' She pointed to a photograph on the wall. 'She was here for Rosanna's birthday but it was a flying visit before she took off again. She's a nomad, that one. Takes after her mother and her granddad.'

Lorraine knew what she would find when she looked at the image. Megan was standing with a group of young people at a function in this room. Her black hair was tied in a ponytail that emphasised her long, narrow face.

Lorraine transposed the face she had seen on a hospital bed – bruised, slashed, stitched and swollen – with Megan's vivacious smile, her pale, smooth skin, and those dark brown eyes with their startling brilliance, and knew it was a perfect fit.

The phone rang from the bar and Maggie hurried to answer it. Lorraine used her camera phone to capture the image. She sat back down and dipped the spoon into the broth. It was tasty and warming. She stared out of the window at the road leading to the harbour. It forked into a secondary road that must lead to houses behind the Running Stag. *Two roads diverged in a wood.* The words from the Robert Frost poem came to mind. Which one would she travel?

Maggie had returned to the room. It would be so easy to tell her about the accident and the chain of events that had brought her here. What then? Carl Sheridan would be on the scent immediately. He had his sources within the gardai: to write his explosive reports on gang crime, he needed contacts within and outside the law.

Information about Victor would be immediately passed on to him. She imagined him sinking his inquisitive fingers into Lochanar, his thin lips smiling as he wrote his copy and prepared to trash Victor's reputation and destroy everything Lorraine had achieved with the marriage retreat.

Nothing of what she had uncovered in Lochanar must touch Rekindle Connections, the brand she had managed so carefully. Nor could it touch Serenity Falls, the home she had relinquished so obediently to Victor.

'Have you decided on what you'd like to do?' Maggie sounded concerned, her forehead puckering. 'Are you okay, lass? You're looking rightly washed out, and that's a fact.' After hearing about Lorraine's loss of consciousness on the harbour, she must be anxious in case it happened again.

'I'm fine, Maggie. Just a bit woozy from the drink. Thank Geoff for the offer but I'd prefer to stay overnight and catch another flight tomorrow – if the room is still vacant, that is?'

'Aye, it's free. I'll organise some fresh towels and add your name to the breakfast list.'

'I'd like to meet Rosanna tomorrow and thank her for her help earlier. Buy her some flowers, if I can catch her before she takes the first tour out in the morning.'

'She'll not be sailing tomorrow. It's the sabbath and she takes her day of rest seriously.'

'Maybe I could call to her house—?'

'You could, but you mightn't get an answer. She'll be at Sunday worship. But you could catch her in the graveyard afterwards. She never misses a Sunday since she laid Candice down.'

'I'd hate to disturb her.'

'You won't.' Maggie spoke with conviction. 'Rosanna's visits to the graveyard are more like a soirée. We often have a blether together when we're sitting around Candice's grave.'

Lorraine finished the broth, ate the toastie, and drank the

tea, amazed that she could still perform such basic tasks without her hands shaking uncontrollably. But she knew she needed sustenance if she was to meet Victor's wife and discover what lay under the skin of her brief, unhappy marriage. Somehow, she had to persuade Rosanna Ross to disclose the facts behind her husband's disappearance – and the reason why she had never removed her wedding band.

In bed, the muffled sounds from the bar reached her. She welcomed the distraction, yet images came at her like flash photography. Stalwart Rosanna Ross with her weathered skin and sturdy limbs had once slept by Victor's side. They must have loved furtively at first, then openly, as man and wife. Lorraine could not endure the thought of them together, their lips opening to the slow stroke of tongues, the mingled groans and breathless eagerness, the drowsy aftermath, sweat cooling on their naked skin... Such memories should have belonged to her, but they were forever tarnished by a discovery that was still unfolding.

She pressed her face into the pillow to silence her rage. An exposé had been Megan Ross's only reason for coming to Ireland. She would have destroyed Lorraine's marriage – if that was what it could still be called – had a Polish truck driver not suffered a fatal heart attack and changed everything. She would have ruined Rekindle Connections – and could still do so, if she recovered consciousness.

The night had talons that scratched deep into Lorraine's anger until it bled and forced her to confront the truth. Rosanna Ross was Victor's lawful wedded wife. As such, she was entitled to inherit Serenity Falls. Lorraine would lose her home. The marriage retreat would be subjected to ridicule and media exposure, with Carl Sheridan leading the pack of investigative bloodhounds. Everything she had achieved would be destroyed. As the talons dug deeper, she accepted that there was only one way forward. Sympathy for the young woman's predicament was a luxury she could not afford. This toughening she was experiencing was not only in her heart, but felt like a physical stiffening of her limbs. A bracing sensation that warned her to be cautious and courageous as she moved to the next stage of revelation.

ELEVEN

LORRAINE

Sweet Buds, the only flower shop in Lochanar, was closed on Sundays.

'Let's see what I can do,' said Maggie, and led Lorraine through the back of the pub to a small garden, where she picked a bunch of peonies and tied them into a bouquet. Refusing payment, she walked with Lorraine to her car and gave her directions to the kirk.

The town was quiet as Lorraine drove towards the harbour. The kirk was already crowded for Sunday morning worship when she arrived. She slipped into a back pew, conscious of the curious glances from the people nearest her. They soon directed their attention towards the female minister who began to conduct the service.

Lorraine could see the Ross family seated in one of the pews. Looking at the back of Evan's long, slender neck, she experienced a rush of recognition that enraged her even further. His two sons sat between him and Nessa. Rosanna, at the end of the pew, had the erect posture of someone who knew the importance of her position in the community. Memorial plaques on the walls honoured residents who had been killed in wars or fishing tragedies.

The joyous atmosphere created by the minister when she brought the children to the altar to sing blew away the cobwebs of history. Lorraine's hands were clenched in an effort to hold back tears, especially when Evan's younger son sang a solo verse of 'I, The Lord of Sea and Sky'.

When the service ended and the minister had shaken hands with the departing congregation, Lorraine walked towards the graveyard. She had a view of the loch from where she stood. The harbour was out of sight and it seemed from her vantage point as if the little kirk was floating on the loch's sun-struck ripples.

She walked between weathered tombstones, and shiny, marble ones that bore a newer date. A swathe of forget-me-knots were in bloom on Candice's grave and Rosanna, sitting on a fold-up chair beside it, was reading *The Sunday Post*.

Hearing Lorraine's footsteps, she glanced up, her eyes widening in surprise. 'My goodness, Eloise, what are you doing here? I thought you were leaving us yesterday.'

'That's correct. I'm afraid your brother-in-law led me astray.'

'I heard you shared a dram or two. He's a wicked man when it comes to the bottle.'

'Well, it gave me a chance to say "thank you" properly.' She handed the peonies to Rosanna. 'You were very kind to me.'

'T'was nothing, lass. These are lovely but they weren't necessary. I was just doing my job.' She gestured towards a second fold-up chair. 'Take the weight off your feet. I always bring another chair in case friends come along for a blether.' She spoke as if it was perfectly natural to sit by her daughter's grave and read the Sunday newspaper. 'How are you feeling today, Eloise?'

'Still a bit rough, to be honest. But I'll be okay.' She leaned forward to read the inscription on the gravestone. 'Candice. What a beautiful name. I'm so sorry you lost your daughter. Andy told me about her.'

Rosanna touched the photograph of the black-haired woman who must have been in her mid to late twenties when she died. She had Victor's gaze in all its persuasive intensity; the same eyes that Megan Ross had inherited.

'She was a headstrong girl and this is where it took her.' Rosanna gestured towards the grave.

'It must have been heart-breaking for you and your husband.'

'He never knew she died. To be honest, Eloise, he was hardly aware of her existence.'

'That's very sad.'

'Aye, leaving his family didn't bring him much luck. He drowned a few years later.'

'How tragic.'

'That's one way of looking at it. Tragedy is relative. He was well gone from my life by then.'

'Was his body ever recovered?'

'No. Hopefully, the sharks got more pleasure from him than I did.'

'Do you ever think about him?'

'Occasionally, when I have indigestion. I see you're married, Eloise?'

'I've been recently widowed.' Instinctively, filled with a sudden urge to run, Lorraine covered her wedding ring.

'Oh, lass, I'm sorry. This is a tough time for you, then.'

'Very tough. I loved him dearly.'

'That's the hardest blow. There's never a day passes that I don't feel grief at Candice's passing and blame myself for the way she went.'

'I'm sure you did everything you could—'

'Today's worship was all about joy and light but that wasn't always the case. My father was one of the elders. He was dedicated to the kirk but pitiless when it came to matters of the heart. He believed it was his duty to put my daughter into an orphanage. Today, we'd call it "going into care", and I'd be acknowledged as a vulnerable young mother under stress. But, not back then. I'd one son, and the husband who shook the dust of Lochanar from his heels as soon as he heard there was another bairn on the way. My father claimed I was drinking heavily and incapable of coping with another child. Putting Candice into care was meant to be temporary but it took six years before I was able to take her home. My father was dead by then and Candice unmanageable.' She stopped, her eyes narrowing in concern as she stared at Lorraine. 'Here I am blethering on about things that are of no concern to you—'

'No... no, please continue. What happened to her in that orphanage?'

'She never spoke about it, but it shaped her for life. She was sulky and beautiful and mad as hell with the world. Andy was the only one who could reason with her. He'd fling her over his shoulder when she was in a meltdown and take her out on the loch. She left for London when she was eighteen, had a baby two years later and died from drugs when she was twenty-eight. I reared her bairn and tried to make a better job of it this time. Sadly, Megan has her mother's itchy feet and there was no holding her back when she came of age.'

'Andy said she's in Peru.'

'Aye. She'd a hankering for waves and ancient ruins. We parted on bad terms, sadly.' She sighed heavily before continuing. 'Megan can be as stubborn as a mule when she digs her heels in. It'll take time for her to cool off and contact me. She'll do so when she's had her fill of travelling and realises that all I want is what's best for her.'

'I hope your granddaughter contacts you soon.' Lorraine reached out and grasped the older woman's hands in hers. 'It was a pleasure to meet you, Rosanna. I'll say goodbye now. I've a long drive ahead of me.'

'Thank you for the flowers.' Rosanna picked up the pink blooms she had earlier laid at her feet. 'Do you mind if I leave them here on Candice's grave?'

'It's the perfect place for them.' Lorraine walked back the way she came. Her feet felt heavy, each step a weight to lift. She looked back once at Victor's wife, and watched her arranging the peonies in a vase, her workworn hands gentle as she caressed the pink petals.

TWELVE

LORRAINE

Her return to Serenity Falls was charged with a nervous energy that allowed her to lie with ease when Pamela or Aidan asked questions about her so-called trip to London. *A lie will always corrode the soul.* That was something Victor used to say. It sounded wise and profound at the time, not slick and easy as it did now. A soundbite, like so many of the soundbites he had used.

Hiding in plain sight. The irony of it. Building a reputation for himself with her eager assistance. The risks he must have taken, living on the brink of discovery yet confident that he could carry it off. No wonder she had spotted vulnerabilities in him; those moments when he dropped his guard and remembered who he really was.

When Aidan was in bed that night and the light in his room was finally turned off, Lorraine entered her office. She removed Victor's possessions from his desk and stored them in boxes that would be removed to the attic first thing in the morning. *If only it was as easy to eradicate his memory.* Her hand was steady as she unlocked the shallow drawer and uncurled the letter he had received from Megan Ross.

This time, his office chair held her steady as she flattened the letter on the desk and laid a sheet of tracing paper over it.

Not all the letters of the alphabet were contained in that missive but Lorraine had enough to work on. She held the pencil too tightly and the lettering blurred. Her resolve strengthened as she laid down a fresh sheet of tracing paper and began again to copy Megan's handwriting. When she was satisfied that she could replicate each letter, she watched the paper burn until all that remained of Megan Ross's name was black ash.

It was after midnight when she entered her bedroom and undressed for bed. Rosanna Ross was probably sleeping. Maybe she was dreaming of dolphins or elusive whales. Did she allow space for Victor in her dreams? Remembering the inflexibility of her expression when she spoke about her husband, Lorraine thought it possible. He should be a speck in her past but she still harboured the hurt he had inflicted on her. Forty-six years had passed since then. How would she react if she knew that she had only recently become his widow? A widow with full entitlement to Serenity Falls and whatever else was contained in Victor's most recent will. Finding it was crucial.

If only the heat of Lorraine's anger could act as a detonator and explode its brutal contents. His finished will remained hidden, as hidden as he had believed his past to be until Megan Ross shattered that illusion.

To her surprise, Lorraine fell asleep as soon as her head touched the pillow. When she awoke, the sun was shining. A good omen for a day when decisions had been made.

No time for second thoughts or regrets.

She knew exactly what she must do.

The liaison officer arrived shortly after receiving Lorraine's phone call.

The shallow drawer on Victor's desk was open, the letter neatly folded and displayed on the leather surface.

'I decided to clear out Victor's desk,' Lorraine said to Jean. 'That's when I found this letter. It's from a young woman named Naomi Nelson. I vaguely remember it arriving but, truthfully, I haven't thought about it since. She's the daughter of friends we made in Sedona many years ago.'

'Sedona?' Jean frowned. 'Where's that?'

'Arizona. It's where Victor and I met. Kelly and Seth Nelson were his friends. I only knew them briefly before they left to return to Texas. From what I remember about them, they were living off the grid in some forest commune there. We never heard from them again until Kelly's mother contacted us to tell us they'd died in a fire. Then, a couple of months ago this letter arrived from their daughter. She was backpacking around Europe.' Lorraine linked her fingers together and resisted the urge to wring her hands. 'You mentioned that the gardai think the woman with Victor could have been a tourist. It never dawned on me at the hospital that night... or since... until...'

She stopped, afraid to continue.

'Go on.' Jean nodded encouragingly. 'I can appreciate how distressing this must be for you.'

'I was too stunned to focus on her then. All I could think about was Victor. But I've had time since his death to think more clearly and last night I suddenly remembered the letter we received. I've been searching the house for it and finally found it this morning. However, I could be wrong; I don't want to waste your time.'

'Going up dead ends can be an unfortunate aspect of any garda investigation,' said Jean.

'Could it have some relevance? You can see from her letter that Naomi was just passing through Dublin, on her way to Belfast. She was hoping for a quick meet-up with Victor. He mentioned something about her when we spoke on the phone.

To be honest, I was too distracted to pay attention. It was the final day of the programme and that's always a particularly demanding occasion. I can't believe I didn't remember...'

The tears that ran down her cheeks came from a well that never ran dry. She wiped them away, conscious of Jean's gaze. Was it sympathetic or speculative?

'It makes sense now.' She cleared her throat but her voice still sounded breathy. 'Victor came home earlier than planned to meet her. He must have been bringing her to the airport.' She handed Jean a photograph she had earlier removed from an album she found in the attic. 'This is a photo of the Nelsons. Naomi was just a baby then.'

She remembered when the photograph was taken. Kelly, Seth and Victor, the three of them sitting on the bench outside Hot&Saucy. Ghost-like figures scorched by the searing sun. Naomi Nelson, two months old, just a few days away from dying, was cuddled in Kelly's arms.

Lorraine had heard nothing from the Nelsons or about them until a crumpled but still intact letter arrived some years ago. It had been addressed to Victor at Hot&Saucy, and then forwarded to Serenity Falls. The letter was from Kelly's mother. She had found the restaurant's address among her daughter's possessions. A tragic house fire, she wrote. Dysfunctional fairy lights on a Christmas tree that they had forgotten to turn off when they went to bed in their suburban house in Chicago. Her anguish seeped from the page. Kelly and Seth gone, just like that. They had run as far as possible from what Seth used to mockingly call the 'suburban mousetrap,' but it caught them in the end, Lorraine had thought as she read the letter.

'Maybe this is just a coincidence and I'm wasting your time.' Her emotions were in turmoil as she waited for Jean to shake her head and dismantle her explanation. She was unable to decide if she was relieved or horrified when the liaison officer

pulled her phone from her pocket and spoke quietly to Sergeant
Boyne.

Unable to listen to their conversation, Lorraine rushed to
the bathroom and held her wrists under the cold water tap.
Gradually, her cheeks cooled and her high colour faded. She
dried her hands and returned to the office, where Jean informed
her that Sergeant Boyne would meet them at the hospital.

'How certain are you that you can identify her?' Sergeant
Boyne swivelled her head from the unconscious woman
towards Lorraine.

'I'm not certain at all.' Even now, it was not too late to pull
back. She visualised Rosanna Ross arriving to claim Serenity
Falls. Thinking like this would drive her crazy. The screaming
and head-banging craziness that she longed to let loose but must
rein in if she was to obliterate everything she had discovered in
Lochanar. 'It's only a possibility that she could be the daughter
of Victor's friends. But it would explain why no one has come
forward to identify her yet.'

'What's her name?' the sergeant asked.

The bruises had faded but the young woman's face
remained puffy and shapeless, and her head was still wrapped
in bandages. She bore no resemblance to the photograph
Lorraine had seen in Maggie's bar, and that helped her to
answer clearly.

'Naomi Nelson.' It was so simple to step over a gorge and
move from a sun-filled space into one of shadow. 'Her parents
died in Texas in a forest fire. Naomi was in college and would
have been home with them a day later. She's lucky to be alive...'
Realising how inappropriate that sounded, she fell silent.

A spasm passed over the woman's face and the sergeant,
glancing down, noticed her reaction. She exchanged a glance
with Jean and her nod, slight but significant, assured Lorraine

that an enquiry would be made to the police in Texas. But where to even begin a search in a landmass vast enough to swallow her lies in its prairies, forests and sprawling desert?

Lorraine's step was decisive when she walked from the hospital. No faltering or hesitating, no turning back to tell those charged with the woman's care that she had made a dreadful mistake.

Sunlight slanted through the long sash windows of her office. Lorraine saw the bend on his shoulders as he looked across at her and smiled. Was he a ghost or a figment of her deranged imagination? Did she want to kiss him or kill him?

People seemed to dance in ballerina steps around her. Were they afraid to stir the air in case she collapsed in a heap? They asked her how she was doing, their voices soft and understanding. Such a banal question, so loaded.

What if she answered it truthfully?

I want to drag my bigamist husband from his grave and wring his deceitful neck. I want to scorch his shattered face with the heat of rage. My tears feel like acid on my skin but I do not shed them in grief. I shed them in fury because his deceit and betrayal have turned me into a monster.

THIRTEEN

NO NAME GIRL

His wife came to identify me on the day he died. That's what I hear. I've no memory of her standing there, hurting and angry. They say she was calm when she shook her head, but she was screaming in the mortuary when she saw him lying on a slab?

I wish I could have told her he was careless on the road. That he had had time to veer into another lane if he hadn't been so consumed by his fear of what I was capable of doing. I saw the truck coming towards us before he did and screamed a warning that tore him too late from his thoughts and that was it. That's all I remember: the side of the truck, then nothing. No last words... nothing... nothing.

He said he'd tell her. I didn't believe him. To gain so much then lose it all for my sake. No, that was never going to happen. In the pale light of day, he was rethinking all that had been revealed when we met. What a night that was. So much laid bare, and what were we to do about it? He is silent now. No secrets will pass his lips. Nor mine. His death was instant. Which is better... instant or lingering? Waiting for decisions to be made?

She's back again. A shadow by my bedside. I can tell by her voice how close she is to me. Why is it not possible to flutter my eyelids? Twitch my little finger? Make a noise that is anything other than a grunt of pain. Yes. No. Or a simple, two-syllable word: li-ar... li-ar...

Am I the only one to hear her lies? I'm not a backpacker. Not an American. Maybe I'm an orphan. I never knew my father. Never cared to find him. A mystery I never bothered to unearth.

She knows who I am. A whisper here, a whisper there, as if she is testing me to see how I respond. Lochanar... Rosanna... her beloved boat... Andy... she's been there... tracing the roots to that letter I sent him. Her voice shakes like a leaf in wind when she calls me Naomi. They are deaf and blind to her lies. Sweet Lorraine... sweet, lying Lorraine. I'm bound and gagged, imprisoned by my own body. How certain she is. Sedona. Hippies living off the grid. Seth. Kelly. A forest fire. Texas.

I float and drown. It's time to turn you... wash you... change you... feed you... kill you... tick-tock... tick-tock... ten, nine, eight, seven... six, five, four, three...

FOURTEEN

LORRAINE

Shortly after Lorraine's return from Lochanar, Megan Ross was transferred from the hospital to a specialist unit that dealt with cases of serious brain trauma and coma. St Gorgonia's Medical Centre was only ten kilometres from Potters Glen and was screened from public view by trees and an automatic gate that rolled slowly open on Lorraine's first visit.

A holding station. That is all it can be, Lorraine thought, as she walked along the silent corridor to St Gorgonia's ward, where the unconscious woman lay.

Naomi... she must call her Naomi... was now able to breathe without the help of a ventilator. But the clinical nurse manager, an efficient, sharp-faced woman called Jackie, believed it was only a matter of time before she lost her fight for survival.

The visiting rules were strict but Jackie agreed that visiting the patient on a regulated basis would be possible. Lorraine's knowledge, however limited, of Naomi's family, could evoke some reaction, though her tone suggested otherwise.

How long would it be possible for anyone to live in this hushed environment where existence was suspended in the indeterminate zone between life and death? Was Naomi waiting to say goodbye to her family... to Rosanna? Thinking about the other woman caused the talons to tear at her again. It was the only way Lorraine could describe the clawing sensation that could attack her at any moment and force her to a standstill. She had to learn to withstand the pressure if she was to survive this new reality she had created.

Did Aidan believe the story about a wandering waif? That was what she looked like since the bandages had been removed: a lost urchin, with her shaved head and ribcage skinniness.

Confiding in him would offer Lorraine some relief but she was conscious that information, once shared, could take a different shape, becoming too malleable to handle.

She had waited for him to announce his intention of returning to Vancouver. When she questioned him, she received vague replies about an indefinite leave. What was the rush when there were so many things to do around the place? Sam Wright, the gardener who looked after the gardens, had accepted a position as a groundsman at the Potters Glen golf club and Aidan had taken over his responsibilities. On the south lawn where the guests usually exercised, the grass was velvet-smooth. Weeding, turning the soil in the flower beds, planting vegetables and herbs – there was always something for him to do as the date for the reopening of Rekindle Connections drew nearer.

Aidan was painting the stone balustrade edging the entrance steps when she returned from her first visit to St Gorgonia's ward.

'Do you honestly believe she's Naomi Nelson?' he asked, when he came into the kitchen to wash the brushes.

'Do you have a better idea?' She wondered if there was an accusation lurking in his question.

'You put forward a possibility and suddenly everyone's

acting like it's a fait accompli,' he said. 'Why has no one come forward since the police released her name? If she was back-packing around the country, she would have met people in hostels. She'd be on the passenger list of airlines or ferry ports, but nothing's shown up.'

'I can't believe you still have doubts about her identity!' She had to stay in control. To give way at this stage was unthinkable. 'She could have a different surname for all I know. She could be married. She didn't put her surname on the letter she sent to us, so I'm simply assuming her name is Nelson.'

'Why didn't Victor tell you straight out that he was meeting her?'

'I've *told* you... he did mention it. I was distracted when he rang and wasn't listening to him.'

'Carl Sheridan is convinced Victor was having an affair with her. He rang me—'

'I hope you hung up on him.'

'Only after I told him to fuck off.'

'That kind of language won't help—'

'It fucking well helped me.'

She had forgotten the suddenness of his anger, his height-ened words that were usually directed at his father and were now finding their way towards her.

'So, do you want Naomi to be someone else? Your father's *mistress*? What a story Carl Sheridan would make of that.'

'Why are you getting so annoyed with me?'

'I'm not annoyed, just worried about you. When do you plan on returning to Vancouver? It's nearly a month since Victor died. How much leave were you allowed?'

'I've resigned.'

'What...? When?'

'Yesterday.' He drew back from her astonishment and folded his arms.

'You told me it was your dream job and you give it up... just like that?' She snapped her fingers in exasperation.

'I want to remain here.'

'Really. That amazes me. You couldn't wait to leave when your father was alive.'

'Things are different now.'

'Because he's *dead.*'

No one reacted or appeared to notice the harshness in her voice whenever she referred to Victor.

'Because you need me,' he said. 'You keep pretending you're coping but I hear you crying at night, and you've lost weight. Why won't you talk about him, confide in me?'

'Will that bring him back?'

'Obviously not.' He tapped one foot off the floor. As if aware of what he was doing, he stopped but soon started again. He had developed the habit during his transition from a contented child to angry youth.

'Tell me the real reason you're not returning to Vancouver.'

'I'm not sure what I want to do in the future. I won't find the answer there.'

'Will you find it here?'

'I don't know.' He shrugged, seemingly unconcerned. 'I can fill Sam's shoes while I'm trying to find out.'

Did he feel guilty over the way he had treated his father? Their relationship had never been easy and his contempt for the public persona Victor acquired over the years had barely been concealed. *History repeating itself* – Lorraine would think of her own father when she heard them arguing. *Same emotions. Different wellsprings.*

Aidan had insisted of going to boarding school when he was twelve. Whenever he returned to Serenity Falls at the end of each term, she noticed the distance growing between father and son. She was the peacemaker, soothing, softening the atmosphere, stretching herself to understand both sides of an argument and persuade them to understand each other's point of view.

He had left for Vancouver as soon as he graduated, with a marketing degree. By then, she understood his need to escape from the density of his father's shadow. Victor could bring a sense of lightness into a room, but he could also suck the energy from it when he chose to do so.

It had taken time for her to realise he was incapable of giving Aidan the love his son needed. His pretence at being an affectionate father had not fooled Aidan: he asked her once why Victor's gift of making people feel special and cherished had bypassed him. She had been driving him home after he had scored a winning goal for Glenners United, the local football team. He had been carried shoulder-high off the pitch by his victorious team mates but his father had already left the grounds. He had an excuse, as always, and claimed he had an important meeting with his publisher. Other similar incidents had proved that Victor was incapable of rejoicing over his son's achievements.

Now, too late, Lorraine understood that each triumph Aidan achieved, were they small or large, must have reminded him of the children he had abandoned.

Lorraine discussed Aidan's decision to remain at home with Pamela, who suggested he should use his marketing skills to promote Rekindle Connections. A decision was made to move him into Pamela's small office; she would cross the hall to the main office and take over Lorraine's desk.

Lorraine sat down in Victor's space and locked the shallow drawer. The portrait of her and Victor had to go. It would be unbearable to look at it every day. She asked Aidan to carry it up to the attic, but Pamela insisted it should hang in the hall.

'It'll complement the other portraits and also serve as a

memorial to all Victor achieved,' she said. 'But you are the dominant figure in that configuration. That's the image you have to project. The way you hold yourself shows your resolve. You are moving on and nothing, even the tragedy of Victor's death, will stand in your way. You worked behind the scenes to make this company a success and it'll be even more successful when you're fronting it.'

It sounded as if her friend was placing a crown on her head. One thick with thorns.

Her son seemed taller, straighter than she remembered. She should welcome his desire to be home again. It had been all she wanted when he left but, now, his presence was becoming a challenge to the narrative she had built around Naomi...

Naomi Nelson. She battled with the name. A tongue-twister that never became any easier to pronounce. *Ash on her tongue, a dry, withered lie that screamed to be recognised and, yet, somehow, was not.*

A new introductory video for the guests to watch on their arrival had to be made. It would replace the one that featured Victor. Another step taken to erase his presence from Serenity Falls. Aidan filmed her walking through the marriage retreat and the grounds. She had written the original script and Victor had delivered it with his usual conviction. Could she do the same?

Pamela believed it was necessary if Lorraine was to become the public face of Rekindle Connection. New beginnings created a different vibration, she claimed. Lorraine understood what she meant. Vibrations were everywhere, tugging at memories, the relentless whispering in her ear; vibrations that were controllable when Victor was there to manage them for her.

She was interviewed for a business magazine and photographed in front of the waterfall. The naturalness of her smile amazed her when she opened the magazine. How could she look so relaxed when her mouth was a rictus? In the back-

ground, the waterfall seemed possessed of a thundering magnifi-
cence. It hadn't possessed such power when Victor was alive.
Now, its pull seemed incessant. The images it conjured up were
as vivid as they were in the aftermath of her father's death – she
saw him falling, his arms and legs flailing defencelessly against
the surging water.

His voice came softly to her. That was how he used to
speak: a soft sibilance that made his utterances seem unbelievable for, surely, such cruelty should have a harsher resonance.
'*Snake-oil man... charlatan... Dr Quack... conman... imposter...
He saw you coming a mile off...*'

FIFTEEN

GAIL

Gail was not surprised when she checked her video intercom and saw Carl standing outside her apartment. No advance notice, just an assumption that she would welcome him.

Apparently he had flown to London to interview an ex-member of the Eastly Boys. A gangster who had killed before he took his first shave. Now, in hiding in his thirties, he was unable to distinguish between shadow and flesh.

Knowing Carl would stay the night, she opened a bottle of Irish whiskey and poured two measures. The sofa, not her bed. They were way beyond that.

He pulled a magazine from his pocket and opened it. *Bayview Ventures*. Gail vaguely remembered it: a monthly business magazine with a soft core, mainly specialising in human interest stories with a business angle. A photograph of Lorraine Gordon illustrated a two-page spread about Rekindle Connections. The feature reported on the reopening of the marriage retreat.

'Needless to say, there was no mention of the woman who was with her husband when he died.' Carl stabbed his finger at the photograph. 'All that's been neatly covered up with some fantasy about her being a backpacker from the States who'd arranged to meet up with him.'

'So, she's finally been identified?'

'That's what Lorraine Gordon would like us to believe. My belief is that she's lying through her teeth.'

'What makes you so sure?'

'I have my sources,' he said, as he always did when he refused to answer a question. 'She insists her name is Naomi Nelson. A Texan. And an orphan, to boot. The gardai are checking out the story. Do you know the population of Texas?' He jutted his five fingers one after the other into the air. 'Over thirty-one million on the last count. A needle in a haystack comes to mind.'

'Surely the gardai would know if Lorraine was lying.'

'The fact that no one has made an identification gives her the benefit of the doubt. And the unfortunate woman is in no condition to contradict anything that comes out of her mouth.'

He looked rough. Too much stubble and an unhealthy flush to his complexion. Why did he expend so much energy on a story that had nowhere to go?

'I've also done some background checking into Victor's time in Sedona,' Carl continued. 'He was considered to be some kind of shaman by those who were taken in by him. He brought that mystique with him when he moved to Ireland and she built his reputation around it. Now that he's gone, all she needs is his avatar and she could continue as before. That's all he ever was. She was the brains behind the operation. I have it on good authority that she wrote everything – the books, speeches, even his advice columns. She was the font of it all, he simply delivered the lines.'

He rasped his hand over his jaw. When did he last sleep? He reminded her of a wolf: lean, hungry, sharp-eyed and ready to attack. 'I'm convinced he was leading a double life and it's connected to the woman in the car with him. I have my hands around one-half of this story... if I could just get to her...'

'To Lorraine?'

'No. The woman. If I could get to her before she dies... she's the key.'

'Be careful, Carl. Don't do anything stupid.'

'I don't deal in stupidity.'

'But you play very close to the edges of it. I've been reading your investigative reports. There's a fine line between courage and caution, and you're dealing with very dangerous people. The Eastly Boys, for instance. What if they find out you were interviewing one of their ex-members? As he's in hiding, they must be after him. Not to mention the Charters. They're probably out to get him as well.'

'I know what I'm doing, Abigail.'

'It's Gail... how many times—?'

'Sorry... sorry. Reinvention. I wish I found it that easy.'

'It's not easy. But it's necessary if you ever intend to move on and get a life.'

'I'll move on in my own time,' he said. 'When I've finished collecting the evidence I need, I'm going to blow Lorraine Gordon's cover-up sky high.'

'What kind of evidence?'

'Doesn't matter.'

'Is it something... *illegal?*'

His gaze, sliding sideways from her, convinced her she was right.

'I always abide by the rules.' His laughter was abrupt and humourless. 'Just watch this space.' He waved his hand at an imaginary headline and reached for the bottle.

She could tell by the speed of his voice that he was drinking too fast but he spoke without slurring and seemed content to keep her awake as he rambled on about his sons. The eldest boy blamed his anxiety issues on his father, his younger son had been expelled from school for smoking weed in the bicycle shed.

Gail yawned and wondered what part she had played in turning them into dysfunctional teenagers. Consequences. Who could predict them? Who could escape them? A shared history, however destructive, bound them together and she would stay with him until his words ran dry.

'Enough about me,' he said, eventually. 'What about you? Still intent on saving the world? *Generational Carousels* – that was a mouthful. When are you going to start making sexy documentaries again? That girl band...' He clicked his fingers. 'What were they called?'

'I'm surprised you don't remember,' she snapped.

'Ah, yes, Cherry Ash. Now, they were more your style, but you've become so... *earnest*.'

'At least I obey the rules.'

'Play it safe, you mean? Victor Gordon died with a secret and I intend to get to the bottom of it. You can help me.'

'How so?'

'Get yourself and your camera into Serenity Falls. Pretend you're interested in making a documentary. Find out what's going on there—'

'For goodness' sake, Carl, are you out of your mind?'

'It's a good idea. The set-up is made for a documentary. All those warring couples—'

'Stop it... *stop* it. You're talking rubbish. I've no intention of doing anything of the sort. I'm one of Lorraine Gordon's failures. Do you honestly think she'd allow me anywhere near Serenity Falls?'

Carl laughed abruptly. 'Do you honestly think she would recognise you? I suspect even your own mother has difficulty knowing who you are any more. You didn't just turn your back on your old life when you ran away, you obliterated it.' He was refilling his glass when she left him and closed her bedroom door.

The following morning, the only traces that remained of Carl were the scattered cushions and the rank smell of last night's whiskey.

His presence always sharpened her recollections of those five days in Serenity Falls, and her conviction that Victor Gordon held her future securely in his hands.

The rising purr of early morning traffic reached her when she opened the living room window. She would email Carl and tell him her apartment was out of bounds when he came to London again. She was tired of being dragged into his petty vendetta. It was time to untie the tentacles that bonded them in knots of guilt.

SIXTEEN

NO NAME GIRL

Professor Macken says I defied the odds. No plugs needed pulling. That's what he said before I was taken by ambulance from the hospital to this silent ward, where he expects me to die from pneumonia or some other complication.

New voices... new smells... new touches. Dessie calls me 'Pet' when he tends to me. He sounds older than the others. Gruff. His hands are gentle. Not like Jackie, with her sharp nails. Hard as nails... ha! She turned her back on me. I don't need to see what is going on to know when the atmosphere changes.

The man who put something up my nose was not Dessie. A stranger. Alcohol on his breath. He invaded me. A phantom who came and went from my bedside. Am I thinking or dreaming? Blinking or twitching? Am I dead? Is this hell? That would make sense.

I never believed in hell. Just pictures and words made up by others. Be good, be righteous, or you'll writhe around in flames, kicking and screaming and cursing and howling. But that's wrong. Being trapped inside your skin, immobile, silent, yet able to understand... that's hell. Being invaded... that too belongs to hell.

Jackie knew... she knew... she was there with him. I smelled the talcum powder she dusts on herself every morning – lily of the valley – but not enough to cloak the sweat of fear, of discovery...

I heard her breathing, fast breaths through her nose, counting the seconds until he left, then a gasp, loud and unchecked. No need for silence when she believes I'm beyond thought, emotion, fury.

She's wrong. In hell, I hear everything.

SEVENTEEN

GAIL

Carl was right about the publicity surrounding Lorraine Gordon. Her determination to continue the marriage retreat without the mesmeric presence of her husband was becoming more visible on social media. He had sent her a link to a video that showed her leading a yoga session on the south lawn. Slender and supple in a neon-pink leotard, her long blonde hair twined in a single plait, Lorraine guided her guests through each position with cat-like ease.

Unable to continue watching, Gail turned her attention back to an outline she was preparing for a new documentary, but the lure of the video drew her back again.

Eight years on, the intensity of her recollections of Serenity Falls had lessened yet, sometimes, caught unawares, she was unable to protect herself against the rush of memory.

Couples counselling. Those two words had filled Gail with alarm when her husband slid a Rekindle Connections brochure across the table towards her, his middle two fingers pressing lightly on the glossy cover. The subheading under *Rekindle Connections* read: *Time to take five. Renew your love, commitment, passion, fidelity and vows in the peaceful surroundings of Serenity Falls.*

'Well,' said Matthew. 'What do you think?'

'I'm still reading it.' She flicked through the pages and stared at the photographs. To all intents and purposes, Serenity Falls looked like a luxurious hotel, which, she discovered, as she read on, was exactly what it had once been. It was only towards the end of the brochure that the true purpose of this five-day escape from reality became apparent. She studied the photographs of smiling counsellors whose carefully crafted biographies promised to untangle the knotty problems that had brought each couple to the marriage retreat.

'Well, Abigail,' he asked. 'What do you think?'

'It looks... interesting.'

'*Interesting?*' Matthew's hopeful expression faded. 'That's what you say when you don't understand art but won't admit it. In other words, it means absolutely nothing.'

'That place is all about trying to repair broken marriages.' She turned back to the photographs of the counsellors. How competent they looked, how understanding; particularly Victor Gordon, whom she recognised from his appearances on television. 'Are you telling me that our marriage needs counselling?'

'We both need some time out but you, in particular, are stressed over this documentary—'

'I'm not stressed, just busy.'

'You're burned out—'

'So you keep saying. And I keep reminding you that tiredness does not equate to burnout. I'm enjoying what I'm doing. I'll catch up on sleep as soon as the final edit is finished.'

The bottle of wine he had opened at the beginning of their meal was almost empty. He poured what was left into her glass and tapped the brochure with the flat of his hand. 'This is about getting things back into perspective and focusing on what is important in our marriage. Donna White said it was an amazing experience. She gave me the brochure to show you.'

'Were you discussing our marriage with Donna White?' She imagined them at the water cooler or in the pub for those Friday night drinks after work. *Abigail is too career-driven to consider my needs. She goes off the deep-end any time I try to discuss starting a family.*

'Of course not. Donna was on a high after her five days there and simply wanted to share the experience with anyone who would listen. I can give them a ring tomorrow if you're agreeable.'

She wanted to be outraged, even truculent, but the brochure had a seductive appeal that was slowly winning her over. Perhaps Matthew was right. It was time to take a break and recharge her batteries... except that that was not what would happen if he had his way. Babies changed everything. It turned hard-bitten professionals into nervous, overwrought parents who complained unremittingly about sleep deprivation and what it was like to be at the mercy of a miniature tyrant. Most of their friends were two-time parents, some were even coping with three. She was still young enough to deliver one, two or even three babies when the time was right. Just one more documentary to make – then she would apply her attention to motherhood.

It was more than that, of course, and they both knew it. The nibbling discontent between them was becoming difficult to ignore. Their last argument, which had been centred around her refusal to discuss the ticking of her biological clock, still stung. Matthew had used her age – thirty-three on her last birthday – as a reminder that she was only two years away from being in the AMA category. When she demanded to know what the acronym meant and discovered that it stood for 'advanced maternal age', the argument that followed had lasted a chilly three days and nights.

'Ring them but don't book anything until we talk this through again.' She closed the brochure and cleared the dishes from the table. She was anxious to return to her laptop but Matthew, having switched on the television, was patting the space beside him on the sofa. She sighed, inwardly. The night before she had been editing until three in the morning – he mentioned it twice at breakfast, and made one of his edgy jokes about her obsession with girl bands.

Cherry Ash had enjoyed six years of fame after they won a televised talent show and began their meteoric rise in the charts. Gail had filmed them from their beginnings and had been there to chart their inevitable break-up. Five strong-willed women, it could only end one way and she had had access to the squabbles, ego-tripping, heartache and sabotage. Thinking back to their final break-up concert in London led her inevitably to thoughts of Carl Sheridan. *Don't go there*, she warned herself. This refrain was persistent. She needed to keep a tight lid on the box he occupied. She intended to keep him there for the rest of her life.

They had met at university where they were attending a media studies degree course. For six months they remained inseparable – a brief, blazing love that ended when Carl left her for a student studying graphic art. She had believed she was heartbroken when he told her it was over, but she met Matthew six months later and the painful memory faded. She and Matthew were steadfast in their relationship but Carl was always moving on. Even marriage and two sons hadn't slowed him down, as she discovered when they met by chance in London where she was filming Cherry Ash's sell-out, final concert. What happened on that weekend was the motivating force that brought her and Matthew to Serenity Falls.

Every effort had been made to provide a welcoming environment for those who were embarking on the five-day programme. Despite the convivial surroundings, most couples remained standing, ill at ease and silent until Pamela Blake entered the Chat Room. Her friendly manner suggested she was used to breaking the ice on such occasions and soon everyone was seated. Introductions began and Matthew, as always, spoke for her.

'We're Matthew and Abigail Conlon.' He waved his hand casually in her direction. 'I work with the police in the IT department and my wife's involved in film. We're looking forward to participating in the programme and getting to know everyone.'

Pamela switched on the introductory video that outlined how their days would be organised into workshops, counselling sessions, group discussions and times for reflection. Guests had the use of the large self-service and well-stocked kitchen, where they could eat freely during the day. Attendance at the evening meal was obligatory. Walking through the grounds was encouraged and benches, gazebos and shaded pergolas provided ample opportunities to read and relax. This information was delivered to them by Victor Gordon, whose appearance on the screen was greeted by a muted gasp of excitement from the woman sitting next to Gail. The man beside her glared angrily at the video, a deep flush mounting in his cheeks. Like Gail, he was there under duress and was making no attempt to hide his resentment. His wife, whose name badge read *Brenda,* shushed him with a sharp dig in the ribs and he grunted his displeasure back at her.

How relaxed Victor looked, so natural before the camera.

As a trained documentary maker, Abigail knew how difficult that was to achieve. The video drew mild applause from the audience when it ended. The ice finally cracked as couples began talking to each other about their impressions of Serenity Falls.

Lorraine Gordon entered the room and spoke briefly about the yoga and tai chi sessions she led, along with periods of meditation and mindfulness. She moved confidently and with a smooth graciousness between the couples, her blonde hair sweeping her cheeks as she bent her head attentively to listen to the concerns of a loud-voiced man. He was speaking belligerently about being highjacked into undertaking the programme by his wife. Gail was unable to hear Lorraine's response yet whatever she said must have appeased him if his laughter was any indication. She was in full control of the room yet when her husband arrived, she seemed somehow diminished. And not just her – it was the same with everyone else in his orbit. Success did that. Gail had seen it often. The camera always picked it up. Politicians at the apex of their careers, film stars and singers, tech millionaires. Did they exude an extra-special aura, or did the public project it onto them? She was never certain of the answer but she believed that that aura clung to Victor Gordon.

Some guests, particularly the men, seemed indifferent to his presence, yet she sensed a lifting of the atmosphere, a sudden heat at the back of her neck, and knew it was a collective reaction to his presence. The red-faced man, whom she had labelled the 'reluctant one', spluttered crumbs at his wife and muttered, 'Who does he think he is... an effing love guru?'

She left Matthew talking to Lorraine about the value of mindfulness and moved closer to Victor Gordon. He was hemmed in between a middle-aged couple, who had the complacent married look that always scared her: weight gain, comfortable shoes, a slight peppering of grey in the man's hair and, probably, a family of three teenagers at home. The woman, who introduced herself loudly as Madge Harper-Drennan, even though the name was visible on her name badge, was questioning Victor about the vegetable garden. Was it totally organic and, if so, how did he keep slugs at bay? Her eyes had a slight bulge that suggested a thyroid problem but could also have been caused by wonderment as she listened to him describing the value of corn and wheat bran as a natural method of slug control.

He was American – that much was obvious from his accent. Was he laughing inwardly at the ridiculousness of such a conversation? If so, he gave no indication of it and was equally polite when another woman asked him if regression therapy could prove to her third husband that she had been a contented wife in a previous life?

'Well, what do you think so far?' Matthew asked, when they returned to their room.

'Early days,' she said. 'Give me time to settle into it.'

A folder containing details of the counselling services available to them had been left on the dressing table. The sight of it added to her irritation.

'We should talk to Jan Lyons.' Matthew flicked through the pages. 'Donna said she's particularly astute, especially when it comes to repressed fears around pregnancy—'

'How dare you discuss something so intimate—'

'Hold on... *hold* on.' He held up his hands, palms outwards. 'Donna was talking about her partner's fears. He won't commit to their relationship—'

'You're her work colleague, Matthew, not her counsellor.' Heat rushed into her cheeks. 'And I don't have repressed fears. Which hat did you pull that one from?'

'There's no need to be so defensive, Abigail. I'm willing to open my mind to all that's on offer here. I accept I've got control issues; at least, that's what you keep telling me. I'm prepared to take that criticism on board. Why can't you be as cooperative?'

'Because I don't feel ready for motherhood just yet. Is that so hard to understand?'

He was putting on weight, she noticed. A slight thickening around his middle. She stared at her own reflection and then turned for a sideways view. With or without her glasses, it was not a good look, and she wasn't even pregnant... yet. She needed to lose at least a stone in weight and go down a size before she could even consider having a baby.

'I'm sorry I ever agreed to come here with you to this shamboree.' She liked the word. 'That's exactly what this is... a *shamboree*. Did you see those so-called *guests*? One half looks as though they're bored silly with each other, while the other half were probably dragged here kicking and screaming.'

'Like you were.' His voice rose. 'That's a great start to the programme, I must say. What else would you like to get off your chest? Or what else are you *afraid* to get off your chest?'

Was that a throwaway remark? Or did he know about...? Her heartbeat quickened. Were other couples arguing? Probably. Victor Gordon called this a safe space but he was wrong. She was outside her comfort zone, struggling with a secret that had no place in a marriage.

She could hear doves. There was a dovecote nearby, according to the video. Monogamous birds, the cuddling type.

'I'm sorry,' Matthew said. 'As usual, I'm clumsy with words.' He came from behind and wrapped his arms around her. 'We have to stop doing this. If we don't, we'll have one argument too many and there'll be no going back. I love you, Abigail, but I'm not sure anymore that you feel the same way about me.'

'I've never stopped loving you and I never will.' Was she speaking the truth? How was it possible not to know? Sometimes, like earlier, she actively disliked him, but the feeling always passed and she was back in familiar territory, in love and happy to be with him. Which emotion was real? Did it matter? Was love like a tide, flowing back and forth, sometimes smooth, sometimes turbulent?

She tried to enjoy the communal dinner. Donna had been right about one thing: the food was delicious. But she found it hard to swallow. At one point, looking down the table and noticing that Victor Gordon's eyes were on her, she was afraid she would have to bolt to the bathroom and throw up. Guilt had been controllable up to now. Here, she felt exposed. Scenes from that weekend in London came upon her without warning. The pang of guilt that surged through her was sickening. It never eased, even though it was two months since she and Carl... *stop... stop...* To think about him in this house where love had been placed at its centre seemed profane yet there he was, his face above her, below her, his love-making more demanding than it had been during their student days, which was, somehow, even more arousing. And he, too, had seemed consumed by that same driving force, as if, in pleasure, they could drown out their consciences.

She had rung Matthew and explained that there was a last-minute glitch with the documentary. He had grumbled the usual refrain: why did her work always take precedence over his needs? She had hardly heard him. Carl had been tracing his fingers along the inside of her thigh and she had had to press her lips together to hush an involuntary moan.

What possessed her to take such a risk? She had obsessively asked herself this question on her guilt-ridden flight home, and was still no nearer an answer when she saw Matthew waiting for her in Arrivals. In bed that night, their bodies spooned as they drifted towards sleep, she vowed that she would never burden him with her guilt and would carry her secret to her grave.

. . .

For five mornings the guests gathered on the south lawn for their yoga sessions. Downward-facing dog, low lunge, bridge pose, supine spinal twist – Gail lost herself in the rhythmic moves as she stretched and bent under Lorraine's guidance. She looked to be in her early twenties but she had a teenage son, a sullen youth dressed in black, who slouched past the guests without acknowledging them. *If ever there was a reason not to have a baby...* Gail stopped that particular thought process and concentrated on her chakras.

The atmosphere in the big house was taut with emotions, laughter and tears following each other as naturally as night and day. Couples came apart during group discussions and were together again by the end of the session, which was usually facilitated by Victor. He spoke little but seemed to know when to interject with a question when someone spoke for too long or said too little. She was conscious of his scrutiny. She thought she was being paranoid until Madge admitted that she, also, was under the same conviction. Was that how everyone felt? She asked Liz – whose third husband wore an earring and had tattoos on his arms – if she felt that Victor Gordon was scrutinising her. Liz nodded vigorously. 'That's exactly what he's doing,' she said. 'But then, far as I can tell, I'm the only third-timer here.'

The man who had been so resentful at the start of the programme was called Frederick. Permanently flushed and angry, he seemed particularly sensitive to Victor's attention. His resentment collapsed on the third day when he began to sob and talk about his experiences of being bullied at boarding school. To Gail's surprise, Matthew admitted during a group session that he had a tendency to be controlling and, for once, didn't add, 'but that's according to *you*.'

The tensions of the days were always relieved at night in the privacy of their bedroom. They came together spontaneously and for a brief, blissful time, Gail was lost to passion.

They were familiar with each other's bodies, the pleasure triggers, the sighs and moans, yet they experienced a newness in touch that added to the pitched excitement of their lovemaking. On the third day, they cancelled their appointment with the relationship counsellor. Gail had made up her mind, and was listening intently to the ticking of her biological clock.

By the fourth day, a supportive vibe was evident in the group as they gathered in the Chat Room for the penultimate group-therapy session.

'Warts and all,' Frederick joked. 'What's left to know about each other?'

'What about secrets?' Liz looked towards Victor. 'Can a relationship survive when a secret is not shared?'

'One of the more challenging phases of a growing relationship is the sharing of secrets.' He looked relaxed, his arms folded, his gaze alert as he surveyed the circle. 'Secrets have many shades. They can be embarrassing or painful, and also be heavy with guilt. However, they all have one thing in common. Our secrets become lighter when shared. We can offer them to the person we love in the hope that he or she has shoulders strong enough to carry the weight we now impose on them. To take that step and test the strength of our love is the beginning of trust. But is there a cost when it comes to such a sharing? Only you can make that decision.'

The stillness in the room as they listened to him... Gail would always remember that. And the authority with which he spoke – a man filled with his convictions. It would not have been the first time Victor Gordon had expressed such views about secrecy, yet he did not sound rehearsed or too polished. He stumbled a few times over words and coughed once, as if his throat was dry. These small interruptions only added to the intensity with which he spoke.

Questions were asked and opinions offered on the risks of

total honesty, but she barely heard the discussion that followed. Fresh air was necessary to clear her head.

Outside the grounds, the path rose steeply until she was looking down over a cliff face. She stopped to recover her breath and admire the plummeting waterfall. She felt as if she was being swept away by a similarly powerful force as it crashed downwards, towards the fast-flowing river that wound, snake-like, around the foot of the cliff.

She debated continuing her walk but knew Matthew would be wondering at her absence.

On her return to Serenity Falls, she passed the outhouses at the back of the building. The largest one was fronted by sliding doors. It was where Victor Gordon retreated in the evenings. She could see him through the glass. He had changed into a T-shirt and a pair of dungarees. He glanced up before she could look away and waved her in.

'I didn't mean to disturb you.' She hesitated at the threshold, conscious that he was carving wood. This was a studio, she realised, a private space with a workbench and shelves for his tools.

'Far from it. I'm happy to take a break.' He laid down a chisel alongside a block of wood that carried a yet-to-be-defined shape and gestured towards a well-worn armchair.

She sank down into the cushioned depths, conscious suddenly of an overwhelming tiredness.

'How would you define your time with us, Abigail?' he asked.

'It's been very enjoyable.' The answer slid easily from her and he, tilting his head to one side, began to carve again. The silence stretched between them and was broken only by the scraping sigh of wood being chiselled. His silence was not threatening, more expectant, as if he was waiting for her to reach deeper into herself for the truth.

Finally, reluctantly, she said, 'It's been challenging... and sometimes difficult.'

He nodded. 'Then you are taking the programme seriously.'

'Your brochure doesn't mention pain. Don't you think it should do so?'

'Are you in pain, Abigail?'

'Not physical pain.' She watched curlicues of wood floating from the block to the floor.

'The ancient Greeks believed pain to be a passion – an emotional sensation, similar to our other senses.' He spoke softly. 'Is that what you're experiencing?'

'Yes, perhaps it is.'

'Do you see it as something to be quashed? That's what western medicine is about: numbing, dulling, erasing the physical and the mental. That's why we have an opioid epidemic – but that's a story for another day.'

'My pain won't be alleviated by drugs or by sharing it in front of others, who are also in pain.'

'Pain is easier to see in others when we deny our own reflections.'

'Are you suggesting my mirror is distorted?'

'I'm simply making observations about pain.'

'What you said about secrets... the weight of them.'

He brushed more wood shavings from the block.

'The muscle power of a secret can never be underestimated,' he said. 'Small untruths become outright lies as you battle them into submission.'

'Surely it's our responsibility to carry that weight on our own, not to burden those we love with it,' she said.

'I agree that it becomes a heavier burden when a secret is one of betrayal,' he replied.

'I never said anything about betrayal.'

He bent his head and cut deeper into the carving. The deliberate rhythm of his hands was hypnotically soothing as she blurted out the truth and watched the shape of a stag's head with full-grown antlers emerging from the wood.

'How can I possibly expect Matthew to understand?' she asked. 'I don't know what to do.'

'Do you believe you have the stamina to live with this secret?' he asked.

'Sometimes I think so, yet I'm constantly battling with myself. I've forgotten what it's like to have peace of mind.'

'Truth is the bedrock of a fully lived relationship,' he said. 'Without it, the foundation remains unsteady. Secrecy, on the other hand, corrodes your soul. If you don't believe in the soul, then let's call it your collective unconscious. Your selflessness. A label is not important. Whatever is finest within you will only fester when there is no air, no escape. Secrecy or truth. Only you can decide how that bedrock can be made secure.'

'Would you make such a confession to Lorraine?'

'Yes, I would. It would be a difficult decision but the truth will always prevail over deceit.'

When she returned to their room, her mind was made up.

Matthew was waiting for her, anxious that they would not be late for dinner. It was a formal affair and everyone was expected to dress up for it.

The wine flowed freely around the table. The food could not be faulted yet she hardly tasted the fresh vegetables, the crisp roast potatoes, and the succulent rack of lamb with its rich *jus*.

Lorraine, noticing her scarcely touched plate, asked if she would prefer the vegetarian option.

'This is delicious, thank you.' She gestured towards her plate and dug her fork into a roast potato. 'Unfortunately, I ate late at lunch so I'm not as hungry as I should be.'

'If you're sure...' Lorraine smiled and moved on to

exchange a few words with Frederick and Brenda, who had decided to stay on until Saturday morning to renew their marriage vows.

Later, in bed with Matthew, she loved him fiercely. Twice they came together, shushing their sounds of pleasure with deep kisses. When she began to cry, he held her tenderly and promised to understand. She had never loved him more as she told him how, in London, discontented and afraid that she was losing her identity, she slept with someone else. His name was not important, she insisted. This decision had tormented her ever since. The only positive to take from it was her realisation that her marriage was the most important and precious gift that Matthew had given her.

'We've talked enough for tonight,' he said, when she asked for his forgiveness. 'Tomorrow we'll deal with what you've told me and work out our way forward.'

She tried to read his expression but he remained blank-faced, his mouth slack when it should have been clenched with fury or jealousy. The more she wept the more controlled he became.

As they lay together, she tried to read his body, but his back was rigid, his legs moving away from hers if she made contact with him.

She wanted him to lash out at her. She would take his odium and his rage as natural reactions, but his lack of emotion was more frightening.

She awoke in the small hours. Dawn was seeping into the room, a chink of light escaping between the drawn curtains and slanting across his cheek. He was sleeping on his back, his mouth slightly open and emitting a drone-like sighing.

He stirred and opened his eyes before she could move aside. She saw her future in his sleep-fuelled gaze. Too late, she realised her mistake. What a fool she had been to listen to Victor Gordon's compelling voice and believe it was that easy to upload her guilt. Such secrets should be carried to the grave and remain there forever.

The mood was celebratory when the ten couples who had started the Rekindle programme with such mixed emotions gathered in the Chat Room to discuss its impact on their relationships. People, especially the men, who had seemed tongue-tied at the beginning of the week spoke movingly about what the programme had revealed to them about their selves.

'For me, it was a most informative experience.' Matthew's critical tone was a stark contrast to the previous comments. 'My great reveal is the discovery that my wife has been *whoring* behind my back.' He used the word with such venom that even Victor seemed suspended in the flabbergasted pause that followed. 'If my shoulders are to carry this weight, let's count how many times you did it.' Matthew addressed her directly. 'This is a safe space. Tell us how many times you thought of me during that whole sordid weekend?'

Frederick's open-mouthed surprise revealed the fillings in his back teeth. The whites of Madge's eyes seemed particularly viscid and Liz's expression suggested that Gail's indiscretion had filled her with inappropriate admiration.

Matthew's questions continued to come at her like bullets, their impact having a paralysing effect on all who heard them. He began to cry then, an almost strangled sound that faded when Lorraine moved forward and asked him to leave the room with her. She spoke so firmly that he took the hand she offered him and stood.

The silence continued after his departure, until Pamela sat down on the two-seater settee beside Gail. 'Abigail, let's go somewhere quiet and talk.' She spoke softly, non-judgementally.

Everyone's eyes were on her but she managed to find the

strength to stand and walk with Pamela from the room. Victor was talking, encouraging everyone to conclude the session. In control again, he was as persuasive as ever as the buzz of conversation that had broken out ceased.

Outside the Chat Room, Gail leaned against the wall. She refused to go into Pamela's office to discuss what had occurred. Before her, the staircase, with its magnificent sweep, seemed mountainous. She needed to climb it and pack her case before Matthew came back from wherever he had gone with Lorraine. Her marriage was over. Forgiveness was not an option. She had seen it in his expression, in the cold malice with which he had torn her apart in front of everyone. Being in control meant everything to him. She had shattered that illusion, and he had contained his fury until the moment it would have the most impact.

She was packed and ready to leave when he entered their bedroom.

'I've called a taxi,' she said. 'I'll have left the apartment by the time you return. There's no coming back from what I've done and you've made certain that I've no desire to do so.'

Matthew nodded. 'Make sure you take the smell of betrayal with you,' he said. 'Otherwise, I'll have to fumigate the apartment.'

Even then, her marriage could have been salvaged. The right words were needed. They were surrounded by specialists in happiness and Victor Gordon was waiting on the steps to comfort her. The entire facilities at Serenity Falls would be at her and Matthew's disposal, he promised, but Gail, sobbing uncontrollably, ran towards the waiting taxi and her new life.

The ramifications had seemed unending during those early, chaotic days following their time at Serenity Falls. She refused to divulge Carl's identity but Matthew found out anyway. He was even able to tell her how often she ordered room service and what was on the menu. He contacted Carl's wife, Jessica, and told her everything that had occurred. Jessica refused to forgive her husband, even for the sake of their two sons. By the time evening came, she had changed the locks on their family home.

Gail had been living in London and renting a studio flat in Notting Hill when Matthew and Donna White moved in together. Donna, like him, claimed that her five-day stay at Serenity Falls had proved her relationship with her long-term partner had nowhere else to go but into the trash. The irony of it all. Laughable, ludicrous and heart-breaking.

Carl was right when he said Gail had changed beyond recognition since then. She lost weight following her flight from Serenity Falls, and never allowed her figure to regain its natural curviness. Matthew, when they met some months after their separation, told her she had become 'scraggy'. It was a deliberate slight, meant to undermine her, which he effectively did until she learned to embrace her new shape and maintain it. Her hair, once mousey-brown and curly, was a vivid flash of vermillion, arresting enough to turn heads. *Sculptured*, that was what she ordered from her hairstylist each time she had it cut. Hard to imagine it was once long enough to wind around her fingers and pull violently when she was stressed. And an eye operation had rectified her sight problem so that she only needed to use glasses when working on her laptop. Gone were her chunky frames, and she felt good without them.

By the time her documentary about Cherry Ash was released, Matthew had become a father. Another child has been born since then and a third was on the way. Donna White-Conlon's stomach dominated her Instagram page. Gail checked regularly, and despised herself for doing so.

EIGHTEEN

NO NAME GIRL

I smell fake tan and sunscreen, perspiration. The weather forecasters talk about an unseasonal heatwave. Climate change or just good luck? The nurses can't decide. Their voices are different in the mornings. Brisk and cheerful. That changes as the day goes on. Less laughter, no gossip. They tell me their secrets. Whisper about love. How it hurts. Whisper about dangerous lovers. Unfaithful or indifferent spouses. Their secrets fall into the abyss. Doomed to die with me. That's what they believe. Who am I to argue? This is my world now. The world of the whisperers.

Dessie has twin daughters. My age, he says. How does he know? I'm a blank sheet. The Vegetable. His wife is depressed. Empty nest syndrome, their twins in Sydney. Surfing on Bondi.

I remember the waves. The endless patience, waiting for the Big One. The Perfect One. Astride my surfboard... waiting... waiting...

Sheila's husband beats her. The bruises on her arms must pulse like stingrays. He holds her throat until her eyes bulge. 'I blacked out,' she whispers in my ear. 'What am I to do, Naomi? What am I to do?'

Get out... leave him...! I want to shout at her. My lips won't open. Only my eyelids move, their weight crushing me... blink... blink... blink. Involuntary tics. Part of the vegetative process. Her voice is hoarse with pain yet she laughs with the other nurses.

All the jokes they share, the gossip. But when they whisper to me, their secrets are for my ears only.

Dominique misses her family in Ecuador and is in love with a woman who betrays her. I am the abyss. No echo. The guardian of their secrets. I count the seconds as they whisper and check my oxygen, change my drips, and read the monitor that tells them I'm still breathing.

Lorraine is here again. Her breath smells of mint, her skin of roses. I breathe in something else. A faint mustiness, as if a certain space inside her is too closed to allow fresh air to flow through. Her hatred feels like needles on my skin.

NINETEEN

LORRAINE

Three weeks had passed since the re-opening of Serenity Falls. Lorraine's initial nervousness when the guests arrived had quickly disappeared. Exhilaration mixed with dread was proving to be a potent cocktail. Was that how Victor felt when he lived the big lie? She had created a new reality and must live as if she believed in its essence, yet all it took was a phone call from the family liaison officer for her skin to lift in goosebumps.

Jean arrived one afternoon with Victor's possessions from his car, as well as the clothes he had been wearing on the day of the accident. His suit was in shreds, cut from him in a vain effort to save his life. His phone had been smashed into pieces and a wide-spread search for missing parts, including the memory chip, had proved futile.

'Such a pity,' said Jean. 'It could have shed some light on Naomi's story.'

After she had driven away, Lorraine carried his briefcase to her bedroom. By some fluke, it was relatively undamaged but the leather was darkened by stains that must be blood. The lock still opened. She removed documents, brochures about Rekindle Connections, stapled pages from the Hearts and

Vows speech she had written for him, his phone charger, and some sterling bank notes. His wallet contained a family picture. He had taken it when they were in Canada last year. *The secrets hidden behind smiles.* She grimaced and searched the flaps and zipped pockets in the lining. Nothing... nothing. The gardai would have conducted the same thorough search and been unable to find anything that would identify Naomi Nelson.

The name no longer sounded like a curse when it slid from her lips.

She shoved his briefcase into the back of his wardrobe. Suits and shirts, drawers full of underwear, socks – such a lot of clearing out to do. She should contact Charlotte from the charity shop in Potters Glen and ask her to remove everything that belonged to him. In this new life he had created for her, she must function without the burden of the past.

Lorraine had quickly put herself on first-name terms with the nurses who attended to Naomi. Jackie had a hardness at her core. It reflected in her eyes and the pull of her mouth, yet she was a professional. When she insisted that Naomi was in a deep vegetative state, no one dared correct her, except Dessie. He was older than the others – a late vocation to enter the profession, he told Lorraine. Dominique had dark eyes that told a story of borders crossed and obstacles overcome that must have seemed insurmountable. Sheila was soft-voiced and kind with a quiet efficiency that made her difficult job seem effortless.

She was taking Naomi's blood pressure when Lorraine arrived one afternoon. 'Dessie told me you run a sanctuary,' she said.

Sanctuary? Her choice of this word interested Lorraine. 'We don't offer sanctuary at Serenity Falls,' she replied. 'Couples who need to work on their relationships, or who simply want time together in peaceful surroundings, come voluntarily and partake of our programme.'

'Do most husbands come willingly?' Sheila entered the medical details on a chart and clipped it back to the bottom of the bed.

'Some do. Others need persuasion and that is up to their spouses, not to us.'

'How do you persuade a husband who is dead set against it?'

'Are you speaking personally, Sheila?'

The nurse gathered her shoulders inwards and clasped her hands around her arms. 'My husband is a stubborn man,' she eventually replied.

'And you want to change him?'

'If only it was that easy.'

'What about changing yourself? Should that not be the purpose of undertaking the programme?'

'I've tried to change. You've no idea how many times...' Her gaze skittered towards Lorraine and away again. 'It's difficult...'

'I'll bring some Rekindle literature in with me when I come again,' Lorraine said. 'Show it to your husband. Tell him you're anxious to change, to understand better the areas of your marriage that worry you both. It might persuade him to try the programme, or it might not; but it's worth a try, don't you think?'

The nurse's expression was still hesitant. 'I like the idea but I don't think Terence will be interested. Still, I'll keep your advice in mind. Thank you, Lorraine.'

She had never thought of Serenity Falls as a sanctuary but Sheila was right. Its walls protected her, and its busy tempo allowed her to forget that her life had become a charade. But when was it not? Pausing to reflect, caught suddenly by this thought in the midst of her busyness, Lorraine breathed deeply before moving on.

She dreaded the visits to St Gorgonia's yet believed they

were essential to silence any speculation that Naomi Nelson could have another name.

Victor's death had become old news. No longer a blip in the public consciousness. Gangsters and government squabbles, economic woes and climate change were eating up the news cycles, yet Carl Sheridan was never far from her thoughts. She kept expecting another phone call from him; but when he contacted her again, it was by letter.

Dear Lorraine,

Please do not give way to your initial impulse and rip up my letter. I assure you, that would not be a wise move. Information has come to me that sheds light on your husband's final tragic journey, for which I once again extend my deepest sympathy to you.

As you have made clear, I am not in a position to interview you, but the moratorium no longer applies to Victor. I'm sure you're as anxious to protect his reputation as I am anxious to set the record straight regarding his movements on the day of his death and the identity of his companion. The information I have acquired allows me to write the truth without your contribution but I'd like to offer you an opportunity to give your side of the story.

We should meet to discuss how this can be achieved. So far, I haven't shared this information with anyone else. I'm prepared to meet you privately. The location is on the map I've enclosed. The barracks has been derelict for years and we will not be seen or disturbed. In order to protect your reputation and the future of your company, I urge you not to ignore this letter.

I await your response.

Carl Sheridan

He was right about the compulsion to destroy his letter. Her fingers shook as she held the flimsy sheet of paper between her hands and shredded it.

She checked his Twitter account. ImplacableX. His latest tweet included a link to a peer-reviewed article about messianic delusions. This was illustrated with an iconic poster of Victor, his straightforward gaze into the camera, his dark, forceful eyes.

Five hashtags were included in his tweet. *#messianiccomplex #loveguru #unhappilyeverafter #nonamegirl #naomiwho*

TWENTY

NO NAME GIRL

Professor Shannon smells of jasmine. The night smell that seems to float from nowhere and everywhere. A welcome change from garlic. Her name is Stella and that's what I'm to call her. I heard Jackie sigh, especially when Stella started talking to me about St Gorgonia. Today, apparently, Gorgonia would have been an Insta celebrity and an influencer on positive thinking. She was trampled by a team of mules way back in the day and so badly injured that everyone believed she would die. She cured herself. No doctor. That's willpower, Stella said. She believes I have it in spades.

Lorraine is here again. I always know when she comes. Her breath is warm against my cheek as she waits for me to die. Always the same questions. 'How is Naomi doing today?' 'Is Naomi looking thinner?' 'How much longer can she survive in this condition?'

'She's stronger than she looks.' Same answer from Jackie. 'In her case, that's a shame. Why should her suffering be prolonged? I know what I'd want if I were in her shoes.'

Together, they remove the last splinters from my identity. I blink but they don't read this silent language I've learned. Even Stella, with her encouragement and belief in me, can't read my eyes. I think of those mules trampling all over Gorgonia and see the truck swerving... I blink... blink... blink...

TWENTY-ONE

LORRAINE

Lorraine drove to St Gorgonia's ward twice a week and watched Naomi staring at the ceiling. The neurosurgeon heading Naomi's medical team was willing to discuss her progress. Professor Shannon looked far too young to be addressed as such but calling her Stella, as she invited Lorraine to do, seemed equally inappropriate. She addressed Naomi directly, which was unnerving to hear, and encouraged Lorraine to play music or talk to her. Words stuck in her throat and when she did manage a few, banal comments, her voice sounded so artificial that she was unable to continue speaking.

'I've been in touch with the professor,' Aidan announced one evening, when Lorraine retired to the Nook after the communal evening meal with the guests. 'She's given me permission to see Naomi. Short visits only, but she believes the more stimuli she receives, the better are her chances of emerging from the coma. I'm hoping she'll respond to me.'

'Why on earth should you think that?'

'I sound like Victor,' he said. 'Not his accent, obviously, but the intonations when I speak. You've often remarked on the similarities.'

He was right. Certain inflexions, phrases and a slight drawl that he had picked up from Victor, Aidan's voice was an uncertain echo that had stopped her in her tracks of late.

'Have you any idea how deep her coma is?' she asked. 'I don't want you to get your hopes up and be disappointed.'

'I'm not a child, Mum. I know she was only a step away from having her life support switched off. But she's made it this far. Who knows what could happen under the right circumstances? Stella agrees—'

'Stella?'

'Professor Shannon. She's just returned from Vancouver. Turns out our apartments were quite close together.'

'How did you find all that out?'

'I rang her?'

'You'd no authority to do that.'

'I've as much authority as you have.' He faced her defiantly. 'I left a message on her answering machine and she rang me back. Victor was my father and I want to find out why that woman was with him.'

'You know the reason. She wanted to meet him.'

'So you keep saying. And I'm not disagreeing with you. But we won't really know the full truth until she recovers consciousness.'

'The chances of that happening—'

'—are slim and probably nil.' His voice quickened. 'But Stella is more optimistic than Professor Macken ever was.'

His use of the professor's first name annoyed her. How dare he interfere with the arrangement she had made with Jackie? She bit back an angry retort, anxious to avoid an argument with him. What harm would it do if he visited Naomi? He would find out quickly enough how torturous it was to sit by her bed and stare at her pale, blank features that occasionally twitched, her eyelids flickering as if desperately trying to see beyond her darkness. Meaningless signs, Jackie would assure Lorraine and, sure enough, the fidgety movements usually ceased and Naomi became still again.

'How often do you intend to visit her?' she asked.

'I'll play it by ear and see how it works out. If I feel that I'm distressing her in any way, I'll stop.'

'Promise you won't aggravate her condition?'

'That's what I just said. Give me some credit for common sense, will you?'

'I'm sorry, Aidan. I'm anxious about her, that's all.' She sounded fake, an actor with robotic lines and no emotion to lend meaning to them.

'What will happen to her if she does recover?'

The thought sent a shudder of dread through Lorraine. Those eyes fixing on her, the words she would utter. It couldn't happen... mustn't...

Aidan, his head tilted to one side, was watching her attentively.

'If she does regain consciousness, which seems most unlikely, she'll live here, of course. I'm prepared to look after her for as long as is necessary.'

'That's what I was hoping you'd say.' He took a bottle of beer from the fridge and held one out to her. She shook her head and kicked off her shoes. The murmur of voices and occasional bursts of laughter reached them from the dining room.

'I keep thinking about Victor's will.' He uncapped the beer and sat down opposite her. 'Has the solicitor been in touch about the intestacy?'

'She's working on it and—?'

'I still can't figure it out.' He sounded exasperated. 'Giving Serenity Falls to him, just like that.'

'I've already explained—'

'How depressed do you have to be to give your home away?'

'Depressed enough to make an attempt on my life.'

Her admission came on a rush of adrenalin and his

distressed expression reflected her own surprise. She had not intended to go there... ever...

'Can we talk about this another time?' She was anxious to bring the conversation to a close. 'I've so much on my mind at the moment. Trawling through the past is not what I want to do right now. Everything will be fine as soon as the intestacy is completed. Jennifer Moore will sign off on the final details very soon.'

'Hopefully, you're right...' He stopped, his eyes glistening. 'I wish...'

'What do you wish?'

'To have a second chance with Victor. When I was delivering his eulogy, I felt as if I was giving a performance. People told me how moved they were by what I said, and that I had such a great insight into his personality and character.'

'It was a very moving tribute—'

'All it proved is that I'm good at my job. Marketing and promotions, it's second nature to me. I never understood him. Never tried to, I guess.'

'Stop being so hard on yourself. Victor loved you and I believe you loved him just as fully.'

''The other night I dreamt he was alive. It was wonderful. That relief of knowing I could make things up with him.'

Yearning wishes did not feature in her dreams. Instead, she dreamt of violence, raging fires and tsunamis, shootings that awakened her with a pounding heartbeat. Was Victor at the centre of this carnage? She sensed his presence but had no recollections of him in the mornings. Only of her father – he would be there, an insubstantial figure in the heat and fury of her nightmares.

'You and I mustn't argue so much,' Aidan said. 'There was too much of that when Victor was alive, and I regret the part I played in it.'

Once, she had taken their closeness for granted and never

questioned his love for her. That love should have intensified with his father's passing but, instead, she sensed a resistance in him, a questioning edginess in his voice when they spoke about Naomi. Lorraine was conscious of that barrier and the impossibility of breaking through it as long as Megan... *Naomi...* was alive.

How long could this continue? Who would break first? Naomi with her twitches and tics, her unaltering, blank stare? Or Lorraine, so overwhelmed with a lie that it threatened to run her over should she dare to look away for a moment from its rolling momentum?

TWENTY-TWO

NO NAME GIRL

Aidan came again today. Dessie says I'm always brighter after he's been here. How can he tell? Is it the tear that trickles down my cheek? Or when I twitch my finger or make that animal noise, like a cat caught between bars? Maybe it's because Aidan knows I hear him. He understands my language. So much I want to tell him, but all I can do is blink... blink...

His smell is subtle, a faint, citrusy scent that reminds me of lemon groves. He says his house feels different now. Lighter. Like there's air blowing cobwebs away. Does he think his father was a spider? Spinning webs and trapping those who came within his silky strands? He is curious as to why I was with him. He asks me directly. Did I know him? Really know him? I blink twice.

Welcome to my world, he says. I never knew him either. His regret twangs like bad music when he tells me about their arguments. How large he always seemed. Large enough to diminish Aidan and make him feel worthless. Is that true? Or did Aidan diminish himself because he believed he couldn't measure up to his father's expectations?

Sometimes we say nothing. No words, no blinks. Not hearing is often louder. Insights fall into silence and I understand why Aidan always felt second best.

Hard to be anything else when his father's heart was trapped between the loch and the purple hills beyond Lochanar.

TWENTY-THREE

LORRAINE

July brought heavy showers and some flooding, followed by periods of intense sunshine that set forests alight. Warnings of climate change dominated the media but the quiet efficiency in St Gorgonia's ward never varied, and Jackie was determined to keep it that way.

She was checking charts at the workstation when Lorraine arrived one evening. The time she was forced to spend with Naomi was becoming intolerable yet she must endure it.

What had she and Victor talked about in those last moments before his death? The question was a burn in Lorraine's throat.

'I'm glad you're here, Lorraine.' Jackie sounded angry but that was not surprising. Her life pattern was based on anger. An alcoholic husband with a back problem, who forced her to be the breadwinner in a job she hated. 'I'd like a word with you before you see Naomi. I know that Professor Shannon believed Aidan might trigger some response in Naomi. Unfortunately, that hasn't happened and we need to keep visits to a minimum on my ward.'

'How often does he come?'

'Too often,' Jackie replied. 'He means well...' She paused and clicked her nails on the workstation desk. 'I've seen how people can convince themselves that they are making a difference to a patient's condition. The distress is greater than it needs to be when there's a setback. That's inevitable in a case like Naomi's. I don't doubt Aidan's good intentions but he's convinced that he's communicating with her. To be honest, Lorraine, I've found his attitude to be... shall we say... verging on arrogance. I've had to address the issue with Professor Shannon. I know her view differs from mine but she sees Naomi for brief periods whereas I see the full picture. It's my professional belief that Aidan is causing Naomi unnecessary stress.'

'That's the last thing Aidan would want to do. I'm sorry, Jackie. I'll speak to him. He won't be coming here again.'

'He's with Naomi now. And there's no time like the present.' The phone on the workstation rang and ended their conversation.

Outside the room where Naomi lay, Lorraine paused in the doorway and listened to her son. The similarity to Victor's voice was striking but was without the American resonances, which her husband never lost, apart from that one occasion... *mo grá... mo grá... mo ghràidh... mo ghràidh...* my love... my love...

How *had* Victor managed to do that? The constant checking, listening out for the slightest slip into a familiar Scottish idiom.

'A... B... C... D—' Aidan was speaking slowly, enunciating each letter of the alphabet and pausing between them. He stopped abruptly when he heard Lorraine and spun around.

His initial surprise was replaced by excitement as he gestured to Naomi. 'I know you don't believe it's possible but we're communicating,' he said. 'Watch this.' He moved closer to the bed and stared intently at Naomi. 'Where are you from? Does it begin with E?'

Her eyelids twitched.

'That's two blinks,' he told Lorraine. 'That rules E out. Let's try F—'

Lorraine watched as he tried the next two letters in the alphabet. The tics and jerks, the almost inaudible grunts; it seemed as if Naomi's face was in spasm, yet Aidan was imbued with a fervour that ignored these signs of distress.

'Stop it at once.' Lorraine's sharp command silenced him and the figure on the bed assumed her normal immobility. Her face had lost its unhealthy swelling and her cheekbones protruded above her sunken cheeks. Her hair, so stubby and patchy in the beginning, had become a sleek, dark skullcap and Lorraine caught a sudden flash of resemblance to the girl in the photograph on Maggie's wall.

Unable to look at her, Lorraine reached for a chair and sat down. Sometimes, she was convinced her legs would buckle and she would collapse, as helpless as a doe shot at point-blank range.

'I want you to stop visiting Naomi,' she said. 'Jackie believes you're doing more harm than good. What I've seen now confirms it.'

'Can you hear what we're saying about you?' Ignoring Lorraine, he addressed Naomi.

Her eyelids were slitted. All Lorraine could see were the whites of her eyes. Then, her face quivered, an effect so fleeting and tremulous it must have been imagined.

'No, she cannot hear anything.' Lorraine stifled the sudden rage that swept through her. 'But if she could, she would agree with me. The pressure you're putting her under is disgraceful. Let the professionals do their work and stop interfering.'

'Look at her. Just *look*. Why can't you see what I see?'

Instinctively, Lorraine glanced back at the young woman on the bed. Naomi's eyes were fully open, a dark-brown gleam that held her gaze and did not blink. *Liar... liar...*

Could that word have been spoken aloud? No, that was not

possible, yet Lorraine could hear its echo reverberating across the distance between them. Her son was correct. Megan Ross knew who she was and knew, also, who she was not.

She pushed back her chair and stood up. Walking to the open window, she stared down at the grounds. 'What I see is arrogance, Aidan. And ignorance, also.' Her voice kept rising. Soon it would be a shriek if she didn't control it. 'You are playing with Naomi's life and have no idea of the damage you could cause by your behaviour. Jackie is going to revoke your visiting privileges.'

'She can't do that. Stella gave me permission—'

'Aidan, Jackie is the clinical manager here. St Gorgonia's ward is her responsibility. She has made her views known to Professor Shannon who accepts her right to make such a decision. If you come here again, you will be trespassing. Do you understand what I'm saying?'

He nodded, accepting defeat sullenly before bending and kissing Naomi's death-mask face.

TWENTY-FOUR

NO NAME GIRL

Lorraine has silenced me.

A... B... C... blink... twang... twang. Such a stretch in the hours. Long, long hours waiting for Aidan, yet knowing he won't come... can't come. Her face when she heard him. Her fear was stark. Terrified he'd reach the letter S... blink! C... blink! O... blink! T... blink! And on and on and on.

I wanted to tell Aidan about Rosanna. R-O-S-A-N-N-A. She believes I'm trekking through Peru, thinks of me among the ruins – Saqsaywaman or the Temple of the Moon. She mothered me... smothered me... But if I'd only listened to her! Believed her when she said the past is a monster best kept caged.

And Candice, so much to say there. C-A-N-D-I-C-E. Her name lies on my tongue and tastes as sweet as it sounds. The monster is on me now. Savage teeth. Razor claws. Memories are as fast and fleeting as dreams.

I'm on my knees on a bedroom floor. Anita kneels beside me. She knew my mother and loved her like a sister. This tatty flat is where they lived together when they were young and had space for dreams. Gauzy scarves are draped over lamps and mirrors. The window is open, and the breeze stirs the scarves. The bed is unmade. Lipstick stains on the pillow. A man's tie hangs from the headboard. Is it so very different to the way it was when my mother came here after running away from Lochanar?

Anita leans forward and opens the metal box she's pulled from beneath the bed. What am I hoping to find inside it? Diaries breathing secrets? If so, I'm disappointed. All I can see are pieces of jewellery my mother designed, theatre programmes and ticket stubs from art galleries and rock concerts. And there are photographs of men, all with their eyes on Candice. I can understand why. Her mane of black hair, uncombed and spilling down her back, her brown, challenging eyes, her lips, sullen and kissed so often. I can tell by looking at her photograph that she was made to be loved by many. Any one of them could have been my father and it matters not a jot to me. She died without naming him. All she said about him was that he didn't want to know.

I think of her giving birth to me, as fatherless as she had been. Why? I could have been a problem easily solved by an abortion. Instead, she brought me to Lochanar in a Mothercare blanket, and left me there, running away again and flagging down a trucker who was driving towards the Borders. My cries of hunger awakened Rosanna. From then on, she took care of me.

I call it smothering, that constant watchfulness, her questions... who was I with? Where had I been? Tell me... tell me. Only now, as I lie in hell, do I understand that Rosanna was trying to recreate a past that she could handle without weeping. Her determination to keep me on a short leash failed. Impossible to hold back the tide. I was eighteen and free to make my own decisions. London with its bright, ugly sheen... following in my mother's footsteps.

She sent letters to Candice. Kneeling by the box, I read them all. Such pleas for her to come home and take care of me. There are photographs, taken on my birthdays and at Christmas. I'm like a pale shadow of Candice's wild beauty but she never looked at me, never even opened the envelopes. She had dreams to fulfil. I didn't feature in any of them. The letters stopped after I was eight years old.

Among these fragments of her life contained in the box, I find a CD on meditation. Like the letters, it's unopened, still sealed in cellophane. Victor Gordon's photo is on the cover. His dark, penetrating stare stirs something in me: a creepy sensation, as if Candice is pressing her cold fingers against my forehead and telling me to make the connection.

But of course, I don't. How can I?

Anita says a man gave it to Candice when she was selling her handmade jewellery at a Christmas craft fair. He bought a necklace and matching bracelet from her. Handsome, Anita says, but older. An American. Candice was too busy to pay attention to him. Later, she threw the disc into a drawer. Anita found it after she died and added it to the box of mementos.

The next time Candice came back to Lochanar she was in a coffin. She had injected a lethal dose of heroin mixed with fentanyl into her arm. 'Accidental death' was the coroner's verdict. I've read his report. He bemoaned a life wasted, such talent giving way to a needle.

Am I to go the same route? An early grave before my race is run? No... no... no! I squandered so many years. Always on the move. Nothing stable under my feet. My mother was unable to give me love but I inherited her gift of self-expression.

I drew people. Sitting on dusty pavements, I painted portraits in charcoal, shade and light. I captured what I saw in their eyes, and they were not always pleased. A man knocked me from my stool once and accused me of making him look like a thug... no argument there. Now, I paint internally. Images of hell. It lightens my darkness, those flames with their flickering cruelty. Dante's Inferno. I see it all now, and I paint as if there is no tomorrow.

TWENTY-FIVE

LORRAINE

Jennifer Moore continued to have difficulties with the intestacy. Her reassurances that this was not unusual, especially when dealing with a house as old as Serenity Falls, did nothing to ease Lorraine's state of mind as she continued to erase her husband's presence from the rooms.

Charlotte, the owner of Second Chance Salon, arrived with her assistant. Together, they boxed Victor's clothes and took them away. Aidan wanted to keep only one item: a Christmas jumper, one that had made him groan every time his father wore it on Christmas Day.

Victor's wardrobe door was open. Emptied out now, it was a vacant space that needed to be filled. Lorraine was about to close the door when she noticed his briefcase lying on its side.

Tan-coloured and made from leather, his monogrammed initials on the front, she had bought it for him on Rekindle Connection's tenth anniversary. The salesman had persuaded her to buy one of his most expensive designs. She had told him about the marriage retreat. Six months later he arrived at Serenity Falls with his wife. Lorraine remembered her, an elfin haircut and a smile that hid a multitude. He said she was as secretive as the hidden compartment in the briefcase he had sold Lorraine.

The memory came back to her with the force of a slap.

She pulled out the briefcase and opened it. The salesman had watched with amusement as she searched for this secret compartment. Finally, he revealed it, a discreet pocket that would remain unnoticed in the red, flocked lining, unless the owner knew of its existence.

She ran her hand over the lining and finally found it. The zip was practically indistinguishable yet it slid sleekly across to reveal the opening. Her fingers closed around a sheet of paper. She knew what it contained even before she unfolded it.

The words jumped in front of her eyes and she was forced to sit down so that she could begin to read it.

This is the last will and testament of me VICTOR GORDON of SERENITY FALL POTTERS GLEN in the county Wicklow I HEREBY REVOKE any Will or Wills by me at any time heretofore made I APPOINT my solicitor Jennifer Moore to be sole executor of this my will I DIRECT her as soon as possible after my decease to pay my just debts funeral and testamentary expenses I GIVE DEVISE AND BEQUEATH Serenity Falls to my said wife Rosanna Ross of LOCHVIEW HOUSE LOCHANAR SCOTLAND for her own use absolutely...

Unable to continue reading it to the end, Lorraine laid his will to one side and buried her face in her hands. An *anomaly*. Was that what she had been to him? How could he possibly have hoped to get away with it? It was a will in the making. His writing was clear. No shake of his hand had disturbed his thought process. All it needed was the signature of witnesses. She pulled out a second sheet of paper. It was a copy of his original will. The one he had shown to her only a few weeks ago, when she once again brought up the subject of the ownership of Serenity Falls. He had agreed that it was time to organise his affairs and had made an appointment to meet his solicitor.

Her persistence was upsetting him, he said.

'When have I ever deprived you of anything?' he had argued. 'Have I ever questioned any of the decisions you've made relating to Rekindle Connections or the house?'

'That's *not* the point,' she'd argued back.

'What is the point when what's mine is yours and vice versa. Just think back to what could have happened if I hadn't been there to take care of you during that time. It suits you to forget what you were like. You couldn't even feed yourself, not to mention looking after Aidan. I gave you peace of mind, and you gave me a home when I needed one. I've no problem signing the house back to you—'

'Then why are we having this conversation *again*?' she had demanded. 'Co-ownership, that's all I'm asking. We're supposed to be a partnership.'

'That's what I intend doing,' he had insisted. 'You sound as if you don't trust me, yet I gave up everything to make a life with you here. I've never regretted it but this constant harping—'

'I don't harp, Victor. I simply want what rightfully belongs to me.'

He had known then that his life expectancy was finite. She had asked his doctor for details about his condition but, like Jennifer Moore, he claimed that patient confidentially continued even after death. The web of lies surrounding Victor was becoming denser. Would he soon disappear into the centre of it and become unrecognisable?

All she knew was that he had kept his illness from her so that he could sign away her home to another woman.

What was he thinking as he wrote those words? Was his conscience screaming at him – or had Megan Ross forced his hand? How many furtive meetings in furtive places had taken place between them? What pressure had she applied? What threats? Had he shown his will to her? Was she smugly thinking about her ill-gotten inheritance before fate intervened?

Carl Sheridan would rub his hands with glee if he knew. The ruination of Rekindle Connections. His big scoop. The 'love guru' exposed. All those years of hard work and dedication could be destroyed by Victor's guilt or whatever twisted emotion he felt as he betrayed her. She thought about Megan's dark eyes. The awareness she saw in them before the sweep of her eyelashes hid them from view. Lorraine imagined them together in his car, his speed increasing as he thought about what lay ahead.

Her rage had no circumference, nor had her fear. She operated with both, balancing one against the other, and was lost in between the cracks. As she walked swiftly to the bathroom, she tore his will in two, then quartered it, ripping it into fragments that she flung into the toilet bowl and flushed twice before the last shreds of his deceit swirled from view.

TWENTY-SIX

NO NAME GIRL

Dominique was crying this morning when she massaged my feet. Last night, she flung a brick through the window of the house where her wife betrays her. She thinks love will drive her mad and hate will keep her sane. Who am I to disagree with her? Sheila's husband threatens to hunt her down and kill her with a knife if she leaves him. She whispers... whispers... What am I to do, Naomi, what am I to do? She knows the answer yet her questions never change.

Dessie's wife plans on going to college to study Greek philosophy. He's afraid she'll outgrow him and discard him like a coat that has grown too small for her. That's what I think, too... but am I thinking or dreaming? Blinking or twitching?

Rosanna never wanted to talk to me about Max, fobbing me off when I asked questions, her mouth puckering as if she'd sucked on lemons. Her secrets were hers alone, and not for sharing. Perhaps, if she were here now, she would whisper them to me. Just as Dominique does, and Sheila... Dessie, too...

Jackie's in a mood today. Back-up staff   not enough – and Sheila is on her day off. Is she safe with that wife beater? Will she whisper to me about her bruises tomorrow? Will I live to see tomorrow? I know how easy it is to steal away. Dessie has gone to an end-of-life meeting with the family of the old woman in the next room. Like me, she is trapped, but death is coming to release her.

Lorraine is here. Her perfume is light yet strong enough to reach through the antiseptic mist surrounding me. My head feels tight. Like there's a gong inside it beating time... tick-tock... tick-tock... tick-tock... The phone is ringing again at the nurses' station. Jackie's gone to answer it. I know her footsteps, her left foot heavier than the right. I want Sheila to come and tell me about her brutal husband... I want to hear about Dessie's twins on Bondi... the memories it brings back... those carefree days.

Megan... Megan... why are you still here?

My name – she always whispers it. Her lips close to my ear.

Megan... no one knows where you are. No one cares... vegetable... aubergine... fleshy... my head... oh, my head, it's ready to burst... St Gorgonia's mules are trampling all over me.

The truck... veering... Max... Victor... Mo ghràidh... mo ghràidh... Did he breathe those last words or did I dream them? Does it matter?

My head... my head... tick-tock... tick-tock...

Her warm breath on my face... mint... her hand on my nose... my mouth...

Tick... tock... tick...

TWENTY-SEVEN

LORRAINE

Her stare as the light in her eyes dimmed held a terrible knowledge that brought Lorraine back to another time. Another instant when a decision must be made and carried through without hesitation. She pressed her hand harder against Naomi's unresisting mouth and tightened her thumb and index finger on her nose. Her own breathing was loud and fast, a jagged sound that was soon drowned in a crescendo of bleeping alarms, running footsteps, commanding shouts.

She remained rooted to the spot as Jackie rushed into the room, brushing aside her stammered explanation that Naomi had suddenly gone into a seizure.

Outside in the corridor, she slumped into a chair. She heard the emergency crew arriving, doors opening and closing, the wheeze and crash of a defibrillator, the wheels of a trolley moving rapidly past her, and then silence as the door closed.

She lifted her head and rubbed her eyes. For one glorious instant, she believed she was awakening from a dream. The relief that overwhelmed her barely registered before she recalled the arch of Naomi's body that had, until then, been lying still, a stillness akin to death, apart from her eyes.

Jackie, entering the room, didn't seem surprised to discover she was convulsing. The medical team were used to such emergencies, she said, as Lorraine was hustled outside.

She waited in the corridor without any idea where Naomi had gone until the tall nurse with the wounded eyes – *Dominique, that's it* – came down the corridor towards her.

'What's going on? Is Naomi... is she...?' Lorraine tried to swallow but her throat muscles refused to work.

'She's still alive.' Dominique laid a reassuring hand on her shoulder. 'It's a serious deterioration but Professor Shannon thinks she has a chance. It's going to be a long wait. You should go home, Lorraine. Get some rest. You've done more than enough for Naomi and you need to look after yourself. Eat something in the café before you drive. You look devastated.'

'Do you think she'll survive?'

'Professor Shannon has miracle hands. We call her "the decoder". The brain is a mystery that she believes she can decode. If Naomi has any chance of surviving, she'll make it under the professor's care.'

In the café, Lorraine carried a cup of coffee and a sandwich to the table. Would Stella Shannon discover what occurred before Naomi had that seizure? But what exactly did occur? Lorraine gulped coffee and scalded her lip.

Welcoming the sting, she lowered the cup and stared at two nurses who were taking a break at the next table. Her mind was filled with fog. It prevented her from making sense of those few moments when she had been alone with Naomi. Her teeth chattered as she sank deeper into the chair. Her hands began to shake.

She spread her fingers on the table and gradually the trembling stopped.

Dominique entered the café and came straight to her table.

'How is she?' Lorraine whispered the question through stiff

lips and forced herself to sit still as she waited for the nurse to reply.

'Naomi is still in theatre,' Dominique said. 'It's too soon to know how she's doing.' She pulled out the chair opposite Lorraine and sat down.

'Same as usual, Dominique?' A woman behind the counter shouted across at the nurse and brought a cappuccino to the table when Dominique nodded.

'I feel as if I'm to blame in some way.' Lorraine raised her voice slightly but the feeling persisted that if she spoke too loud she would shatter the fragile shell surrounding her. 'The seizure she took—'

'It's not uncommon for someone in Naomi's situation,' Dominique was quick to reassure her. 'You mustn't blame yourself. You and your son have done everything you can to bring her out of that pitiless coma.' She scooped froth from the coffee and licked the spoon. 'Dessie told me your sanctuary is open again.'

'It's not a sanc—yes, Serenity Falls has reopened.'

'My wife...' Dominique hesitated, desolate and anxious. 'She and I, we're lost. She wants us to be together but she has wounded me. I don't know if I'm able to forgive her. Dessie showed me your brochure. Your sanctuary helps people to forgive, yes?'

'It's people who forgive each other.'

'Karla and I have talked about Serenity Falls. We believe we could heal there.'

'I'll discuss it with you again, Dominique.' Suddenly exhausted, Lorraine felt her shoulders slacken. 'Please let me know if there is an update on Naomi's condition.'

Twilight was falling when she left the hospital. The sky was full of starlings. Giddy in flight, they seemed possessed by an inner radar that guided them through their chaotic choreography. She paused for an instant before entering her car. Starlings had darkened the sky on the evening her father fell to his death. Her knees sagged with such suddenness that she was forced to hold on to the car door.

She boxed the memory safely away and wondered if she should take a taxi. She could collect her car tomorrow when she was of sounder mind. This clogged sensation was strange but not new – the fog, that same breathless bewilderment, and the belief that this time she would collapse from lack of air... the instant passed. It always did. That was her only certainty.

Her foot was steady when she pressed the accelerator and exited the carpark.

Arriving home, she drove between the poplars. Sentinels at arms, their leaves fluttering to the rhythm of her heart. She parked her car in the courtyard and climbed the steps. The waterfall thundered in her ears. An illusion. It was impossible for sound to travel such a distance. Her father's arms reached into the hazed air, seeking support where there was none to be found.

She refused to go there. Not now, but later, when word came back that Professor Shannon had been unable to decode the tortured wires in Meg—*Naomi*'s brain, Lorraine would finally be able to thrust the past into a safe space where it would be unable to touch her.

'How could that happen?' Aidan's rigid stance signalled his alarm. 'She was doing well when I was with her. I still don't understand why she should suddenly have a seizure.'

'According to Dominique, it happens. But Naomi is in excellent hands. They call Professor Shannon "the decoder", apparently. If anyone can save her, she can.'

'You looked stunned. I'm just glad you were there when it happened. Otherwise—'

'I know... I know. I'm still shaking from the experience. Dominique has promised to keep us up to date on her progress.'

'But what if—' Aidan's haunted expression reinforced the horror of what she had experienced when Naomi's frail body convulsed.

'There's no sense imagining the worst,' she said. 'We focus only on the *now*.'

Mindfulness. Be kind to yourselves. Love yourself first and that love will flow to others. *Platitudes.* She gathered them like a downy blanket around her, and it was possible to concentrate on the guests who had arrived to begin a new Rekindle programme.

Three days passed before the phone call came from Dominique. 'Professor Shannon has performed a miracle.' Her voice rang with delight. 'I thought you'd like to know. Naomi is awake.'

'Awake?' Lorraine struggled to understand her. Did it mean more movement, those awful blinks and kitten whimpers? 'What's happened?'

'She's recovered consciousness and is communicating with us.'

'*Really!* That's astonishing.' Splinters of pain shot through Lorraine's temples and forced her to consider how much unendurable pressure the brain could endure.

'Absolutely. I shouldn't be surprised. Dr Shannon is a miracle worker.'

'What has Naomi said, Dominique?'

'Just a few words, like yes and no. She is still a very sick woman.'

'How soon can I see her?'

'Not for some time. Professor Shannon believes there could

be memory issues. I'll keep in touch with you, Lorraine.' She paused then gave what sounded like a short squeal of excitement. 'Guess what? Karla is looking forward to staying at your sanctuary.'

'And I'm looking forward to welcoming you both.'

Lorraine ended the call and rested her arms on the kitchen table. Would she make it to the bathroom before everything in her stomach was expelled? Breathing deeply, she waited until the heaving eased and was replaced by a cold sweat.

'What's the matter?' Aidan entered the kitchen and hurried across to her. 'My God, Mum, you're ashen. What's happened?'

'I'm okay.' She held his hands and leaned into him. 'Dominique was on the phone. Naomi is awake. She's able to speak a few words.'

'Are you *serious*?'

'According to Dominique, that's what's happened.'

'I can't believe it.'

'Neither can I. Professor Shannon has performed a miracle, it seems.'

'When can she have visitors?' Aidan's face was flushed with expectation.

'She's still critical. We mustn't get our hopes up.'

'I can't wait to hear her voice. She was able to understand me, I know she was.' He fisted the air in triumph.

'Dominique said she could have problems with her memory.'

'How serious?'

'Hard to tell at this stage. She's not allowed visitors until she's stronger and, even then, only *I* will be allowed into the ward.'

He accepted this information with a shrug. 'I wonder how long it will take before she's able to come here to recuperate.'

'I don't think that will be possible—'

'Not possible? You said—'

'I know what I said, Aidan. But the authorities may not allow it. Effectively, I have no control over where Naomi goes when she's discharged.'

'But you'll put forward the case for her to come here, won't you? After all she's been through, she needs somewhere safe to stay.'

'I'll see what I can do, depending on how well she recovers.'

Lorraine was poised to run; she knew not where, but there had to be a reckoning.

TWENTY-EIGHT

LORRAINE

Drips and tubes were still attached to Naomi's body. A nasal cannula aided her breathing, yet the difference in her appearance was startling. It had to do with her eyes. Eyes that Lorraine dreaded seeing – but their clarity held only a mild puzzlement when Naomi turned her head towards the open door.

Her mouth, no longer clenched, opened a little as Lorraine approached the bed. She touched her top lip with her tongue as if to moisten the dryness on her cracked lips.

Jackie said she was confused and forgetful. She spoke one word at a time, yes, no, thanks, okay.

It is her accent that will give the lie away, Lorraine thought. In her head, she heard Andy's rolling burr and Rosanna's strong voice describing the life cycle of dolphins.

'How are you, Naomi?' She pulled a chair to the bedside and sat down.

'Okay.' She sounded hoarse, the word forced from her. She tried to smile, a lopsided grimace that brought Victor achingly to mind. She was propped against pillows, her hands flaccid against the sheets. A wad of cotton wool and a strip of gauze covered the vein used to take blood.

'My name is Lorraine. I'm very happy to see you looking so well.'

The woman remained silent.

'Do you know where you are?'

She nodded. 'Bed.'

Contrary to what Jackie had said, her gaze was alert.

'Do you remember the accident?'

Her forehead puckered as she shook her head.

'Can you remember your name?'

'Na-om-i.' She pronounced it as a child would, taking care to enunciate all the syllables.

'Naomi *Nelson*,' said Lorraine.

'Nel-*son*.' She did not flinch when Lorraine leaned closer to the bed. Instead, as she lifted her head from the pillow, she seemed eager to hear the name.

'You are so like your mother.' Lorraine smiled at her. 'I used to know your parents.'

'Parents?' Her head flopped back again, her eyes widening as if she could picture them.

'So, what do you think of our Naomi?' Jackie entered and spoke directly to Lorraine. 'Doesn't she look lovely today?'

Did she think the woman was incapable of hearing or understanding her? Hadn't she seen her eyes? That dangerous glint. Not easy to miss, but Jackie's attention was on Lorraine. 'Sergeant Boyne has arrived and would like to speak alone with Naomi.'

'I'll visit again soon.' Lorraine lightly pressed her hand and stood, relieved by the interruption. 'Goodbye, Naomi.'

'Bye...' The effort to speak contorted the young woman's mouth but she seemed calm, with nothing hidden or wary in her expression.

Outside the ward, Lorraine watched the garda sergeant coming along the corridor. The woman's bulkiness seemed more pronounced, more threatening. Had she put on weight since they last spoke? Probably not. Lorraine was projecting, walking a tightrope that refused to remain steady.

'No positive results yet from Texas,' Sergeant Boyne said as she drew nearer. 'We've been up quite a few cul-de-sacs, but nothing that brought us any closer to making an official identification. If only you could remember where exactly her parents lived in Texas.'

'They never settled anywhere for long. I don't think they ever had a fixed address. I'm sorry I can't be more helpful.'

'According to her medical team, Naomi is very fragile and susceptible. I hope you haven't been questioning her about the accident.'

Lorraine cleared her throat before replying. As always, she had to brace herself to respond to the sergeant's brusque authority.

'No, of course not. I just wanted to see for myself that she was okay. I'm anxious to help her in any way I can. If she recovers and is discharged, I hope to look after her at Serenity Falls.'

'That's a very generous offer.'

'It's the least I can do. We have professional counsellors who'll be able to help her. It's the perfect place for her to regain her memory.'

Professor Shannon, overriding the head nurse's objections, insisted that Aidan's presence was beneficial to Naomi's recovery. Although she was receiving speech therapy, it seemed as if, with her memory loss, she had forgotten the vibrations of speech, the nuances and inflections, the pitch and lilt of normal conversation. Her accent remained neutral, and difficult to place. It was known that she was a wanderer, perhaps that was the reason.

Lorraine knew that, sooner or later, those Scottish intonations would define her. But as the days passed and Naomi continued to speak in monosyllables or sentences that were short and abrupt, Lorraine tried to take comfort from the belief that she was still holding all the strands that tied Megan Ross to her.

She tried to relax, but the wall she had built with lies had no foundations and could tumble at the slightest push. Would Aidan be the one to pull it down? She questioned him each time he returned from St Gorgonia's ward. He appeared to answer candidly yet she sensed he was withholding information from her. What could that be? And why?

Naomi's eyes, once filled with a terrible awareness, were now blank, devoid of memory. Lorraine had to believe this was true. Otherwise, she would lose it and rip away the subterfuge that protected her. What would happen then?

Somehow, she had to find foundations that were sturdy enough to make her wall insurmountable.

TWENTY-NINE

NO NAME GIRL

Aidan says I talked to him with my eyes. Was that possible? Blink once, blink twice. He wants to know about me. What can I tell him? Naomi Nelson is my name. I weigh thirty-eight kilos. I have a scar on my right leg from my knee to my ankle but no broken bones. My brain is a cobweb that has been reassembled. It took most of the damage. I feel the welts when I run my hand over my scalp. I'm five feet seven inches in height, have brown eyes, stubby black hair and a caved-in face. Was I ever pretty? Was this vacant orb that is my head once full of information, facts and figures, memories? What was my past... other than what I've been told? I call it the dead zone but that's a contradiction because I'm alive. My fingers move; my legs too – admittedly, badly – but my mind exists in the moment.

That's a phrase Lorraine uses a lot. Be in the moment. Don't stress.

What was it like, the blank space I occupied for two months? Strangers surrounded me when I woke up. I could tell by the way they lifted me that they were familiar with my body. They told me their names. Sheila with her broken smile. Sad Dominique. Bitch Jackie. Dessie, I like him best. He told me about his twins.

The things they got up to in Sydney. Sometimes words go like a nail into my head. Sydney. I close my eyes and see waves – but no faces. The nail is just that – with nothing to hang on it.

Stella believes it will all come back to me. They don't call her Decoder for nothing. My brain is my internet. All my memories are there, it's just the algorithms that are confused. Should I believe her? Take hope from her? I was in hell. Then I was not.

Two men are dead. Is that not a monstrous thing to forget? My parents are also dead. A fire in a forest, their home destroyed. Another monstrosity that I cannot recall.

Lorraine wants me to live with her until I'm strong enough to manage on my own. The big policewoman doesn't think that will be possible but I'm too old to be a ward of court. Aidan says I'm capable of making my own decisions. Is that what he wants? He nods when I ask. He stumbles over my name, like the sound of it bothers him. Unlike Lorraine. Bit by bit she reveals my life, but only the slice of it that belongs to a place called Sedona.

THIRTY

LORRAINE

Naomi was sitting on a chair beside her bed watching a girl band performing on television when Lorraine entered St Gorgonia's ward late one afternoon.

Cherry Ash. Lorraine vaguely remembered them. They became overnight celebrities after winning a televised talent show. She remembered Aidan's scorn at the time, his dismissive attitude towards what he considered to be their manufactured success. Their fading was as swift as their rise to fame, and each stage of their heady journey had been captured in a documentary.

She sat on the edge of Naomi's bed to watch the band members being interviewed at the end of their performance. Since their break-up, they had survived divorce, substance abuse, mental issues and, in one case, a brief period of homelessness. Now, they were together again for a reunion tour. *Was it possible to be so unmarked by life's ravages?* she wondered, as she listened to them recalling their experiences. Falling and rising, scarring and healing – was that what the cycle of survival was all about?

Naomi lost interest in the television when the programme

ended. She muted the sound when the evening news came on and answered Lorraine's question in her hesitant, monosyllabic way.

Lorraine resisted the urge to glance at her watch. Time seemed to run on a slow motion track during these visits, yet she was unable to stay away.

She stiffened as she glanced back at the television and recognised Carl Sheridan.

He was standing outside a bleak warehouse in an industrial estate, his lips shaping inaudible words. Without the distraction of sound, these utterances accentuated the sharpness of his features and the stretch of his thin lips. He seemed to be everywhere these days. His knowledge of the prevailing drug gangs meant that he was regularly interviewed about their activities. This led to him receiving death threats and, in acknowledgement of his fearless reporting, he had received a journalist of the year award the previous month. The crime correspondent who was interviewing him was speaking now and Carl, turning his face to the camera, appeared to be staring directly at Lorraine.

Despite his busyness, he continued his personal vendetta against her on social media. ImplacableX. The ridiculousness of his username did nothing to lessen the toxicity of his tweets. They smacked of his obsession, the need to cling to a vendetta that no longer made sense.

A gasp from Naomi forced Lorraine's attention from the television. Naomi had lifted her shoulders and pressed her body back into the chair. Reaching for the remote control, she increased the volume.

Carl was being interviewed about a shipment of drugs that had been seized at an isolated landing jetty in West Kerry and stored in the warehouse off the M50 motorway. He spoke with his usual assurance, tracking the route he believed the shipment had travelled on its way to Kerry, then on to Dublin.

But Lorraine's attention was on Naomi. Her eyes glistened,

not with tears, Lorraine realised, but from a rage she could barely contain as she rocked back and forth in the chair.

'He was here,' she said. 'Asking me...' As if she needed this rhythmic movement to help her to speak, she swayed faster.

'What do you mean?' Naomi's sudden interjection had gripped her with an instant, quivering panic.

'*Questions.*'

'How could he ask you questions?'

'Here,' she repeated. 'Dessie sent him away.'

'Think carefully, Naomi. Are you sure you're not mixing him up with Aidan? We're the only two people allowed to visit you.'

'No.' She pointed at the television. 'It was *him.*'

The news item ended and the newsreader turned her attention to a scandal involving money laundering.

'I'm going to check this out for you right now.' Unable to believe what she had heard, Lorraine left the ward and approached the nurses' station where Dessie was working on a computer. 'Naomi seems confused this evening,' she said. 'She claims there was a journalist in her room. Carl Sheridan—'

'Ah, yes, I see.' Dessie turned his attention from the screen to her. 'Unfortunately, she's right. He blagged his way past Jackie by claiming he was from a voluntary group that visit patients who have no family links. He got away with it until I recognised him. I needn't tell you, I gave him short shrift and threatened to report him to the gardai.'

'Did you do so?'

'To be honest, no. He was only with Naomi for a few minutes before I twigged who he was and Jackie... well... it's unlike her to be fooled so easily. We all make mistakes and she was very upset. Something like that will never occur again.'

Naomi was lying down on her bed when Lorraine returned. 'I've sorted it out with Dessie,' she said. 'You needn't worry.

Carl Sheridan will never come back here again. What did he say to you?'

'The crash. Your husband... I don't know... I don't know.' She lifted her arms and clasped them behind her head, her swaying movement becoming less frantic as she struggled for words. 'He hurt... me... before...'

'How did he hurt you, Naomi? Look at me. Tell me.'

Something was unravelling, a skein loosening from its tightly bound spool. Lorraine would rewind it but it would unravel again... and again. She leaned towards Naomi. 'Tell me,' she repeated.

'My nose... he pushed...' Naomi's glassy stare was more unnerving than usual. 'When I was in hell.'

'Hell?'

'Yes.'

'Do you mean when you were in the coma?'

Naomi nodded.

'But you've no memory of anything that happened to you during that time.' She mustn't lose control... mustn't look away from Naomi's angry gaze.

She fell silent when the door opened and Dessie wheeled a blood pressure monitor into the room. 'I'm afraid I'll have to ask you to leave now, Lorraine.' He smiled across at her.

'Okay. I'll be in to see you soon again, Naomi.' She bent and kissed her cheek. 'Do you want to tell Dessie what you've told me?'

Naomi reached for the remote and switched off the television. 'You tell... I can't find... words.' Flushed and close to tears, she rubbed her knuckles fiercely against her eyes.

'She claims Carl Sheridan also visited her when she was in a coma. He did something to hurt her nose.'

'That certainly never happened here.' Dessie shook his head decisively and hunkered down until he was eye level with Naomi. 'You're probably remembering your nose being swabbed by the nurses, Naomi. There was no way anyone would have been able to get near you when you were in a coma, apart from Lorraine and Aidan, of course.'

'In hell,' Naomi repeated. Her earlier animation drained from her as she lapsed back into the half-world she occupied. Her hands were cold and clammy when Lorraine grasped them before leaving. Was there a slight resistance, barely noticeable, to her touch? Nothing in Naomi's dulled gaze suggested she was inwardly pulling away from her yet Lorraine, attuned to her every mood, sensed it.

Was Dessie right about the swab? It made sense. How could Naomi remember something so specific? She had been unconscious, unresponsive, her mind lost to sight and sound, yet her rage had been authentic when she spoke of hell. She was not confused, or delusional, and despite her memory loss, she was able to clearly recall that specific incident. Was that a one-off or had she been more cognisant than anyone, apart from Aidan, had believed.

Lorraine pushed the possibility aside and concentrated on the reason why Carl Sheridan had infiltrated his way into St Gorgonia's ward on that first occasion. Only one came to mind. DNA. No second guessing what he was trying to prove: Victor's love child... what a headline that would make. Was that why his letters had become more threatening, more confident, more demanding that they meet at his agreed location? He had created a narrative and was determined to shape it his way. Calculating and ruthless, his eyes were on Lorraine, and, as she had discovered, on Naomi.

A summer of mixed sunshine and showers was drawing to a close. Lorraine felt as if she was living inside a bubble that allowed her occasional glimpses at the changing season yet she was unable to break through the quivering membrane. Weeks passed as meetings were held between the various authorities involved in Naomi's care to discuss her future. Despite difficulties with her speech and mobility, Naomi was growing stronger every day. Her insistence that she wanted to accept Lorraine's invitation to live with her at Serenity Falls instead of being confined to a nursing home was finally accepted as the solution to her homelessness.

What had been a distant prospect in Lorraine's mind was suddenly becoming an alarming reality.

Naomi arrived in September at the Nook. Naomi Nelson... her name chimed like a bell. Even Aidan now accepted it. Was Lorraine the only one to hear its out-of-tune pitch?

Naomi's agitation eased as she settled into her new home. She was safe from intrusion or speculation by the guests participating in the Rekindle programme. She didn't have to leave the safety of the Nook as a speech therapist and a physiotherapist visited on a twice-weekly basis to work with her. Barring them was impossible, but their presence added to Lorraine's fear of discovery. Naomi's past continued to elude her, but how long could this continue?

Sometimes she would open the door to Naomi's bedroom and watch her sleeping. How easy it would be to press a pillow to her face. This thought was insidious and horrifying enough to hurry her back to her own room, only to lie awake and imagine those trusting, doe-like eyes narrowing as Naomi finally began to speak in coherent sentences.

THIRTY-ONE

NO NAME GIRL

I live behind a door marked Private. *The Nook is big and wide and all on one level so I can manage my wheelchair. I want to thank Lorraine for her kindness but my tongue twists the words out of shape. My voice is an echo. How do I know that? An echo of what? The speech therapist says the same as Stella: words will come back.*

Aidan gave me a sketchpad. He thinks I can draw my way back to my other life. This pad and my ring are the only things that are mine. The ring was cut from my finger but Aidan had it repaired. I've nothing else that belongs to me; not even the clothes I was wearing that day. Sergeant Boyne said they were rags when they were removed. Rags and blood... there must have been screams.

Even the letter that began it all, the one I wrote to Victor telling him I'd like to meet him, is held by the police. My handwriting has to belong to me, but I felt nothing when I read it. But for that letter I'd still be No Name Girl.

Lorraine has opened her home to me. What does she want in return? Her husband is dead and I'm alive. That has to suck. I look at his portrait in the hall. He swallows me with his eyes.

THIRTY-TWO

LORRAINE

Serenity Falls was filled with light when Lorraine accelerated down the avenue and turned right onto Cliffside Road. Rain was due later but, for now, the night sky was clear. She had refused to meet Carl Sheridan in the abandoned army barracks he had chosen. It was essential that she control the situation from the start. His agreement to her demand that they meet elsewhere indicated that he was as equally anxious to avoid exposure.

This gave her courage as she parked her car on the edge of a ditch. She walked a short distance along Farren's Lane to a lone and desolate cottage that was practically invisible behind over-grown ash and hazel and the ever-clinging ivy.

It was the only building still standing in this forgotten wilderness. The old, country lane was too narrow for traffic and too pot-holed for cyclists. Its only redeeming feature was the profusion of wildflowers that grew along its banks in the summer. She used to bring Aidan for walks along its mean-dering length when he was small and the lane not so overgrown.

She could tell by the dash of water against stone that the river was flowing fast. Tall water reeds wove a silvery silhouette against the night sky and the new moon, as thin and gently curved as a cutlass, was visible briefly as the clouds parted.

She passed his car and opened the gate. Stone slabs were strewn around the front garden and rusted overhead girders in the porch dripped with the fetid moisture of captured raindrops.

He was waiting for her in the kitchen. An old-fashioned dresser, the wood bleached and rotting, was still standing. She imagined it collapsing into dust should she lay a finger on it. A lantern on the table emitted a harsh glare and made it possible for her to see the flare of his nostrils. Glass crunched under her feet as she walked to the other side of the kitchen where a sink held the skeletal remains of a rat. The window frame, minus the pane, funnelled wind through her hair.

'I'm glad you came,' he said. 'It was a wise decision.' His confident voice created a murmuring echo but, perhaps, that was only the sound of ghosts stirring in the cobwebbed gloom.

'You have ten minutes of my time then I'm leaving,' she said.

'I want to talk to you about Naomi Nelson.'

'Then talk.' No ghosts, no echoes, just determined threats that she must outface.

'Firstly, let me commend you on your kindness. The lost orphan now has a home.'

'Get to the point.'

He shrugged. 'If that's how you want to play it, that's fine by me. I've good reason to believe you've falsified her identity.'

The crash of her heart against her ribs, a pain, knifepoint sharp. 'That's a ridiculous accusation.'

'It's an accurate accusation.'

'You're lying. Her name is Naomi Nel—'

'I know she's related to your dead husband.'

She clenched her fists, the bite of her nails against her flesh forcing her to concentrate on what he was about to reveal and which she knew she must deny... deny... deny.

'Nothing to say, Lorraine?' His voice pushed outwards through the murky light.

'What do you want me to say, Carl? That you're deluded. I agree. Now what?'

'I'm far from being deluded. Fact-checking, that's how I work.' He seemed barely able to contain his elation. 'You, on the other hand, have built an elaborate fantasy around this woman for reasons you're about to reveal to me. You've given me ten minutes so let's get down to facts. You and your late husband had the arrogance to hold up a mirror to the rest of us and claim to have the answer to eternal wedded bliss. But your mirror was tarnished with lies. I can prove beyond doubt that Victor Gordon and your so-called Naomi Nelson were related. That means your identification of her is either a deliberate lie... or a mistake. I've evidence to back up every word I intend to write. It's up to you to clarify your side of the story.'

'As easy as that, Carl? A simple clarification?' It was possible to speak firmly and tremble at the same time. To see a clear direction ahead while walls were buckling around her.

'I always offer the right to reply before an exposé,' he said.

'That's not how I remember your last so-called exposé about us.'

'A lot of water has passed under our bridges since then, Lorraine. The gardai will be more than interested in hearing what I have to say.'

'Then why haven't you spoken to them?'

'I'm offering you the right to reply,' he said. 'But if that's not forthcoming, then I'm afraid they will need to be informed about what I'm assuming – in my kinder moments – was a case of mistaken identity and not a deliberate attempt to hide crucial information about her.'

She ignored his grating insincerity, aware that he was

playing with her and that she was playing for time. 'A lot of water may have passed under our bridges, as you say, but you're still a liar... and a thief. I know what you did to Naomi. You took DNA from her while she was in a coma. Unfortunately for you, she remembers.'

His hesitation before speaking was barely perceptible but she registered it.

'Forensic evidence doesn't lie.' He waved a piece of paper at her, seemingly magicking it from the air. 'She and Victor were related.'

'Forensic?' She caught the word and examined it. She understood how he had been in contact with Naomi, but how could he have acquired such a sample from Victor?

She moved closer to the lantern and forced herself to look at the sheet of paper he held out to her. All she could read was the heading, which revealed the business name of a DNA testing centre.

She ran her tongue over her lips to moisten them. 'How did you acquire these DNA samples?' She reached for the document but he folded it and shoved it into an inside pocket in his jacket.

The rain came suddenly, a soft patter at first, and then a heavier shower dripped through the broken tiles. A small nocturnal creature, probably disturbed by the rain, scuttled across the floor, pitter-patter paws.

'You violated my husband when he was laid out in the morgue.' She stated this fact coldly. 'What did you take from him? A strand of hair? Yes, I suspect that's how it was done. Do you really believe you can get away with this?'

'You're not in a position to talk about illegalities.'

He laughed dismissively, but she sensed a crack in his self-assurance. Somehow, she must turn that crack into a break.

'And Naomi? You abused a woman in a coma. How is that

going to sound when it's reported to the gardai. Which I fully intend to do.'

'Let's see how far you go with that,' he retorted. 'All I have to do is publish an article outlining my investigation into the background of Naomi Nelson and suggesting that the gardai consider the option of DNA testing to validate my theory. Don't underestimate my influence, Lorraine.' He looked at her. 'You interfered with a garda investigation and gave false evidence.'

'So why am I here, if that's what you intend to do?'

'I want an exclusive interview.'

'Which is?'

'The truth. The full story. You'll tell the world what I've discovered. That Victor Gordon was a fraud who was driving on the M1 with his lovechild when he was killed.'

He had followed the scent of Victor's death to this desolate place. Was he enjoying his revenge? Eight years coming, yet each involuntary movement and intake of breath convinced her that his confidence was a façade.

'Why did you arrange to meet me here?' she asked.

'I knew you'd want privacy—'

'You're wrong. Unlike you, I've nothing to hide. You've concocted an elaborate lie—'

'DNA doesn't lie. I want your husband exposed for what he was. A charlatan.'

Her father's word for Victor. And here it was again, spat out with the same cruelty. Arthur Kilbride was whispering in her ear, as he had done in the months following Aidan's birth, his voice reaching her from beyond the grave: '*Chancer... charlatan... spiv... snake-oil man.*'

His body, radiant with fear, came before her in a flash that disappeared just as swiftly.

'The woman behind the man.' Carl was openly mocking her. 'What did you get out of it? I've wondered about that. All the hard work you did to carry his voice way beyond where it was capable of going. You managed him so skilfully that you fooled everyone except me.'

He knew too much, yet his information just skimmed the surface of the life she had made with Victor. 'You desecrated the dead—'

'I investigated a crime—'

'That report is a sham.'

'Believe me, it's genuine.

'How many copies have you made?'

'None... as yet.'

She believed him. Such evidence would incriminate him.

'So, did you make a tragic mistake when you identified No Name Girl?' he demanded. 'Or did you tell a deliberate lie? That is the choice I'm offering you, Lorraine. Your story told in your own words.'

He must have violated Victor's cold body in the mortuary, while his 'source' looked the other way. Had he been indifferent as he plucked hairs by their roots from his scalp? Strong, silver strands that she saw every time she picked up his hairbrush. And Naomi, lying so still and helpless as he shoved a test swab up her nostrils. A thief, plundering. The chill of the mortuary had entered her bones.

'Show me that report.' She moved so swiftly towards him that he had no time to step aside. He stumbled back against the dresser and knocked it over. It fell backwards, breaking apart when it hit the floor.

Dust rose and caught at the back of her throat. Cutlery spilt, clanging, clattering, spoons, knives and forks that had been rusting in a decaying drawer for decades. Her hand closed over a blade that would once have cut deeply into flesh and bone, split ribs, and sliced through sinews, hearts and gizzards. She struggled to breathe, to see through the murkiness to where he had risen from his knees. He was waiting for her to talk and spill out the lie that Max Ross created on the day he walked away from his wife and son, and their daughter, still to be born.

An edifice had been built on the lies he told, and Lorraine must keep it from collapsing.

Did Carl lunge towards her? Did she slip and stumble? Afterwards, she would replay the instant when her grip, slick and clammy, tightened on the handle of the knife. Was his face frozen in a rictus of pain or astonishment as he collapsed? Death was merciful and swift.

When he lay still, she removed his phone and the sheet of paper from his pocket. She walked outside and held her face to the sky. The rain was harsh and stinging as it washed her clean. She heard a shriek. A banshee or a nocturnal fox? It did not come from Carl Sheridan who lay dead on the rain-damp floor, a severed artery in his neck.

The sweeping force of the wind carried her cries from her and heaved them through the trees with their tossed branches and sheltering boughs.

She returned unseen to Serenity Falls, where the waterfall was crashing down with ever-more ferocity on its plunge to the river below. Her boots were soaking and covered in mud. In the wood shed, her hands trembling, she untied the laces and kicked them off.

She had not intended to kill tonight, but under Victor's tutelage, she had come to respect the primal power of the unconscious mind.

THIRTY-THREE

GAIL

The phone call came as Gail was preparing her evening meal. No name on the screen, just a number that she recognised immediately. Eight years since she deleted Matthew from her contacts; and she could count on one hand the number of times her ex-husband had contacted her since their break-up. In those days, his reasons for ringing had always been about documents, ones she was slow to sign or was questioning. Those calls usually led to angry exchanges. Tonight, Matthew sounded sombre, even sympathetic, when he asked how she was doing.

'I'm keeping well, thanks. Busy, as usual.' Polite small talk between them was new. 'How are you and your family?'

'All good. The girls are growing too fast but that's the way it is these days.'

'And Donna? When's the baby due?'

'Another month.' He cleared his throat, a prelude to introducing a difficult subject, she remembered. 'Abigail...' She winced at the drag on the three syllables. Her full name sounded alien, even unpleasant to her ears.

'What is it, Matthew? Is something wrong?'

'I'm afraid so. I thought I should contact you before it breaks on the news. It's about Carl Sheridan...' He coughed softly, his voice trailing away.

'What's happened to him?' She knew immediately that the information he was about to reveal would be bad. What other reason could he have for phoning her?

'His body was discovered this afternoon.'

'His body—'

'I'm sorry, Abigail. He was murdered.'

'Murdered?' She sank to the floor, her legs sliding from under her. Her shock was tempered by her lack of surprise. Carl had been in touch with her by phone when he won the award, triumphant and – though his life was under threat – convinced he was untouchable. He had been warned by the police to protect himself, but his investigative reports had still continued to create headlines.

'I'm afraid so. The gardai are still at the scene. His body hasn't been removed yet.'

'How long was he there before he was found?'

'He hadn't been seen for two days. It wasn't unusual for him to go off radar, especially if he was following up on a story. He was reported missing this morning when he failed to turn up for an editorial meeting at *Capital Eye*. His death hasn't been announced publicly yet, but I wanted to let you know in advance.'

'What happened to him?'

Matthew listed the details with the professionalism of someone who remained one step removed from the impact of tragedies.

He had recognised Carl's name when a report came through his department. Carl's car was found first. A dog walker had noticed it was parked in the same place for two afternoons in a row. A phone call to the police with the car registration had resulted in an immediate search of the cottage.

A boreen wending off the Wicklow Way, a forgotten landmark on that vast tract of mountain and lake. How could he have been so careless of his own safety?

Matthew was still talking. No murder weapon was found and rain had washed away any incriminating evidence from the scene.

'Carl was an excellent reporter but he was reckless. Then there was his drinking, those binges...' Matthew pronounced judgement. At least that hadn't changed. She had forgotten how righteous he could sound.

'Was he shot?' she asked.

'He died from a knife wound. I'm sorry to ring you with such difficult news. Is there anyone there with you?'

Voices reached her from the background of his home: a radio playing, a young girl calling her mother, and the sudden bark of a dog, quickly hushed.

'I'll be fine, Matthew. Don't worry about me.'

'I'm not worried, just anxious. Carl was...' He seemed lost for words. 'He was important to you—'

'No, Matthew. He was never important, not the way you believed. But he was a friend and I'm horrified that he died the way he did. Do the gardai have any leads?'

'Not from what I've heard. The rain has made it difficult but there's always something that will lead an investigation in a certain direction.'

'Can you keep me posted?'

'I'm not sure—'

'Matthew, I'm not trying to rewind the clock. Just an occasional text.'

'If it's relevant, I'll be in touch. Goodbye, Abigail.'

'Just Gail. Goodbye, Matthew.'

She opened the fridge door and studied the contents. Eggs and cheese – an omelette for her evening meal.

She sliced tomatoes and added onions to the frying pan. She was furious with Carl. Her hands shook as she cracked eggs and whipped them into a frenzy. How dare he disregard the threats he received? Tears streamed down her face. She thought of his sons, and his ex-wife, who married again a year after they divorced.

Unable to eat, she scraped the omelette into the bin and switched on the RTE nine o'clock news. Carl's death headlined the bulletin. The cottage was as desolate as she imagined. It crouched at the edge of a lane, a forlorn witness to a time when its walls must have rung with voices until the isolation became too much to bear. Figures in white coveralls moved in and out of the entrance. Gardai in uniform stood outside the house where Carl's body still lay. A narrative was already building around his untimely death. Slain in the course of his duty. Fearless in the face of organised crime, unheeding of their threats. How vigorous he looked in his photograph, how clear-eyed and courageous. He would be posthumously honoured for his intrepid investigations. He used to joke about that: 'I want it now,' he'd say. 'Not when I'm six feet under.'

Her mother rang as soon as the report ended. Knowing that Noreen never missed the nine o'clock Irish news, Gail had been expecting her call.

'Matthew has already been in touch,' she said before Noreen could speak. 'He told me about Carl.'

'I simply can't believe it.' Noreen sounded tearful. 'I'm *absolutely* stunned. That poor man. What a terrible way to die. Two days... it doesn't bear thinking about. Are you alone, Gail?'

Gail sighed. Why did people automatically assume that shared grief was easier to handle? 'Yes, I'm alone and that's all right. I've had time to come to terms with the shock.'

'I'm surprised Matthew rang you.'

'Me, too. I guess death has a way of levelling bitterness.'

'Death levels *everything*,' said Noreen. 'That's our only certainty. Will you come back for Carl's funeral?'

'I don't think it would be appropriate. I'll commemorate his death in my own way.'

She brought their conversation to an end and turned up the volume on the television.

Talking to her mother about Carl had never been easy. Noreen's reaction when she discovered what had been revealed at Serenity Falls had been a mixture of disapproval and disappointment. This was combined with the hope that, somehow, Gail and Matthew would salvage what was strong in their relationship and stay together. She could have handled her mother's disapproval but Noreen's constant reaching towards that shining star of hope was one of the reasons Gail had moved to London.

The headlines flashed on the screen again as the news came to an end. Carl smiled back at her. Matthew said the knife severed the carotid artery in his neck. He would have died swiftly, cleanly.

Her stomach heaved. She ran to the bathroom and retched. Her eyes streamed. She would take a sleeping tablet tonight. Her dependency on them had increased of late but she would not worry about that for now.

Despite the pill, and still sleepless, she wondered what would have happened if she had ignored Victor Gordon's advice and borne the weight of her infidelity. Surely, it would have lightened with time, blurred into an inconsequential mistake that would cause her a shiver of embarrassment if it inadvertently came to mind during a busy day when children called her name and dogs barked a sharp staccato before falling obediently silent.

She went online and checked Carl's Twitter account. The usual hashtags had been included in his last tweet, along with a new one. *Implacablexposé*.

Stupid... *stupid* man.

. . .

Footage from Carl Sheridan's funeral service was relayed on the news four days later. A priest extolled his courage and dedication to his profession. A profession to which he gave his life so that the lives of others could be made that much safer.

Gail had reconsidered attending his funeral but coming face-to-face with his ex-wife and his sons, now sturdy teenagers and, doubtlessly, filled with resentment over her interference in their parents' marriage, was more than she could endure.

The general belief, according to Matthew, who texted sparse but regular updates to her, was that the gardai were interviewing members of the two gangs whose activities Carl had been covering for *Capital Eye*. Suspects from the Eastly Boys and the Charters had been arrested and released.

Carl had worked in mean city streets, dark, clattering alleys and urban wastelands where stolen cars smouldered. He didn't deal in stupidity, or so he told her when they were together on that last occasion.

So why had he been in such a derelict location with no back-up or protection?

She reread his last email to her. She could recite it by rote now.

Hiya Gail,

Thanks for your latest detailed dissection of my aimless life. I agree with everything you wrote. The drinking has to stop. I promise... promise. But I've something to do first. That's the big reveal and Lorraine Gordon will be the centrepiece. She's got No Name under wraps at Serenity Falls but I'm going to uncover each lie she's told.

Yes, Gail, I hear you sighing and calling me an obsessive prick. I agree with you that hatred is a cross not worth carrying because the drag is always on my side. But I'm also a good judge of character and there was something about Victor Gordon that triggered my 'suspicious' gene from the beginning. I was convinced the man was a fraud even before you went to Serenity Falls. I was prepared to live and let live until he torched my marriage, family and career – thanks to that fucked-up advice he gave you.

But you don't need me rehashing cold facts so I'll cut to my point.

I now have the means to bring his whole fake edifice down. Watch this space.

Thinking of you, as always,

C

She opened his Twitter account and stared again at his last tweet. Someone should take down his account but who, apart from her, knew who ImplacableX was? She wanted it gone. Otherwise, she would keep checking and staring at that last intriguing hashtag #*Implacablexposé*.

A tweet was supposed to be sweet and tuneful but Carl's last one had an eerie, irritating persistence. Gail compared it to the screech of a barn owl. She used to hear them at night during childhood holidays on her grandparent's farm.

'Graveyard screechers,' her grandmother had called them. 'Easy to mistake their song for the wail of a banshee,' she added.

The screech of an unresolved story. Carl had planted one in her head and Gail was unable to shake herself loose from it.

She awoke one night from a dream that was forgotten by the time she struggled into consciousness. Her mind was filled with a clarity that often came to her during those early hours before daybreak. Reaching towards the bedside table, she pulled her laptop to her knees. Her fingers flew over the keyboard.

The pitch she prepared was short and concise. Can love survive marriage? No hesitation as she laid her idea down. Before she could change her mind in the calmer light of morning, she attached her pitch to an email and sent it to Kathy Myles, a producer with Bayview Stream.

THIRTY-FOUR

LORRAINE

How should Lorraine feel when she turned on the evening news and watched a hearse being driven slowly along a lane, a coffin visible through the window? There were no self-help books to advise her, no scholarly theses to help her to analyse her emotions. Her world had tilted off balance and reformed itself in a shape that was unfamiliar to her. Solid objects seemed movable, walls transparent and corners no longer capable of hiding what was around them. When she stared at her reflection, searching for clues that would define her as different, her face had a polished sheen that she barely recognised. Her eyes were clear, her skin smooth, and her blonde hair, which should have turned white by now, swirled around her shoulders instead of hanging lank and lustreless. When her voice failed to shake over the enormity of her crime, she wondered if this calmness was a thinly disguised cover for numbness.

No. She shook her head. *Numbness is rejection, calmness is acceptance.* And she accepted what she had done.

Guests mistook her detachment for serenity. They commented on her ability to listen, really listen, and hear the pain they tried to disguise in group therapy sessions until it rushed to the surface and spilt over her.

All that mattered was the ending of an ordeal. Carl Sheridan no longer had the power to harass her or besmirch Victor's reputation. No more threatening letters, no more insinuating phone calls.

Arrests were made but inevitably ended with the release of the suspect when the allotted time for questioning was up. Statements from the Garda Press Office insisted the investigation was ongoing and expected to yield results shortly, but these assurances were becoming less frequent.

Death had enhanced Carl Sheridan's reputation as a fearless investigator. Politicians called out for stronger action against criminal gangs, some going so far as to suggest a return of the death penalty. His murder must never become an unsolved mystery.

Pamela was convinced his execution had been carried out by the Eastly Boys. She was an avid reader of crime novels and had been following Carl's reports about the feuding gangs. The Eastly Boys were more ruthless and reckless than the Charters, she insisted. The latter would have considered the consequences of drawing attention to their operation and decided it would be too risky.

Aidan was also fascinated by the developing story, questioning Pamela on the gangs' family networks and intermarriages.

What was Naomi thinking as she listened to these conversations? Was she remembering Carl's hands on her face, the sting of a swab, the rage of helplessness? Unable to continue that train of thought, Lorraine's mind went elsewhere, travelling far beyond Serenity Falls, drifting her across the Atlantic to safer shores where red, sculpted rocks with their tortured faces loomed over the landscape like fortified castles from an ancient century.

· · ·

Pamela called a meeting to discuss promotional strategies. Word of mouth was always a good endorsement but the numbers booking into Serenity Falls needed to increase. Something stronger than occasional interviews and social media exposure was needed to lessen the impact of Victor's absence.

Aidan believed a documentary would work. One that explored the concept of marriage in modern-day society, and had Rekindle Connections at its centre.

'Have you looked at the links I sent you?' he asked Lorraine.

'What links?' She forced herself to concentrate when he repeated his question.

'Gail Robinson. I forwarded her CV to you, and samples of her work.'

'I don't remember seeing them.'

'I like what she does,' said Pamela. 'She's very innovative.'

'So do I.' Aidan nodded in agreement. 'It's an interesting proposition. I can't believe you haven't checked my email, Mum.'

'We need a quick decision, Lorraine.' Was there a hint of impatience in Pamela's voice? 'I mentioned this to you only a few days ago. Gail operates from London but she'll be in Ireland for the next month. She has quite a reputation as a documentarian.'

'Let me look at what she sent and I'll make a decision this afternoon,' Lorraine promised.

She opened her laptop after the meeting ended and found the link. They were right about Gail Robinson. The short samples she provided of her work were excellent, and the outline of the documentary she envisaged looked interesting.

Make an appointment and I'll meet her here to discuss her ideas she emailed Aidan, and forgot about Gail Robinson as soon as she pressed Send.

Everything seemed to be moving at a speed over which Lorraine had less and less control. Perhaps the speed was her body's race to keep ahead of her thoughts.

THIRTY-FIVE

GAIL

The first thing Gail noticed when she entered the hall was the portrait. The perfect couple, a configuration of togetherness. It hung beside three other portraits who, presumably, had lived within the same walls. Victor Gordon's forceful brown stare had been captured by the artist and his smile – that slightly sardonic slant to his lips – was instantly familiar. Lorraine looked radiant beside him, slender and winsome, young enough to be his daughter.

Could he have been unfaithful to her? Had that mysterious, still unidentified woman been his mistress or someone even more personal, like a lovechild? A daughter he had never acknowledged?

Carl was inside her head, prodding and poking, just as annoying in death as he had been in life. Gail had argued obsessively with herself. Two voices, one advocating sanity, the other encouraging her towards stealth and deception. The impulse to flee was strong, and the suspicions that led to this place seemed more outrageous than ever as she stood in the hall, breathing in a subtle lavender aroma.

She turned from the portrait to be greeted by Aidan

Gordon. Any resemblance to the surly teenager in black who had slouched in and out of Serenity Falls all those years ago had disappeared. Admittedly, his T-shirt – with an environmentally aware slogan on the front – had a black background, but the khaki shorts he wore showed off his long, tanned legs. With his blond hair and hazel eyes, he resembled his mother but he had inherited his father's penetrating stare, which sized her up immediately.

She had already been in touch with him by phone and knew he was receptive to her proposal.

He took her on a tour of the house. She tried not to react when she entered the Chat Room and saw the grouped settees and armchairs. A Rekindle programme had ended the previous day.

What vibrations had been stirred, assumptions challenged or lives changed over the five days?

Aidan asked if she would like a tour of the grounds. Lorraine emerged from her office as they were walking towards the front door. Was there a pause, a jolt of recognition? Gail tensed but Lorraine's handshake was firm, her gaze unclouded as Aidan introduced them. She seemed taller than Gail remembered, which was impossible. Maybe it was her posture, so erect and poised, so confident. Aidan returned to his office when Lorraine offered to show her the gardens.

Everything was the same as Gail remembered: the orchard ripe with apples and pears, the woods showing the rich tinges of autumn. The trunks of felled trees had been carved into sculptures. No mistaking Victor Gordon's signature handiwork.

Lorraine opened the gate that was set into the railings dividing Serenity Falls from the Silver Falls Café and providing a short cut to the café, and suggested they stop there for coffee.

'I've read Victor's books,' Gail said, when they sat down at a table on the veranda. 'They're full of interesting insights. You must miss him very much.'

'I'm coping.' Her voice quivered, a lost sound that she quickly steadied. 'Victor believed that the energy of the person who dies lingers on long after they have passed. I feel as if his presence is close to me.'

'That must be a tremendous comfort.'

'Tremendous.'

Gail looked at the woman seated opposite her. Did she really believe that energy was an indefinable source flowing between the living and the dead? Carl had called her a 'widow encased in ice.' At the time, Gail assumed he was being sarcastic. Now she understood what he meant. Lorraine's smile never reached her eyes and her face, which had been so spirited eight years ago, seemed frozen and flawless.

'How wonderful to be born in such beautiful surroundings.' Gail stared across at the waterfall. 'You must never get tired of looking at it.'

It had rained earlier and a rainbow shimmered through the spray.

'It talks to me,' Lorraine replied. 'Sometimes it's a whisper, sometimes a roar.'

'What does it tell you?'

'That dreams can come true. Sometimes the paths to their fulfilment are twisted but they will eventually straighten out.'

'What an interesting thought. I agree with you,' said Gail. 'You've a unique set-up at Serenity Falls. I believe it would make a perfect location for my documentary. I'd like to film the Rekindle programme over its five days. Is that something that would interest you?'

'What exactly would it entail?'

'I'd work with the clients who are participating—'

'*Guests*. We look upon everyone who participates in a Rekindle programme as our guest.'

'Apologies, Lorraine. Obviously, I'd need your guests' full cooperation if they agree to be interviewed.'

'I'm not sure they would want to expose their relationships in that public way.'

'You'd be surprised. People like to talk, even if the subject is a sensitive one. Their faces can be blotted out and their voices changed, if they wish.'

'The Rekindle Programme is about relationships. Not all couples who come to us are married.'

'That would also be factored into the documentary, of course. Overall, I want to document modern-day relationships with all their complexities.'

'Why choose Serenity Falls?'

'"To love is to invite pain to the party." I read that in one of your husband's books. I understand pain. I've suffered a loss in my own life and picked up the pieces again, only they were different pieces. That is what you are doing, Lorraine. I think Serenity Falls is the perfect setting to talk about love and loss and the enduring quality of relationships.'

Lorraine's eyes had moistened as she listened and the nod she gave signified her agreement.

They walked back to Serenity Falls and shook hands in the courtyard. She was still standing on the steps and watching the car when Gail glanced in the rear-view mirror.

Lorraine's stance, statue-like, was hidden from view when she accelerated and rounded the curve on the avenue. As she drove through the gates Gail realised her hands were trembling on the steering wheel, her knuckles white.

THIRTY-SIX

NO NAME GIRL

The woman who is going to make a film about love is sleeping upstairs. What is love? They come here to find that answer. Was I ever in love? Been kissed? Missed? Wept over? Aidan tells me he hated all of that analysing when he was a teenager. Those people took time from his father when he should have been loving his son.

He asks to see the pictures in my sketch pad. I pretend not to have drawn anything yet. Who wants to see lines and circles and squiggles? No shapes to form an image... a memory... a face... What would he make of those squiggles... ripples...? A boat... is it a boat? Draw another and another... yes, a boat on water. Ripples spreading.

Does it mean anything or is it just more scribbles... like the ones stuck on fridges that children draw? How do I know that? Is it another surge... like the boat? Bits and pieces with no joins.

THIRTY-SEVEN

LORRAINE

In the weeks leading up to Gail Robinson's arrival to Serenity Falls, Lorraine was unable to pinpoint what it was about the filmmaker that triggered a particular kind of nervousness in her. The feeling was familiar but, unlike the other jolting sensations that overcame her at unexpected moments and weakened her knees, she could find no explanation to account for it. It had remained undefinable yet persistent enough for her to call a meeting with Pamela and Aidan to consider cancelling the documentary.

Their horrified intervention when she made this suggestion made her realise there was more than her uneasiness to be considered. Rekindle Connections needed the publicity the documentary would create if the company was to survive. The numbers booking into the programme had plateaued and showed no sign of increasing, despite Aidan's efforts through print and social media. Bayview Stream belonged to the Bayview Universal Media Corporation and the possibilities for the documentary being also shown on their other channels made Gail Robinson's offer irresistible.

'We need Gail Robinson,' Pamela insisted. 'We couldn't

buy that kind of publicity, even if we could afford to do so. Why are you having *such* doubts at this stage?'

Lorraine, looking at their faces, struggled to put aside her uneasiness and focus on the positive exposure the marriage retreat would receive.

'I don't have doubts. Just worries that Naomi will be distressed by the upheaval. Professor Shannon says it's essential that she lives in a calming, regulated atmosphere until she's stronger.'

'That's exactly what you're doing, and she's becoming much more relaxed,' said Pamela. 'I wouldn't be surprised if her memory starts coming back. Wouldn't that be wonderful?'

'It certainly would.'

'But difficult for her to realise that she's alone in the world.'

'She's not alone, Pamela. We're her family until she finds her way back to those who love her.'

Hearing herself, Lorraine wondered how anyone could believe her. Was Naomi conscious of her watchfulness? Her persistent checking for signs of recovery? If so, she gave no indication. She remained trapped in the present, determined to walk unaided, and still struggling with words she was unable to remember.

The arrival of Gail Robinson with her cameras and sound equipment increased Lorraine's apprehension. She led the film-maker upstairs to the bedroom she would occupy and flung open the door to number seven

Gail hitched her camera bag a little higher on her shoulder and asked if it would be possible to sleep elsewhere.

'I have a phobia about the number seven,' she admitted. 'Would you mind if I occupied another room?'

'I thought that kind of phobia only applied to the number thirteen.' Lorraine shrugged and chose another bedroom further along the corridor.

Returning downstairs to the Nook, she watched Naomi in

the walled garden doing the exercise regime her physiotherapist had organised for her. Lorraine had discussed the documentary with Naomi and made it clear that the increased activities taking place during the filming would not have any impact on her. She would be safe from any disturbances within the walls of the Nook where she must stay throughout the making of the documentary.

As usual, Naomi had not argued or demanded more freedom. Quiet and pliable, she seemed grateful for everything Lorraine did for her.

The guests being included in the documentary would arrive in two days. They had signed contracts agreeing to the conditions laid down by Gail. Five couples would be enough, she had told Lorraine. Too many voices would only clog the narrative and become repetitive.

Sheila and Dominique had accepted Lorraine's invitation to be involved. Dominque agreed willingly but Sheila's agreement was a surprise. Dessie had initially hoped to participate until his wife decided that her studies could not be distracted by side issues. He had looked crestfallen at being considered a side issue, but their places were taken by Amy and Gerard Foster. The two other couples had been chosen by Pamela.

Their costs would be covered by Rekindle Connections. All they had to do was love, laugh, argue, make up and bare their souls for five days.

Undressing for bed that night, Lorraine tried to relax. If she wasn't careful, people would begin to see through her brittle composure. Gail was anxious to film her before the guests arrived, and would interview her tomorrow about the history of Serenity Falls and the success of Rekindle Connections.

Lorraine sank to the edge of the bed and pressed her fingertips to her temples. She increased the pressure until a pain forked across her forehead. Now that the documentary was actually happening, she knew she should have gone with her gut instinct, which had been to keep Gail Robinson from poking her inquisitive camera into the inner sanctum of the marriage retreat. Too late now. Somehow, Lorraine had to find the resilience to cooperate fully with her.

Next door, Naomi was moving around her bedroom. This was not an unusual occurrence. Lorraine often heard the thump of her crutches and, sometimes, her sobs. Such desperation in the sound – but it was only a minor intrusion, and failed to silence the gurgled death sound Lorraine had carried with her from the cottage. This penetrated her days and invaded her nightmares, a tuneless dirge that forced her awake in the small hours, her body coiled and trembling.

She had no idea what startled her awake. Two o'clock in the morning. She would be unable to sleep again. These bouts of insomnia were becoming more frequent but Lorraine knew immediately that this was different.

Switching on the light in the corridor, she saw Naomi's open bedroom door. Her bed was empty. She was not in the living area and the door leading into the marriage retreat was also open. The hall light was always left on in case guests came downstairs in the night to snack or walk outside, if the mood took them.

Naomi was standing under the portrait. One of her crutches lay on the floor and she appeared to be about to strike the portrait with the other one. It was obvious from her blank expression that she was sleepwalking and in danger of falling.

'I'll look after her.' Aidan hurried across the hall towards them. 'I know what to do.' He spoke softly to Naomi and moved her back from the portrait. She was awake now, though still unaware of where she was.

A noise from the stairs alerted them. Gail Robinson must have been working late; a pair of glasses were shoved into her startling red hair with its buzz-cut sides and sculpted, upward sweep.

'I was burning the midnight oil when I heard you.' Her gaze swept over Naomi, who was leaning on Aidan's arm as they walked towards the Nook.

'Naomi was sleepwalking,' said Lorraine. 'She's okay. There's nothing to worry about. Sorry we disturbed you.'

'Not at all.' She descended the stairs as the couple disappeared into the Nook. 'I presume that's the young woman who was injured in the car crash?'

'Yes. She still has a long way to go before she recovers.'

'I heard her talking from my room. I couldn't make out what she was saying, but from what I could catch it sounded as if she was speaking in Irish. She kept repeating the same words... I think she was saying... *Mo grá*? Could she have been speaking in Irish?'

'As she's an American, I think that's highly unlikely.'

'I'm sure you're right.' Gail nodded, then looked at Lorraine. 'I've read about her on social media.'

'Really?'

'Some of the posts and tweets were appalling.' Gail seemed either unaware that Lorraine wanted to end the conversation or was deliberately ignoring that fact. 'You must have been quite hurt by the speculation.'

'I had other things on my mind, like the death of my husband, to pay any attention to such drivel.' Her lips moved stiffly as she replied. It was possible to feign interest in everything and nothing. This was nothing. Just murmurings in a vacuous whirlpool of communication and contradiction, stirred by Carl Sheridan, who no longer had the power to destroy her.

'I'm sorry.' Gail took a step towards her. 'I didn't mean to upset you.'

'I'm not upset. But I think you should try to get some sleep. Goodnight.'

Naomi's door was closed when Lorraine returned to the Nook. She could hear their voices inside the bedroom. No mistaking Aidan's deeper tone and Naomi's hesitant replies.

He was sitting on the edge of her bed when Lorraine entered. Naomi, looking pale and confused, was lying on top of the duvet, her eyes fixed on him. She claimed to have no memory of leaving her bed. Her confusion was palpable, her hands fluttering so helplessly that Lorraine feared she would have another seizure. How had it begun the last time? The scene in St Gorgonia's ward was becoming increasingly hazed in her mind. Her forehead tightened when she tried to remember the sequence that had led to that sudden, convulsive spasm.

Naomi's eyelids were closing then opening again, her hand sliding away from Aidan's clasp. She said goodnight to Lorraine, her voice expressionless.

What had Gail heard? Had she interpreted Scots Gaelic as Irish? Surely that wasn't possible? *Mo ghràidh... mo grá... my love... my love.*

Lorraine headed for the kitchen and switched on the kettle. 'How often has this happened?' she asked, when Aidan joined her. She slapped two mugs down on the table and ordered him to sit. One glance at her face warned him not to argue.

'Just once before tonight. I woke up—'

'Why didn't you tell me?'

'I was able to bring her back to bed. It wasn't a big deal—'

'What an irresponsible thing to say. We can't have her roaming around Serenity Falls at night. Anything could happen to her. She's frail enough as she is, and—'

'She's not frail, Mum.' His interruption was curt and definite. 'She's always exercising and it's beginning to make a difference. I'm surprised you can't see it.'

'I see enough to worry me. She's my responsibility as long as she remains here. Where did she go when she was sleepwalking the previous time?'

'The same place you found her tonight.'

'The portrait?'

'Yes. For some reason she's drawn to it.'

'We have to lock her bedroom door at night.'

'That's too extreme.' He sounded outraged. 'What if something happens to her and she's not able to get out of her room? I'm amazed you'd even consider doing that.'

'It's her welfare I'm considering. What would Professor Shannon say if she had an accident? And the police? She could be made an adult ward of court.'

'That's highly unlikely. Why are you turning what happened into a drama? By locking her door you'll endanger her rather than add to her safety.'

'What do you suggest then? That we allow her to fall down the stairs should she climb them?'

'What if you lock the door into the hall.'

'And during the day?'

'There's no need to do it then.'

'I disagree. We're running a business, Aidan. Our guests come here for only one reason. Having Naomi wandering around will be a distraction, especially when the filming starts. I've given our home over to her and this is where I expect her to stay.'

'If you insist.' He shrugged and gave in. 'I'm going to take her out for a while every day. Not far to begin with. I'll start with the café. She needs stimulation. If she's tired at night she'll stop walking in her sleep.' He picked up his mug of tea and took a sip. 'It must be horrendous to lose your memory.'

It would be impossible to disagree with him and yet how comforting not to carry dangerous baggage. No secrets to shame or terrify her. No worries that she would plunge into depression and be unable to climb back up the side of the abyss.

Her mood remained constant but that in itself suggested a denial deep enough to be called madness.

Overriding Aidan's protests in the morning, she demanded that he carry the portrait from the hall and leave it in her bedroom.

A short while later, she watched from her office window as he wheeled Naomi along the path at the side of the house. They were wearing jeans and identical Hozier T-shirts with a print of the singer on the front. He had ordered them online and they had arrived yesterday.

Was there a coquettish turn to her head as she glanced back at him? They were laughing at something, sharing a joke, perhaps. Their growing closeness was beginning to disturb her.

She watched the filmmaker follow in the same direction. Gail had mentioned her intention to check the grounds for the most suitable locations to interview the couples. That must be what she intended to do.

Returning to her desk, Lorraine opened her computer and brought up the promotional material Aidan planned to use throughout the making of the documentary. It was good, she thought, as she glanced through his notes, yet she was unable to relax her guard.

Naomi was out sight, which meant she was outside her control.

Pamela arrived, flushed from cycling up the avenue. Her hair, usually tied back, was loose and wind-tossed. 'Are you okay?' she asked, when Lorraine rose abruptly and returned to the window. 'You seem edgy this morning.'

'I'm fine. I've been checking over Aidan's ideas.'

'Good, aren't they?'

'Promising. Did you see Gail on your way here?'

'No. Why?'

'No reason. I'm just nipping across to Silver Falls. Will I bring you back a coffee?'

'No, I'll have one later in the kitchen. I want to look over the menus with Nick.' She switched on her computer, a half-smile playing over her lips as she stared at the blank screen.

'Since when did Nick need advice with menus?' asked Lorraine.

'There's a first time for everything.' Pamela laughed and lifted her hand in an absent-minded wave as Lorraine left the office.

She followed the same path her son and Naomi had taken earlier. Was something going on between Pamela and Nick Tobin? The thought was fleeting, whereas it would once have warranted an immediate discussion between them.

Life continued to revolve around the ordinary while Lorraine struggled with increasing desperation to hold on to its boundaries.

THIRTY-EIGHT

NO NAME GIRL

The waterfall is amazing. All that crashing water. Moss and mud and fallen branches, and something decaying. It's all there in the flow, that earthy smell. Aidan laughs when I tell him and says all he ever smells is the coffee from the Silver Falls Café.

Did I always have such a keen sense of smell? Strange not to know my own name yet be able to list the scents I smell throughout Serenity Falls: camomile, rosemary, vanilla, sandalwood. It was the same in the hospital, only the smells were different there: sickness and death wrapped in antiseptic wipes. And my hearing? Was it always so sharp? I can even hear the waterfall from my bedroom. Lorraine insists that the sound couldn't possibly travel as far as the house. She thinks what I hear is the roar of the accident. It must have been so loud. Maybe she's right and the sounds I imagine belong to terror.

It's too early for customers but Lily lets us in. She's doing preps – chop... chop... whizz... whizz... clunk... clatter... I know those sounds... but they belong to the surges that go nowhere.

Aidan talks about music. He tells me he used to play Hozier on his phone when I was in a coma and ask what I thought. Did I like his music? One blink. What about Dashin' Boyz? Two blinks. That's so weird. I don't know their music. He showed me pictures on his phone of Dashin' Boyz. Four man-boys in white suits. Then Hozier, brooding like Jesus in a sulk.

'Jesus.' I say it just like that. He asks what's wrong. All I can do is shake my head. No words to explain what I've seen. Something floating on water. Not a boat. A building with stained-glass windows. The picture goes so fast. Is my imagination playing tricks again? I can never tell when the surges come. Like a wave that swells but refuses to break.

It's time to leave. Slow, steady steps along the ramp. Flowers are dying in the big pots outside Silver Falls. I can name them. It's as if there are lists inside my head and the names just come, pop, pop, pop – bougainvillaea, petunias, begonia, portulaca, sweet alyssum.

Gail Robinson is outside with her camera. Her hair is shaved at the sides and swept up in a quiff. Why do that? I had no choice. Dessie said my hair was soft as duck down when it began to grow. She's taking photos of us. Aidan keeps pulling funny faces. Now, when I laugh, I sound more normal. It was strange at first, like a cough catching against my breath. It's easier when I'm with him.

Lorraine must have been running to get here. I've never seen her flustered. She's always so cool. The way she presses her hands to her heart is the same as I do when the surges come. She walks back to the house with us. I wish she wouldn't hold my hand. I want to pull away but that would offend her. She is so protective that sometimes it feels too much. Like being smothered in a blanket. It's a familiar feeling. I don't know why.

Jesus. A boat on water... smothering... mothering... smothering... stop... stop...

I'm going to ask Gail for a photo. The camera never lies, not like the mirror where nothing in the glass reflects any truth back *at me. Were my cheeks always so bony, my eyes so muddy and sunk in shadows?*

Does my face really belong to Naomi Nelson?

THIRTY-NINE

GAIL

The couple had been unaware of her presence on the veranda of the Silver Falls Café. Gail suspected that even if she stood beside their table, they probably wouldn't have noticed her. To be so absorbed in each other. It reminded her of those early months with Carl when they were students, their charged sexual energy refined into intense conversations until they could be alone again. Was that how Naomi and Aidan felt about each other? Gail doubted that they had even kissed, but it was there between them, an energy yet to be explored.

Aidan was doing most of the talking. Naomi gestured a lot and moved her head in response. She reminded Gail of a fawn. Those thin, gangling legs and bewildered eyes, their darkness highlighted against her ashen complexion, her short hair emphasising her ears. Gail used her camera phone to photograph them through the café window. Impossible from that position to get a close-up of Naomi's face.

Last night, when she sleepwalked, she had kept repeating the same phrase. It had been eerie listening to her. Like hearing a chant in a place where it didn't belong.

When they emerged from the café and into the autumn

sunlight, the incident seemed surreal, almost imagined. Naomi was quiet and withdrawn at first, yet nodding when Gail asked if she could photograph her, even laughing a little when Aidan started clowning around.

Gail used her Canon camera to get a better effect and had taken a number of shots when Lorraine arrived. Her presence silenced the giddiness between the young couple. She fussed over Naomi, feeling her forehead and insisting that she sat back into the wheelchair, which had been left outside the café.

Aidan pushed her back to Serenity Falls and Lorraine, walking beside them, held onto Naomi's hand. The bond between them seemed close yet Gail found herself thinking about the jailor and the jailed.

A ridiculous thought to consider in such spacious surroundings.

On reaching the house and waiting until Naomi was inside the Nook, Lorraine asked her into the communal kitchen.

'As you mentioned last night, you're aware of the ugly spec-ulation that surrounds Naomi,' she said, when they were seated at the breakfast bar. 'My husband is dead and unable to defend himself against certain vile insinuations. Naomi has been the innocent victim of these rumours and they will increase a hundredfold should a photograph of her appear on social media. I don't have to tell you how vitriolic the online community can be.'

'I'd no intention of putting anything about Naomi online,' Gail protested. 'It was just an impulsive decision to photograph them. They looked so happy together.'

The chilly silence that followed this comment was finally broken by Lorraine. 'Aidan assumes Naomi is stronger than she actually is. I have to constantly remind him that she's still extremely fragile, health-wise. Her memory loss has made her highly vulnerable to triggers, so her behaviour can be unpre-dictable.'

'From what I saw earlier, Aidan is very caring. I wouldn't worry about him endangering Naomi in any way.'

'Obviously, my son's intentions are altruistic but I'm in constant contact with her medical team.' Lorraine inclined her head towards her mobile phone on the breakfast bar. 'They share my need to protect her from unwarranted exposure. It would ease my mind considerably if you would consider deleting the photographs you took.' She spoke politely, but Gail knew that this was an order, not a request. 'I'm sure you appreciate my concerns.'

'You're worrying unnecessarily, Lorraine, but I'll do as you ask, of course.'

It was hard to tell what was different about Lorraine. A watchfulness that hadn't been there during Gail's ill-fated visit to Serenity Falls. Her gaze had become more forceful. Ridiculous as it seemed, its intensity reminded Gail of Victor Gordon and the belief that he could pierce her innermost thoughts. Could Lorraine possibly have recognised her? Could she have found out about her link to Carl and the suspicions he had implanted in her mind about Naomi's identity? Suspicions that had grown more demanding after his murder.

Lorraine had spoken about an energy source that existed between the living and the dead. If such a source existed, then Carl was calling out to her to be alert and notice any cracks in the story Lorraine would spin.

Gail would interview her today. Hopefully the awkwardness between them would have eased by then.

Aidan had studied media production for a year before deciding that marketing was his area of interest. The skills he had gained during that time were useful and he was anxious to be involved. He would handle the sound equipment and, when necessary, operate the camera during Gail's interviews.

The waterfall would have made an arresting backdrop but after checking it out Gail decided it would be too noisy. The orchard was a better option. Lorraine said it was a much sought-after retreat by guests who needed an escape from the simmering tensions that were inevitable, especially after group discussions. Her husband had carved a loveseat from the trunk of a tree that had fallen in a storm and set it beneath the over-hanging boughs.

That was where Lorraine would sit.

As the interview began, Gail was convinced she could hear Carl ordering her not to be distracted by other people's stories. His was the only one that mattered – but making her way through the filaments Lorraine Gordon spun around her seemed even more daunting than she had imagined.

FORTY

LORRAINE

Aidan had wired her for sound and was filming her while Gail conducted the interview. It was easy to talk about her great-grandparents, the original owners, from the diaries and notes they had left behind. Her grandparents had died when she was young but their lives were also well documented. Gail had already filmed their portraits and was anxious to include the one propped against Lorraine's bedroom wall. Tomorrow Aidan would take it downstairs again and hang it up long enough for it to be filmed.

'When was the decision made to transform Serenity Falls from a hotel into a marriage retreat?' Gail asked.

Lorraine had prepared herself for the question and answered it calmly. 'My father developed a medical condition that forced him to close the hotel. He was keen to see Serenity Falls being developed in a new direction and shared the vision of a marriage retreat with me and Victor. Sadly, he didn't live long enough to enjoy its success. He would have been thrilled to see what we achieved with Rekindle Connections.'

An apple fell and rolled to a standstill at her feet. She could hear him again, that same refrain: *charlatan... spiv... conman...*

He belonged at the waterfall, not in the orchard, but Lorraine could no longer rely on him to observe his boundaries.

Aidan was moving the camera for a close-up of her face. She relaxed her features and smiled candidly, as her husband must have done so often during their years together. Unable to help herself, she closed her eyes and Aidan, at a signal from Gail, stopped filming.

'What is it, Lorraine?' she asked. 'Are you feeling all right?'

'Just slightly dizzy. I'm not sleeping well these nights.'

'If you like, we can continue the interview another time.'

'No, I'm feeling better now. Let's finish it.' She sounded convincing. Not like a woman with secrets that could never be shared. The loneliness of such a burden.

Victor had claimed that secrecy corroded one's soul. *Fucking hypocrite.* Her nostrils flared, her fury barely contained and yet, contain it she must.

How many times had he felt that same overwhelming weariness from wearing a mask? How often had he yearned to rip it from his face and reveal his true identity? Or had he believed so utterly in his own invention that it eventually became his truth? Was that possible? If so, then his dread must have been all the greater when he heard from Megan Ross.

Just as he was appalled when the Scotsman, Hamish McAdam, invaded his constructed reality in Sedona. The memory raced through her, the heat and the dust, Hamish's rubbery lips pressed against hers. A man like that, canny and well-travelled, the possibility that he could have seen through Victor's façade had been too great a risk for him to take. No wonder his thoughts had turned to Serenity Falls and the escape route it offered him. How confident he must have been to come with her to Ireland and build a public persona so close to the country where he was born. This stranger with whom she had shared her life had been brave, audacious and monstrous.

Her father laughed in agreement. *Chancer... charlatan... spiv... snake-oil man... swindler... conman...*

They had arrived at Serenity Falls in time for Pamela and Edward's wedding.

The hotel had been reopened for the occasion and catering staff hired to keep it running smoothly during two days of celebration. On a sunlit afternoon, the couple exchanged their wedding vows in the orchard. The purple hue of Lorraine's bridesmaid dress reminded her of irises. Sleek and close-fitting, it gave no indication that she was now four months pregnant. Time enough to break the news to her father when the wedding was over.

The bones of the vision she had presented to Victor had been fleshed out by him and it was becoming difficult to remember that it had originally belonged to her. Soon it would collide with the hard reality of her father's reaction.

It was starkly apparent from the beginning that he disliked Victor but the wedding festivities allowed them to keep up the illusion that all would be well when they sat down with Arthur Kilbride to discuss the conversion of Serenity Falls into a marriage retreat.

Pamela and Edward honeymooned in Thailand then continued on to Australia, where Edward had been offered a job with a pharmaceutical company. So much for Pamela's dream of spending the rest of her life with Edward in Potters Glen. Once inseparable, the two friends were passing each other in transit.

On their first evening alone, Lorraine invited Pamela's mother, Rita, to join them for their evening meal in the hope it would defuse the tension between the two men. Victor had taken over the kitchen in the Nook and cooked chilli con carne, one of his favourite dishes.

Throughout the meal Arthur complained about the spiciness of the dish and played with his food. He drank from a bottle of tequila, claiming that as they were doing Mexican, he might as well do so in style.

Rita's efforts to lighten the atmosphere by reminiscing about the wedding were rudely interrupted when Author demanded to know what exactly Lorraine had in mind for the future of his hotel.

'If you'd let me show the plans we've drawn up—' she began.

'I want to hear it in your own words.' Arthur knocked back another shot of tequila and refilled his glass.

'We want to establish a marriage retreat—'

'A retreat from marriage?' She knew he was deliberately misunderstanding her. 'A hideout for escaping husbands, is that what you're planning?'

'Give Lorraine a chance to explain properly.' Rita spoke mildly but there was a warning in her tone that momentarily silenced him. 'After all, marriages go on the rocks for all sorts of reasons,' she continued. 'Some are incapable of being saved, but others can be healed with the right encouragement and advice.'

'And you think a slip of a girl like my daughter is capable of advising wearied marrieds where they went wrong?' His eyes were becoming bloodshot, his voice slurring. This was the wrong time for such a discussion but his belligerence forced Lorraine to argue back.

'Victor is a qualified relationship counsellor—'

'Let the man speak for himself, Lorraine. I'd like to hear more about his background.'

'What exactly do you want to know, Arthur?' Victor's calmness seemed to inflame him even further.

'Where were you born?'

'My birth certificate states that I was born in South Carolina. But I've lived all over the States. My parents travelled a lot.'

'Were they army?'

'No. They were pacifists and free spirits.'

'Freeloaders, do you mean?' He followed his comment with a laugh, though there was nothing humorous in his narrowed gaze.

'That's *so* rude.' Lorraine slammed her knife and fork down on the table. 'Victor is our guest. I insist you apologise to him immediately.'

'Where's your sense of humour, Lorraine?' he asked. 'Did you lose that along with your judgement?'

'It was a joke.' Victor tapped her hand. 'No apology is necessary.'

'It's *not* funny—'

'Nor is there anything remotely funny about you coming home with a complete stranger and demanding that I turn my hotel over to you so that you can experiment with some ridiculous scheme that has absolutely no chance of succeeding.'

'You haven't even allowed me to discuss it properly,' she said. 'Why won't you look at the figures I've put together?'

'Why waste my time when I've no intention of agreeing to it? No more than I've any intention of finishing this meal.' He pushed his chair back from the table and stood. 'Make up your mind, Lorraine. You either do this my way or leave here with your friend. He might succeed in convincing some gullible fool with his proposal, but I'm not that easily conned.'

'I can't stay here any longer,' Victor said after her father left the room. 'He's made it perfectly obvious that he doesn't trust me. I'll book a room in the hotel in Potters Glen until it's time to leave.'

Rita, looking troubled, nodded. 'It's the right decision to move out for now,' she said. 'It will give Lorraine and her father

a chance to talk things through. You can stay at the lodge and
sleep in Pamela's bedroom.'

'Won't he mind—?'

'Falls Lodge belongs to me, not to Arthur. Who stays there
is my decision alone. He's been drinking throughout the
wedding and it's drink that's talking, not him. All he needs is
time alone with Lorraine.'

In the bedroom they shared, Victor flung some clothes into a
back pack.

'Be patient,' she said, as she pressed his hand against her
stomach. The fluttering of butterfly wings was too light yet for
him to feel, but she wanted him to bond with this new life that
was beginning to stir within her.

'Reopening Serenity Falls as a boutique hotel is a dream,
nothing else,' Rita said, when she and Lorraine were alone.
'Two new hotels have opened recently. One's in Potters Glen
and the other is just outside the village. Arthur will be unable to
compete with them. And with his diabetes—'

'What about his diabetes? He told me it's under control.'

'If he does what his doctor orders then, yes, it's under
control. But that's not always the case. Alcohol has been his
form of self-medication for too long. He went to AA shortly
after you left and stayed sober until the wedding.'

'Until I arrived with Victor, you mean. I should have
warned him in advance.'

'Why didn't you?'

'I was afraid. Our age difference...' She paused, unwilling to
continue.

'It's considerable, Lorraine.'

'But irrelevant. Victor is my soul mate.'

'I hope so.' Rita's quizzical expression demanded a
response.

'Why would you think otherwise? You sound just like my father.'

'I don't want to hurt your feelings, love, but he's afraid that Victor's main interest is in Serenity Falls.'

'That's not true.' She had forgotten how forthright Rita could be. 'Victor *loves* me.'

'I'm sure he does, Lorraine. Let me talk to Arthur. He'll listen to me. You're entrepreneurial, as he once was. And determined. He'll respect that.'

'Not if he's drinking the way he was tonight.'

'I'm hoping he'll see sense and go back on the AA programme.'

Rita sounded confident, more knowledgeable about this irascible man than Lorraine could ever be. Was her relationship with him more than that of employer and employee now? Was that why he had sounded so uplifted when he phoned and asked her to come home? Perhaps it was Rita, not a therapist, who had lifted him from his obsessive memories.

Be careful what you wish for. What Lorraine had wanted as a teenager had no place in her plans for the future.

She did not see her father again until the following evening. The wind was sharp when he left on his daily walk to the waterfall. He made no reference to their argument when she joined him on the steps outside the house. He looked flushed and dishevelled, the reek of alcohol on him.

His drinking had been discreet before she left home. She had been aware that he was often quietly and morosely drunk, yet never as openly apparent as now.

'Victor has moved out,' she said. 'He'll stay with Rita until you apologise to him.'

'Apologise for what? he retorted. 'All I did was ask questions that you should have been asking.' He quickened his stride. 'Have I been such a disappointment to you that you need to replace me with a father figure?'

The reference to their similarity in age meant nothing to her. Arthur looked decades older, years of depression taking their toll on him. His features sagged, unlike Victor's firmness, fullness, his lustre. Her lover embraced vitality; her father, apathy. How dare he suggest she needed a surrogate father.

'He's rootless and that always spells exploitation,' Arthur continued. 'Take my word for it. That man has his hooks in you for only one reason.'

'You're *so* wrong. We came to you with a business proposal. It was my idea, not Victor's. In fact, he was reluctant to leave Sedona. He has such a following there—'

'A following?' His scorn was scathing. 'You'll be telling me next he's a messiah. You certainly treat him like one.'

'Why have you taken such a dislike to him?' They had reached the cliff path and she was becoming breathless from the effort of keeping up with him. 'Are you jealous of the life he's made for himself while you've been so steeped in self-pity you hardly noticed I was gone?'

How splendid the waterfall looked, the soaring flow funnelling downwards against the face of the cliff. Everywhere was so soft and green compared to Sedona. Even the Ice Age rocks had been carved by time to a smoother sheen, a gentler countenance.

'You think of me as a failure.' He stopped walking until she recovered her breath. 'Maybe you're right. But that doesn't mean I won't protect you from a conman like Victor Gordon.'

'That "conman", as you call him, is the father of my child.'

She had not meant to tell him like that, the words torn from her and flung wildly at him. She waited for an acknowledgement that he had heard her.

Instead, he turned his back on her and continued walking.

'Are you waiting for me to congratulate you?' he asked, when she caught up with him.

'If you want to know your grandchild, then yes, I think congratulations are in order.'

'Did you really believe it would be that easy to change my mind?' The storm brewing inside him was reflected in his face, the pallor of his skin and the beads of sweat that had broken out on his forehead. 'I've no wish to be a grandfather to that conman's bastard.'

She should have waited until Rita spoke to him but it was too late to stem his vitriol. *Chancer... charlatan... snake-oil man... swindler... conman.* Serenity Falls had always been a hotel and he intended to reopen it, with or without Lorraine at his side.

'If you stay with him, you'll never inherit Serenity Falls,' he shouted. 'I'm going to marry Rita. Everything I possess will pass to her when I die.' His anger had such heat. Was he jealous of Victor? Aware of the years he had wasted pining for what could never be his again?

Did he understand what was happening when he bent over, his hands to his chest? Did he have time to register that he was having a heart attack? That his medication was back at the house and all she could do was stand before him in a freeze-frame of hate.

Hurry... hurry... for Christ's sake, hurry... Help me...! Why are you standing there...? Go... go... Lorraine... go... go...

His uncoordinated movements. A stumble on a tuft of grass. Could she have prevented him from falling? To push him from her; to pull him towards her...? What happened in that instant when she lost her grip on him and he fell?

His body was soon recovered from the river. The autopsy that followed proved he died from a heart attack caused by his diabetes.

She mourned their lost opportunities, the harshness of their parting, and tried to come to terms with what had happened to him.

Victor's support was constant. He held her at night when

she awoke from nightmares or when she was suddenly over-whelmed by a sensation she was never able to name. A sensation that threatened to steal her breath away. She would allow her father's image to fade – his rag-doll body falling and disappearing into the churning water.

He, of all people, should have understood the power of love.

His arms lifting... His eyes... that terrible awareness...

It had seemed possible to deal with her guilt until Aidan was born. Long hours of labour were endured before he tore through her. That was how she always envisaged his arrival: a thunderbolt that unleashed the emotions she believed were under control.

She wanted to rejoice in her baby but his wrinkled, old-man face reminded her of her father. Even when his skin smoothed out and everyone who saw him remarked on how beautiful he was, she still saw Arthur's eyes staring back at her.

Postnatal depression, said Rita, when she called into Serenity Falls one afternoon and found her weeping in the Nook. It will pass. Rita seemed shrunken in the months following Arthur's death. Did she suspect...? But what could she suspect? It was an accident. Lorraine would stand before the mirror and mouth the syllables: ac-cid-ent... ac-cid-ent...

She used that same word when she woke up in hospital with no memory of the number of sleeping pills she took. She had been rushed there by Victor who had been alerted by Aidan's cries.

That was when she broke and told him about those final moments of her father's life.

He didn't seem surprised, nor judgemental. Instead, he guided her through her tormented thoughts and helped her to envisage that final confrontation on the cliff summit more clearly. She saw herself running towards her father. Her desperate attempts to catch him before his foot slipped and flung him off-balance.

Accepting Victor's vision altered the dynamic between them.

He worried that she would make another attempt on her life. What security would he and Aidan have if they were forced to leave Serenity Falls? His quiet emphasis on this possibility penetrated the hazed world she occupied and became an obsession. She refused to listen to Brandon Moore and his cautious words of lawyerly advice, that it would be risky to cede full ownership of her home to Victor. She was beyond hearing anything other than the demented voice in her head.

When she was calm again, and capable of rational thought, the money she inherited from her father was used to establish Rekindle Connections and create an equal partnership. As they expanded the Rekindle programme, yoga and tai chi were added after she qualified as a teacher. A publishing deal would have collapsed if she had not ghost-written Victor's first book. The words he spoke with such authority did not translate to the page. She had been appalled when she read the first draft. His train of thought was too dense to comprehend and grammatically incoherent, as was his spelling. She was nervous in case he took offence at her suggestions but he was happy to let her rewrite the book. She became his voice in print, a ghost-writer for all the publications that followed.

Being busy was essential. Spare moments awakened the past, while the pain of remembering was acute each time she brought up the subject of Serenity Falls. How often had Victor promised to organise co-ownership of their home? How had she allowed the years to pass without insisting on him doing so?

She knew the answer, but would she allow herself to hear it? Her father, reaching from his grave to claim her. No wonder she never wanted to go back there, in her mind. She had loved too much, too desperately. Arthur Kilbride's death had paved her future – and allowed Victor to keep her securely in the palm of his hand. A gentle tyranny with a savage undertow.

Only now, when it was too late for clarity, did she understand how much she had depended on him to protect her from the truth.

The past did not die. It simply reinvented itself in the telling.

FORTY-ONE

GAIL

The atmosphere in the Chat Room was uneasy. Gail remembered it all: the distance separating one couple from another, the tense smiles and nods, the aimless comments that broke out now and then about the weather, the journey they took to reach Serenity Falls and how lovely the gardens looked in their autumnal colours. She remembered her own desire to flee on the opening day of the programme. Why hadn't she been brave enough to give in to that impulse or to refuse Matthew's request when he slid that Rekindle Connections brochure across the table towards her? The whimsical nature of fate...

The couples who had signed the contract to participate in the documentary intrigued her. Four were married, and the other couple was in a long-term relationship. Her main aim, she reminded herself regularly, was to penetrate the mystery surrounding Naomi and see if Carl's suspicions had any foundation but the documentary was building its own creative momentum and she was anxious to begin working with the couples.

She had already met them in the lead-up to today and

discussed in detail what she hoped to achieve. They had been relaxed then but now she sensed a different attitude; an awareness among them that her camera had the power to capture their unwary words, moods and expressions. She hoped they would be less inclined to notice her once they immersed themselves in the programme.

Pamela played the introductory video as soon as everyone was seated. Lorraine's polished performance onscreen lacked the natural appeal that her husband had once presented; the sense that they were all together on a journey of self-discovery and he would be with them each step of the way. *Each step of the way to the divorce court,* she she muttered to herself, then let thoughts of Matthew go as she observed the group, who were beginning to relax in the comfortable settees and armchairs.

Sheila Graham was a quiet woman with a darting, unsettling gaze. In contrast, Terence, her husband, had a firm handshake and a reassuring smile. Dominique Galarzo's broken English was somewhat difficult to understand when she became excited, and it soon became apparent that she was going through a crisis: Karla, her wife, a Danish blonde with assertive glasses and a background in information technology, appeared to have an issue with fidelity. Amy and Gerard Foster were a success story, happy to chart the changes in their marriage since renewing their vows. Two other couples had specific issues they wanted to address: Darren Wise and Isobel Keane were career-driven and unable to agree on who should be the stay-at-home parent should they decide to have a baby. Felicity and Noel Taylor wanted to separate but two children and a crippling mortgage prevented them from doing so. The Rekindle programme offered them a chance to see if there was anything positive left in their marriage to salvage.

Noel's harried expression indicated he was having second thoughts about the documentary; Felicity cast her eyes upwards when he jumped to his feet and waved his hand at Gail for attention after the video ended.

'I assume we're going to be consulted throughout the entire editing process,' he said. 'I, for one, insist on the right to see what you are doing with the information you take from us.'

Did he believe she was intent on a smash-and-grab of their identities?

Looking around the group, Gail was aware that others had the same fear and were relieved that someone else had voiced it for them.

'I'm afraid that won't be possible,' she replied. 'We discussed this in detail at our meeting. Editing is my responsibility.'

'I don't remember coming to any such agreement,' Noel said. He was a triangular-shaped man with a chest designed to huff. 'I'd never have approved those terms.' He lied. His signature on the contract was a flourish that had almost obliterated his wife's spidery handwriting. 'Are we supposed to trust you?' he demanded. 'We all know what the media are like. Anything that we say could be edited and the meaning altered or used out of context.'

'Gail is right,' his wife intervened. 'You agreed—'

'I agreed to express my views on marriage and to have them used exactly as stated.'

'Repetition is inevitable when filming, and editing will always be necessary.' Gail was aware that everyone was watching her, just as they were when she and Matthew... she brushed the memory aside and controlled her anger. Noel was a tiresome bully but he would make excellent material for her documentary.

'This is my area of expertise.' She spoke crisply, conscious that he was raising the nervous pressure of the group. 'If you feel threatened by how you believe you can be negatively portrayed, I would suggest you look to yourself for the reason why. I'm not interested in working with anyone who doubts my credibility. If that's how you feel then this is the right time to withdraw. You're doing this voluntarily. I can't, and won't, have people contributing to the documentary who are not willing to speak frankly about their relationships.'

'Well spoken, Gail.' Terence Graham clapped his hands. 'I'm one hundred per cent behind you.' His teeth were polished to a brilliant white. His mouth was too small for such radiance, and she looked quickly away from him towards Lorraine, who had arrived into the Chat Room during the discussion.

'I understand the concern expressed by Noel, and it may be shared by many of you.' She stood beside Gail and addressed the group. 'A camera can be intimidating but it is also a powerful tool for revealing our strengths. When I gave Gail permission to film the Rekindle programme that I developed with my late husband, Victor, I had the same worries. But, as Terence just said, I have complete trust in her ability to make an excellent and trustworthy documentary. If it meets the standards of her previous ones, then I will have been privileged to work with her. However, if you wish to withdraw, I'll see you in my office where you can invalidate your contracts. For all who wish to stay, I'd suggest taking a short walk through the grounds before gathering for the first session in an hour. The orchard is looking particularly lovely right now, and if you feel like picking an apple or a pear, enjoy.'

Once again, Terence began to clap. This time he was joined by the others – even Noel reluctantly gave his hands a few taps before planting them firmly on his knees. He would be trouble, a natural complainer. The other subjects... *guests* – the language was important – Gail hadn't taken their measure yet, but it wouldn't be long before their personalities emerged.

If she stepped back eight years, she could be looking at the same scene. All it lacked was the persuasive presence of Victor Gordon.

Apprehension and excitement was what he used to engender. Was his ghostly presence, that Lorraine claimed to feel, focused on her? If so, he must surely be aware of the true motivation behind her decision to make a documentary called *Five Days at Serenity Falls*.

FORTY-TWO

LORRAINE

Released from the strain of filming, the atmosphere was relaxed when the guests gathered for their evening meal. Beef Wellington was on the menu, with the vegetarian option for Dominique and Karla.

Sheila was late arriving to the table. Terence came first, apologising profusely for her lateness. Shortly afterwards, she entered the dining room wearing a gold lamé, figure-hugging dress. The low V-neck revealed her curvaceous breasts and a split at the side accentuated the length of her legs. It took Lorraine an instant to recognise this transformation. Terence seemed equally surprised. Heads turned to watch her approach the table. Noel Taylor pulled out a chair for her and bowed with such a flourish that his wife gave an ear-splitting laugh. Felicity's laughter had an unfortunate pitch that was bound to become intolerable by the end of five days. Karla puckered her lips in an inaudible whistle and Dominique clapped her hands, her eyes bright with admiration.

'The butterfly emerges from her scrubs,' she said. 'You look amazing, dear Sheila.'

'I second that,' said Terence. 'My wife never fails to astonish me.'

The conversation flowed around the table. Lorraine longed to be back in the Nook observing Naomi, who had been curled on the sofa watching television beside Aidan when she left them. They were so relaxed together. Words between them seemed unnecessary... *blink... blink.*

Noel sent his plate back to the kitchen with a complaint that the beef was cold, though no one else appeared to think so. As if to make up for her husband's ungracious behaviour, Felicity laughed often. Terence dominated the table; not in an obvious way, but guests fell silent when he spoke. Already, he was establishing himself as their leader, though no such structure was supposed to exist on the Rekindle programme. He was a gesticulator, moving his hands to express an opinion and referring often to his wife for her support. Sheila nodded and smiled but seldom spoke. Even when Terence accidentally knocked over her wine glass which he had just refilled, she accepted his apology in silence. She excused herself and stood. The red wine had soaked through to the back of her dress.

Lorraine closed her eyes against the sight. Blood haemorrhaging, raindrops pattering against a leaking roof.

Terence apologised, called himself a clumsy ox and offered his arm to walk his wife from the dining room.

The cushioned seat on the chair where she had been sitting was also stained. Lorraine removed the chair and used it as an excuse to exit the meal. The guests were free for the rest of the evening to relax in the Welcome Lounge or walk in the garden.

She reached the bathroom just in time. The contents of her stomach were vomited into the toilet bowl with such ferocity that she was afraid of choking. Finally, it was over. She washed her face and cleaned her teeth. Had Naomi or Aidan heard her? She tensed, expecting a knock on the bathroom door, but they were still watching television when she emerged.

Aidan had made popcorn and the buttery smell almost drove her back to the bathroom. Soon the night would be over and she would be able to retire to bed. To sleep undisturbed, a long, dreamless sleep – how wonderful that would be. Instead, she would doze fitfully and her dreams would drag her down dark laneways where there were no directions, no signposts to help her find her way back to normality again.

A blur of white floating through the darkness, that was all Lorraine could see when she awoke.

Ghosts were to be expected. The spirits of the dead would not lie still until she was exposed. The apparition crossed the floor. If there were footsteps, they made no sound. Was she experiencing a nightmare in which she was fully aware that she was in the realm of sleep yet unable to awaken? She was familiar with such nightmares but no... this was real time, and the faint creak of her door being opened had alerted her.

Naomi was sleepwalking again.

She didn't react when Lorraine, using the dimmer switch, turned on the bedside lamp. In the soft glow of light, Naomi made her way across the floor. She was walking without crutches and each step was an unsteady progress towards the wall where Aidan had again propped the portrait after Gail had filmed it.

It was clear from Naomi's expression that she was unaware of her surroundings yet the portrait seemed to draw her like a magnet. She came to a standstill in front of it and slammed her hand against the image of Lorraine's face. The moan she gave was as unearthly as her appearance.

She flinched and turned when she felt Lorraine's hands on her shoulders, so sharp and bony with no flesh to soften them.

'I'll take her back to her room.' Aidan appeared in the doorway, bare-chested and in a pair of jogging pants, his voice a whisper.

'Go back to bed,' Lorraine whispered back. 'I'll look after her.'

'She's more comfortable with me. I don't want her to get a shock when she awakens.'

'We've already had this conversation.' She spoke softly yet firmly as she guided Naomi from her bedroom. 'She is in my care. I'll look after her.'

'Whatever you say.' He shrugged and stood aside for them to pass.

Naomi moved her head from side to side as if she was searching for someone. Her dark eyes stared blankly at Lorraine.

'Anna... Anna.' She whimpered the name, a child's cry so indistinct that only Lorraine heard its dangerous resonance.

'Did she say a name?' Aidan asked.

'Nothing that made sense,' Lorraine managed to reply.

They had reached the open door of Naomi's bedroom. 'Goodnight, Aidan.' Lorraine closed it firmly on him and helped Naomi to bed.

Naomi was still dazed but aware that she had been sleep-walking again. 'I'm sorry,' she said. 'Sorry... sorry.' Tears ran down her face. She held her arm across her eyes but was unable to stem the flow.

'Don't worry, Naomi.' Lorraine hushed her into silence. 'Everything's going to be all right.' The slenderness of her neck. Why hadn't it been broken during the crash, as Victor's was? 'You're safe here with me.'

A book jutted from underneath the pillow. Only half of the cover was visible. As Lorraine leaned forward to see it more clearly, Naomi turned on her side and covered it with her body. Not a book, Lorraine realised. Its shape was too wide – more like a journal.

It had surprised her to discover that Naomi could remember how to write. In St Gorgonia's ward, Lorraine had seen her sign her name on documents. No hesitation as she formed the words, *Naomi Nelson*.

Pamela arrived to work earlier than usual in the morning.

'How's everyone doing?' she asked, as she removed her helmet and sat beside Naomi at the kitchen table.

'All good.' Lorraine put the teapot down on a heat mat. 'Help yourself to tea. It's just made.'

'Exactly what I need.'

'I'll pour.' Before anyone could stop her, Naomi lifted the heavy teapot. It wobbled slightly but she managed to fill the three cups without spilling a drop. She was gaining strength and showing it in small, authoritative ways.

'Isn't Aidan up yet?' Pamela gestured towards his empty chair.

'He's outside with Gail doing sound checks.' Naomi replied before Lorraine could speak. She was perky this morning. No traces of tiredness as she asked Pamela about the bar in Potters Glen, where Aidan hoped to introduce her to his friends.

Nothing about her suggested she had been sleepwalking in the small hours and savagely intent on destroying the portrait.

She was still talking to Pamela when Lorraine left them and entered Naomi's bedroom. It was tidy, almost spartan, the bed already made. She felt under the pillow, expecting to find the journal she had glimpsed last night. Naomi must have left it elsewhere, but it wasn't visible anywhere in the room. Was it possible she had hidden it and, if so, why?

Lorraine opened the drawers on the dressing table, checked the wardrobe, lifted the mattress and peered under the bed. Had she imagined its existence? Remembering that pale, ephemeral figure swaying against the darkness, she believed anything was possible. Admitting defeat, she gave up the search, nervous in case Naomi returned.

But as the morning progressed, it stayed on her mind. She was convinced the journal existed and could only conclude that Naomi, for reasons of her own, was determined that she would not find it.

FORTY-THREE

NO NAME GIRL

Two days since filming began. Dominique sounds the same as ever. Like sparks are coming out of her mouth. Sheila is different here, quivery and helpless. It's as if she expects to be contradicted if she gives an opinion. Her husband spilled wine on her. He hated her dress. I heard them arguing in the hall. Not that Sheila said much, just sorry... sorry... and my heart was beating so hard I thought this surge would definitely bring me something, but it just ebbed away like the others. Maybe that's why I walked in my sleep afterwards? Is that something I always did? I wake up with no idea of where I was or what I'd been doing.

Lorraine said she stopped me from putting my fist through the portrait of her and her husband. I should be used to not remembering but this is too much... too much. She's going to phone Stella and see if my sleeping tablets can be upped.

Sound carries from the Chat Room. Lots of arguments. I wish I could be a fly on the wall like Gail. She reminds me of a rooster with her punk haircut. Punk was all about anger. Why do I remember that? Being angry and rocking the boat. The boats I draw have a shape. I'd like to show Aidan but I'm afraid of losing the shape if anyone else sees them.

He thinks there are some photos of Sedona in the attic. He's going to search as soon as he has time. Maybe they'll help.

Rock the boat... rock the boat...

FORTY-FOUR

LORRAINE

The five couples turned up for the tai chi session on the lawn. This was their third morning to exercise and they followed Lorraine's instructions in a harmonious sequence, apart from Sheila, who seemed unable to concentrate on the simplest movements. None of the authority she showed in St Gorgonia's ward was visible now. She seemed lost without the structures of the hospital to support her, yet that glimpse of her on the first night when she entered the dining room in the figure-hugging dress she had obviously bought for the occasion suggested there was more to her than the quiet personality she projected. Since then, she had worn colours that were either grey or black. If wine was spilt again, she wouldn't look as though she had been bathed in blood.

When the group broke for lunch, Lorraine returned to the Nook to shower and change into casual trousers and a loose top. Aidan and Naomi were in the walled garden, sitting together on a bench in the small wooden gazebo. A large book was open on Naomi's knees and Aidan, leaning towards her, was turning the pages. Was it the same book that had been under her pillow on the night she sleepwalked? Even from the distance of the living room, Lorraine could see how raptly they were staring at it.

Pushing open the patio door, she walked across the terrace. Herbs spilt over their borders and the bushes were ripe with clusters of juicy berries. Her footsteps startled them. When they looked up and noticed her, the animation faded from their faces.

She recognised the album immediately. It had a *saguaro* cactus on the cover, its long-limbed columns jutting upwards. She wondered if her fingerprints were on the dusty cover where the name *Sedona* was embossed. She had hidden it away after removing the photograph to give to the police. Aidan must have ransacked the attic to find it.

'I remembered you mentioning the album once,' he said. 'You were going to show it to me but you never did. It took ages to find but it was worth the search. We've found photographs of people who could be Naomi's parents.'

Who could be... His casual assertion that Lorraine could be mistaken infuriated her but it was mainly dread she felt as she watched Naomi tracing her finger over a photograph of Kelly Nelson.

Kelly was sitting on the bench outside Hot&Saucy and eating a taco, her stomach straining against the blue dungarees she had worn towards the end of her pregnancy. Seth, a beer in hand, his other arm around her shoulder, was grinning at the camera. Underneath the photo, Lorraine had written their names. Her handwriting had faded over the years yet it was still legible.

'They look so happy.' A blush deepened on Naomi's cheeks as she stared at the photograph.

'Why wouldn't they be?' Lorraine sat beside her. 'They were looking forward to your arrival.'

Aidan watched eagerly as Naomi turned to the next page and stared at a younger Victor Gordon, a free spirit at ease in an environment he had wrapped around himself. Nothing suave or smooth about him then, his black hair tied in a ponytail, his skin bronzed from the sun. His denim jeans and jacket looked well-worn and fitted his tall, rangy figure like a second skin. Lorraine was by his side in some of the photographs. She was startled by how thin she was, how pensive. Falling in love with a man who always seemed to be the centre of attention in any group gathering hadn't been easy. The gloss she had applied to that first year with Victor gave back an ever increasingly dulled reflection. Goosebumps lifted on her arms when she recognised another photograph of Kelly.

'That *could* be you, Naomi.' Aidan tapped his finger against the photograph of the baby in Kelly's arms.

His challenge. There it was again.

Naomi, her eyes widening, removed the image and brought it closer to her face.

'You were only a month old when I took that photo,' said Lorraine. 'Would you like me to frame it for you?'

'Okay.' She handed it to Lorraine and continued turning pages. 'Is anyone called Anna in the album?' she asked. The shaky hesitancy in her voice was changing and becoming more confident. 'Aidan told me I called out to someone called Anna when I was sleepwalking.'

'I don't remember you mentioning anyone's name.'

'She did,' said Aidan. 'I heard her.'

'The surge comes when I say *Anna.*' She looked directly at Lorraine.

'What do you mean... "the surge"?' Lorraine understood the power of a surge, its uncontrollable randomness.

'It goes nowhere,' Naomi said. 'I don't feel it now.'

'There is no Anna in the album.' Lorraine spoke firmly, decisively. 'But *this* is you, Naomi. You were such a beautiful baby.'

'Why don't I feel anything?' Naomi pounded her fist against

her chest. 'I can't bear it. It's close... close... but it's thick and sticky. Is it blood, Lorraine? There must have been so much blood.'

She was trembling as the album slid from her knees to the ground. It was the first time she had strung so many sentences together, and her accent had a mellifluous quality that was unnervingly similar to Victor's. That wasn't possible. Or could it be a remembered reaction to the last voice she heard before the crash? The accent that Victor never let slip, apart from the one occasion when he murmured feverishly in Gaelic. Just as Naomi had on her sleepwalking episode, according to Gail.

'You mustn't lose faith, Naomi. Remember what Professor Shannon advised. Small, steady steps day by day. Aidan had no right to put you under this stress.'

'He's helping me.' She gestured towards the garden walls on either side of her. 'I'll never get better if I'm always confined to the Nook.'

'Confined, Naomi? Do you believe I've imprisoned you?'

'I didn't mean it to sound like that.' She held onto the back of the bench as she stood. 'I need to lie down.'

'I'll go with you.' Aidan attempted to rise and assist her.

'I can manage... it's okay.' She gestured at him to stay where he was. Despite being upset, she sounded determined to cope on her own.

'Thanks for the album.' She smiled down at him, her fingers touching his shoulder fleetingly. 'I'm sorry it hasn't made a difference.'

'There's no need to apologise,' he said. Everything will come back to you in time. I know it will.' He watched her as she walked slowly up the garden path, poised to run after her if she stumbled. His stance disturbed Lorraine. Indeed, much about their seeming affection for each other continued to worry her.

'Why didn't you tell me you were going to search for that

album?' She allowed her anger to erupt. 'Had you any idea of
the risk you were taking by exposing her to those photographs?'

'I wanted to help. What's wrong with that?' He was challenging her again, punching holes in the security she had built
around herself.

'Everything is wrong with it! Her exposure to those photos
could have triggered another seizure! I work closely with
Professor Shannon. I don't see Naomi as some plaything to be
experimented with. She's a sick woman—'

'I'm not experimenting with her. How dare you say that.'
His anger matched her own. 'She needs a friend, not a guardian.
The way you hover over her is oppressive. People with amnesia
lead perfectly normal lives and adjust to their lost memories in
time. I want to bring her out to meet my friends. Do some of the
normal things couples do—'

'*Couples.*' She was aghast. 'What on earth are you talking
about?'

'I don't mean like *that.*' He seemed equally taken aback by
his use of the term. 'She's a friend and I feel sorry for her. I
know that Dad would want me to take care of her.'

'What do you think I'm doing?'

'It's not the same. We're on the same wavelength—'

'You know nothing about her. How can you claim to be on
the same wavelength?'

'I told you I could communicate with her when everyone
thought she was a vegetable—'

'Don't use that term. It demeans her.'

'That's how she was treated. But she knew everything that
was going on around her. If she hadn't had that seizure—'

'—she'd still be unconscious.' Lorraine was tired of arguing
with him. 'What's happening to us, Aidan? You've changed so
much. I feel as if I don't know you anymore.'

'Why not take a look in your own mirror if you want to talk
about change.'

'You're right. I *have* changed. How is it possible under the circumstances not to do so? Gail Robinson said that when you suffer a great loss, you pick up the pieces again – only they are different pieces.'

'Is Naomi one of those pieces?' he asked.

'I don't know what she is, and neither do you. If Victor hadn't died, she would have been a passing moment in our lives, as we would have been in hers. Now, through circumstances beyond our control, she's in our care and we have to be protective of her frailty. You must be careful not to give her the wrong signals—'

'What are you suggesting?'

'Don't be so obtuse. You know what I mean. Bringing her out to meet your friends is not a good idea. It suggests—'

'It suggests nothing other than friendship. I just want her to live normally again.'

The thought of her son feeling anything other than pity for that wretched woman was unbearable. Lorraine understood love, its fury and its passion, its consuming greed, hurt, disappointment and bliss.

But this would be a different kind of love; one that was forbidden, and must not be allowed to take root.

FORTY-FIVE

NO NAME GIRL

Sometimes I catch her watching me and my throat goes dry. It's a choking feeling, but more than that. It's as if I only have to reach inside her to find out who I am. She can be cold, like a wind that comes from nowhere and lifts your skin. Does she hate me? Do I even know what hatred feels like? Yes... if I can recognise love then hate must also exist on the end of the same continuum. My breath is short and fast. I'm shaking so much that it's hard to hold the pencil. Squiggles... scribbles... I see a face. It's gone before I can draw it. Turn it into a cloud. An appropriate metaphor. Cloud-brain.

Have I ever been loved? Did I ever love anyone in return? Did my stomach clench with a pain that is indescribable when he smiled at me? If Aidan knew how I felt... stop... stop. Just because someone is kind to me should not make me want to kiss him so hard his lips will bleed into mine.

Lorraine recognises love. How can she not do so when she has flooded her house with its convulsions?

I saw her face when she came into the garden. Were we sitting too close together? Why should she resent her son being kind to me... unless... But that's all it is... just kindness. He was so pleased when he found the album.

I had to pretend to be excited. My parents had faces yet nothing stirred inside me – no flicker of recognition, love, possessiveness. Not like when I repeat her name... Anna... Anna... but it's a stump. Something cut and bleeding... no, not bleeding... crying... crying... Her voice telling me to sit still... stop roaming... be in the moment.

Squiggles... scribbles... a boat with her name written on the side. A boat called Anna...

Is that a clue, or just ripples going nowhere?

FORTY-SIX

GAIL

Gail chose the woodland walk, with its dappling shadows and flurrying leaves, as the backdrop to the interview she did with Noel and Felicity.

They sat together on a wrought-iron, two-seater bench and manged to make the distance between them seem like an unreachable destination.

If Gail had hoped to gain an understanding as to how a couple who were once in love had reached the stale compromise of living in the same house but separately, she was mistaken. They blamed the government, their in-laws, the property market and job dissatisfaction for their unhappiness. After three days on the programme, they gave no indication that they had learned anything about self-analysis or taking shared responsibility for their mutual disenchantment.

After the interview ended, Aidan packed up the equipment and returned with the couple to the house. The guests would break for lunch soon.

Anxious to give them some relief from her hovering presence, Gail had packed a sandwich and flask of coffee in her backpack. She sat down on the bench vacated by the Taylors and unwrapped the sandwich. This area, with its shadowed pathways and overhanging trees was little used by the guests, who preferred the orchard or the lawns to the front of the house.

She had finished eating and was leaving when she spotted a movement between the trees, followed by the rustle of fallen leaves. Her own footsteps were muffled as she walked towards the sound.

Sheila, unaware of her presence, was slumped on the ground, her back pressed against the trunk of a tree. Her face was in her hands and the heave of her shoulders was the only indication that she was crying. She must have sought this isolated location to be alone.

What could Gail say that could stem this tumult of grief? Sheila was unaware of her presence as Gail walked soundlessly away.

The day was warm enough for the guests to use the north lawn for lunch. The Fosters were sitting at a table on their own. Noel and Felicity were sharing a table with Terence. Was he aware that his wife was weeping in the woods? Should she tell him what she had witnessed? A blast of laughter from Felicity in response to a comment he had made decided her. She was an observer, not a participant in the dramas that were unfolding between the couples.

Karla and Dominique were sitting on a rug a short distance away from the others. Karla was leaning back on her elbows, languidly relaxed, while Dominique, sitting erect and staring into the distance, was clearly upset, if the jut of her chin was any indication.

Darren and Isobel must be in their bedroom. Gail hoped they were making a baby and not arguing over who would mind it.

The afternoon group workshop – *Protecting Your Sexual Identity* – was facilitated by Lorraine. She was skilful at moving a discussion forward and concentrating on which comments were worth exploring further, yet Gail had the impression that her concentration was elsewhere, even when she seemed most engaged with the group.

As for Sheila, it was possible for Gail to believe that what she witnessed in the woods had been a hallucination. She listened attentively to her husband whenever he spoke and was in agreement with his opinions, so much so that all she did was replicate them. At one point, Terence stretched his arm around her shoulders and drew her close to him. Was there something clenched about the gesture? A possessiveness that seemed as fake as his wife's smile? Obedience – was that what was at the core of their relationship, or something far darker?

The couples were more relaxed with each other now and less inhibited when it came to sharing their feelings. Sex was the one subject that had hovered around the edges of most group sessions but had not been openly discussed until now. That changed when Isobel claimed that Darren's expectations left her with little control over her own pleasure. He wanted... no... *demanded*... that she achieve orgasm. Such pressure negated any spontaneous pleasure she should feel and reminded her of her teens, when she had been a champion gymnast constantly primed to win gold.

The discussion that followed this admission became even more heated when Karla admitted to being unrepentant about an affair she had had with another woman. She claimed to have a Scandinavian tolerance of infidelity and believed Dominique was overreacting to a trivial transgression that did nothing to destabilise their love for each other.

Gail, aware of its electrifying impact, became the fly on the wall as she captured their body language and unconscious prejudices. Aidan was equally discreet as he recorded their explosive exchanges. They made a good team, able to interpret each other's facial expressions that revealed when a moment was worth recording, and the ones that would end up on the editing floor.

Gerard Foster expressed the opinion that Dominique should be more tolerant because infidelity between wives was not as serious than if it happened in a heterosexual marriage. Amy exclaimed aloud that he had embarrassed her once again with his sexist views.

Dominique was fiery and passionate when she called him 'a chauvinist thug'. Amy seemed undecided as to whether she should nod in agreement or defend her husband. The smugness that had clung to the couple since their arrival was beginning to fray.

The bloated anger on Noel's face was worthy of a close-up when Karla insisted that sex should be regarded as a healthy exercise akin to a strenuous game of tennis, and who would break up a marriage over a spouse's activities on the tennis court? Felicity giggled nervously but didn't offer an opinion.

Terence was a calming influence. He spoke about the complexities of human emotions and the power of empathy. Karla's liberal views had to be respected but true love required sacrifice. Dominique's desire for total commitment must also be balanced against Karla's need to explore her sexuality. This was an obstacle they must surmount if they were to find a way forward and stay together.

He had the power to silence the group with meaningless platitudes. Easy, knowing he worked in public relations. Words were his livelihood but his eloquence threw his wife's silence into even sharper relief.

As if aware of Gail's thoughts, he turned to Sheila and said, 'Sheila and I have had our differences – hands up who hasn't...

yes, that's what I thought.' He laughed softly at the upraised hands before continuing, 'But we are soul mates. She would know instantly if I'd been unfaithful to her. The same goes for me. If it were to happen, our love, as Karla has explained, would keep us secure and still together. Love is a cage. There's no escaping from it and I, for one, would never dream of unpicking the lock. What do you say, Sheila?'

'I agree,' she replied, and looked directly into the camera. 'We exist in a love cage.'

The discussion continued until Lorraine drew it to a close and the group, energised and animated, headed to the kitchen for a coffee break.

'That was an interesting session.' Terence stood beside Gail. 'I hope you're finding our little quirks and caprices to your satisfaction.'

'What I've filmed is promising, so far. Everyone is being very cooperative.' She was aware that he was standing too close to her. He made her uneasy, yet anyone looking at them would have seen only the attentive angle of his head as he conversed with her.

'Yet, in reality, I suppose most of our angst will end up on the cutting room floor,' he said. 'I know how these things work. You have a narrative you want to project and the sludge must be discarded.'

'Sludge? Is that what you consider people's angst to be?'

'Obviously not.' He protested too loudly. 'But to produce excellence you must be ruthless. You strike me as someone who knows how to cut to the essence of the message.'

'Thank you, Terence.' A tremor ran through her as she walked away from him.

Could he possibly know what she had captured on film, when his wife shimmered like a butterfly before turning into a moth?

On that first night, Gail had been filming the table with its soft lighting and abundance of food. The guests were merely a backdrop at that stage but the following morning, when she viewed the footage, she had watched the rapid movement of his index finger as he hooked it around the long-stemmed wine glass that Sheila was using and knocked it over.

FORTY-SEVEN

GAIL

Nick had decided on an Indian menu for the evening meal. Marigolds and jasmines decorated the table, which was laid out with dishes of pilau rice, chicken tikka masala, and aloo gobi for the vegetarians. Side dishes of cucumber riata, tandoori roti, onion bhajis and mixed vegetable pakora added to the colour and spicy aromas.

The mood was giddy, almost raucous as dishes were passed around and wine glasses filled. Everyone had changed for dinner, except Sheila, who still wore the same grey-patterned blouse and plain black trousers.

'Too hot... oh, my God, this food is *so* hot.' Noel coughed and drank copious amounts of water, even blowing his nose on his table napkin.

Darren and Isobel dipped into each other's plates and had the contented, drowsy expressions of a couple who had been making love before they came downstairs. Obviously, today's session had made a difference to the polite and somewhat stilted interviews Gail had conducted until then, and she believed the evening meal – when the guests were relaxed – was another opportunity to capture their true views about love and what it demanded from them.

Dominique and Karla appeared to be arguing again. They were too far down the table for Gail to do anything more than observe their body language. She would talk to them in a few minutes.

Gulab jamuns with homemade ice cream was served for dessert, and Nick, coaxed from the kitchen by Pamela, appeared briefly to take a bow and accept their compliments.

After the dishes had been cleared away, Dominique was persuaded to sing a song in Spanish. Terence followed her with a poem on marriage from Kahlil Gibran's book *The Prophet*. He had a sonorous voice and the confidence to hold the attention of his audience. His eyes were fixed on Sheila as he came to the last verse and opened out his palms towards her.

> *Give your hearts, but not into each other's*
> *keeping.*
> *For only the hand of Life can contain your*
> *hearts.*
> *And stand together yet not too near together:*
> *For the pillars of the temple stand apart,*
> *And the oak tree and the cypress grow not in*
> *each other's shadow.*

The round of applause was spontaneous and noisy. No one except Gail noticed the door of the dining room opening.

She turned her camera towards the entrance where Naomi was standing. Her eyes were open and focused on Terence. Barefooted, she crossed the floor to the table, where the unexpectedness of her arrival created an abrupt silence. One glance was enough to convince Gail that she was not sleepwalking on this occasion. Her eyes were open, yet there was something off-kilter in her gaze as she paused for an instant, seemingly equally startled to find herself caught in their collective stare.

'Oh, my darling girl!' Dominique jumped to her feet and uttered a squeal of excitement. 'How wonderful to see you again.'

Lorraine moved towards her, smiling, arms outstretched. Gail imagined a fawn being corralled, and maybe that was also on Naomi's mind as she swerved from her grasp and stumbled awkwardly towards Sheila.

'Why are you silent?' she asked. 'I hear everyone... always talking... talking... talking.' How slight she looked as she stood there in a pair of pyjama bottoms and her Hozier T-shirt, yet her voice had none of the hesitancy Gail had heard outside the Silver Falls Café. Instead, it was firm and powerful when she spoke to Sheila. 'Why don't you tell them that he beats you?' She pointed her finger at Terence. 'He will kill you with a knife if you leave him.'

It was Aidan who caught her as her legs began to buckle. He lifted her easily, one arm supporting her back, his other arm under her knees.

'Do you want me to bring you back to the Nook?' he asked.

She nodded, her eyelashes sweeping downwards to hide the blankness that was already dulling her expression.

The silence they left behind pulsed with questions. Everyone's attention had turned to Terence, who seemed stunned by the accusation. His face, suffused with red, appeared bloated and shapeless. Had a veil been ripped aside and had the truth, in all its brutal clarity, exposed the real character behind his handsome exterior?

Gail continued filming. She was mining gold and was hardly breathing as she focused the camera on him.

Lorraine signalled at her to stop filming but she pretended not to notice. Terence opened his mouth as if to speak then clamped it closed again.

Gail turned the camera on Sheila, who had not moved since Naomi confronted her. Her fingers were linked together and pressed to her chest.

'I'm so very sorry, Sheila.' Lorraine hurried to her side. 'And you, too, Terence. I can't apologise enough. Naomi is my guest and, for those of you who don't know her history, she was seriously injured in the car accident that killed my husband. She suffered a severe brain injury and is staying at Serenity Falls while she recuperates.'

'No apologies are necessary, Lorraine.' Terence had recovered his smile. Gail wondered at the effort it must have cost him. 'Brain injuries can be catastrophic, which is obviously the situation here. Sheila is familiar with Naomi's case so has a full understanding of her behaviour. As, indeed, do I. Even from a layman's perspective, it's obvious that she has a long road ahead of her to regain her sanity. I'm sure I speak for every one of us when I wish Naomi as speedy a recovery as possible under the circumstances.'

The murmur of agreement that came from the others was interrupted by Sheila, who uncrossed her arms as she stood up and leaned on the table. 'Naomi was not expected to live after the accident so her survival is miraculous.' Her voice flowed evenly over the unsettled atmosphere. 'In the beginning, her medical team believed she was in a vegetative state and would never come out of it. The only question worth considering was when to end her life support.'

'Fortunately, that decision was never made,' Lorraine smoothly interjected. 'We're hopeful Naomi will learn to function again under the changed circumstances of—'

'Aidan believed in her.' Sheila interrupted her with a wave. 'He insisted that Naomi could understand what was going on around her. He was right. I told her everything about my ugly, brutal marriage... whispered all the sordid details into her ear. How Terence assaulted me so often that I could no longer distinguish between one beating and another.' She spoke softly yet audibly, and with only the merest tremble in her voice. 'Naomi may have lost her memory now but that wasn't the case when she was in that coma. She heard me and she remembered.'

Dominique's eyes were swimming with tears as she nodded in agreement.

'Sheila... Sheila... what are you saying? What does she remember?' Lorraine sounded as shocked as everyone else in the room.

Terence stood and slapped the table, demanding attention. 'I'm so sorry, everyone. My wife has obviously been drinking too much tonight—'

In one swift movement, Sheila unbuttoned her blouse. Her plain white bra was a stark contrast to the marks on her skin. Her chest was mapped in violence and more bruises were visible as the blouse slid down her arms.

Terence tried to pull her blouse up again but she pushed him away with such force that he staggered against the table. Shrugging helplessly, he appealed to the group: 'We should have been upfront from the beginning and explained to you about the addiction issues that Sheila—'

'I do remember this beating.' Sheila's attention was fixed on the camera as she tapped the bruises on her arms and chest. 'It took place on the first night here. I dared to wear a dress that Terence hadn't personally picked out for me. This was my punishment for disregarding his wishes. That's what he always tells me before he hits me. I *disregarded* his wishes.'

'You fell in the bedroom because you had too much to drink!' he shouted. 'And not for the first time, I picked you up and put you to bed.' His mouth a gash that opened and closed in a futile effort to turn everyone's attention away from his wife.

'This is your safe place, Sheila.' Lorraine positioned herself between them. She picked up the blouse and settled it around Sheila's shoulders. 'You are free to speak your truth here.'

'How can you believe the word of a deluded alcoholic?' Terence's self-control withered before their combined gaze.

No one in the room could doubt Sheila's reality. The sickening weight of what to do with that knowledge was etched on every face except his.

'My wife is a very sick woman.' He pointed his finger at Sheila. 'I stay with her because I vowed to love her in sickness and in health. I never touched her except with love—'

'You have to stop lying, Terence.' She seemed elated, almost giddy as she confronted her husband.

'Don't you dare call me a liar!' He lifted his hands towards her, his fingers curved in such a throttling position that Felicity shrieked and covered her eyes. Ignoring the group, he continued to berate Sheila.

'I've had to endure your fantasies for years. I don't know what you said to that woman when she was in a coma. You broke medical protocol by spouting your nonsense to someone whose mind was so badly unhinged that she—'

'Please, Terence, this language is cruel and unnecessary.' Lorraine spoke quietly. 'Naomi has been through—'

'Do you think I care what she's been through?' he shouted. 'Sheila is overwrought and unstable. She needs to come home with me now.'

'I'm not going anywhere with you ever again,' said Sheila. 'Do whatever you like to our "love cage". Burn it down, smash it up. It'll make a change from smashing me up.'

Suddenly realising that Gail was still filming, Terence turned his attention to her. No longer the fly on the wall, she felt the heat of his fury.

'Stop fucking around with that camera.' He reached her in a few strides. There was no time to move aside before his fist caught her cheek.

Still holding the camera, she staggered backwards and was held secure in Dominique's strong arms. When he lunged towards her again, it took the combined strength of Karla, Gerard and Darren to drag him away.

Lorraine had already rung the police. They were on their way, she warned him.

The calmest person in the room was Sheila. Had she walked through fire? Fallen from a height that she was always afraid to trust? Emerged from subterranean depths into the light? Any metaphor could apply to someone who had finally found the courage to speak out. A courage that was triggered by the young woman with a broken memory and an uncanny sense of hearing.

Terence had left by the time the police arrived. Running to where? Gail thought back to her own undignified dash from Serenity Falls. The feeling that the bricks of her marriage were clattering around her and shaping a new direction. She hoped Terence's direction led him towards a jail cell. Her cheek was swollen and throbbing as she gave her statement to the police. Her injury was photographed and, eventually, she was able to return to her bedroom.

Collapsing onto her bed, she applied an ice-pack that Pamela had prepared for her to her cheek. How long had she kept her camera running? She would have captured Terence's fist but after that, the images would be distorted.

Never mind. She had enough material to frame her documentary.

She felt that same nerve-tingling sensation again as she picked up her camera and played back the recording. The images she had captured were even more powerful than she had imagined. She watched Naomi enter the room, her blank expression adding a flatness to her features until her eyes rested on Sheila. The awareness that grew from that glance was mesmerising to watch. So, also, was Sheila's reaction. A Rip-

Van-Winkle awakening from a long sleep of denial and delusions. Miraculous. Was such a description possible?

The footage where Terence struck her was as fuzzy as she expected but was perfect material. A niggling feeling that she was missing something important persuaded her to watch the sequence again. She rewound back to Naomi's quiet entrance and watched her unsteady yet determined walk to the table. Gail had captured the reaction of the couple to Naomi's accusation with absolute clarity but it was Lorraine, who was also in the frame, who now held her attention. Her shocked expression when Sheila acknowledged the truth of what Naomi had stated with such conviction was clearly visible, but it was more than that. Gail froze the image and studied Lorraine's wide-eyed stare, the intensity of her gaze, and how her mouth had seemed to open of its own accord, her lips drawn back from her teeth in a slack-jawed instant that betrayed what Gail could only describe as *horror*. She released the image and watched the footage again. In that instant of revelation, Lorraine's body had arched forward slightly as if she was reacting to a blow delivered cleanly to her solar plexus. A few seconds later she had snapped back to her customary self-possession. How had she managed to recover her composure so quickly? It revealed a high level of self-control. No one watching her would have realised how appalled she had been to discover that Naomi Nelson had been alert to the people surrounding her, and their activities, as she lay in a coma.

Gail was about to transfer the footage to her laptop when a soft knock on her door interrupted her.

'Are you okay?' Pamela scanned her face. 'You took quite a blow from that creep.'

'I'll live. The ice-pack helped.'

'You'll have a shiner tomorrow, no doubt about that. Just as well you're behind the camera, not in front of it.'

'How's everything downstairs?'

'All calm again. Lorraine has called an impromptu group session and they're all fussing like clucking hens around Sheila. I'm escaping back to the lodge for a glass of chilled white wine. Would you like to join me?'

She walked with Pamela down the long avenue. It was dark by now and the stars were clear enough to make out the Plough and the streak of the Milky Way.

Was Naomi recovering her memory? Perhaps, soon, there would be answers to the questions Carl had so vehemently pursued.

'Things can get tough during a Rekindle programme but tonight wins the award for the most fucked-up communal dinner I've attended,' said Pamela.

'I thought Lorraine handled it well. I mean, what are you supposed to say and do under such circumstances?'

'My inclination would be to run for the hills but she's made of sterner stuff.' Pamela turned the key in the lodge door and switched on the light.

The small living room was simply furnished with comfortable armchairs, a crammed bookcase and a low coffee table.

'Take a seat and relax,' said Pamela. 'I'll open the wine.'

She disappeared into the kitchen and Gail, sitting down, gazed around her. A framed photograph of a young woman was positioned on the centre of the mantlepiece. She was sitting on a wall, her legs dangling, the lodge in the background. Another photograph taken many years later showed her as an older woman in a strapless sun dress – a beach scene, with Pamela and Lorraine, skinny teenagers in bikinis, on either side of her.

Arthur Kilbride was in another photograph. He looked much older than the formal portrait Gail had filmed in the hall. This photograph had been taken inside the lodge. He was relaxing in an armchair and the same woman was leaning over the back of it, their faces touching.

Pamela returned with a tray, glasses and an open bottle of wine in a cooler. 'You were too busy filming to eat earlier but here's something to stem the hunger pangs.' She nodded towards a cheese toasty she had made, and a bowl of crisps. 'You can't drink on an empty stomach if you want a steady hand for the camera tomorrow. How much of the war did you film?'

'Enough. I wonder what snapped inside Sheila? She was so timid... well, apart from the first night.'

'Tonight reminded me of another bust-up that happened here years ago. Different reasons but a similar scenario, apart from the violence.' She filled two wine glasses and handed one to Gail.

Her voice was guileless, no hidden meaning behind her comment.

'Have there been many failures on the programme?' Gail hoped Pamela would attribute the rush of colour to her face to the blow she had received. She bit into the toastie, as ravenous as she always was when she emerged from the near-trancelike state that took her over when she was filming.

'Lorraine doesn't talk much about the failures,' Pamela replied. '"Never stand on the platform of negativity", that was one of Victor's sayings. Or it could be hers. It was often difficult to tell the difference.'

'How long have you worked with Lorraine?'

'Since I came back from Australia. My marriage had broken up and I was recovering from a rather messy divorce. That must be fifteen years ago.'

'Neither of you have changed much since you were teenagers.' Gail gestured towards the beach photograph.

'Flattery will get you everywhere.' Pamela finished her wine and poured another glass. 'I'm afraid we've both changed radically since those days.'

'You know what I mean. You and Lorraine are obviously very close?'

'We were like sisters then. Eloise, her mother, died young. She was a lovely woman and hugely missed. Lorraine thought her father would be happy again if he married my mother.' She lifted the photograph of the older couple and tapped her index finger against the face of the woman. 'I was terrified that would happen. Arthur was such a grouch in those days. He fell to pieces after Eloise died but my mother finally made him realise that the dead demand nothing more from us than to rebuild our lives and find happiness again.'

'I believe he drowned.'

'I was on my honeymoon when it happened. Lorraine witnessed it. My mother said she was inconsolable for about a year afterwards. I was living in Australia by then, so I wasn't much help to her.'

'That explains why she was somewhat emotional when I was interviewing her about her father.'

'She never talks about Arthur. Now, it's the same with Victor. She keeps a tight rein on her feelings.'

'Your mother looks like a lovely woman?'

'*Was* a lovely woman. Pamela's animated expression faded as she replaced the photograph. 'Rita died some years ago. She used to look after the gardens here. In my family, working for the Kilbrides goes back to when the hotel first opened. And here I am continuing the tradition.'

'What was Victor like?'

'Ah ha... now, that's a million-dollar question.'

'You didn't like him?'

'My feelings were mixed. He had the ability to draw people to him but also to use them for his own benefit.'

She held out the wine bottle to Gail. 'Top up?'

'Just a small glass. As you said, I'll need my head together for tomorrow.' She paused. 'So... was there any credibility to all the online gossip that followed his death?'

'No truth at all.' Pamela's reply was definite. 'I never had any sense that he was playing around with other women... especially someone like Naomi.'

'Yet the rumours persisted.'

'That guy on Twitter – he had some stupid hashtag or other – was barking up the wrong tree. He tormented Lorraine. I know we shouldn't speak ill of the dead, but he was an absolute jerk.'

'When you say he tormented her, what do you mean?'

'The tweets, for a start. And those phone calls. He wrote to her as well.'

'Emails?'

'Probably. And a couple of letters. I recognised his handwriting on the envelopes when I sorted the mail out.'

'How could you do that?' Gail had finished the toastie and was beginning to nibble at the crisps.

'Carl Sheridan signed his name in the book of condolences at Victor's funeral. Graphology fascinates me, so I tend to recognise people's handwriting even if I've only seen it once.'

'What was in the letters?'

She shrugged. 'Probably the usual stuff he went on about. I came into the office on one occasion when Lorraine was reading a letter from him. I thought she was going to show it to me but she shoved it into a drawer on her desk and pretended everything was as normal. That's the way she operates. His death put an end to all that.' Pamela's cheeks were flushed, her eyes bright. She had been drinking during the meal and was about three glasses ahead of Gail. 'I believe they have another suspect in custody.'

'Yes, I heard that on the news.' Gail kept her tone neutral. 'I believe he made a lot of enemies.'

'It's a strange one,' Pamela agreed. 'He was obviously

executed, but I would have imagined whoever did it would have put a bullet through his head. Why a knife? And why would he go to such an isolated place when the gardai had warned him that his life was in danger?'

'I've wondered about that myself. I'm familiar with knife crime. It happens a lot among gangs in London.'

'But not so often here. And when it happens it's usually a bullet. Anyway, it's a relief to go online now and not see all those insinuations about Naomi.'

'It's strange that no one in her extended family has been traced.'

'If she had an extended family, it would be. From what Lorraine remembers, her parents were hippies who lived off the grid and died in a fire. It's possible her grandparents are also dead, or have no contact with her.'

'Why did it take Lorraine so long to identify her?'

Pamela shrugged. 'A sudden death is a traumatising experience,' she said. 'After my mother died, it took months for me to remember things that had seemed important before her death. Lorraine was the same. Going to London and talking to Lucy Strong, who was one of the last people to see Victor alive, helped to clear her mind. That's when she recalled the letter Victor had received from Naomi. She seems to have been as footloose as her parents and was backpacking around Europe.' She stood a little unsteadily. 'It's time I made some coffee, black and strong. I don't drink very often. I'll be bedridden tomorrow at this rate. Would you like a cup?'

'No, I'm okay. I'll just finish this glass and head back to the house.' The painkillers Gail had taken earlier were wearing off and her cheek was throbbing.

As if reading her thoughts, Pamela returned to the room with a cup of coffee and said, 'Terence was a class act, wasn't he? Imagine coping with that kind of violence and still being able to hold down a full-time, responsible job, as Sheila does.'

'I filmed him knocking that glass of wine over her dress on the first night.'

'My god! He's such a swine. I wonder if Felicity will stop laughing now that he's gone?'

'We should be so lucky.' Gail sighed. 'I feel as if I've been living in a cocoon since I came here.'

'These programmes are absorbing.' Pamela nodded. 'Are you happy with what you've filmed so far?'

'Some good. Some bad. Tonight has added a whole new dimension to it. I've a lot to think about.'

'We need this documentary, Gail. Lorraine is finding it hard to pick up the pieces after Victor's death. *Five Days at Serenity Falls* will really help to publicise the retreat.'

FORTY-EIGHT

NO NAME GIRL

What happened was not a dream. Not another sleepwalking episode. It was a surge that couldn't stop. Someone was pushing me, telling me what to say and do. I wasn't allowed to have doubts or to ask questions. I believe that person was me. The part of myself I've lost. It was wonderful to be whole again, if only for a few minutes. It's gone again and I can't stop shaking.

Aidan pulls the duvet over me and sits on the edge of the bed. He thinks tonight was a breakthrough. Maybe he's right but nothing else comes back to me.

Outside the Nook, it sounds as if another kind of hell has broken out.

We're still together when Lorraine opens my bedroom door. Her face is shadowy and white. She's been calming the atmosphere. That's what she calls it. Calming the atmosphere that I stirred with a hand grenade.

She smiles but I don't think she's being funny.

'Naomi needs to rest.' I can tell by her tone she's annoyed that Aidan's in my room. She stares at his hands: he's holding mine, and he pulls back, sits up straighter.

After he leaves, she asks what else I can remember about

being in a coma. Think... think... My head hurts from her questions. When I begin to cry she leans over and kisses my cheek. Her lips are cold, like her eyes. She hates me.

I think I've always known that, but now she's no longer able to pretend.

The light is out in her room when I open Aidan's bedroom door. I watch over him as he sleeps. I can barely see him but it doesn't matter. I'm content to listen to his breathing. Am I in his dreams?

He stirs and whispers my name. He reaches for my hand. The heat of his skin flames with mine when we kiss. I lie beside him. Oh, the feel of him, the wonder of his body and mine together... but there is an instant, a shuddering pause, that warns me to have a care.

I'm beyond heeding it but her door has opened. We are stilled by fear of discovery. Her footsteps sound on the floor as she walks across the Nook and enters the marriage retreat.

Aidan tries to hold me. He reassures me that she will never come into his room without knocking first – but she will enter mine, without a thought for my privacy.

The wrench when I leave him is an ache that needs relief but I dare not stay any longer. We cling together before I leave and return to my bedroom.

What drives me to him? Passion or loneliness? Fear or my need for comfort? All of these, I guess, but mostly it's love – the need to belong to him fully.

I wish I could believe we are on the cusp of something wonderful but the voice I hear in my head sounds a warning that I can only ignore at my peril.

FORTY-NINE

GAIL

Apart from a light in the hall that was always kept on at night, Serenity Falls was in darkness when Gail returned.

She had reached the top of the stairs when she heard a door opening. Glancing over the banister, she swayed, overcome by a sudden wave of nausea. The drop to the hall below was dizzying.

She gripped the banister to steady herself before hurrying along the corridor to her room. Accepting Pamela's invitation had not been her wisest decision. She wondered about the friendship between her and Lorraine. It was difficult to imagine Lorraine having friends. There was a remoteness about her that suggested sharing – as friends inevitably did – would be a difficult commitment for her. Pamela had even suggested they could have become half-sisters if Arthur Kilbride's untimely death had not put paid to his decision to marry her mother.

Once inside her room, her stomach settled enough for her to download the footage from the night's filming to her laptop.

The knock on her door was soft and rapid. She knew before opening it that Lorraine would be outside.

'Is something wrong?' Gail stood aside for her to enter.

'Nothing that can't be fixed,' Lorraine replied. 'I was looking for you earlier to sort it out.'

'Pamela invited me to the lodge for a drink.'

'You probably needed one after such an appalling experience. That's why I'm here. I was unable to sleep and when I heard you returning, I decided to tackle the problem right now. I need to ensure that Naomi is not exploited in any way through the footage you filmed.'

'I have every intention of protecting Naomi's privacy,' Gail replied.

'I trust your professionalism but excluding her from those scenes could be difficult and, dare I say, challenging for someone whose main motivation is to create drama and impact.'

'I'm also sensitive to her situation.' Gail's only wish was to lie down and close her eyes. 'Everything is negotiable, Lorraine. You'll have the opportunity to see the finished version before I submit it to *Bayview Stream*.'

Lorraine's eyes narrowed, just a little. 'That's not a satisfactory solution, Gail. I'd like to see the rushes now and decide what needs deleting.'

'I made myself clear from the beginning.' Gail spoke just as firmly. 'I've never worked with anyone breathing down my neck and I don't intend to start now.'

'I'm aware that I'm over-protective of Naomi.' Lorraine's palms, spread outwards, sought her understanding. 'The slanderous online gossip following Victor's accident was deeply scarring for both of us. Admittedly, it's ceased in recent times but I'm not going to risk it being triggered again. If footage of her exists, there is always a risk of it being exploited by others who are not a scrupulous as you. This documentary is important to me but I'll break our contract right now if my wishes are not respected.'

Was it the hardness in her stare that gave her eyes a slight protuberance? She seemed capable of carrying through her threat. Arguing further would not change her mind.

'What about the confrontation between Sheila and her husband?' Gail demanded. 'Is that also to be cut? It's a powerful example of domestic violence and it would be a shame to lose it.'

'I agree with you. As long as Naomi is edited out, and, also, any reference to her, I'm happy to keep it in. From what we both witnessed tonight I believe you have more than enough material to reflect the truth of their marriage.'

Gail nodded in agreement. Her editing skills would be tested to their limits but she was in no doubt that what Lorraine demanded could be achieved.

The footage that was removed also included Lorraine's reaction to Naomi's startling appearance. She gave no indication that she had noticed her sudden change of expression, apart from an abrupt nod at Gail to delete.

When she was finally satisfied, she left as quietly as she had come. Alone at last, Gail opened the window and leaned out into the night. The cold air brushed against her throbbing cheek and her hands trembled as she pressed them down on the window sill. She was haunted by Carl's whispering insistence that answers to his questions could be found in Serenity Falls. The more Gail tried to convince herself that she was imagining his presence, the stronger it grew – especially when she was with Lorrain Gordon, who was protecting this mysterious waif with a ruthlessness that brooked no opposition.

Gail was walking a tightrope, and her balance was becoming more uncertain with every step.

Sheila was ready and willing to be interviewed in the morning. Her transformation from the nervous woman Gail had first met was startling. She spoke freely about her marriage. How

Terence's violence had gradually stripped her of her confidence and self-belief.

'He terrified me so much that I was afraid to confide in anyone I knew in case he found out,' she said. 'So, I chose Naomi, believing my secret would be safe with her. But I was wrong. She knew about the mind games he played and, last night, she reflected them back to me in all their brutality. She wasn't afraid of him and, somehow, her awareness broke my chains... if that doesn't sound too dramatic?'

'It sounds defiant and brave,' Gail reassured her. She was still unsettled from the previous night. Her confrontation with Lorraine had had more impact on her than the blow she received from Terence. She concentrated on Sheila, who was outlining her plans for a future without her husband. She would move in with her sister until she found her own place. The house where she had endured ten years of violence would be sold and divorce proceedings would begin immediately.

'You'll have a battle on your hands with Terence,' she warned Gail when the interview ended. 'He'll do everything in his power to prevent that scene from last night ever seeing the light of day.'

Gail sighed. So many forces were ranged against her, yet they only added to her determination to complete the documentary.

The guests had broken for lunch when a taxi arrived for Sheila. They gathered in the courtyard to wave her off then made a beeline to the kitchen. Gail filled a mug with coffee and decided which sandwich to choose from the delicious selection prepared by Pamela. One couple less had not decreased the noise level but Karla and Dominique were holding hands for the first time since their arrival. Noel and Felicity appeared to be rudderless since the departure of Terence. They would have to find a new conduit if they were to continue communicating with each other. From the way they were smiling at the Fosters, Gerard and Amy appeared to be their target.

The day was sunny, an autumnal warmth that had lasted for almost a week. Gail decided to take her lunch to the orchard and eat in peace.

As she emerged from the communal kitchen, she saw Lorraine leaving her office and walking towards the open front door. By the time Gail reached the entrance, she had descended the steps and was heading towards her car, which she always parked in the courtyard.

Gail waited until she had driven round the bend in the avenue before running upstairs to her bedroom. She printed out the photograph she had taken with her mobile phone of Naomi through the window of the Silver Falls Café and slipped it into an envelope.

Aidan had mentioned that the door of the Nook was locked at night to prevent Naomi from sleepwalking again. Was it locked during the day? Swiftly, before she could change her mind, she turned the handle. The door opened easily.

She entered a circular, open-plan living area. Wooden beams supported the ceiling and windows with frames in matching wood overlooked a walled garden. It was a relaxed, comfortable environment that included a kitchen and a walled-off area at the far end, where the bedrooms and bathroom must be located.

'Naomi.' She called her name softly as she closed the door and moved further into the room.

Naomi appeared to be asleep on the sofa, her face buried in cushions. On hearing her name, she uncurled and sat up.

She rubbed her eyes but was unable to hide her tears. 'I'm okay.' She grabbed tissues from the table beside her and blew her nose. 'Lorraine's not here.' Her nasally tone suggested she had been crying for some time.

'It's you I came to see.'

'Really?'

'Yes... *really.*' Gail smiled at her obvious surprise. 'Do you remember the first morning we met at the café?'

'Of course. You took photos. Lorraine said you deleted them by mistake.'

'Ah... yes. A stupid mistake.' Let the lie stand for now. The room was full of light, a harsh, sunshine glitter spilling through the glass patio doors, yet the air felt cold or, perhaps, Gail was once again being prodded by Carl's pale, determined shade.

'I used my mobile phone to take this photograph.' She reached into her jacket pocket and handed the envelope to Naomi. 'It's not as good as the others. A bit blurry, I'm afraid, and the angle was wrong, but I thought you'd like to have it.'

'Thank you.' Naomi studied the photograph and blushed. 'You're very kind. I can't see myself in the mirror... the *real* me, I mean. I thought maybe a photo could tell me what's genuine and what's my... my... craziness—?'

'Don't even think like that, Naomi. You've been through the most serious trauma. I'm amazed you're doing so well.'

'I'm not... not *really.* My memory's gone. Without it, how can I put my life back together? Last night I broke up a marriage.'

'You liberated Sheila—'

'He said I was unhinged.'

'I can guarantee that that's nothing compared to what he's said to Sheila over the years. You haven't done anything wrong—'

'How can I know that?' She reached behind her and pushed the photo into the back pocket of her jeans. 'It makes me sick to...'

She stopped, tears spilling down her cheeks.

'What is it, Naomi?'

'Lorraine's husband and me. What people think about us?'

'They don't think—'

'A man said they did. He visited me in Gorgonia. The questions he asked... horrible... *horrible*.'

'What man?'

'Carl. He's dead now.'

How was it possible that Carl had been able to question her. Aidan had told her about the visiting rules – how he had been banned when he was the only person who could tune into Naomi's mind.

'I'm sorry you had to go through that experience, Naomi.'

'He came twice. The first time he put something up my nose.'

'What do you mean?'

'When I was in hell—' Her voice was slower, more forced.

'Do you mean in a coma?'

She nodded. 'I call it hell.'

'Maybe it was one of the male nurses taking a swab?'

'No, it wasn't Dessie. He's gentle. This person was scared.'

'If you were unconscious, how could you have known?' Gail asked.

Naomi tapped the side of her head. 'Everything is scrambled in here. Sometimes things escape. A memory... or a dream. It's hard to tell the difference. I saw him on television. He was a shadow that suddenly had a shape. Like Sheila last night.'

'Who knows about this?'

'Lorraine and Dessie. Why would someone do that to me?'

'I've no idea...' Gail was floundering in unknown waters, and Naomi's tearful expression indicated that she was reliving those moments in what she called 'hell'.

Dream or reality? Gail imagined trying to separate those two spheres. To be struggling between them must be petrifying. She remembered Carl's face when she asked him if he had done anything illegal; his furtive sideways glance that confirmed her suspicions. He had been pushing at the margins of the law in his efforts to uncover the story behind this woman.

If what Naomi claimed had actually happened, then he had been taking her DNA. No other explanation was possible. She was appalled yet not surprised by his behaviour: he had been so intent on proving she was Victor's lovechild.

'I don't know what was going on, Naomi,' she said. 'All I know is that he had no right to do that to you. And, for sure, he will never be able to bother you again.'

Soon after Carl's murder, Gail had walked in his footsteps and followed the scent of his death. Her idea of making a documentary was a half-formed concept with nothing to hold it together except a nagging, ghostly voice demanding her attention. If she had hoped to silence him by visiting the scene of his murder, she was mistaken. To die alone in such desolation, Gail had been unable to absorb that reality until she entered the cottage. Tape still fluttered around the environs of the crime but it was already in tatters. The white tent had disappeared, as had the gardai, yet there was cutlery strewn across the floor and the dresser that held it had become a heap of mouldering wood. Someone had left flowers that had long withered inside their plastic wrapping.

Matthew had fed her snippets of information. The knife that ended Carl's life had had rust on it. What kind of self-respecting gang member would carry a rusting blade? The gardai were now convinced that this had not been a planned execution, as originally suspected, but an impulsive crime, something that had gone wrong; a falling out, perhaps, between Carl and one of his sources.

Speculation was all the gardai had to go on. Gail had been relieved to drive away from that desolate site but now, comforting Naomi, Carl's voice sounded even more forceful as he urged her onward in her search for answers.

FIFTY

LORRAINE

Behind the wardrobe. That had to be where Naomi had hidden her journal. Lorraine had searched the bedroom thoroughly on two occasions but had never considered the possibility that Naomi would be devious enough to hide it there.

It was evening time and Naomi was exercising in the walled garden before Lorraine finally had an opportunity to check out this possibility. The exercise routine looked exhausting but Naomi was definitely growing stronger, and moving with more agility. *If her mind is progressing at the same rate...* Lorraine shook this fear aside and hurried towards the bedroom.

She shifted the wardrobe easily; a quick shove was all it needed to reveal the journal jammed between it and the wall.

Not a journal, she realised, as she sat on the edge of the bed and turned the pages, but a sketch pad. At first, it was impossible to make sense of anything Naomi had drawn. She used charcoal sticks, which added to the density of her scribbles.

Shapes began to emerge when she was halfway through the sketch pad. It seemed to happen suddenly yet, looking back over the pages, Lorraine recognised a pattern in the shading effects Naomi had used. *Storm-tossed clouds in an ominous sky,* she thought, but changed her mind a few pages later when she recognised the shape of a boat.

The back of her neck was suddenly clammy as letters appeared on the side of the boat. *Rosanna.*

The name became clearer with each drawing. In the final one, she could make out a figure on the deck. The face was featureless. Impossible to tell if it was male or female. But that too would emerge in the way the boat had, and when that happened, the resolute countenance of Rosanna Ross would be recognisable.

She had not been imagining Naomi's secretiveness, a closing-in on herself, as if she needed to guard her thoughts. Something was going on. A hum in the atmosphere and Lorraine had been unable to tune into it.

Silently, she shoved the wardrobe back into position and returned to the living room. Shortly afterwards, Naomi came in from the garden. She slid the patio door closed and smiled too brightly when she saw Lorraine. What else was she hiding? Those drawings told their own story. Her memory was returning. It could be a slow process or come like a thunderbolt. Either way made no difference. Something had to give, and when that happened, the powers of hell would be let loose.

FIFTY-ONE

NO NAME GIRL

I try to draw myself from the photograph Gail gave me. The real me. Stupid... stupid... I've no idea who I am. I never will.

Gail could not look at me when I told her about Carl Sheridan. Talking about him brought it back again. The ticklish sensation in my nose. His breath. Whisky. Reminding me of Andy.

Who is Andy?

And Jackie, pretending to be busy, her back turned.

I knew what Gail was thinking. It came to me in a flash. Carl was taking my DNA. He could only have had one reason for doing that. It's so obvious now.

After Gail left, I looked through the album, searching for clues. Kelly and Seth are in love. But him... that man who died by my side... he dominates all the photos with his big, open smile and weird stare... Did he and Kelly...? I'm going crazy thinking about it. Over and over and over... a whirligig, that's the way my mind has gone.

I kissed Aidan and everything changed. Now, all I want is to believe that I'm Naomi Nelson, backpacker, hoping to cadge a bed for the night from my parents' one-time hippie friends... whose son put his hands over my heart and captured it.

Please let it be the truth... please... please...

Lorraine has been in my room again. I know it, even though nothing is out of place. I can tell by the air. It's chilly... like her voice when she tells me that all she cares about is my welfare.

FIFTY-TWO

GAIL

It was after one in the morning when Gail hurried along the corridor. No sounds from the other bedrooms, no night sighs of pleasure or heated arguments.

Two-seater settees and low tables were spaced at intervals along the landing, and a wrought-iron staircase spiralled upwards to the attic door.

The portrait of Lorraine and her husband was balanced against the railings of the banisters. Earlier that evening, when the guests were gathering for the communal dinner, Aidan had removed it from the Nook.

'Orders from above,' he said when he had passed Gail in the hall. 'Lorraine wants it dumped in the attic.'

'That's a shame. It belongs with the other portraits in the hall.'

'Try telling her that. She wouldn't listen to either Naomi or me. I'm supposed to put it in the attic but I can't find the key to open the door. I'm going to leave it on the landing for the time being.' He sounded harried as he hurried up the stairs with the portrait and disappeared from view.

Why was Lorraine consigning the portrait to the attic? Was she unable to look any longer upon the features of a man who preached truthfulness at all costs yet died and left a mystery behind? Gail's nervousness increased as she paused to stare at the painting before going downstairs.

Was Carl's hand at her back? Probably. Otherwise, why was she risking everything on a casual remark Pamela had made when they drank wine together the previous night?

She opened the office door and, switching on the torch on her phone, crossed to the desk Lorraine used. The pale glow when she turned on the computer illuminated the tidy surface. She entered Carl's name into the address bar. No response. The result was still the same when she entered *Capital Eye*.

If Carl had been emailing Lorraine, she must have removed all traces of their correspondence.

She opened drawers, tensing when the whine of wood on wood came from one of them. A quick glance was enough to convince her that she wouldn't find anything there with his signature on it.

Just as she was about to give up the search she noticed the trim running across the width of the desk. The tiny keyhole was easy to miss and, at first glance, she thought it was simply another ornamental flourish. After a quick search through the main drawers, she found a key that was small enough to fit it. The shallowness of the drawer would have made it impossible to fit anything of significance into it, yet she realised her search was over when she found an envelope addressed to Lorraine.

It consisted of only a few lines, but left her in no doubt as to Carl's intentions.

Lorraine, you've chosen to ignore my previous letters. So be it. Your marriage was nothing but a sham built on a bedrock of lies, as your late husband would have said. I intend to reveal that truth about No Name Girl to the public. This is your last chance to meet me. I have questions that need answering and you'd better be willing to talk. You have the directions to the barracks. I'm waiting to hear from you but my patience can only be stretched so far.

FIFTY-THREE

NO NAME GIRL

Anna... Anna... Rosanna... Her name is a tremble on my lips. I didn't mean to say it out loud but sometimes words erupt like mud bubbles and splatter... splatter.

We were in the kitchen tonight and Lorraine had her back to me. When she turned around she looked as if she was trying to smile but her lips wouldn't move.

She poured water into a glass and swirled it around before drinking it down in one swallow.

'Did you say something, Naomi?' she asked.

'No.'

'You said something. A name?'

'No, I didn't.' The atmosphere was strange: a vibration that was shaking me, clattering my teeth. Her stare was hard, a question that demanded an answer. One that I didn't have and even if I had, I wouldn't have revealed it to her.

Does Rosanna exist? Is she whole? She belongs to a boat... Rosanna... a boat on grey water... and a wave coming... so high... dashing towards me... rising higher... the Big One... waiting so long to rise on the swell... Ros-ann-a... Ros-ann-a...

She is waiting on the shore. All I must do is ride the surge.

FIFTY-FOUR

LORRAINE

Uncoiling her body, Lorraine lay ramrod straight in her bed and listened to the sounds from next door. Naomi was more unsettled than usual tonight. Her constant pacing was only interrupted by the opening and closing of drawers. The whirr of an electric toothbrush, shoes falling to the floor and, finally, the creak of her bed as she climbed into it. Somehow, while Lorraine was absorbing these sounds, her body had once again tensed into a foetal position. She seemed incapable of lying any other way. Even during the day, the longing to fold in on herself was constant.

Soon, Naomi would sleepwalk. The signs were evident. Lorraine must be alert for the twist of the handle on her bedroom door. Naomi's footsteps would be silent, her movements sylph-like as she swayed towards something over which she had no control.

The door opened as expected and was followed by silence. Lorraine visualised the young woman's slow progress across the living room towards the door into the hall.

When it opened, she pulled herself upright and left her bed. Ghosts watched her from behind pillars of darkness. Carl

Sheridan, his mouth an open gash, was no longer able to mock her. Her father's forehead was heavy with the burden of her sins. He carried them uncomplainingly, knowing that he had forced her into doing a terrible deed, as Carl, also, would realise in time. It always took time.

The door marked *Private* was open when Lorraine walked across the living room. A glance into the hall revealed Naomi as she approached the bottom step of the stairs. Instead of following her, Lorraine crossed to the patio door, which she opened and closed behind her. She walked through the walled garden and entered Serenity Falls by a seldom-used side entrance.

This led her up the back stairs and through a network of corridors and bedrooms until she came to the main landing overlooking the hall. As she expected, Naomi had reached the landing and was standing in front of the portrait.

The lost attic key had angered Aidan. Naomi had helped him to search for it and listened patiently when he insisted it should be in its usual drawer, where he had left it after bringing down the Sedona album.

What was the compulsion that drew Naomi to this painting? Was it a random urge or something deep-rooted and destructive? Lorraine stood behind the spiral attic stairs and watched as she touched the canvas.

Her movements were gentle, with none of the force she had used on the previous occasion. From Lorraine's vantage point, she appeared to be using the oiled surface as a form of braille that she could read. Her fingers ran over Victor's face, tracing his eyes, nose and mouth.

Suddenly, she bent and forced her fingers under the bottom of the frame, her body braced to take the weight of the portrait. She moaned, the sound torn loose from somewhere deep within her as she lifted it. The portrait was forced halfway over the banisters. Bending her knees, she tilted it up even further. The effort this cost her was obvious and her movements became more unsteady as she tried to send the portrait flying downwards to the hall.

Lorraine moved softly, swiftly, towards her.

She was so easy to lift. How unresisting her body, so slight and fearless as she allowed herself to move with the portrait. To become one in flight as the tilt became more dangerous, the propulsion more unstoppable.

It wasn't necessary for Lorraine to do anything except gently guide her into space.

FIFTY-FIVE

GAIL

Looking upwards when she emerged from Lorraine's office, Gail could see the portrait balanced precariously over the banisters.

Behind it, she saw the pale oval of Naomi's face.

The scene was unreal, a staged tableau with props that caused illusions and flights of fancy for it seemed as if – from her vantage point – that Naomi was possessed of wings that floated her into view with swanlike ease. But this was a deadly flight and when Gail screamed, the spell was shattered.

'What's going on?' she yelled. 'For Christ's sake, Naomi, what are you doing?'

As she tore up the stairs, she heard the thud of Naomi's body falling backwards and the heavier weight of the portrait breaking apart.

Naomi was dazed and incoherent when Gail reached her, her legs and arms spreadeagled, the portrait frame broken, the canvas torn. The guests, disturbed from sleep by Gail's warning scream, emerged from their rooms. Aidan, taking the stairs two at a time, knelt beside Naomi.

Ignoring her insistence that she was able to walk on her

own, he gathered her in his arms, as he had done on the night she confronted Terence Graham, and carried her down the stairs. When Lorraine emerged from the Nook, wearing a dressing gown and slippers, Aidan was already walking across the hall. He stopped briefly to speak to his mother before closing the door behind him.

'What on earth is going on?' Lorraine demanded, as she reached the landing. 'I heard a crash... oh, my god! What happened to the portrait?'

'Naomi was sleepwalking again,' said Gail. 'She was trying to throw it over the banisters. She had no idea what she was doing and would have fallen if I hadn't heard her.'

'She was lucky you were still up,' Lorraine said. 'You saved her life.' Her hair was tangled and her face, free from make-up and with the sheen of moisturiser, looked vulnerable and shocked.

'How did she get up here?' Gail stared down into the hall. 'I thought that door into the Nook was locked at night to prevent something like this from happening?'

'I locked the door myself,' Lorraine replied. 'But the patio door was unlocked. She must have discovered the side entrance into the house. What were you doing downstairs at such a late hour?'

'I couldn't sleep so I went outside to study the stars. I never see them in London but they're brilliantly clear here.' She sounded convincing and Lorraine, nodding in agreement, asked no further questions.

Gerard and Darren had been gathering up the pieces of the portrait, and now laid them out on one of the low tables.

'It can be repaired,' Gerard began, but Lorraine put up her hand to silence him.

'Some things can't,' she said. 'This is one of them. Goodnight, everyone.' Her breathing was still laboured. Beads of perspiration glistened on her forehead, and the stillness of her pale features reminded Gail of an alabaster bust.

Stepping from the shower the following morning, Gail rubbed steam from the bathroom mirror and surveyed her reflection. In the harsh morning light, the bruise on her cheek was more pronounced. A warning that Terence Graham would do everything possible to prevent her documentary from being aired.

Last night was still a mosaic of impressions in her mind, but one thing was clear: if she had ignored the compulsion to search Lorraine's office, Naomi would have fallen to her death. Gail could not imagine her fragile body surviving such a drop.

Before going downstairs, she sat on the edge of the bed to reread Carl's letter, which she had photographed on her phone.

The scene that she had witnessed when she stepped into the hall from Lorraine's office had lessened the impact of his letter but reading the words again, she was shaken anew by his threats. Threats that now sent her thoughts spiralling in unimaginable directions.

Had Lorraine given in to his request to meet up? A secret meeting in a desolate location? *You have the directions to the barracks.* The cottage with its rank smells and skeletal walls was once a family home, not a base for soldiers or gardai. Unless the meeting place had been changed. But, surely not... she shied away from the possibility that such a meeting could have taken place yet there it was, flashing like neon, and forcing a grotesque possibility on her.

She should delete the letter from her phone and rid herself of thoughts too caustic to be entertained.

This was the last day of filming. It was bound to be an emotional one as the couples spoke about their experiences and what they had learned about themselves and their relationships.

After Sheila and Terence Graham, anything else was bound to be an anti-climax, yet their views were essential to round off the documentary.

The guests were already breakfasting in the communal kitchen when she came downstairs. She had no desire to join them. A brisk walk to the Silver Falls Café was necessary to clear her head.

She left Serenity Falls by the back door. The studio where Victor Gordon used to retreat in his spare time was locked but, looking through the window, she could see his workbench and tools. The untidiness of the studio suggested that it had remained undisturbed since his death. A mallet and chisels were visible on the table, alongside a half-completed carving, its shape still undefined. Unable to continue looking at such an arrested scene, Gail hurried past.

A few customers had already settled around the tables but the Silver Falls Café was quiet. Was she any nearer to the answer Carl had been pursuing, she wondered, as she drank the double espresso Lily brought to the table?

The door opened and Naomi entered. She had walked from Serenity Falls using one crutch. It thudded rhythmically against the wooden floor as she approached Naomi's table, the strain of the effort visible on her face.

Rising to assist her, Gail pulled out a chair and helped her into it.

'How are you feeling this morning?'

'Apart from this lump on the back of my head, I'm okay.' She leaned forward to allow Gail to feel her skull. The lump was visible through her short hair and must have occurred when she hit the landing.

'I owe you my life, Gail.' She was breathing normally again

and the flush had faded from her cheeks. 'I don't know how to thank you for something as momentous as that.'

'I did what anyone else would have done under such circumstances. I don't need thanks.'

'Yes, you do.' Naomi pulled off a canvas satchel that she had worn crossways over her chest and removed a sketch pad. She was dressed casually in her Hozier T-shirt under a denim jacket, and her indigo jeans emphasised her skinniness. 'I'm very lucky to be alive. In fact, it's all quite miraculous.'

Her hand shook as she opened the sketch pad and pushed it across the table towards Gail. 'Will you look at these drawings, please?'

At first, it was impossible to make sense of the sketches but gradually the images became more coherent.

The repetition of the name 'Anna' quirked Gail's curiosity. Aidan had mentioned that he heard Naomi call out the name during one of her sleepwalking episodes. She was definitely creating a story with her drawings, but Gail had no idea where it was going until she saw a boat named 'Anna', followed a few pages later by a similar boat with 'Rosanna' drawn on the side.

It reminded Gail of a small tour boat with a viewing deck and rows of seats, some double, some single.

'Do you think she's Rosanna?' Gail asked, when she saw another sketch with a woman standing on the deck. Her features were blurred, as if Naomi had rubbed out successive attempts to draw them.

'That's the only name that stays with me when I'm doing these drawings.'

'Let's check online and see if there's a similar boat called "Rosanna".' Gail picked up her phone and googled the relevant details. Nothing came up that resembled the sketches Naomi had drawn.

'That's no reason to give up,' Gail said, when she saw Naomi's disappointed expression. 'Memory, especially a lost one, must find its own way back to us. There was a purpose to your drawings and they'll eventually make sense. I'm sure of it.'

'I often believe I'm on the edge of something and then it's gone. It's *so* frustrating.' Naomi frowned as she slid the sketch pad back into the satchel and fastened the straps. 'Does it hurt?' She tentatively touched the bruise on Gail's cheek. 'It's badly swollen.'

'I'll survive.'

'Why do you think Terence came here?'

'I believe it was a game for him,' Gail replied. 'He could play the perfect husband to a captive audience while undermining his wife in private.'

'Do you think the Rekindle programme had any impact on him?'

'I doubt it.' Remembering the viciousness of his punch, Gail shook her head. 'He's beyond redemption.'

'*Redemption...*' Naomi blurted the word out with such force that it seemed to knock her back in the chair. 'That's the name of the boat,' she said. '*Rosanna's Redemption.*'

Gail googled the name on her phone again. A response came up immediately. A boat on water, the name visible on the side. A tour company, Scottish, owned by a woman named Rosanna Ross. She was an older woman, probably in her mid-sixties, with a broad face and a smile that promised sightings of whales and dolphins to those who booked her tours.

Naomi studied the photograph intently before admitting defeat. 'I don't recognise her,' she said. 'It must be just a coincidence.'

'It has to be more than that,' Gail insisted. 'I believe your memory is returning.'

'But what have I to do with Scotland?' she asked. 'Nothing matches. I've gathered all these scraps but don't know how to put them together. Are they dreams? Fantasies?' She tapped her forehead in exasperation. 'Even lies?'

'What does Lorraine have to say about your drawings.'

'I haven't shown them to her.'

'Why ever not?'

'I can't explain it. She's been kind to me. I don't want to sound ungrateful.'

'If there's something you need to get off your chest, you can trust me, Naomi.'

The younger woman sighed. 'I don't feel as if I'm in the right skin. Like someone is pulling strings and I'm jerking to each pull. Does that sound crazy... or "unhinged", as Terence said?'

Gail closed her laptop. 'It must be hugely confusing to be deprived of memory. Those strings you mentioned. Who do you believe is pulling them?'

'I'm afraid to say—'

'Naomi, it will go no further than this table. Do you think it's Lorraine?'

Naomi nodded, reluctantly. 'I don't understand her. I made Aidan show me those tweets Carl Sheridan wrote. They must have upset Lorraine dreadfully, yet she's given me a home. I'm grateful to her for doing so. It's just... she's always watching me. What does she want from me?'

As if on cue, the door opened and Lorraine entered the café. Naomi hastily shoved the satchel towards Gail. 'Keep it for me,' she whispered. 'I'll collect it from you later.'

'I thought you might be here.' Lorraine's anxious expression eased when she saw Naomi. 'I brought the wheelchair with me in case the walk back is too difficult.' She smiled at Gail. 'The guests are gathering in the Chat Room and Aidan has already set up the recording equipment.'

'Thanks, Lorraine.' Was her tone as casual as she hoped? She slung the satchel over her shoulder and stood. 'I'll run on ahead, then. Nice talking to you, Naomi.'

. . .

The final day passed without incident. Dominique and Karla decided to renew their vows in a simple humanist ceremony on the south lawn. Alyssa Grant, the celebrant, bound their hands loosely together with a ribbon of lace to signify freedom and they exchanged Claddagh rings – hastily purchased that afternoon in Potters Glen by Aidan – to express trust in each other. The final meal was treated as a wedding feast and the group dispersed in high spirits with plans to meet again for the unveiling of the documentary.

Gail should have been happy. The impromptu ceremony would make a satisfactory conclusion to the documentary. That must be her aim for now. But ordering herself to concentrate on recording these tender moments between Karla and Dominique failed to lessen her suspicions. More than ever, she was convinced that the real story behind Serenity Falls was shrouded with mystery, and she had barely scratched the surface.

FIFTY-SIX

NO NAME GIRL

Rosanna... Rosanna. I see her on the deck of her boat but more than that. Narrow streets – she knows them all – and houses jostling as if they are reaching out to claim her. She wears a long coat and a tartan scarf. Her face is lined and burnt from the wind rather than the sun. All those things are true but then the pieces separate, and my conviction falls apart. But this I know. She is my grandmother... my smother-mother who wanted to keep me locked in a box. All in the name of love. Just as Lorraine does... only she has a different reason. Can she read my thoughts... splatter... splatter...? Does she know that there are memories coming at me so fast I can hardly breathe.

I've made lunch for Aidan. A new Rekindle programme has started. The marriage retreat is alive again with angst, but we've more time together since the filming ended. He shows me a compact disc he took down from the attic. Lorraine finally found the lost key and he was able to dump her broken portrait.

All my fault... all my fault...

I have to stop blaming myself...

Aidan says his father's voice is on the compact disc. He used to record meditation sessions when Aidan was a boy. An old CD player was also in the attic and he thinks it might help my memory if I hear his voice.

The disc spins for a bit before he begins to speak. Velvet... that's how he sounds. So smooth. I imagine a roll of velvet... dark purple... rolling... rippling like waves... and it comes again.

Another surge.

My body talks to me now, shivers plucking my skin, my breath coming short and fast. I see silvery-grey water and a horizon that looks close enough to touch.

Lorraine is back. We never heard her coming into the Nook. She puts her hands to her ears. The sound of her dead husband's voice must be more than she can endure. She shouts at Aidan to switch off the CD player.

The back of my neck is wet. I'm going to faint. He presses my head between my knees and tells me to breathe... breathe. Lorraine brings water. Icy cold, shuddery. I drink the water and inhale... exhale... inhale. She orders Aidan to put the player and CD back in the attic. She's tense, ready to snap if he argues with her. He slams the door behind him. She still locks it at night, but I haven't sleepwalked since the night I almost flew.

The picture is clearer now.

Anita, blonde and petite, elfin. A London elf. We're rummaging through a box... jewellery... unopened letters... photographs of a dark-haired woman... and a disc like the one Lorraine has silenced. I take it with me when I leave that room of drifting scarves and a breeze that can't dispel the smell of Anita's cigarettes and weed.

Why am I in London when I belong to Texas? It makes no sense. Other pictures come to mind. A bedroom with Hozier posters on the wall and photographs of a woman stuck around my dressing table mirror. Her wild, beautiful face looks beyond me but, now, I hold onto her until her name comes to me.

Candice... not Kelly... Candice... this disc once belonged to her.
My bedroom... where is it? Not Texas... that I know for sure... the
name Lochanar floats effortlessly into my head and becomes a
perfect fit.

I'm flooded with memories.

Anita... London... Candice... a loch that drags the silver from
the moon... Lochanar... my mother is dead... drugs... not a fire...
and my father is nothing... no shape, no beginning or end. An
anonymous sperm...

Rosanna... Rosanna... mother me... smother me...

His voice on the CD. I play the disc in my own bedroom in
Lochanar. Rosanna's face twists with hate when she finds me
meditating to his deep-throated commands.

She orders me to turn off the player. His voice annoys her
because he sounds like Max. Not the accent, she says – it's the lilt
of his persuasion. What does that mean? Max Ross had a way
with words, she says. Most of them were as empty as a politician's promise. If she wants to meditate, she'll listen to her
whales singing.

Who is Max Ross? Why is there such hatred in my grandmother's
voice when she speaks his name? I must roll with that hatred to
see where it brings me.

Lorraine is watching me.

Can she guess what's going on in my mind? The churning of
truths and lies? What would she say if I told her how that disc
affected me? The memories that come like buffeting clouds,
shaping and reshaping; algorithms clashing in my brain and
forming a path to the past.

Is Victor Gordon the man who gave it to Candice?

.   .   .

Handsome and American, that's what Anita says. I look him up online. He heals marriages in a Wicklow village and makes love sound like a gift that never stops giving.

When I discover that he's booked to speak at a motivational conference in London I go along. He's introduced as a 'love guru'. I suspect he must hate that name, it's so tabloid, but he smiles like he's used to it. He tells us to respect our dreams. Their path to fulfilment is within us if we're prepared to dig deep enough.

I sit in the front row and study him. I take out my sketch pad and draw as he gesticulates and convinces us that our belief in ourselves must be robust, unflinching. He looks unchanged from the photo on the cover of the meditation disc but it must be years since he made it. It must be his stare. Do people ever see beyond it?

He's easy to draw. It's as if I know his face. My hand and mind travel on separate paths and the face in my sketch resembles the young, angry man in the photo Maggie once showed me in secret. Rosanna and Max on their wedding day.

Why have I connected the two men with a few strokes of charcoal?

After his speech, he sits at a table and signs copies of his book. People crowd around him and tell him he is inspirational.

I buy a copy and wait my turn to have it signed. He smiles and asks my name... my name... my name...

No Name Girl... Not Naomi... Not Naomi... there's a whispering in my head and it's growing louder. A surge that brings me back to that moment... that memory...

When I tell him my name he puts down his pen and stares at me. The others in the queue seem to disappear and I know I'm the only person who matters to him. He picks up his pen again and signs his book.

Pictures spinning... I want to see my name... show me my name... and there it is... written clearly in his copperplate hand-

writing... the whispering has become a roar but only I hear it as I read his message.

To Megan Ross. May your thoughts always lead you to a peaceful oasis. Victor Gordon.

But he remains an enigma. I try to forget him. Australia, Bondi, surfing, drawing faces, waiting tables. Six months in New York, three in California.

I continue to meditate and begin to imitate his American accent. It reminds me of movies I've seen. Cotton plantations and crinolines, white-pillared mansions, and honeyed Southern voices drowning out the songs of slaves. He is always on my mind. Even in my dreams he calls to me. His face is cast in pain.

FIFTY-SEVEN

NO NAME GIRL

Lorraine has gone to Dublin to meet her solicitor. She tried to keep her voice down when they were speaking on the phone. Her anxiety seeped through the bedroom wall. Victor's will. Problems. Intolerable ones.

I was only in her room once before – sleepwalking and intent on destroying her portrait... or so she tells me. I can't remember. That's my theme song... except that it's not true anymore. Keeping this truth from her makes my head ache.

Her perfume bottle is half-empty. The scent of summer roses. I spray it on my wrist. The smell sickens me. So many triggers. Like his briefcase. Battered and covered in blood stains, it's the only thing left in his wardrobe. His initials on the leather are still visible. I see the swing of his arm as he flings it into the back seat of his car. I've no time to brace myself against the surge that comes and goes as fast as wind gusting through a tunnel.

What came after? Tell me... tell me.

I leave this room where her presence is so strong and go into the walled garden. Is this how prisoners feel when they look up at the bricks surrounding them?

Victor's presence remains with me in the gazebo. Will he stay longer this time? Will he answer my questions? The sky is murky. Rain will come soon. I can cry then, and no one will notice.

Pamela asks if I'm okay. Where did she come from? The patio door is closed. I'm the only one who came through it. She picks parsley and rosemary. Tonight, she's cooking dinner for a man. Just a friend, she says, and sniffs a sprig of thyme. She's talking about Nick. Her big secret, or so she thinks. Aidan says he's left his wife. Nothing to do with Pamela but it's not a good look for the administrator of a marriage retreat to be in love with a married man. The guests left yesterday and she's doing the cooking for a change. She leaves the garden by a side door I never noticed until now.

It's set into an alcove that is partly shielded by overhanging ivy. It can't be used often if the hinges that creak when I pull the door open are anything to go by. The air smells musty and thick cobwebs quiver from the rush of air. Stone stairs rise up in front of me, framed by the wall and a thick, wooden banister.

A corridor to my right must lead to the hall. That is the way Pamela went if the sprig of parsley that fell from her bunch of herbs is any indication. The stairs are covered in a layer of dust. Whoever climbed them before me has left their footprints behind.

It's a maze at the top, one corridor leading into another with small rooms on either side. I open the door into a room that's filled with sheets and pillows. Another has toiletries. I walk faster and faster... and there it is before me – the main landing where I should have died but for Gail, her scream freezing the moment. Sleepwalking. Such a dangerous thing to do.

Did I imagine a shadow moving as I fell back to safety? A blink and it was gone. A shadow behind the white, spiral stairs that lead to the attic. A ghost? A figment of my imagination? Or someone bent on harming me? It should have been so easy.

A push and it would have been over.

The perfume on my wrist threatens to steal my breath. Was

that what I smelled when I woke up that night, lying on my back and still clinging to the portrait? The waft of roses? It came from nowhere or so it seemed. I thought Lorraine was nearby but she was sleeping in her room when Gail saw me rising into the air... like a swan taking flight, she told me.

This time when a memory comes it rips through me. I'm gasping for breath... Lorraine's hand on my forehead to check my temperature. Her hand offering me pills. Her hands on my mouth... my nose... my body arching...

No... no... why would she want to harm me...? Kill me...?

Yes... kill me... that is what she will do if she knows I'm becoming whole again.

FIFTY-EIGHT

GAIL

London seemed to be moving at a faster pace than Gail remembered. All eyes straight ahead, escalators, elevators, underground, overground, no sharing or spilling of secrets, no embarrassing confessions, no confrontational outbursts.

She quickened her step and tried to shake off her hideous suspicions. Her apartment closed around her like a well-worn blanket.

She rang Matthew for an update on the investigation into Carl's murder. Nothing new to report, he said. No further developments. No further arrests of suspects. The belief was that an unplanned but violent fight had broken out after Carl upset one of his criminal sources. The knife was probably lying at the bottom of a lake somewhere in Wicklow.

Matthew sounded distracted. In the background, Gail heard a baby crying, that kittenish, new infant meow. His son had arrived early and safely.

She would concentrate on editing. That was when hidden gems revealed themselves as she burnished raw footage into a coherent storyline. So much work to do if she was to meet her deadline. A date had been set for completion of the documentary and its airing. It was a tight deadline. She must strive to reach it rather than allowing herself to be tormented by a question.

Why had Lorraine deemed it necessary to visit London so soon after Victor's death? Pamela had mentioned a meeting with Lucy Strong. Admittedly, Lucy must have been one of the last people to speak to Victor before his death but it still seemed a strange decision for Lorraine to make. Surely there must have been many other more pressing matters demanding her attention at that fraught time. Not to mention the grief she must have been enduring.

Ringing the organiser of the Hearts and Vows conference would be a time-wasting exercise. Even as Gail argued this fact with herself, she was ringing Lucy's number.

Lucy's clipped tone suggested that her time was a valuable commodity that should not be wasted. She warmed slightly when Gail reminded her that they had met at the Harlequin House Hotel on the day after Victor Gordon's death.

'What a tragic accident.' Lucy sighed. 'Victor was such a charismatic speaker. What can I do for you?'

'I'm working on a feature about Rekindle Connections. When you met Lorraine in London after Victor's death—'

'Can I stop you right there, Abigail—?' A phone rang, it sounded as if it was by her elbow, and, though the ring was quickly silenced, she sounded more anxious to finish their conversation. 'I've never met Lorraine,' she said. 'On a few occasions we've spoken on the phone and emailed, but we haven't met face-to-face.'

'Oh, have I been misinformed? I was sure—'

'The success of my business is my ability to remember people and dates. I can assure you that I've never had the pleasure of meeting Lorraine Gordon. Is there anything else you need to ask me? I'm about to begin a meeting with my marketing team.'

'No, it's fine. I'll check my notes. I'm sorry to have disturbed you.'

FIFTY-NINE

NO NAME GIRL

The Chantry was once a church. Church of Ireland, says Aidan, and not enough parishioners to fill it. Now it's deconsecrated and packed to the rafters with his friends. All those names. I try to hold on to them... Amy, Jess, Alan, Jake, Melissa... and others whose names I've already forgotten.

The stained-glass windows remind me of jewels. Jewels in a metal box. Not real, Anita says. 'Just good imitations.'

Aidan must have told them I can't stand for long. The bar is crowded and it's hard to find a table that everyone will fit around. Finally, only the women can sit. Someone, I think it's Melissa, makes a joke about a 'girly gaggle'. No one laughs until the cocktails arrive.

When I look again, Aidan is further away and surrounded by the other men.

Jess asks where I'm from and they all go 'Wow!' when I say Texas.

'What's it like living there?' asks Melissa.

Jess nudges her to stop asking questions. 'Aidan told us about your accident,' she says. 'Not remembering things must be difficult.'

'I wish I could forget Jonathan Adams,' says Amy, and pretends she's wiping tears.

'He's a dickhead.' Melissa hugs her and I'm forgotten when they start talking about Jonathan. He drives a Porsche and breaks hearts. Someone orders shots and chasers. The music thumps. They drink faster.

More friends arrive... more introductions...

I feel sick. It comes so suddenly, rising up. I force it back, my hand over my mouth. The women pull away, as if I've got a contagious disease.

Melissa almost lifts me to my feet and pushes with me through the crowd to the bathroom.

I kneel in front of the toilet bowl. I've done this before... a scrap of memory that goes nowhere.

Aidan is waiting outside. 'What was she drinking?' he asks Melissa.

'Same as the rest of us. Cocktails, a few shots—'

'I told you to look after—'

'Aidan, if you want a babysitter, pay me babysitting fees.'

I'm so angry. Hot and shivery spasms grow in my stomach. I think I'm going to be sick again. I make it outside before vomiting into the bushes. He helps me into the car.

I don't want him near me. He brought me out for a night then abandoned me with strangers so that he could be with his mates.

Serenity Falls is a prison. I fall on the steps and can't tell if I'm hurt. He's guilty, afraid Lorraine will find out what's happened and say she told him so.

He reminds me of Evan.

The name comes from nowhere. It's like a parcel tied with string. If I pull the string, what will come out?

'I'm sorry, Naomi.' He sits at the side of my bed and starts explaining. 'I hadn't seen some of the lads for years. I couldn't get away from them and I thought you were okay with the girls.'

'*Evan looks like you,*' I say. '*Only older.*'

'*Who's Evan?*'

'*My uncle, I think.*'

'*You remember?*'

'*Yes.*'

'*What else?*'

'*He's my dead mother's brother.*'

'*Oh, Naomi—*'

'*Don't call me that name.*'

'*What's wrong?*'

'*Everything. Tonight was awful. I wanted to be normal for a change, instead of being a prisoner.*'

'*A prisoner. Is that how you see yourself?*'

I keep whispering '*Evan... Evan... Evan...*' as if the repetition of his name will act like a catalyst and give me back my memory.

'*How else can I see myself when your mother wishes me dead?*' There... I've said it out loud. No... not loudly... just a whisper, and Aidan hears me.

'*I'll never forgive Melissa.*' He puts his hands over his face. '*I bet she was the one who encouraged you to drink those shots.*'

'*I'm not drunk—*'

'*You should try to sleep.*'

'*What if I sleepwalk and Lorraine tries to kill me again with her killer hands? It's a long drop to the hall.*'

'*Stop... stop...*' I've never seen that light in his eyes. Fury. He struggles to speak then shakes his head.

'*Did you hear me, Aidan?*'

'*I heard you,*' he replies. '*You called my mother a killer. She was right about mixing alcohol with your drugs. You're hallucinating—*'

'*Is that what you call the truth?*'

'*Just shut up, Naomi. Shut up! Mum took you in and did so out of concern—*'

'*Even though she suspected I could have been fucking her*

husband?' I hate what I've said, and can tell by his expression that I've crossed a line he's tried to ignore for too long.

'Were you fucking my father?'

I try not to laugh but it bubbles up. Froth, it will choke me. I can't stop. I'm still laughing when he lays me down on the bed and covers me with the duvet.

'Sleep it off,' he says. 'I'm going to try to forget this conversation ever took place.'

He will try and fail. I've destroyed whatever was gentle in our relationship.

I won't sleep tonight. The taste in my mouth disgusts me. Did it taint the things I said to him? Poisonous words planting thoughts in his mind. Aidan... I'm sorry... sorry...

Three days have passed since that night in The Chantry. Aidan is waiting for me to apologise. I can't do it. I didn't mean to call his mother a killer but that doesn't mean it isn't true. I still feel the pressure of her hands on my face that time in Gorgonia's, my nose blocked, my mouth trapped under the cold force of her palm. Her eyes staring into mine, so merciless. The memory wiped out in the trauma of a seizure.

But is that what really happened? Or was I hallucinating, as Aidan believes? And on the landing, when I was lifted high? Was that real or the stuff of dreams? All I know for definite is that my name is not Naomi Nelson and that Lorraine Gordon has forced another identity on me.

He still hasn't told her what I said. If he had, she wouldn't be able to look me in the eye. I've studied the cracks behind her self-assurance. I've heard her breath shorten. Is she as horrified as I am by the pretence she created? Sometimes, I believe she is. Does she suspect that the argument we had was about her? She walks on quicksand and must be aware of how easily she can sink.

She wants to know what happened in The Chantry to put me into such a mood.

'Ask Aidan,' I say.

'It would be easier to ask a sphinx.' *She flutters her eyelashes and smiles.* 'All I know is that he's miserable and you've locked yourself away from us. Whatever went on between the two of you can't be that serious, surely?'

She suspects there is something different about me. It is safer to stay silent.

'You can trust me not to take sides, Naomi.'

I turn away from her and face the wall. Aidan comes again and tries to speak to me. I don't respond... not even a blink... blink.

SIXTY

LORRAINE

The phone call from Lucy Strong came as Lorraine was waiting for the arrival of the new guests. Twelve couples on this occasion.

The desire to ignore her call and allow the answering machine to take her message was balanced by curiosity as to why the Hearts and Vows events' organiser was making contact.

'Congratulations on managing such a successful reopening.' Lucy sounded business-like yet effusive. 'Victor would be very proud of what you've achieved. I must say, your son is doing a stellar job on publicising your forthcoming documentary. How very exciting. I can't wait to see it.'

Aidan had kept up a steady stream of social media content throughout the five days of filming, and was continuing to build up interest in the forthcoming release of *Five Days at Serenity Falls*. Tantalising glimpses of group discussions, the yoga and tai chi sessions, evening walks by the waterfall and the communal dinners, Dominque and Karla arguing, then laughing together, Noel and Felicity glaring at each other, Sheila, her blouse sliding off her shoulders, her bruises visible, and many other images had created a wide-ranging picture gallery. His campaign was obviously attracting the right attention.

'When will the documentary be released?' Lucy asked.

'We haven't settled on a date yet. I would imagine it will be within the next month.'

'Excellent. I'm looking forward to seeing it. As you know, Victor played such an important role at our Hearts and Vows conferences, which must be worth mentioning if the filming is still ongoing.' Lucy paused to allow her hint to settle.

'I'm afraid it's at the editing stage, Lucy.'

'Oh, well, no harm in asking. I hope you'll consider being one of our guest speakers at our conference next May. You might even consider delivering our keynote address.'

'How kind of you to think of me.' The first car came into view on the avenue. Soon it would reach the courtyard. She needed to be at the entrance to greet the couple. 'Would you like to email me with the details? You've caught me at a busy time. We're beginning a new programme and our guests are about to arrive.'

'Absolutely. I'll mail you this afternoon. I'm sorry I wasn't able to contribute to that article about the reopening of Rekindle Connections. I was swamped with meetings on the day the journalist rang and had to cut her short.'

'I wasn't aware you'd been contacted. When was that?'

'About a week or so ago.'

'Who was the journalist?'

'Abigail. I'm afraid I can't remember her second name, though I did meet her previously when she was reporting on Victor's tragic accident. On this occasion, she seemed to believe you and I had met personally. As I've never had that pleasure, I wasn't able to help her with a quote.'

'The interview must have been organised by Aidan. I'll check it out with him.'

'His social media skills are impressive. We must make full use of them for your debut at Hearts and Vows.'

'We certainly will.' Lorraine laughed politely and ended the call.

Aidan was working on his laptop when she entered his office. 'Did you arrange with a journalist called Abigail to write a feature about me?' she asked.

'Not that I can recall,' he said.

'Check back over your press list.'

'Okay.' He scanned the screen and shook his head. 'No one by that name. Why are you asking?'

'Just checking something. How is Naomi this morning?'

'Same as yesterday. She's still refusing to come out of her room.'

'I warned you about taking her to The Chantry.'

'It's got nothing to do with that.' He spoke defensively, and she was too rushed to challenge him any further.

She had heard them coming back from the pub, their raised voices finally falling silent. What had Naomi said to him that caused his expression to be so stricken the following morning? Since then, he had refused to discuss what occurred. His silence was unsettling, as was Naomi's stubborn refusal to answer her questions or leave her room. Something had changed. Control was slipping away from her. It felt physical, this slippage, like the burn of a rope, yet Lorraine was unable to understand what was pulling it from her grasp.

Shaking that thought aside, she hurried towards the front door to greet the first couple. They walked at a polite distance from each other as they climbed the steps. She knew instantly that one was the persuader, the other the persuaded. A glance at their faces told her who was who. This knowledge was stored for further use, while her mind turned over the information that Lucy Strong had so casually tossed to her.

Gangland feuds and killings had kept Victor's name from

the headlines in the aftermath of his death, yet in London a journalist had been interested enough in the circumstances of the crash to interview Lucy.

Where had her feature appeared? If it had been in one of the Irish newspapers she would have seen it. The media monitoring service she used to source any publicity from abroad would have sent the clipping or link to her.

That same journalist had contacted Lucy a second time with the intention of doing a feature on Rekindle Connections. Again, nothing had appeared in print. *Abigail... such a pretty name.* She had only come across it on one other occasion. A face came to mind. A Rekindle guest, nervous and reticent on her arrival. One of the persuaded. Untidy corkscrew curls, her hair such a nondescript shade that Lorraine was unable to remember if she was blonde or mousy-brown. Round-faced and slightly on the plump side, glasses that were unsuitable for the shape of her face. She had said little over the first few days. Lorraine had sensed a deep-rooted nervousness within her and she only seemed to relax towards the end of the programme.

On the final day, the reason for her nervousness was explosively revealed during the wrap-up session in the Chat Room. Infidelity. So many ways to view it. For Karla, it was a recreational pursuit but this woman had dipped her toe into traitorous waters and her husband had left her in no doubt about his reaction. His abusive comments, followed by his tight-lipped fury, had made it impossible for anyone, especially his wife, to reason with him.

Lorraine had lit incense in Room 7 after their stormy departure, clearing the air of negativity and restoring positivity. Was it possible that she had believed in what she was doing? That negativity could so easily be dispersed on the fumes of some obscure scent?

The odds that she was the same woman were not worth considering yet the nagging feeling persisted as Lorraine continued to welcome the guests and settle them into their new environment. The communal dinner was over before she had time to check her records.

How many years had passed since that embarrassing confrontation had taken place? She entered the name *Abigail* into the spread sheet of past guests and it came up immediately. Only one listing.

Abigail Conlon.

Occupation: Filmmaker.

Lorraine held onto her desk as she stood. The shadow that had stalked her since her first meeting with the documentarian had finally caught up with her yet to equate the dynamic persona of Gail Robinson, who wore an outrageously sculpted hairstyle and had an authoritative yet pleasant manner, with that adulterous, hysterical wife was an impossible jump yet she made it effortlessly.

She rang Lucy back. 'Just in reference to the journalist you mentioned, is she a redhead?' she asked.

'If you're asking me if scarlet is her chosen colour, then yes.' Lucy laughed. 'She is most definitely a redhead with attitude.'

Why hadn't Gail revealed her true identity? Why had she contacted Lucy Strong for information on Victor's death? Why had she lied to Lucy about features she never intended to write then or now? The questions continued, each one adding to Lorraine's belief that undercurrents flowing below the surface were moving at a faster momentum. One that would soon become impossible to contain.

SIXTY-ONE

GAIL

Lochanar had the closed-up face of a small tourist town whose main revenue would not return until the spring.

In the harbour, where a flock of seagulls was savagely attacking a discarded beefburger, a fishing trawler lay at anchor, alongside a fleet of smaller boats. One of the tour boats had been docked and was being wheeled towards a boathouse.

The elderly man in charge of the operation barked commands at three younger men who were doing the main work. Gail had difficulty understanding his accent but they followed his instructions with certainty. He nodded at her and touched his index finger to his forehead as he passed her by. His beard was white, a jutting tuft of hair that vibrated every time he spoke.

Rosanna's Redemption was written on the side of the boat. Even if she had not been able to see the name, she would have recognised it from Naomi's drawings. Looking at their concentrated expressions, Gail knew it would be impossible to interrupt them while this delicate operation was underway.

She continued on down the harbour. Kiosks and small offices were closed, their posters of cloudless skies and leaping dolphins fading and blown to ribbons. The kiosk where *Rosanna's Redemption* cruises were booked was equally bleak and empty. She peered through the window but was unable to see anything beyond the counter and a row of shelves with pamphlets.

The door of the boathouse had been pulled down and the seagulls were swooping elsewhere when she left the harbour and drove into the centre of Lochanar. Parking was available on the town square. Here, as on the harbour, some of the boutiques and galleries were shuttered for the season.

An open fire burning in the grate of the Running Stag drew Gail like a magnet, its erratic flames proving it was the genuine thing.

As if she needed further proof, a woman came from behind the bar to fling a log onto the grate and send a smattering of sparks up the chimney.

Gail sat at the counter and ordered a light ale.

'Irish?' The woman handed the foaming glass over the counter and smiled at her.

'Originally, yes. I live in London now.'

'I spent years there myself in my younger days. Loved the vibe, but I was glad enough to return here.'

'Everything seems to move at a much slower pace when I go home,' Gail agreed. 'Yet when I'm in London, I've no sense that I'm living on a fast track.'

'There's some who can cope and some who can't. I got tired of moving through crowds and not recognising a single face. Not much danger of that happening here. Are you hoping to meet up with someone?'

Gail nodded. 'Rosanna Ross. Do you know her?'

'Who doesn't? But I'm afraid you're out of luck. She's in Glasgow visiting her sister.'

'Oh, that's a shame. I was hoping to talk to her about her cruises.'

'Aye, she's made a good success of them. They've stopped for the winter, of course. She'd love to run them year-round but the conditions of the sea loch make that too dangerous.'

'I was down on the harbour and saw her boat being taken out of the water.'

'I heard that was the plan for today. It needs an overhaul after such a busy season.' The woman walked to the other end of the bar to serve a customer and stayed chatting with him for a few minutes.

Gail photographed the bar with its selection of Scotch whiskies and the painting of a massive stag running between trees.

What is Naomi doing now? She was unable to think of anyone else. Her drawings had led Gail to this small town but fitting her into the sea-faring community was difficult. The accents she heard around her had a lilting fullness that emphasised the vowels and added a musical intonation to even the most ordinary conversation. Naomi's accent had proved difficult to pinpoint. It was neutral enough not to have a home. Even the slight American drawl Gail had noticed when they first met had been less pronounced the last time they spoke.

'Have you any idea when Rosanna Ross will be back?' she asked when the bar woman returned.

'I afraid I don't, hen. Is this something that can wait?'

'Yes, it can. Her tour was recommended to me by a friend who visited here some months ago.'

'Word of mouth. The best advertisement of all. Name's Maggie, by the way.'

'Gail.'

'You're welcome to Lochanar, Gail.' She had a firm handshake and darting bird-like eyes that probably sized-up the entire needs of the bar in an instant.

'My friend stayed here,' Gail said. 'You may remember her. It would have been sometime in late May. Tall and blonde, long hair. Here's her photo.'

'Aye, I recognise her all right.' The woman glanced at the screen on Gail's phone. 'I'm glad she recommended our town. It's an undiscovered treasure. We need more people like Rosanna to put us on the tourist map.' She turned her attention towards the door when it swung open. 'And while it's a pity you missed her, here's a man who should be able to help you. Andy, come over here.' She shouted at a customer who had just entered. 'Andy is Rosanna's brother-in-law. He'll be able to give you an update on her travels.'

Gail recognised the older man who had been supervising the transportation of *Rosanna's Redemption* to the boathouse. He hoisted himself up on the stool beside her and offered her his hand. His complexion had the raw sheen of a seasoned sailor.

'Do you remember Eloise?' Maggie poured him a Scotch without being asked and handed it over the counter to him.

'Eloise?' he pushed back his cap and his head. 'Remind me.'

'The two of you had a right session together if memory serves me. Show him the photo on your phone, Gail.'

'The blonde lass?' He squinted at the screen and chuckled. 'Aye, she took a powerful shine to me.'

'Her name's not El—' Gail began but Andy was talking about a woman called Eloise, who had collapsed down by the harbour and his valiant efforts at reviving her. She lost track due to his accent until Maggie slowed him down with another drink.

Eloise... why would Lorraine have used her mother's name when she came here? And what had caused her to collapse?

She felt utterly out of her depth, which was nothing new when it came to understanding Lorraine Gordon.

'Gail was hoping to meet Rosanna,' said Maggie. 'Any idea when she'll be back from Glasgow?'

'Another week at least. She needs a wee break after the season she's had.'

'Will you have the same again?' Gail asked him.

When he nodded, she signalled to Maggie, who busied herself at the dispenser.

'Why don't you and Andy take your drinks over to yon table?' She gestured towards an empty table near the fire. 'There'll be regulars coming in soon who'll think the sky is about to collapse if they see a stranger sitting on the stool that they believe is theirs by God-given right.'

'Do you have family, Andy?' Gail asked, when they were seated.

'Nae. I'm not the marrying kind. Spent most of my early years at sea. Damned if I could find a woman to take me when I found my landlubber legs again.'

'He's a far better grandpa than many around here.' Maggie set another drink on the table for him, along with coffee and a sandwich for Gail. 'The way you look out for Evan's two, not to mention Megan.'

'Aye, when she stands still long enough to be loved,' he replied.

'Who's Megan?' Gail asked.

In reply, he pulled his phone from his pocket and showed her a photograph of a young woman with an abundance of sleek black hair and a Cleopatra-style fringe. The bold stare from her dark-brown eyes brought Victor Gordon instantly to mind. She dismissed the thought immediately yet she found herself taking the photograph from him and studying it intently.

'She's beautiful, Andy,' she said. 'Her eyes are so striking.'

'Aye, she's that and more... and those eyes are always set on the faraway hills.'

'Where is she now?' Gail handed the photograph back to him.

'Peru. Searching for waves, she told me before she took off.

She's a fair judge of the big ones and the surfing is good there, I'm told.'

The sudden rush of excitement Gail had experienced faded as quickly as it came. 'I've heard that, too, Andy. But Peru is a long way to go for a wave, no matter how big?'

'Distance is nothing to that young one,' he said. 'She's had itchy feet since she first started to walk.'

'She's a heartless lass,' said Maggie. 'Not a word to Rosanna since she took off.'

'Harsh words were spoken then,' he replied.

'Harsh words can be forgiven.' Maggie spoke sharply. 'But silence never solved anything. Better get back to my station,' she said, when her name was called. 'The natives are getting restless.'

'When did Megan go to Peru?' Gail asked when they were alone again.

'Och, I canna recall.' Andy's hand shook as he raised the glass to his lips. 'Early summer sometime. She and Rosanna were like two fleas looking for the same crease in a bed and always hopping off each other. Started when she was eighteen. London first, then Australia and the States.'

'She sounds like an adventurous young woman.'

'Just like Candice.'

'Is Candice her sister?'

He idled with his glass, rolling it between his gnarled hands, before taking another sip. She waited out his silence. No sense in hurrying him along.

'Her mother.' His eyes, clouded by cataracts, closed briefly as he shook his head. 'She was my bonnie bairn.'

'Your bairn?' Gail asked. 'Do you mean your daughter?'

'She was my brother's lass.'

'Where is she now?'

'In the ground.' His face crumpled as if his admission had caused his facial muscles to collapse.

'I'm sorry.'

'Aye, indeed.'

'Was that long ago?'

'Not long enough to heal the cut in my heart.'

He seemed content to sit in silence. She suspected that that was his usual form when drinking, yet he must have talked to Lorraine if his coy comment about her taking a 'shine' to him had any validity.

She partially opened the window beside her. The welcoming chill of the evening forced his attention back to her.

'I'm sorry—' she began, but he waved her sympathy aside.

'Will you take a dram with me?' he asked.

'I will indeed.'

He caught Maggie's attention and raised two fingers.

'I'm hoping to meet another young woman while I'm here.' Gail checked the gallery on her phone and showed him the shot she had taken of Naomi through the window of the Silver Falls café. 'Do you know her.'

He glanced at the screen and shook his head. 'Nae. Can't say I've ever seen her. She looks thin enough to scare the crows. Not a local, that's for sure. What do you say, Maggie?'

Maggie set the drinks on the table and took the phone from him. 'Such thin shoulders,' she remarked. 'Is she ill?'

'She's recovering from a car accident.'

'Poor bairn. What makes you think she's from around here.'

'Something Eloise said. She gave me the photograph and told me to look her up but I've forgotten her name.'

Maggie rubbed her hand across her forehead as she looked back at the photo. 'She's definitely not local but there's something...'

'Something?'

'If I could see her face more clearly it'd come to me.'

'I know it's not a good photo. It was taken from an awkward angle and it's the only one I have.' She thought bitterly about the footage that had been deleted from her documentary and, also, the photographs taken outside Silver Falls, all at Lorraine's insistence.

Would their reaction be any different if they saw Naomi confronting Terence Graham, her thin face taut with rage but each feature clearly visible?

Maggie handed the phone back to her and returned to the bar.

'What happened to Eloise on the harbour?' Gail asked.

'Landlubber legs,' Andy replied.

'Did she stay here long?'

'A day or so. She'd a blether with Rosanna in the graveyard so that must have been on a Sunday.' Unable to keep his eyes open, he lowered his chin and sank into a reverie.

'He'll be like that 'til I close up,' Maggie said, when she came to clear away the glasses. 'There was a time he could drink the bar dry and walk home with a steady step. Age... age... we should be grateful for it, but it's one hell of a taskmaster.'

'Would it be possible to stay the night here?'

'Och, aye. You can choose any room you want.'

Andy was still snoozing when she left him. Her room was warm and comfortable. She sat by the window and looked down on the street. Most of the buildings were in darkness. Downstairs, Maggie was calling last orders. *It will be impossible to sleep*, she thought, as she lay down. Too many thoughts pushing for space in her mind.

But when she opened her eyes, the sun was up and Maggie had laid out her breakfast on the same table. The fire was still burning. The smell of stale beer mingled with smoke was strong but not unpleasant.

'I close the dining room when the season ended,' Maggie said. 'This is cosier.' At Gail's request, she had prepared scrambled eggs and toast. 'Are you sure you wouldn't like some fried tatties with that?' she asked. 'It's a skimpy breakfast to start the day on.'

'I usually only have black coffee for breakfast,' said Gail. 'This is a feast.'

'It's no wonder you're built like a greyhound.' Maggie laughed and poured coffee for her.

'Did Andy stay long after I left?'

'He cleared off shortly after. He's like a dog without a bone when Rosanna's not around.'

'Is she worried about her granddaughter?'

'She wasn't at first. But Candice's anniversary was last week and Megan still didn't get in touch. That upset her a lot. Megan's headstrong and they were very cross with each other when she took off, but she always contacts Rosanna on that date, no matter where she is in the world.'

'What about Rosanna's husband? What does he think?'

'It's a long time since he thought about anything. He left her when she was pregnant on Candice. Evan was barely a year old. Couldn't cope with the stress and headed off to God knows where. He drowned some years later. Took a swim from a beach in California and never came out of the water.'

'How awful.'

'Awful for those who were left. It took Rosanna seven years to be recognised as his widow but she was lost in herself for a good part of that time. She pulled herself together and bought the boat with his insurance money. Hence the name. It kept her sane when Candice... but all that's behind her now. If only Megan would get in touch, she'd be content. That's one of her sketches.'

Maggie pointed towards a framed drawing that hung on the opposite wall.

Boats on the harbour, seagulls swooping.

Gail's hand shook so much she had to put her cup down.

'Is Megan still in Peru?' she asked.

'Either there or somewhere else in South America. Surfing and waiting tables, that's her lifestyle. She does portraits – sets up her easel on the pavement to make some extra money. She gets by but Rosanna wants her to settle down. I think she's afraid of her going the same way as Candice.'

'Andy told me about her.'

'Poor man. He's still heartbroken over losing her but life goes on. Can I get you anything else?'

'Just my bill. I've a long drive ahead of me.'

'Give Eloise my regards when you see her. She was troubled when she was here. How is she now?'

'What makes you think she was troubled?'

'The look in her eyes. She was haunted by something but managing to cover it up well enough to fool the others.'

'You don't miss much.'

'Even if she hadn't fainted on the harbour, you get a sixth sense about people's troubles when you run a bar.'

Down on the harbour, a piper was busking for a charity. His kilt swerved in the October wind but he seemed oblivious to the cold as he played his bagpipes to the passers-by. Gail recognised the tune but was unable to name it.

The door of the boathouse was open. Parking nearby, she walked to the entrance of a cavernous interior where *Rosanna's Redemption* rested on a massive plinth.

'Can I help you?' A man approached her from a workshop at the back of the boathouse. 'This is private property and dangerous if you don't know the ropes.'

'I've been photographing the harbour.' Gail held up her camera. 'Do you mind if I take some shots of the boat?'

'Are you the lass who stayed at the Stag last night and had a dram with my uncle?'

'Yes, that was me.'

'He's nursing a cruel hangover this morning.' He laughed and waved his hand at the boat. 'Not a lot worth photographing right now but she'll be a rare beauty when we finish with her.'

She was unable to take her eyes off him. 'Do you work on the boat with Rosanna?'

'Yes. I'm at the controls. Andy said you're friends with the woman who fainted a few months back after one of the tours.'

'Eloise, yes. She recommended Rosanna's cruise.'

'Glad to hear she bore no ill will. She took a hard knock when she collapsed.'

'You were there?'

'On the spot. She looked across at me and that was it. She went out like a light. Doesn't say a lot for my fatal attraction with the opposite sex.'

His dark eyes gleamed with good humour as he remembered.

'I'm Gail.' She held out her hand. 'You must be Evan.'

'That's me. You told Andy you were hoping to organise a group trip on the boat sometime in May. It's a good month for spotting whales so you're right to book early. We've had a few sightings and we're hoping that'll improve.'

'I'm sorry I missed your mother but Andy was good company. I was also sorry to hear about your sister and your father.'

'Secrets don't stick around for long in this town. Who was blethering about them?'

'It came up in conversation last night. Andy became quite emotional talking about Candice.'

'He loved her, as I did, even though she made it hard to do so. I think about her every day.'

If he was surprised by the intimacy of their conversation, he showed no signs of it. 'The only thing I've learned from my father's disappearance is the importance of family and the heartache it causes when that is trampled on. We were fortunate that Andy was more than able to fill his space.'

'It's sad that his body was never recovered.'

'It happens all the time.' He shrugged. 'The oceans are deep and, unlike here, they keep their secrets.' He fiddled with his phone then held it out to her. 'I discovered this a few years back. Some paper in the States put their archival material online. It included a report of his drowning. That's the only picture I have of him, apart from a wedding photo in Maggie's album, which my mother would rip to pieces if she knew it existed.'

The young man in a T-shirt and jeans had been photographed with a group of surfers outside an ice-cream parlour. Surfboards were stacked against the wall and one of the women was holding an old-fashioned transistor radio on her shoulder.

A hank of dark hair hung over his eyes and his hand was raised, as if to protect himself from the camera.

Aidan, she thought. *He's the image of Aidan, except for his colouring.*

That was when she knew. The truth delivered with a slick shove that pummelled her heart so hard she instinctively pressed her hands to her chest.

'The newspaper claimed he entered the water an hour later.' Evan didn't seem to notice her shocked reaction. 'He was never seen again.'

Her phone rang. Stepping outside with a muttered apology when she saw Lorraine's name on the screen, she took her call.

A letter from Terence Graham's solicitor had been delivered by courier to Serenity Falls. It outlined the actions that would be taken by the law firm if Gail dared to include any reference to their client in her forthcoming documentary.

The strains of the bagpipes added to the pressure in her head. She pressed a finger to her ear to soften the sound.

'We must meet and decide what to do,' Lorraine said. 'How soon can you come here?'

'Hopefully, I'll be able to organise an early flight for tomorrow,' Gail said. 'I don't believe Terence Graham has a legal leg to stand on. His contract was water-tight.'

'Forget Terence and his threats.' Lorraine sounded terse. 'I'd like to see what you've done with the documentary so far. Aidan's social media campaign is paying off and we're having a substantial number of enquiries about the programme.'

'The editing is quite advanced,' she said. 'I believe you'll like the result.'

'That's wonderful to hear. What time shall I expect you?'

'Hopefully, late afternoon. I'll rent a car at the airport and book a room in Potters Glen. I've no problem staying overnight, if necessary.'

'You're welcome to stay here again.'

'Thanks, Lorraine. That sounds perfect.'

The sheer normality of their conversation made it even more difficult to believe what she had uncovered in Lochanar. Should she go to the police and present them with the evidence she had acquired? But what if she was making a ghastly mistake... what then? It was possible that Megan Ross really *was* in Peru, surfing confidently to shore on a wave of gigantic proportions. One that would drown Gail if her suspicions turned out to be nothing more than a coincidence. No one who saw the photograph she showed them had recognised Naomi. Even Evan had shaken his head. A face in profile and slightly blurred, sharp shoulder blades jutting: how could anyone who knew Megan Ross equate her with the fragile figure Gail had photographed?

The drawing Maggie had pointed out to her in the bar had the skilled sweep of a professional hand, unlike Naomi's sketches, which were undeniably similar, but were more like the work of an amateur.

She thought back to the libel action Lorraine had taken against *Capital Eye* when Carl wrote his slanderous report on Rekindle Connections and how the case was only settled on the steps of the courts moments before it was due to go for trial. According to Carl, Lorraine had been the driving force in their demand for retribution.

What would he do under these circumstances? *Control the story. Own it. Dig deeper and sieve the muck until it runs clear. No lumps.*

The piper nodded his thanks at her when she passed him and dropped a pound into his collection box. Cancer was his charity of choice. She remembered the name of the tune now. 'The Skye Boat Song.' Snippets of the words came to her, *bonnie boat* and something about a *bird on a wing*... the words would follow her all the way from Lochanar to Potters Glen.

SIXTY-TWO

LORRAINE

Earlier, before speaking to Gail, Lorraine had contacted Matthew Conlon, her ex-husband. Looking again at the records of guests who had undertaken the programme, she had discovered that he was a member of *An Garda Siochána,* but he was no ordinary police officer on the beat. He was a specialist investigator who probed the slimy world of the dark web.

She had checked social media for traces of him. Whatever direction his personal life had taken, he had not been prepared to share it with the public. In contrast, Gail Robinson's social media profile was slick and professional. No traces of the distraught, weeping woman Lorraine remembered. Her phone number would be different to the one on record, but perhaps Matthew's was still the same.

To her surprise, that turned out to be the case, and he had answered after a few rings.

'Conlon here.' He had spoken abruptly, as if his calls were only made and taken to impart and receive information.

'Matthew, it's Lorraine Gordon. I don't know if you remember me—'

'I remember you.' His surprise had been evident but she also detected his hostility. 'What's the purpose of your call?'

'I'm looking through our old records and came across your number. I remember the unfortunate circumstances under which—'

'Unfortunate is not a word I'd choose. Eye-opening would be more appropriate.'

'Whatever you say, Matthew. I regret that our programme failed you. As you may have heard, my husband died—'

'Yes. Please accept my condolences.' Despite his expression of sympathy, she was conscious of his impatience. *He must be at home*, she thought, as a child began to cry.

'I've never forgotten the distress experienced by you and Abigail,' she said. 'Nothing like that had ever happened on the programme before, nor, thankfully, since then. But I've reopened Rekindle Connections and I'm anxious to learn from that incident. In an effort not to make the same mistake again, I wonder if I could enquire how you and Abigail—'

'—divorced?' He brusquely interrupted her.

'I'm sorry.'

'But you're hardly surprised.'

'Saddened, Matthew, particularly as it was Victor's counsel that precipitated it. He believed in honesty at all costs and I'm not so sure Abigail was well served by him.'

'Your husband was only a minor part of a bigger problem. I'd suspected Sheridan—' He had stopped abruptly and shouted at someone to lower a television that was playing in the background.

'Sheridan?' In the sudden silence that followed, his name came at her like a hammer blow. 'Are you referring to Carl Sheridan?'

'What if I am? It hardly matters now.'

'You're wrong, Matthew.' Once again she felt that swaying

sensation and the nausea that came with it. 'It matters hugely to me. Are you talking about the journalist?'

'Yes, we are.'

'Am I to believe Abigail was having an affair with him?'

'What exactly do you want from me, Lorraine?' His snapped question had suggested he was on the verge of ending the call.

'We received very negative publicity from Carl Sheridan after your and Abigail's departure.' She pressed two fingers to the gap between her eyebrows and inhaled deeply. 'I often wondered what the link was. Now I know it was your wife who was responsible for the nonsense he wrote then, and continued to tweet, until his death.'

'My ex-wife. But she had nothing to do with that drivel. Sheridan was a man who carried a grudge. And he wasn't the only one with a grudge, as he discovered to his cost. Why exactly are you ringing me, Lorraine?'

'I was anxious to know how your life turned out after you left Serenity Falls.'

'My wife... *Donna*... has just given birth to our third baby and I'm a very happily married man. A fairy tale ending, you could call it, but not exactly the one you would have anticipated.'

'Do you know how I can contact Abigail?'

'I doubt if she'd want to hear from you.'

'She can always hang up. I'd like to talk to her.'

The phone number he gave her matched the one she had for Gail Robinson. She was not surprised to recognise it, yet having it confirmed had only added to her fury.

'If you do manage to contact her, call her Gail,' he said. 'She abbreviated her name along with her marriage.' His laughter was as brittle as their conversation.

'You've obviously moved on.' She managed to speak quietly.

'As she has. Time heals. That's such a cliché but it's true. I wouldn't say she and I are friends but we've learned to be civil to each other.' He laughed mirthlessly and hung up.

How had she allowed herself to be so deluded? That warning prickle of recognition... how many times had she ignored it throughout the time Gail had been filming? She longed to crawl into bed. The foetal position was the only one that would work.

Was Carl Sheridan's death the reason Gail Robinson had approached her? Was her documentary merely a decoy that had allowed her to poke and prod the truth from others, while all that time she was seeking a path that would lead her from that derelict cottage to Serenity Falls? What had she discovered during her time at Serenity Falls? What truth did she believe she possessed?

Lorraine was unable to answer those questions but one thing was certain. Gail Robinson, who was once Abigail Conlon, had returned to the marriage retreat for reasons that breathed danger. She had made a documentary about love without understanding its murderous demands. What did she know of the price Lorraine had paid for loving too much?

Victor's death had removed that yoke, but settled another heavier and more deadly one on her shoulders.

Gail must have been out in the open when she answered Lorraine's call – a gusting wind, blowing hard, had made her difficult to hear. Also that background music, hauntingly familiar. Bagpipes, no mistaking their pitch or the tune being played. The song learned in school... *loud the winds howl, loud the waves roar, thunderclaps rend the air...*

Music of the mind, that's all it was. Her imagination transporting her back to the harbour at Lochanar, that same swirl as the sky spun and dark clouds descended.

SIXTY-THREE

NO NAME GIRL

I go out walking when they are working. Leaves rustle underfoot, trailing gold and copper across my path. I study the sculptures Victor Gordon did on the stumps of fallen trees: an eagle in flight, a vixen at play with her cubs. In the garden at the back of Rosanna's house, he'd carved the stump of a fallen tree into an eagle. It had disintegrated by the time I was born but I'd seen it in old photographs. His skill had grown since those early years. I stop to study a stag's head with antlers.

That's when I remember the Running Stag and Maggie phoning me yet again, asking me to collect Andy, who was too drunk to walk the short distance to his home. Grizzled and belligerent and as soft as putty underneath it all, he loved me and wanted me to stay still for long enough to be at ease with myself.

My memories come at me like reels of a film. I see myself in London, nightclubs and concerts, working in cafés and drawing on pavements. I remember a man called Nathan who I loved for a mad three weeks. And other men, Lachlan, Malcolm, Jack, Finn – none were serious. Buds that never opened. Only when I met Aidan did it happen. Love, coming at me like a thief and stealing my senses.

Aidan does not know how I feel. We came home from the Chantry and all he heard were the cruel taunts about his mother that I flung at him. He will never realise that another truth was hidden behind my fury.

If I'd known in the beginning that he was my half-uncle, would it have made a difference? No wonder Lorraine was panicking. She saw it happen. After all, she is an expert on love. She understands how easily it can fly in the wrong direction and she knew right from the beginning that I could never be in love with her son. Consanguinity. Blood will out.

Victor Gordon's name is the brightest reel of all. I remember him clearly now, with no confusion or scattered thoughts, no gaps. What I see is a journey I undertook with the deliberate intention of righting a wrong so buried in the past that it no longer had an identity. How ironic that in doing so, my own identity was wiped from me... until now.

No more surges. My story now has a beginning, a middle and an end. When I think about him, he comes to me in the past tense and I know that I'm reaching the end of my search.

Anita contacted me again. She'd found something else that belonged to my mother and wanted to pass it on to me.

The sculpture she gave me was made of wood, a sturdy-backed Clydesdale horse, exquisitely sculpted, from its knotted mane to its shaggy feet. The American gave it to Candice along with the CD, she said. She'd forgotten about it until she cleared out the bedroom where Candice used to sleep and found it.

In his book, Victor Gordon wrote about the importance of a hobby. Something that could lift the mind to another dimension and silence its clamour. His hobby was wood carving. It was a clue, slight and easy to overlook, but I was convinced of its importance.

I returned to Lochanar and entered the kirk where my great-grandfather once preached. Rosanna believed her father's intolerance was only equalled by his belief that guilt and repentance formed the steps to heaven. The kirk is a gentler place these days and the air of serenity that settles over all who enter, especially when it's empty, never fails to calm me. On this occasion calmness was not an option when I compared Max Ross's signature on his marriage certificate to the one in the book Victor Gordon had signed for me.

To be certain, I sent a copy of the certificate and the flyleaf with his signature to a handwriting expert. Her verdict came back. The two signatures belonged to the same person.

How was it possible that this 'love guru' with his mesmeric eyes was my grandfather? He'd polished away any resemblances he once had to the gauche young husband in Maggie's photo gallery yet, once I discovered the truth, I saw the man behind the façade.

My hatred towards him grew like bindweed. How dare he speak of love and commitment? Of truth as the edifice of marriage? I wanted to tear it all down and rent his false life asunder.

On my visits home I left the book with his photo on the cover on the dining table and on any other surface where Rosanna would see it. She didn't even give it a second glance. How would she have reacted if she had discovered what I intended to do?

'Did you ever miss Max?' I asked her. 'Did you ever mourn him?'

'I shed my tears after he left and had none to spare when he drowned,' she replied. 'My only regret about his death was that I never had a chance to dance on his bones.'

She had that closed-up expression she always got when his

name was mentioned. What was I stirring? A hornets' nest that would be better left intact?

'What if Max was still around?' I asked. 'What would you say to him?'

'Will you stop your blethering?' she said. 'His life insurance bought my first boat and put me on my feet. My widow's allowance puts bread on the table. If he appeared before me this minute, I'd tell him to go back to hell and stay there.'

Some memories never grow gentler with time. Before I returned to London she offered me a future chasing dolphins and whales. The wind whipped the waves into a frenzy when I refused and told her I was going to Peru, where the waves are a surfer's challenge and the wildness in me would be satisfied.

I leave the woods and walk back to Serenity Falls. A tree sculpture of a boy and girl at play carries his chiselled mark. On their hunkers they are playing marbles or a game with a ball, rolling him back to Lochanar and the children he left behind.

SIXTY-FOUR

GAIL

Inside Serenity Falls, all seemed quiet until Gail's ear adjusted to a low murmur from the Chat Room. She recognised the voice of Martina, one of the relationship counsellors, who specialised in emotionally focused therapy. The low clack of Aidan's laptop sounded from his office. Familiar sounds, yet Serenity Falls felt different, as if the walls with their tasteful, relaxing hues were merely shields to hide the secrets behind them.

Pamela emerged from the main office to welcome her. 'I'm delighted you're back,' she said. 'Things have been rather strained since you left.'

'In what way?'

'Hard to tell. Aidan took Naomi out to meet his friends in The Chantry and, apparently, it was a disaster. Naomi was quite sick afterwards. Alcohol doesn't mix with her medication so she didn't need to drink much before it had an impact on her. She's hardly been out of her room since.'

'I'm sorry to hear that. I'm hoping to see her while I'm here.'

'I'll tell her you've arrived. That might cheer her up. I've heard of lovers' quarrels, but she and Aidan have been at logger-heads since that night.'

'You think they're lovers?'

'Not it the physical sense, but there's a strong attraction between them. It's been there from the beginning. Haven't you noticed?'

'I suspected so, yes. What does Lorraine think about it?'

'It's hard to know what's going on in Lorraine's mind. We were once so close. I never believed that could change but it did. Probably not surprising, considering the death of Victor. It's had a massive impact on her, understandably. As for that creep, Terence Graham, with his threatening letter... that's really upset her. I've never seen her so tense.'

The number seven was written on the door Pamela opened. She stood aside for Gail to enter the bedroom she had shared with Matthew for five turbulent days and nights.

She hesitated only briefly before stepping inside. Was there a snap as her last link to Matthew was broken? If so, Gail was too far removed from her past to hear it.

Driving from Lochanar, she had believed she had stumbled on the truth, yet the nearer she had come to Serenity Falls, the more outrageous it seemed. Her only certainty was that Lorraine Gordon had gone to that small, remote town seeking information before returning home and identifying the young woman with no name as Naomi Nelson.

She would have expected her to die. According to Aidan, end-of-life discussions had been held but the spark within Naomi had prevented the plug being pulled. How panicked Lorraine must have been as she grew stronger and eventually regained consciousness. Then, the relief of realising that her memory was lost. No wonder she brought her to Serenity Falls. Control – it was all about maintaining control of a narrative that Lorraine was determined to maintain at whatever cost.

Gail was no longer in any doubt that Lorraine Gordon with her swaying hair and persuasive smile was capable of diabolical deceptions. Naomi Nelson, who could be Megan Ross, was being held prisoner in Serenity Falls. Her bindings were soft and undetectable. Only someone like Gail, who was being haunted by a ghostly voice that had been cut off in mid-sentence by a rusted knife, would notice them.

Lorraine was on the phone in her office when Gail came downstairs.

'I appreciate you agreeing to meet me at such short notice, Jennifer.' Gail, overhearing the conversation, hesitated at the door. 'It's vital that there are no more delays.' Lorraine ended the call on this emphatic note and gestured at Gail to enter.

'Welcome back to Serenity Falls.' Her tone softened as she stood, then gestured towards a chair and waited until Gail was seated before sitting down again. 'I'm looking forward to seeing what you've done – especially that exchange between Sheila and Terence Graham.'

'I hope the letter hasn't upset you too much.'

'His solicitor can send as many threatening letters as he likes.' Lorraine brushed aside the suggestion with a dismissive wave. She was as impeccably made-up as always but her cheeks were too highly blushed and the dark-red lipstick she wore gave an unsettling hardness to her mouth. 'He can't deny his own words and actions. If he meant to frighten me, he was seriously mistaken. I've no intention of interfering with your documentary and will back you one hundred percent when it's released.'

'That's reassuring to hear.' Pamela must have been mistaken. Whatever was worrying Lorraine, it was not Terence Graham.

'He signed a watertight contract that allows you editorial control over the footage and was arrogant enough to believe he would play the starring role,' Lorraine continued. 'Thanks to Naomi, we now have a different ending.'

'How is she? Pamela says she's hardly been out of her room.'

'Unfortunately, Pamela's right. Naomi was making good progress and this is a setback, though not unexpected, according to her neurosurgeon. Professor Shannon believes that Naomi will have problems figuring out what's real and what is fabricated if she ever begins to remember her past. She's just had an episode like that, and it's left her... troubled.'

'Tell her I was asking after her,' Gail said.

'I will, of course. Now, let me see what you've done.'

Gail switched on her laptop and brought up the file. 'It still needs tweaking but this is a rough idea of what the documentary will look like when it's finished.'

Lorraine watched in silence, nodding now and again, and making notes at certain points. She stiffened as she watched the footage of the scene in the dining room with Terence unfold. Gail had worked hard at creating a seamless account that focused on the confrontation between husband and wife; one that culminated in Terence's attack on her. The documentary, ending with the renewal ceremony between Karla and Dominique, offered a soft focus to what had gone before.

'I intend showing it to the solicitor I use to legally vet all my documentaries.' Gail closed her laptop and sat back to wait for Lorraine's reaction. 'He's very thorough and I trust his judgement.'

Lorraine nodded in agreement. 'I like what you've done so far.' She paused and picked up the pen she had been using to write the notes. Tapping it against the desk, she created a beat that soon became as irritating as it was rhythmic. 'I only have one issue.' She tapped faster. 'You never included the waterfall in any of the shoots. It's such an essential backdrop to Serenity Falls.'

'I considered it before I did the interview with you but decided it would be too noisy.'

'For an interview, yes. But as a standalone shot, a motif, it would add greatly to the atmosphere of the documentary.'

'I'm not sure...'

'It's what I'd like, Gail. The forecast is clear for tomorrow morning. You can get some wonderful shots from the summit and from below. It shouldn't be difficult to incorporate them into the documentary.' She waited for Gail to reply, the pen poised in mid-air.

'No, it won't be difficult,' Gail agreed. 'In fact, it's not a bad idea.'

'If you shoot from the base of the cliff, you can use the bridge over the river as a vantage point.' She laid the pen down and linked her fingers together. 'But for sheer spectacle, you could try the promontory on the summit. It definitely offers the most dramatic view.'

'You can show me—'

'Unfortunately, I won't be here. I've an appointment with my solicitor. It's a personal matter and nothing to do with the documentary. And while I'm with Jennifer, I'll ask her to point me towards a solicitor who deals with the film industry. Better to have two legal heads to deal with Terence Graham.'

'I agree.'

'I'm satisfied with what you've done so far. We'll have to organise a reception to publicise it. Are you happy to launch it at Serenity Falls?'

'Absolutely. It's the perfect location.'

'Leave the organisation to us. It's Pamela's domain.' She held out her hand. 'You won't be here when I return from Dublin so I'll say goodbye now. I look forward to seeing the documentary in its entirety.'

The hall was empty when Gail left the office. She heard voices from the Chat Room where guests were relaxing between sessions.

She knocked on Aidan's office and entered the small room.

'Good to see you again.' He crossed the floor in a rush and embraced her. 'I can't wait to see the documentary.'

'It's still a work in progress. I've just shown it to Lorraine and will send you a file. How is Naomi? Pamela said the two of you had an argument.'

'A stupid one,' he admitted. 'I took her out to meet some friends but I didn't take care of her.'

'Don't you believe she can take care of herself? Naomi is stronger than she looks.'

'Not that night.'

'It's hard to imagine the two of you arguing.'

'When drink talks it's either balderdash or hurtful truths. In her case, I'm not sure what category fits. She hates Lorraine. She made that perfectly clear.'

'What did she say?'

'I'd rather not talk about it. She's hardly come out of her room since. I keep checking on her and encouraging her to eat. She won't even open her door, let alone talk to me.'

Whatever had split them apart was bitter enough to shatter the fragile relationship they had established.

'Maybe she'll speak to me. I know Lorraine is sensitive about the privacy of the Nook—'

'It's my home, also, Gail. If you can persuade Naomi to talk to you, then please try. I'm very worried about her. The way she behaved...' He stopped and rubbed his hand across his forehead. 'I think she's beginning to remember things and when she started drinking, everything she's going through became even more confusing.'

'Tell me what she said, Aidan.'

'I don't want this to get back to my mother.'

'I promise it won't.'

'She accused Lorraine of wanting to hurt her... or worse.'

'I can understand why you're upset. People say the most ridiculous things when they're drunk.' *They also speak the truth,* Gail thought. The fear she was trying to keep at a distance swept away any lingering doubts.

'I know they do. I keep hoping she'll apologise and we can move on from that night. I thought we were friends... or even more than that—' His phone rang and distracted him from whatever he had intended to say. 'If you talk to her, tell her I care. Her bedroom is the middle one.'

The living area inside the Nook was empty. Swiftly, Gail crossed to the bedrooms.

The middle door was locked. No sounds came from within when Gail tapped on the door. If Naomi was awake and listening, she gave no indication that she had heard her or that she saw the note Gail slipped under the door.

Back in her room, she sent a copy of the documentary file to Aidan and did some further editing. A light knock on the door startled her. Opening it, she was surprised when Naomi slid past her into the room.

Breathing heavily, as if she had been running, she collapsed onto the edge of the bed.

'I heard you in the Nook,' she said. 'But I was afraid Lorraine would find you there. She's constantly checking on me.'

'Did she see you going up the stairs?'

'I've found another way out of the Nook.' She glanced back at the door and whispered. 'I don't have to go through the hall.'

She could not have afforded to lose weight yet she looked thinner than before, and there was a jitteriness about her that was new.

'Aidan says you've had an argument.'

'I said terrible things to him. Now, he thinks I'm crazy.'

'He doesn't think that...' Gail paused before drawing a deep breath and speaking the name that had been tormenting her since her visit to Lochanar... '*Megan*.'

'*Megan?*' She repeated her name with such wonder that Gail felt her throat constrict. 'How did you find out?'

No wonder she had remained in her room. One look at her expression would have alerted Lorraine that the masquerade was over.

'Let me show you some photographs first. Then we'll talk.'

Megan's eyes widened as she stared at an image of *Rosanna's Redemption* being hoisted from the loch. She nodded at another image with Evan standing outside the boathouse and one of Maggie behind the bar. Her tears came when she saw the jut of Andy's white beard, a glass raised in his hand.

'Were you going to expose Victor Gordon when the accident happened?' Gail took the prints back from her and pulled a chair around to face her. 'Tell me everything you remember.'

SIXTY-FIVE

MEGAN

Gail brought the final pieces back from Lochanar for me to assemble. I recognise my voice now. It has the softness of a burr yet it's tinged with the echoes of places I have been: London, New York, Sydney... There should have been a few phrases of Spanish in the mix, but I allowed myself to be side-tracked by a mystery I needed to solve.

The letter I sent to my grandfather scared him enough to contact me by email, with an arrangement to meet at a Dublin hotel. I flew from London and travelled light, just the clothes I'd need for an overnight stay, along with my wallet, flight details, phone and passport.

At Dublin Airport I took the shuttle bus into the city. I'd hours to spare before we met. I kept rehearsing what I'd say to him then changed my mind a few minutes later.

On O'Connell Street, I sat on the steps of a statue. Daniel O'Connell loomed above me with his cloak and angels, and surveyed the street that was named after him. He did good deeds. Many people believe my grandfather was also a man of action. I ate a burger and drank a takeaway coffee.

The man who sat beside me said his name was Justin. He had the dazed look of someone who seldom ventured into sunlight. I moved slightly away from him when he rubbed his shoulder against mine.

'Sorry... sorry.' He hitched his offending shoulder and stared at my half-eaten burger. 'If you're not going to finish it, miss...'

I handed it over to him and he downed it in a few ravenous bites.

'American?' he asked.

'What makes you think that?'

'Your effing accent. Sure you'd know the yanks a mile off.'

'South Carolina,' I replied as my lying grandfather must have done so many times.

He laughed and burst into song, his voice out-of-tune as he sang about Carolina in all its morning glory.

Where did he hear a song that belonged to family parties and elderly relatives?

He had the sloped resignation of an addict and I wondered about his story.

He offered to show me around Dublin if I gave him enough money for a hostel. He took the twenty euro note I offered him and nodded when I refused his invitation.

We parted amicably but, later, as I cut through a laneway on my way to the hotel where Victor had arranged to meet me, Justin was waiting. A knife at my throat. He said Americans were loaded with dough and I wouldn't miss what he took from me... which was everything.

People hurried past at the top of the lane. Too fast to see what was happening within its shadows, and when he ran past them with my backpack, no one noticed him.

I found my way to the hotel and met my grandfather for the first time. My mugging helped us over that initial awkwardness. He ushered me into his room where he washed away the blood that trickled from my neck. I hadn't realised Justin had pricked the skin with his knife before he took my backpack.

My passport was probably floating on the Liffey, my grandfather said, and my sim card must be blocked before my personal information could be hacked. He made phone calls to prevent this happening and ordered food from room service.

Everything I needed to say to him was forgotten as I gave way to the authority and compassion in his voice. As had happened before, it was easy to believe I was the only person in the world who mattered to him.

Did he recognise me from our meeting at the motivational conference? His expression gave no hint of it. The vibrancy I had seen in him on that occasion had drained away and there was a waxiness to his skin.

I told him about Candice. The orphanage and the heroin, and the men she loved briefly before discarding them, as she'd discarded me. Tears rolled down his cheeks as he described meeting her in London when she was selling her jewellery at the Christmas market. He was there for a conference and saw her name on a poster in a shop window. He remembered Rosanna telling him that if they had a girl she would call her Candice. He had known as soon as he saw his daughter's tumbling hair and dark eyes that she was his.

Twice he saw her before returning to his other life. All he had to carry back from those meetings was the briefest of indifferent glances from her.

It was after midnight when I left him. He had booked a room for me next door to his own. I stared out of the window at the Liffey as it flowed like a multi-coloured ribbon through the night city.

To my surprise, an hour or so later, he knocked on my door and begged me to let him in. He still needed to talk... so much talking through those early hours. He had been trapped in a marriage he never wanted. Nineteen and restless, and Rosanna's *love was not enough to keep him by her side. He went to California where he planned his disappearance. A merman who ventured into Davy Jones's locker and emerged victorious. A new identity and the self-belief that he could see into people's hearts. He could touch their grief. Comfort them. Give them new eyes with which to view themselves.*

He never intended to marry again. No commitments – until Lorraine took his skills and moulded them into Rekindle Connections.

Did he love her? He considered my question then shook his head. He depended on her... and used her. This last statement sounded like a confession and he blinked as if hearing himself for the first time.

He told me about his son, about how hard he tried to love Aidan, but that all he could ever see was the first son he abandoned. Lorraine once told him it was easier to pretend love than to understand its absence but he was sure that Aidan knew, somehow, he was second-hand material. The gulf between them had grown so wide it was impossible to bridge.

He was dying. That was what he told me next. His heart was failing him. I recognised the signs then, the bluish hue to his lips, subtle yet recognisable when the reason had been revealed. He'd made a new will. His house would belong to Rosanna.

I was familiar with Serenity Falls from social media. What would Rosanna do with such a house? She belonged to the loch, not to orchards and crashing waterfalls. He spread his will before me and asked me to read it. His eyes were as dulled as sunbleached pebbles. He'd take that document to his solicitor as soon as he returned home, he told me.

I asked about Lorraine, this woman who believed she was his wife. How would she react when she discovered she was homeless?

He shrugged and said I was to leave that to him to sort out.

All he asked from me was to allow him to tell her the truth in his own time.

We were exhausted from talking and it was easy to believe him.

In the morning he was still sitting beside my bed. He said I'd slept soundly and he kept watch over me.

What did I feel as we left the hotel? Kinship? The satisfaction of a journey ended? None of those feelings touched me. He had buffed them all away, honed his accent and lost himself in the shell he became.

He intended to drive me to Belfast where I could contact the passport office about my stolen passport and organise some form of identification for my flight home.

'As you're a UK citizen, it makes sense to take a domestic flight rather than trying to organise one from this jurisdiction,' he said.

I suspected his main intent was to banish me from his life as swiftly as possible. He had offered Serenity Falls to Rosanna in exchange for my silence but in the harsh, bright light of morning, I knew that that would never happen. He would change his mind again once the intensity of our meeting faded.

As he drove along the motorway, I called him a liar. A bigamist. A criminal. His will was merely a ploy, a pitiful fob to buy me off. He was still denying my accusations when the articulated truck veered towards us and we were swept aside like flotsam. The screech of metal was deafening yet in those seconds we shared between life and death, there was another sound that I'd forgotten until now. A gasp from him that was swiftly extinguished, but I hear him still... 'Mo ghràidh... Mo g—'

Lorraine knocks on my bedroom door and asks permission to come in. My heart beats in time to the clacking of her black boots as she walks towards me. It drums a warning that she is intent on harming me again. Her coat is pewter-grey and a faux-fur collar surrounds her face like a silvery nest. She is a bird of prey, her voice soft when she says goodbye. She is on her way to Dublin and won't be back until later tonight.

I smile and wish her safe travelling. The air is lighter after she leaves.

The door marked Private sealed my prison and now that I'm leaving I have only one regret. A weakness that I will never share with anyone. A memory that will never leave me.

I loved Aidan and never knew it was forbidden. How can such love be suppressed because it is tainted with blood? Nothing will change how I feel, but I understand that we can never have a future together.

I entered his room again last night. As before, he sensed my presence and awoke, the hint of lemon soap faint on his skin. I apologised to him for the hurt I caused him and the brutal remarks I made about his mother. He said he was sorry for turning our first night out together into a nightmare but there would be others... many others...

I let him talk. When we kissed it would have been so easy to forget my warnings and stay with him until our river had run its course. He begged me not to leave him but I knew it was time to go.

I didn't say goodbye. Goodbyes need explanations, and how could I tell him that Megan Ross is going to destroy his mother.

I can't allow myself to be inside his head or hers. I'm dressed and ready to leave. Nothing to pack, apart from essentials and my Hozier T-shirt. The sketch pad is in tatters: a spiral earring, tiny enough to go unnoticed in the fluff of the carpet surrounding the wardrobe, was caught in a glint of sunlight. It told me that Lorraine's fingerprints were on my drawings, just as her footprints marked her journey to the landing on the night I almost flew.

Now, with nothing to ground me to Serenity Falls, I'm as weightless as a balloon when the string is cut.

SIXTY-SIX

LORRAINE

The sun was rising when Lorraine left Serenity Falls. Turning right on Cliffside Road, she entered a network of narrower roads.

Doubling back towards the waterfall, she drove into the site of the long-abandoned pottery that had given the village its name. Only one chimney remained standing and the main building was an empty shell. Quickly, she parked behind the pottery and changed her clothes for a black tracksuit and trainers, bunching her long hair into a woolly cap which she pulled over her forehead.

The approach she had chosen to reach the summit of the cliff was a more difficult climb than the one nearest to the hotel. This one was seldom used and overgrown. She had to force her way through dead bracken and heather that was withered and stalky. It offered her more cover as she neared the summit yet she gasped with relief when she reached Potter's Folly and was able to hide within the walls.

The folly was a landmark, a low, tower-like structure, neglected and crumbling. Council workers had fenced it off but the wire was broken in places and access was easy, as evidenced by the beer cans and fast-food wrappings strewn on the ground. A circle of stones had been used to create a make-shift fire pit to warm the young people who gathered there at night. The half-burned logs suggested it had been a failure.

Narrow slits in the walls allowed light to stream into the interior. From one of these slits, Lorraine had a view of the cliff walk where Gail would set up the tripod for her camera. It would afford the documentarian the clearest and most spectacular view of the waterfall.

The spot where Arthur Kilbride used to pause and marvel at its flow.

She sank to the ground and pulled her knees to the chin. It had to end where it first began. This time she could not pretend and allow her thoughts to dissolve into mistiness. Nor could she arm herself with justifications. Victor was no longer around to cushion her from the reality of her deeds or allow her the luxury of denial. Her father's body flailing, falling through eternity.

That vision should have been seared into her brain but time had allowed it to fade from neon to a grainy grey. One that could almost be ignored.

Carl Sheridan's fall had been more of a buckling, more of a thud, and one that still forced her hands over her ears.

Then there was Naomi. So easy to press down on her, so light to lift up, thistledown falling... she should have fallen... and soon she would. It had to be done.

But, first, Gail Robinson must be silenced. Her pathetic affair with Carl Sheridan was responsible for his death.

Consequences, there were always consequences.

She checked her watch and rose to her feet. Gail would arrive soon to capture the early morning light. So glorious, that wintery sun reflecting its blood-red hues on the waterfall. The glare was merciless, forcing her to see what was to come. Gail would climb the steep steps to the summit. She would stand for a few moments to take in the view and imagine it transposed onto celluloid. Picking her vantage point, and knowing the exact image Lorraine wanted to portray, she would be too absorbed in capturing the relentless flow of water to notice anything else.

Lorraine watched a black smudge form a shape and become distinguishable. Gail was wearing jeans and a navy hoodie, her camera bag slung over her shoulder. She had pulled the hood over her red hair with its ridiculous quiff. As Lorraine had anticipated, she stopped to admire the view before striding confidently towards the promontory. Kneeling down, she removed her camera and moved back and forth along that protruding stretch of grass until she was satisfied she had chosen the best vantage point. She must have left the tripod back at the house and was using her shoulder to balance the camera. She was in no hurry to start filming and seemed content to stand motionless, gazing into the distance.

Finally, she moved closer to the edge and leaned downwards, focusing her camera on the opening in the rocks where the waterfall dashed into being.

Her stillness suggested she was utterly immersed in what she was doing. She had spoken to Lorraine about a trance-like state that sometimes took her over when she was filming. It seemed to merge her and her camera into one entity as she captured what was visible through the lens.

A bird broke the silence with flute-like notes that filled Lorraine with a sudden desire to weep. She resisted this unexpected response. Honesty, she had to embrace it. She killed Carl Sheridan. She killed her father. She would have killed Nao —*Megan Ross*... that slithery cat with nine lives... but for the intervention of others.

This time there would be no mistakes, no sudden interruptions. When it was over, she would drive directly to Dublin to meet with Jennifer Moore. The long, drawn-out intestacy was almost complete. Just a few more documents to sign and Serenity Falls would once again belong to its rightful owner.

She waited until Gail began to film. Soon, the early morning walkers would appear, dogs would bound free from leads and joggers, elbows rigid, would run past her. Gail never stirred as Lorraine moved from the folly. Swiftly – she could not afford to hesitate – she ran towards the promontory, where the noise from the waterfall silenced any other sound as she flattened her hands and thrust her arms forward.

SIXTY-SEVEN

MEGAN

'Tell the gardai everything you can remember,' Gail says as she drives from Serenity Falls. 'Every little detail, no matter how unimportant it seems.'

We both agree that when Lorraine is questioned by the police, she will arch her eyebrows and press her hands to her chest as she admits to having made a dreadful mistake. A clear case of mistaken identity. She will talk about hallucinations and disturbances of the mind when she hears that I've accused her of attempted murder.

But she will falter when Gail reveals what she discovered in Lochanar.

What of Aidan in all of this? I couldn't tell him that I intended to bring her to justice. He would have betrayed me. How could he not do so? She is his mother. That has to matter more than any feelings he has for me.

Gail drives past Falls Lodge. The curtains are still drawn. No sign of lights or of Pamela's car. Did she spend the night with Nick? She'll never know what I discovered on the day she gathered herbs in the walled garden. Parsley, sage, rosemary and thyme.

The automatic gates slide apart and we are on Cliffside Road. As yet, the peak hour traffic hasn't started. Nothing to delay us as we drive towards the police station in Potters Glen. Is hate as passionate and obsessive as love? Can the hate I feel for Lorraine be balanced on the scales of my love for her son and find it has an equal measure?

I knew him before he was aware of my existence. Megan, the sleuth. Facebook, Instagram, LinkedIn and the blog he wrote about life in Vancouver. I saw photos of the women he dated, wine glasses clinking and plates of scrumptious food. The tittle-tattle of a carefree life, as was mine. An open world to be explored until my horizon was compressed into a white ward and a blink or two.

He came with me into that world and it was impossible not to fall in love with him.

Clouds streak across the rising sun and cast red shadows on the river. It's running high and fast this morning. The waterfall is behind us and inaudible.

I hope Aidan is able to film the waterfall from the angles his mother wants. He offered to do the filming when Gail told him I needed a break from my four walls. He smiled, as if he understood my need to breathe in great dollops of fresh air.

SIXTY-EIGHT

LORRAINE

In Vancouver she went shopping with her son. He bought her a pair of earrings, gold and curved in a spiral. She bought him a hoodie, dark navy and made from the finest Mongolian cashmere. The embroidered motif on the back of the hoodie was a small maple leaf, a symbol of Canadian national identity... and there it was, with its angular lobes and orangey-red hue, impossible to miss as she tried to stop the momentum of her lunge, her body moving forward even as her mind screamed at her to stop... stop... *stop!*

When she gasped, a sound louder and more violent that the gushing spray, Aidan staggered forward, the camera still resting on his shoulder, one arm raised as if the morning breeze was something he could grasp to hold him steady. As the camera tilted forward and fell at their feet, she clutched her son and held him to her. A dance began, their bodies entwined as they swayed on the precipice, one step forward, one step back, and he, collapsing to his knees, dragged her down to the grass with him.

He lay still, his breath pumping in short gasps. He was

dazed and shivering uncontrollably but his eyes never left her face. Such terrible awareness...

Once again, Lorraine was forced to see herself reflected in the horror of another's gaze. This time there would be no erasing of her crime, no slate wiped clean in memory loss, or death.

The earth was damp from the morning mist and the rising spray from the waterfall. She was conscious of it seeping through the light fabric of her tracksuit. Her elbows hurt and she suspected she had strained her shoulder. Sensations of damp and pain were momentary distractions that helped her to gather her wits about her. She needed to be in control when her son was finally able to speak. She still clung to him, her hold so hard and desperate that he was forced to press against her as he pushed himself upright.

'What the hell...? You could have pushed me over the edge.' Unable to continue speaking, he leaned over to stare down at the waterfall.

She was inside his head. Where else could she be in those moments after the random tilt of the world had righted itself and held them safe? His mouth must be parched, she thought when she heard him gasp and struggle to swallow. 'What were you trying to do?'

It was a question, not an accusation, and she needed an answer that made sense of the madness.

'I slipped on the grass and fell forward.' She managed to rise to her knees, a penitent kneeling before him. 'I mistook you for Gail Robinson. I needed to speak to her. The ground is damp...' Looking up at him, she found it impossible to believe she had been so mistaken. A mist before her eyes had caused it... the same mist... she must stop and concentrate. 'You stepped back just as I touched you and—'

'Why are you dressed like that?' His brusque interruption

cut short her explanation. 'You're supposed to be driving to Dublin.'

'That's where I'm going now. I'll be driving for most of the day and I wanted to take a short run before I left.' She found the strength to stand. 'I'd just started off when I saw Gail... or thought I saw her. I was going to ask her to film the pottery ruins. After all, that's how the village got its name. Then I slipped.' She slid the sole of her trainer along the scummy grass, flattened now by the impact of their bodies.

'You never made a sound. Why didn't you call out?'

'I should have... but you know how she hates being interrupted when she's filming. My voice would have been recorded.' She was unable to take her eyes off the maple leaf motif that was also embroidered on the front pocket of his hoodie. So small and delicate, yet it had saved his life. 'Where is Gail?' Her shock was beginning to ease. 'How come she isn't here?'

'I offered to do the filming. She had other things to do this morning.'

'Other things? What exactly—?'

He picked up the camera and turned it over to examine it for damage. 'I felt your hands on my back.' He continued to concentrate on the camera before lowering it carefully to the ground. 'Naomi was telling the truth when she said you had killer hands.'

The ugliness of his words. Unable to believe what he had said, Lorraine reeled away from him.

His mouth opened and closed. She caught some words. The Chantry. Naomi having taken some kind of seizure... no, not a seizure... she had been drunk and violent with words. *Killer hands.* His voice hardened as he repeated what Naomi had said.

Lorraine turned her palms upwards to watch the blood run from them but all she could see were the lines of fate that had brought her to this moment. Her son, unaware of her suffering, continued talking about Naomi and her terrible accusations, which he had disbelieved, and hated her for making. But he had just felt his mother's touch, the determination with which she had tried to send him over the edge and to his death.

'Naomi believes you tried to kill her,' he said. 'I was convinced she was hallucinating, but you've made me think the unthinkable.'

'How can you make such an appalling accusation?' She had to save him from himself. 'Naomi didn't know what she was saying! The loss of her memory has affected her mental state and when you add alcohol to the mix, what else can you expect? She's twisted your mind with her fantasies. I'm driving to Dublin to sign off on the intestacy. When I return this afternoon, we're going to sort out this ridiculous situation. I've tolerated her for long enough. When she repays my generosity with these slanderous remarks, then it's time for her to go.'

'I believe her.' Such implacable conviction. How did that happen? Pity masquerading as love. Anything else was impossible.

'You *can't*.' She slapped his cheek with such force that he took an involuntary step closer to the edge before moving back to safety.

'Gail would be dead by now if you hadn't realised your mistake.' He was unrelenting. 'You knew exactly what you were doing, just as you did when you tried to push Naomi over the banisters. Your bedroom was empty when I looked into it that night, yet you claimed to be asleep when she was sleepwalking. I'd forgotten about that but it's been nagging at me ever since she told me you wanted her dead.'

He was barely audible about the gush of the waterfall yet she heard every accusatory word.

'The key to the attic was never lost. You knew exactly what you were doing when you told me to leave the portrait on the landing.'

On the evening she had identified Victor, she had screamed.

It had been the only way to release the swelling in her chest. This time, experiencing it again, she knew that screaming would not bring relief. Her son was pronouncing judgement when he knew nothing about the reasons that had led them to this confrontation.

No more lies. Aidan would support her when he understood her motives. Her need to protect what was hers... and his. Mother and son, that bond could not be broken.

'I lied about her identity,' she said. 'Her name is Megan Ross. She is your father's granddaughter.'

'What are you talking about?' The mark of her hand on his cheek was stark against his ashen complexion.

'Your father was married before. He never divorced his wife. It was easier to walk out on her and create a new identity. He abandoned a young son and a daughter who had yet to be born. Consequences, Aidan. There are always consequences to our actions.'

'You're lying. I can't be related to her.' He spoke hoarsely, his head flung back as if her admission had struck him with the force of a fist. 'This is another one of your lies. We *can't* be related.'

'You asked for the truth. Now you have it. Your father was a bigamist. The "love guru". It would be hilarious if it wasn't tragic.'

'When did you discover the truth?'

'Shortly after his death.' Sweat beaded her forehead and stung her eyes. Mist... she had to feel her way through it. 'You believed I was in London. I wasn't.'

'Where were you?'

'Meeting his wife in a town called Lochanar in Scotland.'

She allowed the silence to stretch and watched his lips move as he attempted to speak, the words strangled before he could utter them.

'Why didn't you tell me?' he finally demanded.

'A shared secret loses its shape,' she replied. 'It was the code by which your father lived. He left me to deal with the skeletons in his closet... only they were alive and we would have lost everything to them. I saved Serenity Falls for your sake, Aidan.'

'What else are you not telling me...?' His voice cracked as he strove to continue. 'I need to know about Megan Ross.'

He fears me, she thought.

Not for his physical safety, but for the truths she would reveal to him.

'She would have taken everything from us and exposed your father. I did what I had to do to preserve what we have.'

'You imprisoned her—'

'I gave her a home and tried to control an impossible situation. Can you imagine if Carl Sheridan' – his name still had the power to bend her with its blunt force – 'had discovered the truth? We would have been destroyed.'

'So, you believed he had to be silenced.' The pitiless words he spoke seemed to come from deep within him, from a space he hardly knew, such was their bewilderment, yet they were also vehement and certain.

'I had a thought,' he continued before she could speak. 'One of those crazed thoughts that was gone as quickly as it came. Your boots...'

'My boots?' She had no idea of what he was going to say, only that it would be bad, and the hairs at the back of her neck lifted in anticipation.

'I'd noticed them in the wood shed,' he said. 'The mud and yellow petals caught between the ridges on the soles. I wondered if you'd been walking through a quagmire in the rain.'

'What are you talking about?' His eyes... she had never noticed their compellability, but had she ever looked that deeply into their depths? Now, doing so, she was shocked by their ferocity.

'Two days later Carl's body was found,' he said. 'That's

when the thought came to me. I remembered those walks we took along Farren's Lane when I was a child. You said the flowers that grew there were the tallest in the world, especially the buttercups. They glowed on our chins—'

'I've no memory—' The tightness in her chest was agonising.

'A thought that lasted for a nanosecond before I let it go because it was too ludicrous to *even* consider... His voice wobbled. 'And I didn't until now. That's what you've done to me... you've shown me that anything is believable when it comes to your self-preservation.'

Was it possible for his face to become even more drained of colour? For his expression to quiver, as if he had accepted the reality of a once unimaginable deed?

'Aidan, you don't know what you're saying. Stop before it's too late. I'm begging you, put such thoughts from your mind. My only crime is lying about Megan's identity! Those accusations you've made are delusions. You have to believe me.'

'How will I ever know if you're telling me the truth?' he asked.

She loved him with a desperation born from loss. The burn of her hands on his back had become an indelible branding. It signalled the end of trust. She could see it evaporating like sun on mist.

Aidan was still talking about murder and its convenience when she interrupted him.

'Why isn't Gail here?' She snapped the question at him.

'What does it matter? She was taking Naomi for a drive... what's *wrong*?'

'Naomi is in my care. Gail has no right to take her anywhere.'

'Naomi is free to go anywhere she wants with or without your permission. She's not in prison, even if that's how you make her feel.'

'*Aidan,* where were they going? It's vitally important that you tell me.'

'I thought Gail was taking her for a drive until Pam arrived for work. She'd stayed overnight at Nick's place and saw them going into the garda station. Naomi's trying to get her passport sorted. She can't wait to leave her *prison.*'

Lorraine barely registered what he was saying. Gail had lied to him about the passport. Just as she had lied to Lorraine about the reason for her documentary. She had gone into the garda station with only one purpose in mind.

Sergeant Boyne's shoulders would be rigid with determination when she came calling. The younger garda – Lorraine had forgotten his name – would be chewing his lip as he mounted the steps behind her. Just as he did on that sunny day when she was foolhardy enough to enjoy a tableau of perfection that was as false as it was beautiful.

Would they use the siren? A bell tolling. She had the steel to withstand a garda interrogation. A case of mistaken identity. Was it a crime to make a mistake? If so, she was guilty as charged. Killer hands... what did that mean? An accusation made in the throes of drink. Megan Ross was delusional, profoundly impacted from the trauma to her brain. What evidence would Gail Robinson bring forward? Lorraine had opened the marriage retreat to her and cooperated fully with her documentary. Nothing to hide. Nothing to link her to the tragedy that Carl Sheridan's reckless disregard for his own safety had brought upon him. The knife she had wielded with such savagery was buried in bogland, along with his phone, sunk deep in the mire of antiquity. Her son's withering gaze, his unanswered questions, his dangerous suspicions, all that could be handled. She would appease Aidan as she had done so often when he was a boy and Victor's indifference had reduced him to tears.

It all began there, on the promontory. Her father threatening to steal her dreams and Victor with his comforting reassurances had allowed her enough rope to believe she was free from culpability. And all he ever had to do was yank it a little – a nod, a few words, a frown, an unspoken warning that knowledge was power – and she, his marionette, danced to his tune until death did them part.

Aidan eyes were locked with hers in a merciless hold. He would keep her secret, as Victor had done, but knowledge was power... knowledge was power... and nothing would ever erase that instant when he turned and witnessed her lethal intent. Killer hands, palms flattened. Memory was as pitiless as the deed she had been about to commit.

To think otherwise was to chase rainbows, to stir fairy dust with her fantasies. Reality was cold and factual.

When she phoned Gail, believing her to be in London, and somewhere out of doors, with a hard wind blowing, Lorraine had been convinced she imagined the almost inaudible strains of a familiar tune. Now, when it was too late, she realised her mistake. Gail Robinson had been standing on Lochanar Harbour when the swirl of bagpipes penetrated their terse conversation. Lorraine visualised the piper standing ramrod as he played 'The Skye Boat Song' with an energy that suggested it was his first time performing it.

What was she revealing to the gardai? And Naomi... *Megan*... she was so far outside Lorraine's control that nothing could rein her in. Within the stillness of her captive world, Megan Ross had known what was about to happen when Lorraine leaned over her bed and laid her hands upon her. Armed with that awareness, lost for a time and found again, she was now the one in control, the one with knowledge... and with power.

Lorraine pressed her hands to her ears and began to run.

Aidan shouted at her to stop, a warning that was lost in the clamour of the dead.

How loudly they called out to her. How vivid their appearance. Her father, standing on the promontory, was smiling, his arms outstretched to welcome her. Carl was beside him, a darker vision who was still journeying towards the light, all enmity gone. A puff of smoke. Was that what life in all its tremulous uncertainty was about? Yes, Lorraine Gordon thought, as she ran towards the men whose lives she had cut short yet who, in death, had found the will to forgive her.

Above her, the streeling clouds resembled a backbone, cleanly fileted, each bloodied vertebrae reminding her of Sedona and the red, pulsing energy that had transformed her. Victor was waiting to catch her as her legs gave way. Dominant as always. Such radiance, such laugher as he lifted her in his arms and flung her, light as a butterfly, into the air. The waterfall was the only song Lorraine heard as she fell into its pulsating vortex.

SIXTY-NINE

MEGAN

Frost comes in the night and shrouds her in ice. In the melting morning glaze, it thaws on the black branches and hangs like a shimmer of tears about to fall. A dog named Bruce, trained to detect the odour of those who drown, traces her to the reeds. She is buried deep in a mouldering undergrowth that foiled the efforts of dredgers and divers who tried, without success, for three days to find her.

The river ran high on the day she fell. Currents swirled and curved through the froth as it charged past the deserted cottage where Carl Sheridan was murdered. The reeds reached out to claim her and that was where her journey ended. I imagine her face beneath the ice, the weaving filaments of her long blonde hair, her golden stare looking upwards at the world she left behind.

Aidan talks about her last moments. Her confession to him about my identity and her realisation that the subterfuge was over.

The tracks where she fell are still visible. A scum of dead leaves reveal the print of her trainers as she skidded inexorably towards the edge of the cliff. What did they say to each other during those final moments? All he tells me is that she understood that he could never forgive her and, more importantly, that she could never forgive herself.

On the morning of her death, I sat with Gail in the Potters Glen garda station and told them who I was. We were still there when Aidan's distraught call came through to emergency services.

I knew then that she would never be held accountable.

Gail believes she killed Carl Sheridan with her own hands. No proof exists, she admits. She is just going on intuition. That is where I also struggle. That same hand on my mouth. Her hands lifting me high. Hallucinations? Delusions? Intuition, no matter how honed, will never equate to evidence. Even the letter from Carl that she found in Lorraine's desk is no longer there. The will that Victor Gordon showed me has also vanished. I know it existed but now it doesn't.

It would be comforting to believe that false identities don't fit. That they scratch and itch the skin and will eventually fester, as mine did. Victor Gordon's identity fitted him like a membrane. He grew into its stretch, flexed its muscle until it gave him the arrogance to grow a public face. One that would never be overlaid by the shadow of Maxwell Ross. He played the part so well that he become a legend. Is it that easy to sway a multitude with fine words and a gaze that seemed to strip the veneer from one's soul?

Lorraine loved an illusion, and was prepared to kill to maintain it. These are truths that cannot be proved, and she will take the answer to the grave that she will share with Max Ross for eternity.

She was dead before she reached the river, her body dashed against the cliff face on that fatal downward plunge. This information was given to Aidan by Jean, who found herself once again acting as liaison officer to a member of the Gordon family.

I refused to return to Lochanar until her body was found and buried. I've spoken to Rosanna and kissed her face on Zoom. The others were there, boxed and constrained on the screen. Evan and gossipy Nessa with their boys, and Andy, who wore a suit for his first online conversation. His expression told me it will be his last. Rosanna couldn't stop crying. She looked old and vulnerable, stooped from the shock of hearing that the man she loved so briefly, and mourned so bitterly, had been masquerading in full view of the world.

At her funeral we listen to Aidan's eulogy. He speaks about love, its unselfish transcendence, and how his mother used it to shape him into manhood. His description of her last moments ring with anguish as he describes how he had been filming on the cliff top when he saw her on her morning run. She stepped too close to the edge to admire the waterfall and slipped.

His eulogy is his parting gift to her; but behind his fulsome words, he knows what she was capable of doing.

I see the swing of her long, grey coat and the silvery snuggle of fur around her neck. Her high-heeled boots clacked a warning that I never heard. When she fell, she was wearing a black tracksuit and trainers.

Gail reaches for my hand as Father Smithson recites the final prayers.

We could be standing by her graveside if she'd followed Lorraine's instructions and taken her camera to the clifftop.

Rosanna does not want her status as his widow to change. Too many complications for her to sort out legally. All she wants to do is captain her boat. Aidan will inherit his parents' estate. He intends to remain at Serenity Falls and work with Pamela to create a new retreat for those who believe that love is worth the pain.

Are they right? My heart aches for a forbidden love. I see that same turmoil in Aidan's eyes. How can we have a future when *his father's dark reflection hangs over us? How can I lose myself in his embrace without thinking of his mother's determination, her ruthlessness?*

Fate flings random boulders in our direction and it's how we catch them that counts. Would Max have been happier if he'd stayed with Rosanna? Would Candice be alive today? Would I exist? Too many questions for my brain to consider. All I have right now are sensations. Loss and sadness mixed with anticipation as the date for leaving draws nearer. And heartache... oh, that ache. I'll never again hear the words of love Aidan spoke on the night I came to him. Will he whisper them to other women... Melissa, Amy, Jess? Will I allow another man to kiss me so deeply that even now, thinking back to that night, I'm weakened by longing?

The service is over. We bow our heads as Lorraine Gordon is lowered into the earth. After we leave the grave diggers will cover her with clay. They wait at a discreet distance as we stand awkwardly before the fake grass cover that hides her coffin. It is strewn with flowers from those who believe she walked in light.

Tomorrow, Rosanna and Evan will arrive and bring me home. Aidan will welcome them and meet his half-brother for the first time. Passion can fade and love can be weakened by too many demands, but family bonds have a different energy. Blood and kinship now hold us together. Maybe, in time, what I dared to dream with Aidan will fade and we will be at peace with each other.

He kisses my cheek when it's time to say goodbye. A kiss that is chaste. One filled with awareness that we're embarking on separate life journeys. We don't need words to express how we feel. The burn of other kisses is on our lips, and that's the memory I take with me when I leave Serenity Falls.

In spring, I'll go to Sedona to draw rocks and tall saguaros.

I'll walk in the dust of my grandfather's footsteps and meditate within the silent might of a vortex. If there are answers to be found, perhaps that's where I'll find them.

On Cliffside Road the waterfall surges into view. What secrets does it carry on its downward plunge? Does it purge and forgive? Was that what Lorraine sought when she submitted to its embrace? On the clifftop, she could have saved herself at the last minute if she had gripped the handholds that were within her reach. Roots that budged obscenely from the earth, clumps of strong heather, rocks as jagged as broken teeth.

She chose not to do so.

The rain has washed away the tracks she left behind but the trail of unanswered questions remains. Is it possible for the dead to reveal their secrets? Do they send answers to us in dreams and other mysterious ways? Or do their secrets wither with them and cease to have power over us? Perhaps, someday, I'll know the answer.

She told me I was imagining the waterfall's thunder when I said I could hear it at night. She twisted strands of her long blonde hair around her fingers and said my imagination was playing tricks again.

Perhaps she was telling the truth, and what I heard as I drifted off to sleep in the Nook was the rise of dolphins as they splashed waves against the sides of Rosanna's Redemption.

A LETTER FROM LAURA

Dear Reader,

I want to say a huge thank you for choosing to read *The Marriage Retreat*. If you did enjoy it, and want to keep up to date with all my latest releases, just sign up at the following link. Your email address will never be shared and you can unsubscribe at any time.

www.bookouture.com/laura-elliot

I hope you enjoyed *The Marriage Retreat*. Writing it was a pleasure and also a challenge, which is the way it goes with every book I write. Each one leaves a particular memory behind. This will vary between each book, yet they all share one thing in common. I call it the spark that comes suddenly and triggers the question—what if...? 'What if' can lead the imagination down many paths. These include infuriatingly inviting cul-de-sacs, long, broad avenues, and high speed motorways with no traffic jams. Usually, the motorways only come into view after the cul-de-sacs have been explored and deleted, and the hidden trails along the avenues thoroughly investigated. Metaphors help me to visualise the journey of a book towards completion but there has to be something more concrete to give substance to plot and character.

When I sat down to write *The Marriage Retreat* the character of Victor Gordon was a shadow, a flicker in my imagination yet the dominance he projected was startlingly familiar. It is projected by the men (some women but predominantly men) who have the charisma and power to draw people to them. I've watched them in action in self-help workshops, religious settings, on the political stage, in philosophical and celebrity circles, at parties, book launches, conferences and anywhere that offers them a public arena to charm and mesmerise. Such personalities can influence to the good but that same power can also be used to exploit people's vulnerabilities and have destructive consequences. All too often, times will show that such feet are made from clay.

These thought were mulling around in my head when I was creating Victor Gordon and following the trail of 'what ifs' that explored the story behind the brand? The story that didn't make the headlines. The story that revealed how damaging—or enhancing—such personalities can be to the lives of others...which, of course, is what created the cast of characters that inhabit *The Marriage Retreat*.

Thank you for taking time to read my latest book. I love to hear from readers. You break the silence that is such a large part of the writing experience, especially that waiting period when a book is finally released into that great, unknown space outside the writing room. If you've enjoyed *The Marriage Retreat* and would like to a leave a review on Amazon, it would be greatly appreciated.

With warmest regards,

Laura Elliot

www.lauraelliotauthor.com

facebook.com/lauraelliotauthor
twitter.com/Elliot_Laura

ACKNOWLEDGEMENTS

Writing The End is always an exhilarating experience. In the euphoria of bringing the book to its conclusion, it is easy to forget the often challenging journey it underwent to arrive at its destination. So many people help in many different ways. Their ability to listen, advise, encourage and offer support breaks the isolation of being in a space that is silent expect for the clack of a keyboard and the occasional deep sigh...or muttered expletive.

To my family, my husband, Seán, my son, Tony, my daughters, Ciara and Michelle, my daughter-in-law, Louise, and sons-in-law, Roddy and Harry, and my precious grandchildren, Romy, Ava, Nina and Seán — thank you for being the centre of my world and the happiness you bring to my life. Thank you for the practical and caring help you give when it's needed – as well as your endless patience when I ring you once again with my conspiracy theory that my computer doesn't understand me.

I've had the pleasure of visiting Scotland many times but there is still much I do not know about this lovely country. Lochanar is a fictitious location but I wanted to make it as authentic as possible. Thank you to my Scottish friends, Morag Dunbar (Scottish Tourist Guide), Sandra Gibson and Janet Weatherston for taking the time to read through the Scottish sections of *The Marriage Retreat* and steer me on the right course.

To my friends, those who write and those who don't – thank you for your support, the meals we share, the conversations we enjoy, the listening and the sharing.

Zoom and other such platform have allowed the world to virtually link hands and I'd like to send a special shout out to Brenda Brown and her students at Saydel High School, Iowa, with whom I've had the online pleasure of discussing my work. Also to Larry Okun, my Floridian 'pres' and to Shirley Oppen-heimer, whose invitation to visit Arizona inspired me to use Sedona as one of my landscapes in *The Marriage Retreat*. Renita D'Silva's wonderful books are always enhanced by her mouth-watering descriptions of Indian cuisine. Thank you, Renita, for helping me to set the table when my characters sat down to enjoy their communal Indian meal.

I've been very fortunate when writing *The Marriage Retreat* to work with two excellent editors, Claire Bord and Natasha Harding. Thank you Claire for your insightfulness, sensitivity and friendliness during my years with Bookouture. I was equally fortunate to experience a seamless transition to my new editor, Natasha, who has brought that same professionalism and warmth to our working partnership. A special thanks to Jess Readett, who devised a detailed publicity programme for me, also to my eagle-eyed copyeditor and proof reader Belinda Jones and Claire Rushbrook, my *very* patient typesetter Lizzie Brien and my cover designer Lisa Horton, who evoked that haunting image of a space where secrets brood.

Finally to my readers, I'd like to extend a very special thank you. Your reviews, emails and messages add an extra special warmth to my days and are always welcome and appreciated.

Printed in Great Britain
by Amazon

27021561R00229